KNIVES FOR THE PEOPLE

PETER MOLNAR

ISBN: 978-1-945263-43-9

CONTENTS

PART THREE
RUN TO ME, RUN FROM ME

For all the kids in their garage with a guitar right now, figuring it out…

PART ONE
LOVEBUG AND EVERYTHING AFTER

"Anything that's worth doing is worth overdoing."

-Steven Tyler

"Some girl asked me for an autograph, and I asked her why.
She said because she admires me. I said she should see a
shrink. Then she started crying and I started
laughing."

-Nikki Sixx

ONE

Gretch Solomon wakes with tears lying on her cheeks, the smell of burning in her nose, and the bedside phone's metallic shriek beside her head that nearly stops her heart. She can't remember the dream that made her weep. There's no time to try. The ringing phone in the dead of night, beside the red digital readout of an alarm clock that reads 3:20 am, is like a corpse's kiss in the dark. She pulls herself up onto an elbow, switches on the bedside lamp, and snags the phone from its cradle halfway through its fourth ring.

"Hello?" she croaks into the receiver, her heart clenched between her teeth now.

"Yes, is this the Darius residence?" a prim, female voice asks.

"Mm-hmm. What is it? Who's this?"

"Mrs. Darius?"

In any other situation, she would have gently corrected them. *Solomon. I kept my maiden name. But how would you know that? Of course you couldn't possibly—*

"Yes. Who is it?"

"Mrs. Darius, I apologize for calling at such an hour, but you've been listed as an emergency contact for one of our patients here."

"Emergency contact?" The face of her brother, Damon, breaks the shimmering surface of her guarded thoughts. He's finally done it. The wayward son has gone and gotten himself killed or taken his own life. She swings her legs over the side of the bed now, grasps the receiver with both hands so tight its plastic shell clicks. "How?"

"A drug overdose," the caller tells her. "Heroin."

"*What?*" Gretch cries. "An OD?"

"Yes … Mrs. Darius—"

"Wha-now wait-just *wait* a goddam minute!" The blood has flooded back into her brain. "You want to tell me how the hell my brother got his hands on H in your clinic?"

"Mrs. *Darius*—"

"What kind of circus are you running over there? I've been paying you all a small fortune to house and heal him and it comes to this?"

She hears the familiar creak of a box spring in the next bedroom, followed by a craggy raised voice, made all the rougher by its heightened volume. "I said no! *Goddammit!* Bring the lights down! Until tomorrow!" The sound of her husband's voice, a mockery of what it used to sound like, is like the sound of a ghost speaking in a broken and bastardized language.

It sends a shiver up her spine.

My own husband's voice frightens me.

I ought to be ashamed of myself.

Gretch rejoins the conversation halfway through the caller's reply.

"—think we're at cross-purposes, Mrs. Darius. I'm calling from the ER at Cedars-Sinai."

"Oh," Gretch sighs, the tightness in her shoulders oozing somewhat. "And who put me down as their emergency contact?"

"Her name is—er—Gloria R. Tizione"

The bedroom walls seem to shudder then compress, bearing down on her. In the foyer, the tock of the grandfather clock which had come over on the boat with her Irish grandparents, sounds close enough to have climbed the stairs and relocated itself in her doorway like some monolith of doom.

Hang up the phone.

Unplug it from the wall.

Go back to sleep—

"Okay" Gretch manages, in a small and mystified voice. "Alright."

There is a heat in Gretch's cheeks. Blood boiling in response to the sudden dizzying array of spliced images from her past. All of them featuring various situations she has shared with Gloria Tizione. They project themselves against the blank screen of her frontal lobe and remind her of what seems to be an endless list of reasons why she ought to end the call right then and there.

To soothe Stevie, her husband, back to sleep.

She will have a bear of a time calming him after this disturbance.

She thinks he's started crying in the next room, a low and gelatinous sound that pulls her chest muscles into a vest of knots.

"Do you know this woman?" the caller asks, impatiently now.

In the background, a loudspeaker pages someone with an unintelligible name and rings off again with a cursory beep.

"I … I do. I do know her." Biting her bottom lip and sucking it, Gretchen feels a stirring in her gut that has always spelled trouble in the past.

A bad omen.

A poor decision.

"An … an overdose, you said?" Gretch says. "How is she?"

Down the hall, Stevie whimpers. "Hang up! *Won't you just … hang up on them?*"

If only he'd spoken his peace a second before, she would have done just that and shut the light.

"Someone dumped her out in front of the ER. She was unresponsive when we wheeled her inside. Sadly, this happens more often than you'd think. The things people will do to avoid trouble, even if it means leaving someone for dead. I'm glad we were able to locate someone connected to her. She's talking now, but it was touch and go for much of the night. Otherwise, we'd still have a Jane Doe on our hands. She's not carrying any ID on her. But she asked for you."

Raking her auburn curls back out of her face, Gretch shuts her eyes and digs deep for an ore of compassion when it comes to Gloria Tizione. The last time she'd seen her was backstage at The Mud Festival in Glasgow where Grifters Anonymous was headlining, the band Gretch was managing, and her husband was playing bass for. Someone had struck her from behind while in mid-conversation.

The last face she'd laid eyes on before the black of unconsciousness claimed her had been Gloria's.

The big brown eyes, blinkless.

Fascinated.

"I'm sorry," Gretch says, "what is your name?"

"My name is Sheila. Would you like my extension?"

"Yes, please." Gretch rummages in the bedside table drawer and snags a loose pen mid-roll, along with a hand-held notepad. She rips off the uppermost page, rife with doodles and an unlabeled phone number that had hopefully not been important.

Fresh page. Pen uncapped. "Go ahead."

Just as Gretch finishes writing down the contact information, Stevie let's out a shredded, unnerving shriek from down the hall. *"DON'T TELL THEM ANYTHING! NOT YET! I'M NOT READY TO PAY THE DEBT!"*

It's all Gretch can do to cup the receiver and mute the outburst as best she can.

Gretch quickly reads the numbers back to Sheila.

They are correct.

"I have to go." She bites her lip once more, rolling it around until it elicits a twinge of pain. "Will you call me in the morning to update me on her condition? That will give me time enough to make plans for her pick-up and … helping her with her next move."

"Of course. Good night."

Sheila's smile shines through in her tone of voice.

Rising from the bed in what feels once more like a waking sleep, Gretch crosses the room to the wide window overlooking the lush expanse of rolling hills framed by the crowded, seemingly impene-trable screen of redwood trees on all sides. Parting the sheers, she sees a curious wine stain splashed across the sky, even though sunrise is a good hour and half from now. God is getting sloppy before the start of yet another California shit show.

Still, it could be worse.

She and Stevie could still call Malibu home and their obscenely oversized palatial mansion their mailing address.

Stevie.

It's not that she's forgotten him. There's never been a moment, let alone an hour he's slipped her mind. Even now, Gretch is not remiss in this.

No, she is running through various scripts in her mind about how she will explain to him that they will very likely be allowing *the enemy* into their home for an indeterminate period.

Will he even grasp the weight of it?

Who knows?

His weeping has started again. She follows its sound like the condemned on the way to swing.

TWO

Stevie Darius lay with the blankets kicked down to the foot of his Instamatic hospital bed. The full deterioration of his thirty-five-year-old body is on unnerving display. Gretch forgoes switching on the overhead ceiling-fan-lamp, which casts too garish a luminescence that it would startle him. She steps up to his bedside. His weeping halts at the sight of her in the half-light cast by the full moon sitting in the upper left corner of his bedroom window. Sniffing at the air, which is thick with the smell of Lysol and the residual odor of feces, he grabs for a side rail and curls one palsied fist around its steel.

Gretch had to bring in a home-healthcare worker, a kindly Guatemalan named Flora, once it became apparent she could not care for Stevie herself and meet the daily obligations of various errands and food runs that maintain the household and provide her with the occasional respite.

Stevie tries to haul himself up into a sitting position and holds it for just a moment before collapsing back against his pile of limp, flattened pillows.

"Damon always used to say … it's not enough just to rip the phone out of the wall," Stevie wheezes, his sunken chest tremulous. "You gotta leave it all behind. All the machines that've come to own us.

Otherwise, they can track you. *And ...* you gotta pay your debt. But I'm not ready."

Gretch smooths the thin, wispy strands of gray-blonde hairs that stick to his considerable brow with a sheen of sweat. The mention of her estranged brother (for the second time that night) does not phase her, as Stevie always felt a deep connection to Damon ever since they first met. Perhaps they'd recognized the shared mental illness in one another before its full manifestation.

It is not hard for her to remember the Young Lion Stevie from only a year ago, with a full head of feathered blonde hair. Shoulder length. Now, it'd be a considerable task to gather a decent hunk of his hair to make a ponytail. It wouldn't hold and she'd learned this and had to tell him so after he'd pressed for her to tie his hair back, ignorant of his baldness.

Mouth twisted and tongue lolling, he pushes more words out, even as his eyes flutter beneath the weight of fatigue and confusion. "It hurts to sleep. Always hurts."

"What hurts, baby?" Gretch asks.

"The waking up. Sick of it."

His black Slayer t-shirt pools on either side of him where a year before it had gently hugged his ribcage. His Umbro soccer shorts, one of ten pairs he alternates in and out of because of their slippery comfort, clings to his inner thighs. His manhood is a mere bump in the center, a reminder for Gretch of how long it's been since they've had sex.

Thirty-five years old. With early onset dementia.

It is still hard for her to fathom. The rarity of such a condition in one so young and once so vibrant he'd thrilled and enthralled millions of loyal, diehard rock fans with his swaggering persona onstage and the running of one complicated bass line after another. He was a classically trained musician. A Juilliard dropout and proud of it.

And here he lies, drenched in his own sweat with bones like tent poles barely holding up his clothing.

The doctors say Stevie had a 0.16 percent chance of developing such a profoundly rare condition.

"Babe," Gretch whispers, lowering herself down onto the edge of his bed and taking his hand in hers. "Babe, I've got to tell you something. Can you hear me?"

Stevie rolls over onto his side, facing away from her. Then he spins back around like he's been pinched by an unseen thumb and forefinger. His blues eyes, typically lusterless, now shine with the spark of knowing. This is something Gretch will never get used to, the coming and going of her husband's ability to recognize and reason.

"Gretch?" He squeezes her hand. "What's wrong? Did somebody die? Is it … Davey?"

"No-no-no," Gretch says. "No one died."

"Not that-y'know-I'm pulling for that. I don't wish death on nobody."

"I know. That's not your way, babe."

"Tell."

In a quiet, cautious tone, keenly aware of how the news could trigger him, Gretch begins.

"You remember Gloria?"

His eyes suddenly retreat to their usual thousand-yard stare.

How could he not remember that day at Mud Festival. The biggest show of Grifters Anonymous' short-lived but legendary career.

Their last.

The riot that ended their set one-song in and resulted in twelve audience members trampled to death. And a handful of others stabbed to death

Backstage? The part Glory played in someone striking me so hard in the back of the head I was in a coma for forty-eight hours?

He's gone again.

It would be better that he not know who is coming to stay with them tomorrow. Of course, Stevie could experience another lucid moment like this one and he would recognize Gloria.

Such fleeting instances as this are so few and far between, Gretch decides to roll the dice.

"Gloria," she says, ignoring the knot forming in her stomach as the lie comes barreling out of her like she's been rehearsing it for months in advance. "An old friend of mine. We go way back but something happened-I can't remember-and the friendship turned into a burden for both of us. She was always troubled though. I have always worried about her. Thought of how she was doing whenever my mind was clear enough. And it turns out she's, well, she's been struggling after all. Really *struggling*. So much so that she landed herself in the hospital. She's been into drugs, and they say she overdosed. Someone-probably one of her shitty drug *buddies*-dumped her outside the ER and left her there."

He blinks up at her, his mouth open and jaw slightly askew. Says nothing.

Squeezing his hand, Gretch says, "Gloria listed me for her emergency contact. She must have burned all her bridges and has nowhere else to go. She needs a place to dry out and get clean. But I promise you I will keep it temporary."

Stevie presses his ring finger into her palm.

"What is it, baby?" Gretch says, leaning in towards him. "Are you trying to tell me something?"

Something, a ligament or vertebral plate, clicks as Stevie hoists himself up until they are nearly nose-to-nose. There is the faintest current of electricity which passes between them. She longs to kiss his lips. For her husband to moan against her and press his lips harder into hers until they are mashing mouths and exploring with roving, greedy tongues. *Oh, how exciting and dirty it all used to be when we got together!*

"What?" she whispers, afraid to blink for fear of jinxing the moment. "Stevie? Are you … are you—"

"What are you doing in my fucking room?" Stevie screams in her face, his breath hot and spoiled. *"I don't screw the help! Get the hell outta here, Flora! Let me sleep! YOU BITCH! YOU FUCKING—"*

And Gretch flees the bedroom. Her hands flailing to switch off the bedside lamp and palsied fingers that curl around the doorknob to shut the door against the now unhinged cries of the man who is and *is not* your husband.

It will die down.

She hopes sooner than later.

Sleep is a lost cause.

Gretch waits out the rest of the night curled up inside the reading nook that overlooks her prized garden, now a tangle of dead vines.

She's been meaning to clear it but is finding she could care less what becomes of it.

She's going to take Gloria in.

Something stirred in her while talking to the nurse, and then that something sat up and opened its long-sealed eyes while she was talking to Stevie. She hopes Gloria, once she's lucid again and past the withdrawals, can help her to fill in some of the blanks involving her time as manager for Grifters Anonymous.

Help her to fill the holes and somehow act as her memory. Names. Events.

Dispel any untruths for her.

Lately Gretch has started to mistrust how *she* remembers her time with the band.

False memories of conversations.

False revelations. Rumor. Speculation.

Some of it turns her blood cold.

Scares the hell out of her.

When she'd been in a coma for two days, Gretch had lost significant blocks of memory.

Vignettes from her childhood as well as more recent experiences, some of them tragic in their loss.

The inability to conjure her own mother's face in her mind.

A wine stain has spread across the sky. It brightens in its brilliance against the rising Crescent City sun. It lulls her into a shallow doze, which is more than she could have hoped for.

THREE

Gretch Solomon and Stevie Darius have never been ones to flaunt their celebrity. No denying they could if they wanted to. She was one of the most infamous and sought after rock managers since Peter Grant entered the rock scene alongside the new gods, Led Zeppelin. Stevie was the bass player in the legendary hard rock band, Grifters Anonymous, which critics have roundly praised as the last *real* rock band of the twentieth century.

When you consider the century still has five more years to go, such praise seems just as impressive as it is provocative.

Before his illness left him no choice but to surrender his driver's license and general freedom, Stevie and Gretch were avid travelers. They went on long hikes into the hills of northern California, sometimes even overshooting their route at the last minute and crossing over into Oregon. They rode on Stevie's Harley Roadmaster, sharing a cigarette as the rubber devoured the road and blasted AC/DC so all the countryside thumped to *Back in Black* and *Highway to Hell*.

So, Gretch's decision to hire a car service to collect Gloria Tizione from Cedars Sinai the next afternoon at 11:30 am did not come easy. Given the two women's history, the thought of riding the hour home, trapped in a car with the likes of Gloria, sent waves of anxiety through her.

For the sake of preserving her nerves, she dialed the car service and managed to dismiss any qualms about this *celebrity move*.

Now, the black leisure sedan rolls across the driveway and into view of the front door a little before 1 p.m.

The driver tips his hat to Gretch and cranks his door open. He's a swarthy man with a considerable beer gut he must hike the waist of his black slacks up and over before opening the back door for his passenger.

As it stands now, she doesn't even know she's holding her breath.

Waiting.

Gretch lays eyes on Gloria for the first time in four years and steps out into the driveway, wide and accommodating and framed into perfect seclusion by dense, fuzzy-looking high hedge.

Gloria steps out from behind the opened back door, one hand clutching a clear plastic bag with the words Cedar Sinai stamped onto its front in flowing script. Crumpled articles of clothing are crammed inside.

Her starved, threadbare appearance stops Gretch in her tracks.

She would never give voice to this, but Gretch is glad she agreed to take this young woman in after all.

Gloria Tizione, let back out onto the wild and bruising streets of Los Angeles, would be dead in days. And there would be no one around to dump her outside an ER a second time.

In the moody, overcast lowlight of early afternoon, Gloria Tizione stands at a spare five-feet tall. Her short stature is a reminder as it was then when Gretch had first met the girl that she is still quite young, and had been downright illegal when Davey Grifter, the lead singer of Grifters Anonymous, had taken her for a child bride.

Ten years ago, when she'd become a permanent fixture at rehearsals and recording sessions and shows, Gloria had been a sullen sixteen-year-old. With a shockingly whip-smart wit and dour sarcasm that no doubt charmed Davey Grifter.

She's traded in her former waist-length, poker-straight black hair for a bleach-blonde pixie cut and her arms are both sleeved in what looks like an overcrowding of self-administered tattoos. To the untrained eye, the tattoos do a decent job of concealing the track marks. Gretch spots the red and raw punctures almost immediately.

The former cocky smirk on Glory's face has vanished, replaced now by a hunted look. Her eyes do not blink as they used to. Now they twitch. She's dressed in an oversized white V-neck men's t-shirt and baggy green cargo pants. The ensemble looks borrowed or gifted to her out of pity. *Alms for the little junkie girl.* But the black, heavily scuffed Doc Martins are Gloria's property and Gretch remembers the day the girl bought them. The band had been playing the Spectrum in Philadelphia, and they'd gone shopping on the famous South Street.

She'd bought them at a store called Zipperhead.

Gloria smiles thinly and drops her gaze to the blacktop.

The best Gretch can offer in return is a single shallow nod.

The driver crosses in front of Gretch, breaking the line of sight and thus the standoff. It's not immediately clear what he's up to with his back to Gretch and full attention towards Gloria. Then, the oversized chauffeur starts digging in the pocket of his slacks and brings out a pen.

Gretch hears Glory laugh. It is an obscene sound like a giggle graveside.

The driver moves back to the front seat and gracelessly leans across it. He emerges clutching a small spiral notepad.

And it's only then that Gretch realizes what this is.

It's no surprise.

Gloria Tizione ("Glory" to those who know of her and her former celebrity), had been such a fixture in pictures and magazine layouts and interviews and documentary footage alongside the rest of the band she'd gathered as much fame for herself as the band. Interviewers had treated her with the same reverence as Davey Grifter or J. Germanian or Gretch's husband Stevie.

All due to the fact she spent her nights under the lead singer of Grifters.

Glory scribbles an autograph in the pad, wearing a sideways smirk.

The chauffeur waves the signed notepad and pen at her with a shit-eating grin, climbs back behind the wheel, and backs all the way out of the driveway.

The screen door behind Gretch bangs open and Stevie's exhilarated voice explodes the tension of the meeting.

Gretch holds her breath, praying his ignorance has held and will continue to hold even as he lays eyes on Gloria.

This is the true test.

She'd banked on his not recognizing Gloria so heavily Gretch had called Stevie's nurse, Flora, bright and early that morning to let her know she would not only have the next two weeks off, but that she'd be compensated with double her usual salary for that time away. That way, Gloria could come to fill the role of live-in nurse in the interim.

This cleared the way for such a ruse, and a necessary one at that.

"What's all this?" he blurts out. He's wearing a beat-up Lakers baseball cap. "Who're you?"

Stevie comes rolling out onto the Welcome mat, the wheelchair he's riding banging the left and right threshold and digging chips out of the all-weather paint.

The last thing Gretch could have asked for, a wild card throwing himself into the awkward mix. But at least he does not recognize Gloria Tizione. The dementia has fogged over yet another block of memory where Davey Grifter's wayward wife is concerned.

Gloria's jaw drops at the sight of this man who now barely resembles the young, hot rocker she'd known four years ago. "Oh God, Stevie—"

Gretch cuts her off, sharply. "I would ask that you address him as Mr. Darius. At all times. For the duration of your ... *employment* ... here."

Befuddled, Glory's mouth works but she cannot coax the words out. "I don't—"

"You're here to care for my husband, yes?" Gretch widens her eyes at Glory and prays the young woman will pick up what she's laying down.

"I-er-right." Tears stand in Glory's eyes.

"You're here to assist him from the day-to-day. I can only assume your temp agency failed to inform you of my request that you never,

ever call my husband by his first name. You're a stranger. And he has his challenges when it comes to certain fears and … oh honey, I hope you don't mind but she should know everything …*my husband's* fears and paranoia."

Gloria switches her gaze between Gretch and Stevie, who looks to have not even heard his wife and her warning. She nods curtly.

"No, the agency didn't tell me. Now I know. Whatever you like."

Gretch swears the girl looks like someone who wishes at that moment she could flag down the driver who'd just dropped her off and hop back in. Tear it out of there without so much as a backward glance.

"Is that all?" Gretch asks Glory, jabbing a thumb at the plastic bag dangling from her hands. "No other belongings?"

Glory acknowledges the light load in her hand, shrugs. "I travel light," she lies for Stevie's sake.

Stepping behind Stevie's wheelchair, Gretch mutters something in his ear and spins him all the way around so they can enter the home again. She reverses with him, making room for Glory to go first.

"Have you eaten? I just brewed a fresh pot of coffee and there's half a tuna salad in the fridge. It's all yours."

"That sounds … that sounds awesome," Glory says, and hurries along. She pauses before Gretch but does not meet her gaze. Eyes lowered and mouth drawn into a bloodless line of humility. "Thank you. Really."

FOUR

After wheeling Stevie into the solarium just off the kitchen where he will appear to watch Oprah without *processing* much at all, Gretch shows Glory to the guest room where she will be staying. Having stowed Stevie out of earshot, Gretch is better prepared to field Glory's inevitable questions. The young woman could not have looked more blindsided by it all

The room is spacious. There is a handsome cherry wood desk with a small lamp aimed down at a journal that is opened to a crips, blank page. A pen has been laid the paper to hold it open. A queen-sized bed is shoved up against the left wall. Its quilting and abundance of pillows are inviting in their lovely plushness. Gretch has been meaning to replace the wallpaper, a busy yellow pattern that reminds her a bit too much of the very design on the walls in the short story "The Yellow Wallpaper, a tale of paranoia that has stayed with her since she read it in high school.

The direct sun pouring in through the bay window seems tailored for someone in need of brightness and rejuvenation.

Gloria seems to approve as well, taking it all in and turning back to offer Gretch a thankful smile before moving towards the bed and dropping her bag of meager belongings. She perches on the edge of the mattress.

"Gretch, I don't know how to thank you—"

"Why me, hmm?" Gretch interrupts, folding her arms.

Gloria stiffens. "What?"

"Oh, come on, Glory," Gretch scoffs, coming all the way inside the room and stopping at the foot of the bed. "We've never been what anyone would call *close* or *friends* for that matter. I think you know I've never exactly been a fan of yours. So, you can imagine my surprise when I'm woken from a dead sleep to find out Glory Tizione, wife of my sworn enemy-and yes, Davey is an enemy of both myself and my husband—has named me as her emergency contact. What about one of your groupie whore friends? What about Davey? What about your mother or father? *Why me?*"

"Oh really, Gretch? *Really?*"

"Yes, really? You're telling me I'm all you've got? That there is nowhere else to turn?"

Clearly stung, Glory considers her folded hands in her lap. "That's right. You're all I've got. We haven't seen each other in years. I-I don't know what happened. Everything's turned to shit!"

Something shifts in Gretchen, and the start of a softening towards the troubled young woman is enough to push her headlong in the opposite direction, that of callousness and disregard. "We've all got our shit," she says. *Jesus, I ought to put that on a t-shirt and just wear it indefinitely.* "I'll ask you again. Why me, when you could just as easily have called your mom or dad or Davey?"

"Oh, you think that would have been the *easy* way to go? You know my father. You know what he did."

"I do. I also have no memory of you complaining about the arrangement. Never once. You loved being married to a rock star."

"Oh yeah right! Mom and dad were all too happy to trade me and turn me into someone else's problem. It was a business transaction. My father took money to let me go. Enough he never went back to the plant or dirtied his fucking fingernails ever again. He signed over all parental rights to the man who would eventually become my husband. Please let's not pretend I could've ever turned to him. Ever!"

"I'm not getting into the weeds about that, Glory. That's another conversation. I'm not interested in bringing my blood to a boil about all that today. So, no mom and Dad. Fine. You've got a husband. Where's Davey now?"

"Oh, I'm sure you know."

"Glory, I know nothing when it comes to the *scene* or your husband or any of the other tiresome bullshit that comes with any of it. I turned my back on all of it. You're just going to have to tell me."

Gretch had, in fact, heard rumors and she'd seen the grainy photographs of someone who looks a hell of a lot like Davey slumming all the way across the continent in Brooklyn or getting baptized on a riverbank down Mississippi or (and this was Gretch's favorite) performing in an Arabesque show while going by the name Dreamy Genie.

"He's dead to me. I don't want to talk about it." Glory rolls her shoulders in a hapless gesture.

As much as Gretch would like to convince herself otherwise, she can't deny the stab of disappointment. Then she realizes there is nothing useful or healthy in knowing and she would better serve herself by dropping.

"Fair enough," Gretch acquiesces.

Silently, Gretch moves to switch on the overhead light and ceiling fan. The breeze builds and lifts Glory's close-cut hair into chunky blonde tufts every few seconds.

"Some ground rules."

"Alright," Glory murmurs.

"You're not a prisoner here. I'm not your keeper or your sponsor or anything like that. I've got enough on my plate caring for Stevie—"

"What happened to him, if you don't mind my asking—"

"I'm not finished. You are going to have be your own cheering section. *You are going to have to keep yourself clean.* I can't be responsible for that. I will say that if I gather even the slightest of suspicions you've brought drugs of any kind-and I'm talking anything that is not presently in my medicine cabinet-I will immediately search your things. And you will let me. I find you've brought anything into this house, and you'll be forced out. I see the way you're looking at me right now. Shall I call you another taxi?"

Glory wets her lips, stares straight ahead. "No. I understand."

"I'd rather you stay out of sight when Stevie is out of his room. I know we've given him the impression that you're his interim caretaker. That was just to quash his curiosity. I'll be caring for him exclusively over these next few days, so there'll be no need for you to talk to him or really have any contact with him at all. We can't take the chance of him remembering who you really are. And he has his moments when the fog lifts and … well, his mind is sharp as a tac for a short while."

Before Glory can question this, Gretch holds up a hand and continues.

"Early-onset Alzheimer's. I can't predict how he'll react, but I do know he has never forgiven you for the part you played in my attack backstage at the Mud Festival."

"Gretch, please! It happened so fast I couldn't have possibly done anything to stop him. He acted on his own!"

"And you left me lying there on the cold concrete, unconscious and bloodied, for my husband to find. You just stood by like I was a goddam curiosity."

"Gretch—"

"Just stop right there, Glory," Gretch says, her green eyes flashing with ire. "For your safety, *do not allow yourself to be seen by Stevie.* Check around to see before you go wandering the house. Understood?"

"Jesus," Glory gasps. She looks like she's about to cry. "O-okay."

"We'll try this arrangement for two weeks, Glory. If in that time I find that you're making progress and you need a bit more time here, I'll take that into consideration. Any arguments or even the slightest raised voice and you will have to leave."

Gathering herself, Glory straightens up and out of the slouch she's in. She lifts her chin, regards Gretch with a calm resolve. "Okay."

"I will provide you with the following. Anything in the refrigerator or the icebox is fair game. Help yourself. Through that door behind you, to the right of the bed, you'll find a full bathroom. It's spotless. Never been used. There is a stack of fresh towels and washrags inside, along with a toothbrush, toothpaste, hand soap, and other toiletries for a week's stay. You'll take your meals in your room … for obvious reasons. I can provide you with magazines. Books. Music. A small boombox. Play at a reasonable level, and nothing after 9. That's Stevie's bedtime." Gretch nods her head at the writing desk, the fresh page and the pen. "I also bought you a journal." She feels a sudden lump in her throat. It gives her pause. "I've heard it helps when you're getting clean. Use it or don't. Choice is yours."

"Alright," Glory mutters. "Can I … ask a question?"

"Yes?" Gretch sighs.

"How will I know Stevie is out and about?"

Gretch considers this, then does a half turn. She turns to the side in the doorway, points at a light sconce set into the outside hallway. "I will hang Stevie's red tie on this whenever he's out of his room. All you'll need to do is poke your head out, check it, and you'll know what to do or not to do."

"That works."

"Okay then, so—"

The squeak of Stevie's wheelchair sounds in the doorway.

"Let me talk to her!" he says, glazed eyes hinting at a foggy mind. "What's her name again?

Glory freezes, her mouth in a bloodless line.

The two women nod to one another, a gesture bearing some small semblance of momentary camaraderie.

"What did you want to ask … Dana? That's her name." Gretch can feel Stevie rolling his chair into her knee, trying to inch forward and have a look.

"Oh, come on, lady!" Stevie erupts. "I want to talk to Dana in private!"

"About what exactly, Stevie?"

"You don't listen to the things I tell you," Stevie gripes, the color flooding into his sunken cheeks. "I hope this one will take me seriously. I've been telling you and telling you! About my feet! Hey … Dana? Somebody gotta protect me. They come at night!"

"Stevie—" Gretch mutters, laying a hand on his shoulder.

He shrugs it off. "You had your chance. You think I'm crazy. Have a look at this, Dana!"

Stiltedly, Glory rises off the mattress, only for Gretch to frown at her and wave her back down. Mouthing the words *I've got this!*

When Gretch turns her attention back to Stevie, he already has one knitted sock peeled off his left foot to reveal a pale and seemingly shrunken appendage that looks like it's turned in on itself like a wilting daffodil. Groaning, he wrangles the bare foot up across his other knee. "Here now! Have a look at this! Always at night! See what they do to me!"

"Dammit, Stevie!" Gretch cries. "I did *not* ignore you! Be fair! I could *never* ignore you!"

"Yeah, you and Flora both! Dana! *Look!* For Chrissakes!"

Fresh stress sweat stands on her brow, Gretch draws a deep breath. Turns back to Glory. Waves her closer. "Alright, have a look! There's nothing there, Stevie. I swear to—*what the fuck!*"

Glory gasps, claps her hand over her mouth.

Stevie slams the flat of one palm hard along the right wheel rail. "I *told* you! They come at night!"

Gretch takes a knee and grasps his foot in her hands to have a better look at the angry, red and swollen skin of Stevie's heels.

Behind her, Glory cannot help herself. "Who did this?"

"I'll handle this!" Gretch snaps. "Why don't you go have a bath! And-and get settled *in!*"

She does, but not before getting an eyeful of Stevie Darius' exposed sole. Quickly, she turns and scurries into the bathroom.

Closes and locks the door.

"Stevie ... *how?*"

The bottom of his foot is the color and texture of raw hamburger meat. Sear marks show along its center where the foot becomes some-what concaved. And there is the smell, which only now hits Gretch's nose like a punch in the face.

It is the rancid odor of rotting flesh and decaying vegetables.

Her husband's foot smells like a compost heap.

It takes Gretch's breath away and before she realizes, there are tears standing in her eyes.

No-no-no! Don't do this to yourself, lady! You checked both of his feet the first time he complained and there was nothing even remotely wrong with them! This is new!

Still.

"Can I touch it?" she asks, her voice small and apologetic. "It's got to hurt."

"Only when it's happening. When they hold the torch to it."

"What? *Stevie*-who are you talking about? It's only ever been you and me here. This? This is fresh!"

Nothing.

The window has closed just as quickly as it was raised. The small spark behind her husband's now roving blue eyes is extinguished, leaving behind the all-too-familiar vacancy that sits inside of his stare like two onyx stones. With a graceless jerk, he kicks his leg out of her grasp and quickly sets about pulling his sock back over his bare foot. Wordlessly. With his bottom lip pulled up over his top lip in such a way that he looks like the little boy he'd been long ago when first learning to tie his own shoes.

Since the dementia has claimed more of his mind, Gretch has seen more of the child he'd been in him now than the man he is supposed to be. It is a cruel regression. A Benjamin Button effect. Only there is nothing of fascination in bearing witness to this horrid phenomenon, and all the mounting horror that will one day culminate not just in his death but a complete and total deletion of his life.

She reaches out, touches the side of his cheek. She smiles, sadly. "Honey, I'm sorry. I'm so … I'm *so sorry*."

Stevie starts to sob and shake.

Gretch curls her arms around his legs and clings to them for dear life.

In a broken, watery voice, Stevie cries out. "It's Hell!"

"Oh, Stevie. Please … *stop—*"

"It's Hell knocking at my door. The devil and the angel all in rolled into one—"

"*Stevie … please … just stop …*"

FIVE

Despite having a new person in the house and another stricken with a raving illness, the farmhouse sat quiet and felt hollowed out as a Halloween pumpkin by the time the waning moon hung high in the night sky. Gretch assumes Glory has had a long day and gone to sleep. The queen mattress in the spare bedroom is heavenly. As for Stevie, he had not gone so gently into that good night. It required coddling and even lying beside him on the hospital bed until he started to snore.

She had applied healing ointment to both his feet, as they both were burned. Closer inspection convinced Gretch there would be no need for a visit to the ER, or even a consultation with a plastic surgeon. Satisfied in her own mind the wounds would heal, Gretch wound both feet in a thick layering of gauze.

You don't really *believe there's a* They *who comes at night and sets fire to your husband's feet. You may as well be talking about the damned Tooth Fairy.*

This *They* exists only in his mind.

Now, in the silence of the house, Gretch creeps from one drawer in the kitchen to the sideboard in the living room, collecting the two long-stemmed candle lighters stowed in the spots. She will hide them in a safe place or just toss them in the garbage cans out in the garage, where Stevie would have easy no access.

All the while, she can't shake the visions of disembodied hands, delicate but boasting long, black talons, at play inside Stevie's skull. Prodding at parts of his brain. Digging its long nails into the slippery gray folds arbitrarily. Killing regions of her husband's mind, touch by touch.

Gretch does not sleep well that night and abandons the effort around two in the morning.

"This arrangement," she whispers, rocking to and fro in a rocker set up before the double windows overlooking the expansive yard and the redwoods beyond, "it's not going to work."

If only she were referring just to Glory.

SIX

But the household defies Gretch's dire expectations. It falls into a smooth and simple rhythm of co-habitation that brightens her mood once she sees it for what it is.

Normalcy, if not a semblance of it.

There were no unwelcome *visitors* to Stevie's bedroom the first night. Upon opening his foot wounds to the air, Gretch was pleased to find the raw flesh already beginning to heal. He greeted her that first morning with a calmness she can only ever count on when he's sitting in front of a big screen, and the television is tuned to Oprah. The spark of recognition in his eyes lingered longer than usual, also. In fact, Stevie rallied for nearly three days straight in terms of recognizing his wife.

Eventually, this balance put her on guard, anticipating the other dropped shoe. She found herself considering whether Glory's arrival had somehow changed the dynamic of the household for the better and managed to ease Stevie's condition.

Granted, Glory kept herself hidden as best she could and obeyed the tie-on-the-sconce signal dutifully. The second afternoon, Gretch had popped her head into the guest room to find it empty. Later she'd find out Glory had slipped out for a walk in the woods. In the moment,

Gretch feared the woman was wandering the house or dipping into and out of rooms. This did not stop Gretch from behaving like a hypocrite, one she herself would loathe, and sneaking a quick look around the guest room for any contraband. What she discovered warmed her towards Glory.

The journal Gretch had left in there for Glory lay on her bed. A pen was clipped to it, marking the next fresh page. By the looks of it, she'd made serious use of the journal, having filled in at least twenty pages so far. In two days' time.

Gretch is careful not to let any hint of optimism obscure her judgment or lower her guard in the slightest. A woman who'd once been a skinny, plucky, and freckle-covered girl growing up in an abusive house that featured a violent father who daily apologized and wept for his abominable behavior only to fall back into that same violent rhythm of his own hours later, Gretch's skepticism has always served her well. Back then, it had saved her life countless times. Not that she fears Glory would turn to violence. No, if anything the young woman would deceive and manipulate. Hoodwink.

So, it would take more time than this.

Now, Gretch remembers to remove the red tie from the sconce before continuing down the hall that leads into Stevie's bedroom.

The sudden shocking sound of shattering glass calls the hackles up on her neck.

Then she is running towards the noise. It feels like she's trying to sprint through a river of molasses. The door to Glory's room swings wide and she appears, only to have Gretch wave her back inside.

Gretch finds him standing before a broken windowpane in his bedroom. Stevie starts to laugh. A low, rolling sound that sickens Gretch. The sight of him, even with his back turned to her sends a chill up her spine. She hates herself for thinking of her own invalid husband along these lines.

Yet, the way he stands there, dressed in a Motley Crue t-shirt and his favored slippery Umbro soccer shorts, his back stooped and sinewy body barely filling out the clothing, Gretch can't help but feel haunted by his appearance. The wispy, white hairs standing up high and waving atop his head as the air vent above fans him with a cool breeze.

As little as four years ago, (as much as this thought sickens her in equal measure) her future husband had kept a queue outside the dressing room of scantily clad, painted ladies just itching to fellate him.

Today, none of those lascivious young women would so much as help him cross a busy street.

"Stevie," Gretch says, mindful not to yell so not to spook him. "Stay right where you are. I'll come to you." She eases her way towards him because her feet are bare, and the floor is littered in glass shards. "What did you—what *happened?*"

"I sent … that fucking *Moon Man* to the moon! Heh-heh, to the moon *Alice!*"

He does a half turn and cranes his neck to leer at her with a queer satisfaction for what he's done.

"Just *stay where you are, Stevie!*"

"I'm not going anywhere, sugar." He tips a nod to her.

Raising her bare feet over an especially sizeable piece of broken pane, Gretch makes a big grab for him. Her hands find purchase on the right short sleeve of his rock tee.

His feet are not bare, thankfully. He's wearing his Bearclaw slippers, worn to tatters. Gretch takes him by the bicep, noticing she can nearly ring the once bulging muscle with her thumb and forefinger now. "Come along. It's alright."

"No," Stevie drones, allowing himself to be led and keeping his gait small and shuffling. "No. Huh-uh. It's not alright." He slips into what barely passes for a British accent but gets its point across. *"Ever get the feeling you been cheat-ed?"* The words of a bitter, regretful Johnny Rotten at the last Sex Pistols show in '78.

The bureau near his bed looks different on sight, but damned if Gretch realizes right off. Then, as she's easing him down onto the edge of his bed it dawns on her. The *Moon Man* Stevie was referring to is what's missing. The MTV Video Music Award Grifters Anonymous won in '88 for their concept video for "Knives for the People", their biggest hit. She'd always considered it to be the tackiest-looking of all the awards the band took home, the Grammy a much more stoic and classy-looking one that had been relegated to the room in their house they called the "Ego Room". It's where they display all things Grifters, from pins to various t-shirts to seven-inch record singles.

He sent the *Moon Man* award not to the moon per se, but out the window to crash on the flagstones below.

No time to determine the trigger. Best get him into bed, under the covers at once.

She's not ready for the push-back he gives her when she tries to ease him down onto his back.

Baring his teeth, Stevie barks, "I don't wanna lay down, *woman!*"

"Stevie, it's time for bed—"

"I said *I don't wanna do it!* All I been doing is laying around! Just laying all around-all day and all *night!*"

It is like struggling to wrangle a child dead set against sleep.

Still, she persists.

Stevie cranes his neck over at her, his eyes gone dark.

"Bitch!"

Gretch steps back. She must wring her right hand out like a wet rag. It itches to slap him. "Fine. You win. Just-*please*-stay there or you'll get a piece of glass in her heel. Alright?"

Mopishly, he shrugs and makes a study of his hands in his lap.

Quickly, Gretch collects the broom and dust bin from the bedroom closet. She drops to her knees. Maneuvers the glinting shards into the bin. Thankfully, most catch the light cast by the nightstand lamp, and wink up at her from the hardwood floor like a handful of earthbound stars.

A part of her wants to wheel around and scream at Stevie for making the extra work for her, and for *what?*

Increasingly, she's had to bite down on words that would hurt.

She'll need to get the vacuum and run it everywhere before she will be satisfied the floor is safe.

"Will you stay put?" she asks Stevie, her voice winded with exhaustion. "I'll be right back?"

Still perched on the right side of the bed, he stares fiercely down at the hardwood with a slack jaw fascination.

She decides she lacks the patience to figure this new puzzle out.

What's he obsessed with now? Where did his brain go now?

"Stevie!"

He grunts, eyes glued to the floor.

Gretch plants a kiss on his forehead and hurries out of the bedroom. It is during this short trip to the garage where she has stowed the vacuum that he realizes that she is not doing as well as she'd thought or convinced herself. The lie, the denial, that she is enough and can handle this great burden, made larger by the day, has finally caught up with her. And it comes in the form of the sudden tightening of her chest, a closing up of her lungs, a profound shortness of breath, and wet palms. By the time she is on her way back, wheeling the vacuum before her, Gretch's thoughts have spun out of control and it's all she can do not to fold like a card table.

To pull herself into a fetal ball and to scream so loudly her body turns to a tuning fork.

I'm not OK. But I must be. Not Ok *is not an option! Stuff the weakness down!*

"Coming back, Stevie—"

"Let go of it, Stevie! LET GO!"

It's Glory. She sounds frantic.

Struggling against something.

Or someone.

"Do no *harm*, you fucking bitch!" Stevie shrieks. "The longer you keep me alive the more harm! —"

"Drop it, Stevie! M-Mr. Darius!"

Gretch rolls the vacuum in double-time. It snags on the hallway's royal red runner, and she yanks it up and over, snagging the underside matte.

In the bedroom, she finds Glory and Stevie locked in a tug of war over some item out of immediate view. The shock of the scene stops Gretch in her tracks. She rebounds with a fierce overcompensation, skirting the hospital bed to the other side where her husband is splayed sideways on his back and Glory has him pinned by the wrists on either side.

"Dammit, *whore!* What the hell do you think you're doing?"

Gretch seizes Glory by the arms.

Stevie let's out a shriek, recoiling. Blood runs in stark, shiny lines out of his closed right fist. Stevie's face is purple, eyes bulging. "Do no *harm*, you bitch!" he spits, head coming up off the mattress and nose nearly mashing Glory's forehead.

He sighs as the bleeding fist opens.

A piece of glass, roughly the size of a fingernail, drops to the floor, gleaming wet and red.

Oh, dear God! That's what he was fixated on when I left the room.

Before anything else, Gretch lunges for the discarded piece of bloodied glass.

Makes it disappear.

Glory peels herself off Stevie. Raises her hands up like someone has a gun trained on her center mass. "Gretch, I-I-I knew something was off in here when I peeked my head out. I couldn't ignore my gut. And I got here just as he was about to … slit his wrists with the glass! I swear to you I never—"

"What!" Gretch cries, her heart hammering between her ears. "No! No! Stevie? He's-he's *not…*"

"I swear to you, Gretch!" Glory says. Blood stains her V-neck white t-shirt. "I would never … if I didn't think—"

In a blur of motion, Stevie Darius kicks gracelessly out at Glory's hip. He misses by a fair amount, dropping awkwardly back onto the mattress. He grumbles. Mutters something unintelligible. Defeated, he yanks the blankets all the way up over his head. "Get out of my room! *Kill you!*"

"Stevie!" Gretch tugs at the quilts and he makes a quick tug-of-war out of it with her until she lets go. "I'm not done cleaning up in here. I must run the vacuum."

"Gretch," Glory pleads, "please believe me—"

"Glory, wait for me in the hall please."

"Ok, but—"

"The hall!" Gretch barks. "Please." She levels a finger at the entryway.

Glory hurries out of the room, arming fresh tears from her eyes.

Her eyes brimming as well, Gretch approaches the bed and plants a hand on one of the blanketed legs of her husband. "Why, Stevie? I'll always take care of you. You can't leave me. Not like that."

"I'll do it again," he says. "You would've already snuffed it by now. So, save it."

It's like he slapped her.

"Alright," she says, teeth gritted. "I love you very much, but not another word. *Not another fucking word out of you.* I'll make it fast."

In a daze, she runs the vacuum over every bare inch of the bedroom floor.

Finished, Gretch switches off the bedside lamp and slips out of the room, shutting the door behind her. She has forgotten she sent Glory out into the hallway to wait for her until she nearly walks headlong into the young woman.

Glory stands with her hands clasped before her as she launches into a whispered plea of her case.

The lips are moving but all Gretch can hear is a subtle buzzing, a ringing in her ears as the events of the evening culminate into a weakening of her knees and the inability to focus. Her mind is a mason jar full of red and black ants that has just been shaken.

Synapses firing at one another.

Murdering logic and reason.

Before she knows what she's doing, Gretch throws her arms around Glory's neck and burrows her face into the young woman's shoulder. Sobbing. The tears come hard and fast. They rattle her whole body.

They exchange something and the barrier weakens.

Just as Glory moves to tighten her hold on Gretch's body, she pulls away.

"Good night," Gretch mutters and disappears into her room.

SEVEN

"Glory? Join me, please."

Glory had just finished prepping her Eggos by drowning them in a sticky swamp of molasses and making for the kitchen exit with speed. Ringing the rim of her steaming coffee cup before her on the kitchen table with an index finger, Gretch watches Glory make a slow turn towards her, glass of apple juice in one hand and plate of waffles in the other.

"I never thanked you for last night," Gretch says, waving Glory over to the chair beside her. "Please. Have breakfast with me."

It's something Gretch has never noticed before about the young woman, not even when she'd been a teenager on Davey Grifter's arm. Glory's shoulders are stuck in the raised position, reminiscent of Nixon and his own stiff posture.

Glory shrugs and drops her shoulders without any prompting. "You want some of my Eggo. I promise I won't say leggo."

And Gretch can't help but smile.

I've been hard on her, and she's taken every insult and insinuation and veiled threat with a grace I've never seen before. Maybe time to cut her a break. Looks like she's working a program, even if it's not the program. "I think I'll take you up on that offer."

"Black coffee?'

Gretch casts a dismissive hand at her half-empty mug. It's already gone cold as she has been sitting there for far longer than maybe Glory is aware of. Gretch's sleep was hard won at first and eventually abandoned around five a.m., which would have been far more terrible had she not spent it in one of the deck chairs beside the duck pond, bundled into a blanket, and further warmed by the flapping arrival of the mallards along the grassy bank. Then their bath in the murky, standing water.

"Yes," Gretch says, "and it leaves enough of an appetite to eat the elephant. Piece by piece, of course."

Glory is in the process of seating herself when the two women meet eyes. Where Glory expects to find that intimidating fire in her host's green eyes, she instead discovers a touch of indulgence. An invitation to speak plainly, but not too much.

Steadily, Glory saws her waffles into bite-size pieces, head lowered to the activity. "So that's what this is? Cards on the table? A little early."

"Probably," Gretch acquiesces, and sips her cold coffee. "Can I ask you a question?"

"It's your house," Glory says, laying her fork and knife on either side of her plate and sitting back against the wooden slats of the kitchen chair.

"Were you outside my room last night? Around say ... midnight or so?"

Without missing a beat, Glory says, "Yeah. But I wasn't eavesdropping."

"No?"

"No. To be fair, I'd have to be a monster or a drone to just walk past your bedroom door when I can hear you clear as day crying."

"Fair enough."

"I almost knocked."

"I'm glad you didn't."

"Well then," Glory says, and pops a wedge of sticky, saturated Eggo waffle into her mouth.

Looking on and considering her next words carefully, Gretch finally spreads her hands wide and says, "What happened, Glory?"

"I don't know what you mean?"

"How do you come to be dumped and half-dead outside an ER with enough heroin in your system to kill a horse ten times over?"

Glory chews contemplatively, eyes on the scarred wood surface of the table.

Gretch threads the needle a little more. "The last time I saw you—"

"Backstage at the Mud Festival. Yeah, I remember."

"That's right," Gretch says, glowering at her. "Right before your husband—"

Glory drops her fork. "Okay, you wanna know? Davey dumped me. You remember the festival and how we showed up with a *third*?"

"What was that *very young* girl's name? Something like the name of a perfume—"

"Allure," Glory says, with an eyeroll. "She's back to her birth name. Leanne. You should know I had no idea he'd married her until after the fact. There was never a conversation. He never ran it by me because he knew I'd shoot it down. I mean, bigamy? I'm not exactly a prude and it's not like I firmly believe in the absolute sanctity of marriage. Christ, my mother and father are two textbook examples of people who never should have said *I do*! But I don't think it was too much for Davey to have—I dunno—come to me. I thought he got bored with me. I would've spiced things up. Anything for him. All he would have had to do was to … to just *talk to me*.

"Davey banished me three months ago. He set up this fucking commune—he calls it an Artist Colony. Only thing was, anyone who showed up on The Mountain unannounced, looking for the *inspiration* the land granted the 'worthy ones', Davey chased them off. I can't tell you how many times he nearly shot one of them dead. Fired on them while they were running off. And I firmly believe he would have racked up quite a body count of these *visitors* if I weren't there to call him off. To calm him.

"It's not like any of the others would have dared challenge the Great and Powerful Davey Grifter. Until, well, I just couldn't support his dangerous ideas any longer."

Gretch raised an eyebrow. "Now, when you say *others*, who are we talking about?"

"When I left Davey and fled The Mountain, he was *married* to thirteen other women. Not legally, obviously. They held their own ceremonies up on The Mountain and recognized the unions among one another."

"So ... the rumors I've been hearing?"

"If you're talking about that bit of it, then yes. When I made my vow in front of a minister I never could have dreamed I'd be following Davey down into this pit of self-delusion and ... well, madness. He's crazy. I wanted to settle down with him in the Hollywood Hills with his royalty money when the band broke up. When all was said and done and the smoke cleared, he came out of it a millionaire many times over. We had our pick of any high-end real estate we wanted.

"I watched him try and I watched him fail to stage a solo career," Glory says, lamenting. "The music just wouldn't come for him. I'd never seen him so ... so low. Like he'd been betrayed by a good friend or loved one. The Muse just stopped whispering in his ear, I suppose. These things happen and that's what I believed, but I never would have said something so dismissive to him while he suffered. You know, I don't think there is anything more saddening and at the same time terrifying as watching an artist who has lost the ability to create. Far worse when it shows no signs of returning. I propped him up until I lost myself in H. Then, it was all I could do to keep him from snuffing it.

Glory paused, eyes flashing. "Do you want to know how he repaid me for keeping him above-ground?

"He kept me well fed on drugs. All kinds. I'm not blaming him for my addiction, but he sustained it. For his own reasons. I must have been out of my head on something when he proposed we move further up north into Oregon. That he'd spent a good chunk of his wealth on purchasing property. Ten acres of land ... and an abandoned rehabilitation ski resort-type building that sits snugly up against the mountain range itself. He bought the entire valley. Had his broker negotiate terms with the local native American chief council that owned it before him. Just seemed like such a random, reckless purchase, but it's his money. Who was I to put up a fight?

"But … *fuck*, I wish I had! I would have if I wasn't so doped. Useless."

Gretch sips her coffee, peering at Glory curiously over the rim of her mug. "Did he give a reason for making such a strange, out-of-the-way purchase? That alone seems like proof positive he wasn't playing with a full deck."

Not that he ever was!

That's what I have always contended, that he's never been harmless. He's always been dangerous.

A liability.

"He was pretty cagey with his answer," Glory answers. "Something about it being a lesser-known part of Grifters Anonymous history. And the resort was in danger of being demolished by another interested party. He never told me who. Or why they were looking to tear it down. He said the building used to be a rehab clinic. That Grifters spent a short time there in the very early days. Before they mattered—"

"They were never in rehab," Gretch interrupted. "I'd know it if they were. And there would have been no real push for them to do it *before* they made it and started generating money. It may sound harsh, but no one would have given a shit about a bunch of LA riffraff with drug problems. They were a dime a dozen back in '84."

"Oh, I remember," Glory says. "I used to walk the Strip and fall in love with every other rock guy who walked past. So much talent. Rarely an ugly one in the bunch. Must be something in the water."

"No … *no*, Stevie would have told me about any rehab stint. But go on."

"Well, Davey starts asking what Allure—Leanne— felt about moving into what he called a *fixer-upper* in the middle of nowhere. Snowbound and secluded to the point of a frightening disconnect form the rest of the world. It was nothing more than a fake-ass formality that he'd ask *us* if we were on board with this. When we got there, and it's not the easiest place to reach since they stopped plowing the long driveway leading up to it, Leanne and I were surprised to find Davey had already managed to get the lights on inside by way of a massive generator that ran non-stop in the basement of the building. The place was stocked with food, but that would eventually run out and we'd have to take weekly trips into the next town over. Some of the others knew how to hunt and skin their kills. Could be why Davey picked some of them. And I learned to love venison, as well as a spoiled rich girl could."

"You mentioned the *others*?" Gretch asked again, fully engrossed.

"The other wives," Glory says, flatly. Her gaze darkens. "He had … he …" Her voice turns watery. "The women were already there. Waiting for him in the abandoned rehab. They were there all along. In the company of a man. I knew him only as Karl. Apparently, he and the women had been squatting there. Davey moved in and-I'd never seen him so aggressive and threatening-he took the reins away from this Karl guy. Really alpha'd him. Humiliated him. Eventually he would drive Karl off The Mountain altogether. He brought in a minister from God-knows-where and had him perform a wedding ceremony, joining him with the other women. I knew there was more to this. Davey and Karl seemed to have met before. I couldn't imagine how or where. No one would discuss it with me, and I knew this was Davey's doing. He went from confiding in me for all things to shutting me out and shooting me up to keep me docile and compliant. There came to be fourteen Sister Wives, including myself and Allure. And the variety. Jesus! They were young as eighteen and as old as sixty-two. I questioned him one too many times and … he banished me from The Mountain not soon after Karl.

"The other wives slept with the right people in the next town over in exchange for goods and services. Gasoline for the generator. And … Davey not only encouraged it, but he also punished any girl who dared resist this obvious prostitution.

"Made to worship a *god* none of us fully understood or believed in, for that matter."

"A god? What *god*? Has he lost his mind completely?"

"I had the same reaction when he first explained the God of the Mountain to me. I laughed at him. He slapped me so hard I think I passed out for a minute."

"Dammit, Glory, *he hit you? He abused you?*"

"Never before," Glory says. "Not until The Mountain."

Gretch pauses, chewing her bottom lip and glowering at Glory. "Wait a minute," she says, "you believe in all this too. Don't you? He's gotten into your head. You've been brainwashed—"

"No!" Glory exclaims. "No. I hate Davey. I hate what he's become. I'm scared to death of him. All of this. But … please understand. He wasn't lying about the God of the Mountain. I've—"

"Oh, come on, you've *what?*"

"I've seen it."

'You've …" Grasping the edge of the table and shoving herself back with a look of impatience and bafflement, Gretch appears to run the gamut of a range of emotions. "You're away from him. That's good. I … I'm proud of you. For staying away."

Glory shrugs, forlornly, now taken to shoving the thoroughly saturated waffles around in the brown sticky soup.

Sensing she forced Glory back into her shell, Gretch says, "Ok, your beliefs? That's a conversation for another day. I—I didn't mean to make you feel a certain way."

Gathering herself, Glory pauses to breathe deep. Then, she rakes her hand through the tight tufts of her blonde pixie-cut and casts her eyes warily towards Gretch. "Stevie?"

"Yes—"

"It's just … he's so young. This just *doesn't* happen to a guy as young as Stevie."

"Oh, well, it does. It's very, *very* rare, but not unheard of. It did happen. His doctor has been wonderful. Thorough. Bedside manner the likes of which I've never had the pleasure of experiencing before. He ran a battery of tests. An MRI. It revealed an abnormality on Stevie's pineal gland. A CT scan ruled out a tumor. The doctor determined it was …a calcium … deposit. On a part of his brain that is normally about the size of a grain of rice. Stevie's pineal gland? Somehow it had swelled to three times its size. Placing pressure on the tissue around it. It's too risky to go in and remove it altogether. The doctor says it would drastically alter his personality." Gretch laughs, weakly. "That ended up happening anyhow when the dementia really took hold of him. He's … he's just not the man I married. I'm still mourning him like he's passed already. It's the only way I know how to manage all of this."

"Mm, you know, I think I've heard of that part of the brain. Wasn't that long ago. High school biology." Glory's eyes take on a faraway caste, then she rejoins the conversation again. "Healers call it the God Gland. The Third Eye. Ms. Heinrich … great teacher … and the biggest hippie ever to come down the pike."

Distantly, Gretch says, "I hadn't heard about any of that. Only that for such a miniscule portion of the brain, it controls more than you'd think. It regulates everything from the menstrual cycle, circadian rhythms, and bone density" She pauses, rubbing the cleft in her chin. "An abnormal gland can cause everything from hallucinations. Paranoia. Schizophrenia. And violent tendencies. Lovely …"

Glory doesn't say anything and lowers her gaze.

Gretch is down the rabbit hole now. "I'm past asking why. I'm past the anger portion. Right now, I'm sort of easing my way into the acceptance phase. But I'm not there yet. Not entirely."

"I didn't mean to—"

"Stop," Gretch says, "Just stop." It's time to pivot at this point or Gretch knows she will lose her temper and blow a gasket. "He seems to believe this is what he deserves. He's told me as much in his rare lucid moments."

Glory sighs. Shakes her head. "Do you know what became of the other Grifter guys? I feel like I've been living on another planet for the last two years. The isolation."

"Mm, you sure you want to know? There's not one happy ending in the bunch, sorry to say."

Glory stares at her, hesitates, then offers a stiff nod.

"Bobby Royal and Chris Desmond. They're the lucky ones. They're both dead."

Glory glowers at her. Tears stand in her eyes.

"Chris Desmond's death? On its surface, it could pass for an accident to the casual observer. He was riding his Harley. During a hurricane. People who know Chris would say *That's just what he is! He's a fool! Does stupid shit!*" She pauses. "He was riding the Pacific Coast Highway. He was riding to the left of a tractor trailer. Went to switch lanes and went right under it. Decapitated instantly. He had to have seen it. A big goddam truck coming up on one side? Tox report came up clean. He was lucid. Alert. You make of that what you will."

"As for Bobby, there's no other way to say it other than he just went mad. Apparently, he suffered the mother of all nervous breakdowns. Word is he died raving about someone *digging their fingers into his brain and moving things around while he sleeps*. He became an insomniac, afraid to shut his eyes. Mother's long dead. Everyone knows his father! The old man, Nolan Royal, took his son in out of obligation, but he insisted on little to no dealings with him. And the mogul's giant estate allowed for that sort of arrangement. Lots of speculation. Like he went the Syd Barrett route and mistakenly dropped a whole sheet of blotter acid. Either way, he died screaming. With his hands wrapped around his father's throat while the man slept. A member of the old man's security shot Bobby Royal before he could fully strangle his own father to death. They say he'd cut his own eyelids off right before this. His eyes were flooded with blood. Horrific sight."

Now Glory can only cover her mouth with both hands, eyes wide and watery. She has no words.

"Then there's John Germanian. J to his fans. J's always been bipolar. We knew this about him. He took a therapist on the road with him, and he took a cocktail of meds to keep himself even. Of course, the meds can only do so much when you're cancelling them out with a daily bottle of Jack Daniels and you're banging white rails off a different groupies' ass every night. J had a dark night of the soul. He ended up blowing his brains out in front of his fiancée, some French actress."

"But … you said Bobby and Chris are dead."

"That's right," Gretch says, softly. "J survived."

Glory's hands fall away to reveal a mouth set into a twitching O. Tears slip past closed eyelids and skate down her sunken cheekbones.

You could have lied.

You should have lied.

This is enough to knock her right off the wagon again.

Gretch, what were you thinking?

Something dark and deep within her answers the question without hesitation.

(You wanted to hurt her, and you have)

It takes Glory some time to gather herself. A yellow band of sunlight plays across the lower half of her face. She flings her arms around herself. A self-hug. Something Gretch has seen the young woman do when she was still a girl and trying to self-soothe in tenser moments.

"I don't know any more than you do," Glory declares. "Why five young guys would all end up the way they have. Davey's fucked in the brain too. He's developed this Savior complex, and I'm not talking about the usual ego most lead singers end up with. It's stranger than coincidence, but I just don't know. But-and I'm sure you probably already tied it all together-all the Grifters are either dead or crazy due to some mental illness. A malfunctioning brain. I wonder if it's a shared sickness in some way. Something contagious."

"It's not a question of *if* but *when* it's all going to come out. I'd rather know what to expect when it does so I can stave off some of the damage it will cause. Stop up *some* of the bleeding."

"It's … it's Davey."

"I know it is," Gretch says. "He's got you scared of your own shadow. So it's no wonder you'd clam up when it comes to old band business. Especially in the event its damning to him directly. He's got the most to lose … well, because out of all the Grifters, he's suffered the least. But what you should understand is he can't get to you so long as you're here. It might not seem like it, but this house is Fort Knox in terms of security."

"I-I never would have known."

"That's the idea."

"Gretch, listen to me."

"I'm listening."

"I've been thinking of, well, turning Davey in. Of going to the police. He's … he has developed some frightening ideas. And the way he sees the world now? Something is broken inside of him. He needs help. Or prison."

Nausea twitches in Gretch's gut. "What kinds of ideas?"

"Listen, it's all going to come out," Glory stammers. "Then you'll know everything."

But before Gretch knows what she's doing, she has seized Glory by the wrist and wrenches her arm towards her. "Will it incriminate Stevie? In any way?"

The two women lock eyes. The feral quality of Gretch's stare works on Glory by degrees until the young woman can take it no more and reclaims her captive wrist, wrenching it backward and into her chest. "He has delusions of grandeur. He says he has experienced the apocalypse That he plans to write a second Book of Revelation."

"Oh … *God! Glory!* Jesus Christ!" Gretch exclaims, shoving away from the table. Suddenly, this clearing of the air feels like a bad idea. "How could you let this go on? For so long. First the young girl! Now all … this! The Feds ought to be storming that damn compound of his right now as we speak—"

"Don't you *dare sit there in judgment of me,* Gretch! Always judging me! I was forced into the fucking life. I was just a child myself. You knew it. I wasn't old enough to make the best decision for myself. My father? He always hated me! He wanted a boy. I was his fucking biggest failure, and he saw his chance to get rid of me *and* make some serious money at the same time! He took it!"

Disarmed, Gretch sheds her righteous indignation and finds herself on her heels defending herself. "I-I-Glory I tried. You know I tried. And god*dammit,* when I took a serious step to free you *and* that literal *child,* Allure, from Davey, he nearly killed me. So, you tell me, what more I could have done without your *husband* finishing the job. Huh? You stood by and let him attack me backstage at that fucking Festival. I'm sure you knew beforehand he was going to do it—"

"NO! *I DIDN'T!*"

"—BULLSHIT! You saw him coming up behind me while I was trying to talk Allure into leaving with me and Stevie. You gave me no warning. You stood by. And when he knocked me down, you were one of the faces staring down at me with this *fucking look of fascination and-and retribution* in your eyes! So don't you dare put this shit on me, Glory! You could have left Davey Grifter ages ago, but you liked the money, and you liked your own celebrity that came along with it. *The Child Bride!*"

Glory bursts out of her chair, knocking it on its side. "What about *me?* That's my *point!* You were going to take Allure away and leave me to that-that fucking *pedo* bastard!"

"What!" It feels like a stiff, hurricane wind has blown Gretch's body back a couple paces, nearly sitting her down hard on her ass. "I didn't know. I … how would I … how could I have known you wanted out of the marriage? Glory! Shit, I would have helped you."

"Did you know? About the arrangement between my father and Davey?"

"Not until it was too late," Gretch says, solemnly. "Not until much later."

Glory shoves back from the tablet and stomps across the kitchen and comes to lean across the slate island there. Hanging pots and pans above her head shudder against one another as if the young woman's loss of temper was like a force of nature. She leans over, plants her hands, and turns her eyes to Gretch. They're brazen and defiant. "That's the story. True fucking story. My. Own. Father." Dejected, Glory drops her head and shudders as the tears overwhelm her.

Without hesitation, something that in retrospect will surprise Gretch Solomon all things considered, she goes to Glory and pulls her into a tight embrace. They stand together this way, holding fast to one another like two struggling swimmers caught in an undercurrent. She expects Stevie's ragged raised voice to burst from his bedroom upstairs, summoning Gretch for a wet bed or some paranoid delusional rant she must listen to in earnest. When it doesn't come, Gretch feels strange.

A quiet of the mind she thought she'd lost is back.

The two women separate.

Glory turns to walk out.

Gretch touches the young woman's shoulder.

"Stay as long as you need to. Thank you for saving Stevie's life."

Glory turns to face her, suspicion sitting in her big brown eyes. "What changed?"

It's an easy question.

Yet Gretch has a hell of a time answering it. Truthfully, anyhow.

EIGHT

Gretch only stepped out for a quick run to the Circle K. They had run out of the orange juice that she'd only just discovered Glory is most fond of drinking. A citrus drunk. This would be the third gallon of Tropicana she'd had to replace in only a few days' time.

The fact she had run out at all would have escaped her notice for a good week if not for her sudden hankering for a screwdriver once five-o'-clock struck. Permission to indulge, as determined and controlled by rotation of the earth around the sun. The convenient store is only ten minutes north of their home.

No harm.

No foul.

Now, as she tosses her keys in an ornate bowl by the front door and shrugs herself out of her windbreaker, Gretch hears a sound that confuses her. And it is a stark reminder of how joyless her household has become. Joyless, with a side of doom.

It's laughter.

And not just laughing alone.

Laughing with someone else.

Having a real belly-laugh at that.

She stomps up the stairwell.

"Oh God … I haven't laughed so hard since … fuck … I dunno when!"

Stevie.

It's been years since …

When Glory's voice responds, winded herself, Gretch stops cold. Just outside her husband's bedroom.

"If it's not in there already, you *have to* add it," Glory says. "I mean, riding your motorcycle straight into the Grand Hyatt lobby? That's right up there with John Bonham with the shark and the girl up in that hotel room. And it was *you!*"

Stevie cackles. "Yeah. Right. I-er-gotta tell ya'. I forgot all about it. But … I swear I musta' hidden it away for good reason. Didn't wanna … didn't want it to come back and *hurt Gretch* after I'm gone. Couldn't let that happen."

"Oh, Stevie, it's only a memoir. Right? It'd make Gretch a ton of money if you ever decided to publish it—"

"I can remember that's not what it's for." The mirth is instantly gone from Stevie's voice. Suddenly, he sounds stung. Irritated. "It's got no entertainment value. That was never what it was supposed to be."

"Ok … but you gotta admit the Harley burning out the hotel's expensive red rug was fucking priceless—"

Gretch rounds the corner. She considered bursting upon them. Two people she was dead certain could never be in the same room with one another ever again.

Not after the events of The Mud Festival.

And yet, here they are.

And she makes him laugh like I've been unable to do for years. My husband.

Am I the doom?

"What's all this?" she says, slipping inside the bedroom.

Glory looks like the cat who just ate the canary, her face pinched and mouth an open lock-jawed expression.

Stevie says, in a clear and confident voice, "Gretch, look who's here!"

He pats Glory's hand. Glory has enough sense and can read the rage simmering beneath Gretch's pinched grin to pull her hand away and set it in her lap.

"I can see that, babe," Gretch says. "The two of you catching up?"

"I dunno, Gretch," Stevie says, that coveted light of lucidity still flickering behind his eyes. "All the funny-*fucked up*-things we got away with. I don't know that you were there for the Hilton thing. I rode my Harley straight into reception and parked it at the check-in counter. I—"

"Of course I was there for that. I was your manager. There's very little I would have missed. Couldn't exactly leave you boys unattended for very long. It was like herding cats with the five of you most of the time."

Glory's laugh is weak and winded.

Stevie looks at Gretch. His limbs stir with excitement. "Glory helped me to remember some things. And I …"

"You … what, Stevie?" Gretch glowers at Glory, who casts a wry grin over her shoulder at her hostess. *It's obviously nothing to do with The Mud Festival, or I would have found him making some attempt, albeit feeble, to strangle the life out of you, Glory!* "I only caught the tail-end. 'That's not what it's for'. *What's* for? What are we talking about?"

Stevie nods. By degrees, he is slipping away again. "She reminded me. Towards the end of the band. She found out by accident. That I was writing-I dunno what you'd call it-a memoir or something. But … I think … I *think* it was a confess—"

"No no, Stevie," Glory interjects in a doting, parental tone. "Stories about the band. That's what you said they were. You were going all the way back to when you guys were still a cover band. You called it a *chronicle*. Remember?"

He shuts his eyes. His mouth pulls into a bloodless line. "Glory caught me hunched over my Composition book just scribbling it all down backstage at some show. This was years ago. I told her what I was doing. Never told anyone else."

Glory opens her mouth to speak again.

Gretch waves her silent. "Let him tell me. Let him fill in his own blanks. You're not helping him by being his memory."

"I was just—"

Gretch levels a malevolent gaze at her, says, "Go on, Stevie. Take your time. You've got my full attention now."

"I … I don't wanna do this anymore. Read them and weep. I can't stop you. Now you know where I hid em'. I remembered where. Now I don't. So read em'. Then you come back when you're finished and maybe you … y'know, you put me down. With a pillow, like …" He moves to roll over onto his side, facing away from the two women.

"What are you saying, Stevie?" Gretch moves alongside his bed. She reaches for him, and he shrugs her touch off violently.

"I'm tired," he mutters. "Fuck off with you." Covers up over his head again.

Glory stands, hands up. "Gretch, I swear he called *me* in—"

"Out in the *mother-fucking* hallway. Now."

Once out in the hall with the lights switched off in the bedroom and the door closed, Gretch wheels on the young woman, her whole body vibrating rage like a tuning fork.

"You were told to stay away, you stupid …" Gretch bites her lip, barely holding the words back. "For the love of Christ! What the hell did you say to him? Why would you *do this?*"

"Now wait a minute, Gretch. Just hold on—"

"I opened my home to you. I trusted you. And I was just starting to learn how to forgive you. You blew it all up with this reckless, idiotic move! Now you're going to tell me where he hid it. You obviously got it out of him. I have no fucking idea how *you* of all people would have. Not to mention, I'm his wife. His caregiver. And this is the *first* I'm hearing about a goddam memoir!"

Glory's brow furrows. "You don't really think he told me *where* he hid it. For all I know, he stopped writing it a long time ago. M-maybe he lost it somewhere along the way. Or-I dunno-tossed it."

"Why the hell would he just *toss* it?"

"Like he said. I'm sure you heard him when he said it could hurt you. And he loved you too much to let it get out and do any damage."

Gretch steps up to Glory, reminding the young woman of the significant height difference between the two of them, for what it's worth. "Where did he say he hid it? You don't want to stonewall me right now."

Tilting her chin upward, Glory swallows a lump. "He never said. I. Don't. Know."

"He seems to think he told you exactly where it is. Why is that?"

"Come on, Gretch. I-I-I swear he's not remembering our conversation the right way. He never… he *never* said where it is. And I really do-I really do *think* he got rid of it a long time ago."

"And what makes you so sure?"

"Because whatever he wrote in there? H-he seems to believe it will make you want to hold a pillow over his face after you finish reading it. Y-You heard him!"

"Yeah, well, this is your doing. Now I've got to keep a vigil to make sure he doesn't hurt himself. And if anything happens to him? I swear I will beat you into the ground. You … you groupie *whore!*"

Gretch shoves past her. "Pack your things. I want you out of here by morning." She tosses the words over her shoulder.

Behind her Gretch hears Glory slide down the wall, sniffling and gasping and weeping as she comes to hug her knees tight.

NINE

It's another chill night in Crescent City, compliments of a cold front that blew into town from the Central Valley and forces Gretch into a shawl. The heater is going to need another once over from the tech whose already been out twice in the last month. There is no relief when the vents kick on, and she finds herself more uncomfortable after having dragged her rocker just beneath the one in the family room. She drags a quilt off the back of a nearby loveseat, winds it around her upper body, and lowers herself onto her side amidst the billowing, hunter green cushions of the sofa.

The TV flickers across the room, casting blue flames along the walls.

The volume is low so she can hear the baby monitor on the end table at her elbow. Or *the monitor*, rather. More suitable considering it is being used to alert her in the event her sick husband has a nightmare or calls out to her in the dark for food or water or an embrace. The small speaker, no bigger than a fist, gives off a steady hissing sound that can only be attributed to the oscillating fan in his room that is kept running continuously. He is always hot to the touch.

The television is tuned to MTV. It's a replay of Pearl Jam's very raw, unhinged performance on Unplugged. The singer, Eddie, and his subtle eyebrow raises and raw passion haunt Gretch as she cannot help but see the ghost of who Davey Grifter had been as little as six years ago. In his prime.

I think there's been some borrowing going on here.

From their predecessors.

The ones these Grunge guys badmouth every chance they get.

Lips parted as the singer on tv holds her in thrall, Gretch doesn't hear Stevie right away. The low, droning whimper is easy to miss.

Then the whimper turns into a high-pitched scream in mere seconds.

Gretch is in motion before her legs can even get enough blood into them. The quilt unravels and falls from her body like a second skin as she makes her way to him. And there is that familiar, hated gnawing in the back of her brain that asks the dreaded (and-God help her-*hopeful*) question: *Is this it? Is this the end?*

She half expects Glory's door to be opened a crack, the young woman standing just inside with a question on her lips and trepidation in her eyes.

And a quick stab of guilt flares in her gut. She wonders if she went too far with Glory.

Glory's door is closed. For some reason Gretch can't quite place, this gives her a desolate, abandoned feeling.

She finds Stevie spinning slowly in place in the center of the throw rug like a dog getting ready to drop into a doze. The white cottony wisps of his hair stand on end. His face has gone the color of a ripe tomato. He wrings his fists in the air, back stooped slightly. He is shirtless and his Umbro soccer shorts wag and threaten to drop below his bony hips.

"Why-why-*why* didn't I burn it?" he cries. His rotations tighten until he is spinning like a bent top. He starts punching himself in the side of the head. It produces a thick, knocking sound. She struggles to pull his arm down, but eventually his strength gives out, and he relents. "Your brother! He told me to destroy it and I-I didn't listen. It was forbidden. Never should have written any of it down. I knew the consequences. *Fuck! I'm dead! All of us! We're all dead!*"

The mere mention of her brother, Damon, draws the hackles up on the back of her neck. She hasn't seen him since he stayed with them two years ago for a brief spell. It ended badly, to say the least. It's not something she's able to think about right now.

So, Stevie confided in your crazy brother and crazy Glory. About some memoir. Full of what sounds like incriminating stories or-I dunno-forbidden knowledge?

But he held back from you.

Why?

"We are safe, and we are healthy, Stevie," Gretch soothes him, arms slung around his bowing shoulder blades. "There is no threat. Do you understand? I'd never let anyone hurt you. Do you hear me?"

Slack jawed, Stevie looks at her with naked fear showing in his eyes. He is frequently frightened, but never like this. It is contagious and Gretch feels some of that fear as well. "Why would you *ever* let her come here. What were you thinking of?"

"Who? Who are we talking about now? —"

"The-the fucking Child Bride! Glory! Who do you think?"

I can't keep up with him.

It's getting harder to adapt to the way his mind works.

And how it fails.

Gretch takes his hands, places the palms on her cheeks. "It's your wife," she pleads with him. "It's Gretchen. Please. See me, Steven."

His mouth works, emitting a low groan. His eyes are rheumy.

Don't turn away.

See me!

"Bitch thinks she can just come and go … gotta plug the key holes … in all the doors … that's how she got in … drinks the black liquid and it shrinks her … tried to get me to try it but I tell her now … she's mad because I didn't take a drink and she went and she's gonna burn our life with the fucking papers… she thinks she can do this? I get my hands around her throat, and she's done-done-*done*!"

The mistake Gretch makes most often is to try to convince him his thinking is flawed. It is a futile and exhaustive effort, enough to burn out a caretaker faster than anything else. Still, she is human, and instinct moves her to try again. "If you can tell me where your journal is hidden, I could protect it for you."

Stevie nods. "Gotta do something about the keyholes. Call the locksmith."

Gretch sighs, leads him back to his bed and guides him down onto his back. "In the morning, love.

AN HOUR LATER, after having polished off the last quarter of Knob Creek, Gretch finds herself standing outside Glory's room.

She is swaying. The hallway has become a carousel, and she's got nothing to hold on to. She gracelessly grabs for a nearby sconce. The anchoring in the wall that secures the sconce buckles, and a hairline fracture forms in the brown-painted drywall.

Swinging her body back around towards Glory's door, Gretch manages to gain the confidence to once more stand on her own. Still, something of a human pendulum.

"Glo-ri-a!" she cries. "*Come! Out!*"

Nothing.

"No-no-no! I know you're in there! Open this damned door! FACE ME!"

The slightest, smallest suggestion of a smiling face in the white-wash of the door broadens the longer she stares at it. Into it. She feels like she'll fall into its mouth if it opens before her.

Gretch squares her shoulders as if she's about to go to war with this door and whoever is hiding behind it.

"*THIS IS MY HOUSE! I WANT YOU OUT! NOT TOMORROW! RIGHT FUCKING NOW!*"

Smiling grey eyes blink and dance and sing just above the widening smile. No nose to speak of. The door shudders like its cold.

Gretch puts her ear to the door, mindful to place it clear of the face that taunts her. The smile is open and there are needle-point teeth sitting inside those porcelain lips.

She can't hear anything.

A fleeting thought comes to her, but she loses its thread before it can fully occur to her. *You've got to calm yourself. You're going to scare Steven. You know how he gets when he gets woken up—*

She winds up and smashes the empty glass tumbler in her hand against the door.

Then, the floor rises to meet her.

To kiss her hard and fast.

To bloody her lips as they mash against her teeth.

Mouthful of blood.

A sudden sharp pain in her side.

Blackout.

TEN

Gretch's sleep is troubled.

The blinds in her bedroom were left open and heavy rain splashed the windows like she was driving her bed through a car wash. Gretch awakes slowly and finally lies there watching the winding sheet of water hit the panes. The events of the night before are still murky in her mind. Her brain feels like its packed with cotton.

Then she realizes she should have woken up on the hallway floor outside the guest room.

Somehow, she'd ended up safely tucked away in bed.

There's no way it could have been Stevie. Her husband lacks the physical strength to carry her to bed, let alone a few feet. The darkness of her bedroom crowds inward, throwing further shadows across recollection. There are flashes of sneakers walking past her head.

Well-used Doc Martin chukka boots.

Glory.

Really?

Gretch swings her legs out from under the blankets and over the side of the bed. Pain roars from the base of her spine. A reminder of how she'd fallen awkwardly last night. Nearly face-planted. Perched there on the edge of her mattress, she has no choice but to wait out the pain.

Her first stop is to check on Stevie. She opens the door to find him on his side, blankets kicked down to the end of the bed, and a chainsaw snore shredding the heavy air.

She shuts the door.

She knocks three times on Glory's door and waits, hands on her hips and the beginnings of a headache forming.

A part of her hopes she comes up empty-handed after making her search. A larger part than she could have expected.

Knock.

Knock-*knock!*

Gretch laments the optimism that yesterday morning had sparked the start of a reconciliation. *Hatred is baggage. An albatross. I was hoping we'd squashed it.*

No answer.

"Oh, fuck it," she says and turns the knob.

The door is unlocked.

The bed is empty. Meticulously turned down.

The bathroom door across the guest room yawns open.

"Glory?" Gretch calls, making certain.

The torrential downpour answers her, brash and bullish as it splashes the windows.

And it's a strange emotional response she is not ready for.

Her loneliness is revived.

You told her to be gone by morning. Make up your mind, will you?

Shaking off her waking fog, she makes the rounds of the various spots in the home where she's stashed money, her favorite Jamaican red weed (which she dips into with the sensible method of an accountant), and the jewelry which she keeps in an heirloom box on her vanity.

The money, which at last tally amounted to roughly ten thousand dollars in cash, is light a grand.

Why wouldn't she take it all? Nevertheless, she's grateful. This is emergency money. Bail money she's gotten used to storing away ever since she started managing bands on the Strip so many years ago. *Call it a habit.*

Nothing is missing from her jewelry collection.

The weed is gone with the wind. *So much for a drug-free fresh start.*

In the kitchen, she discovers the butcher knife missing from its wooden block. *She's hitting the streets. She thinks that'll keep her safe. Sad as it is comical.*

She pops her head into the Hubris Room. Stevie named it when they decided to use it as a display for Grifters memorabilia they'd acquired over the life cycle of the band. Everything from bobble heads to wrist bands to porn star panties to the framed gold record for their seminal masterpiece *Knives for the People.*

Three mannequins line the far wall of the room, their sole purpose that of displaying Grifters tour shirts. One of the shirts modeled on a mannequin is one of the rarer pieces in the collection, a fan club exclusive hearkening back to the band's early days when their female fans were called *The Massengill Army.* Back then, Glory had pretty much declared herself the president of the fan club and she'd worn the shirt to tatters, often going weeks without even thinking of giving it a good laundering.

The slim wall space sandwiched between two windows along the east wall draws Gretch's attention. The ghost of an 8x10 rectangle stands out amongst its surrounding olive shade. The rectangle stands out in pale, reverse silhouette, and it immediately reminds Gretch of what had hung there.

She casts her eyes about, her attention snagging on various souvenirs and posters and keepsakes displayed all around the room. Gretch comes to locate the missing hanging item, sticking out from under a tallboy caddy-cornered along the north wall. A bit of the corner of a shadowbox frame pokes out from under, haphazardly hidden away by someone restricted to a time limit.

She crosses the room and stoops to fish the frame out. It comes apart in her hands, the rear portion of the shadowbox showing a hairline fracture. The front and back no longer fit together.

The white cardboard that had projected the two memorabilia items inside in such a way they would have appeared to float behind glass, is torn out in a violent and vulgar fashion.

The work of someone not just in a time crunch, but someone who also loathes Grifter Anonymous like the victim of a sexual assault hates their rapist.

Davey had clearly done a number on Glory, well past that of filching her youth and innocence.

Something else is at play here.

The two memorabilia items now lay inside the broken shadowbox, limp and disrespected.

Gretch removes the items and lays them on the rug.

The partially crumpled napkin with the Cantor's Deli, Hollywood logo stamped into one corner and somewhat faded with age. This was the napkin the Grifter boys passed around one night towards the end of their recording. They had been brainstorming possible titles for their debut album. And surveying the other ideas spiderwebbed in ink across the thin paper (*Burning Girls*, *The Ache*, *Glasgow Smile*, etc.), Gretch was thankful they'd gone with *Knives for the People* in the end.

The other item is a rough pencil sketch on a memo pad page, complete with an ugly fringe lining the top of the paper. This was Stevie's surprisingly skillful rendering. A drawing of two hands locked into a shake. The fingers are dark with blood and more of the same drips from the conjoined limbs like they are each squeezing the other into a slow pulp. As he'd told Gretch one night during their pillow talk, he'd been wanting to somehow work it into the band name's logo. The other guys liked it. But Davey had been the one to nix the idea, dismissing the artwork as *too easy*.

She removes the lid of the shadowbox, careful not to catch a splinter. She retrieves the two items and gently sets them back down in the back of the box.

That's when Gretch sees it.

Faint.

But it's there.

The faint, ghostly loops and lines of handwriting pressed into the white cardboard at the back of the box itself. Imprinted. The result of applied pressure upon the back of a page, stamping the writing into the surface. Transforming the shadowbox into a crude substitute of the printing press. She brings it up before her eyes and tries to make out the writing.

Impossible.

What could have applied the pressure on the back page to cause it to leave an imprint like this?

A stack of papers?

"The memoir," she says. "Fucking. Bitch. I'll kill her."

But even then, Gretch Solomon does not allow herself to lose control. Surrendering control was what put her in this situation the night before. That's how she sees it, anyway. Best to remain poised and calculated. Hold it together and make your next move carefully. She channels the hardnosed band manager she'd been (in what feels like another life) and reasons it out.

If she calls the police and reports a robbery, she will have no choice but to leave out the memoirs. She has no idea what they could possibly reveal. The fact Glory had somehow extracted the location of them from Stevie and then made off with them points towards a strong possibility they consist of damning, even forbidden writings. Information that, according to Stevie, would hurt Gretch.

His confession?

Have to finesse this when I talk to the cops.

She hurries down to the kitchen and dials the authorities. She waits on the line for someone to pick up her 911 call.

Something alien catches her eye, winking in her periphery from the refrigerator surface.

The Polaroid pinned to the refrigerator amidst a sea of magnets for various local businesses, photographs, and other disconnected items had blended in with ease until now. But its new and as much as Gretch has paid little attention to what she's stuck to the outside of the fridge in the past, the photo practically rises to meet her gaze.

To beg for her prompt attention.

She stretches the phone cord to have a closer look.

A female says, "Nine-one-one, what is your emergency?"

"Sorry … wrong number."

"I'm sorry, ma'am?"

"Dialed you by mistake. Sorry to bother you—"

"Ma'am, you are aware dialing nine-one-one without cause is a serious offense—"

She hangs up the phone and approaches the fridge.

The photo is unsettling in its spareness. In fact, there is nothing even remotely extraordinary about it. So why does it give Gretch such a sick, haunted feeling. Like she was never meant to lay eyes on it.

At first glance, it is a gray slash just left of center set against a total, nullifying blackness. Like a prehistoric bone rising from a tarpit after millennia. The more Gretch studies it, the more certain she becomes she is looking at a glimpse of either the spindly, elongated arm belonging to a severely starved body or an arm bone. It is the angle in the shape, nearly a right angle, that implies an elbow joint. Not a leg.

Protruding from what looks like a cave wall.

Disembodied. Obviously, a photograph snapped hastily. Covertly captured before its photographer beat an equally hasty retreat for the nearest point of light to escape to.

Something is wedged beneath it.

A piece of paper folded four ways.

Unfolding it as she makes her way to the kitchen table, Gretch pulls up a chair and scans the surprisingly flowing cursive of a letter.

It reads:

GRETCH,

IT WAS NOT easy to do this to you. I'm not a cold-hearted bitch. Yes, this was a long game. Yes, I hate myself for doing what I did.

No, I have absolutely nothing to gain from lying.

So, when I tell you that you have the only known photograph of the Muse of the Mountain then you can take that to the fucking bank. You can't imagine what it took to even capture it. I leave it with you as proof that I'm going back to there to hunt evil. To kill a god older than the human mind could even fathom.

Davey will die also. I'm going to see to it. I just hope I'm not too late. He was talking crazy towards the end there, before he banished me from The Mountain.

I need you to understand I have no intention whatsoever of allowing for the memoirs to see the light of day. Not ever. I'm not looking to make a buck from their publication. And to show some good faith, I've only taken the sections pertaining to the band's time on The Mountain. With the Muse. I've left you the remaining pages from Stevie's memoirs. They will be incredibly difficult for you to read, much less believe. But they are the truth, written before Stevie got sick.

You will find them on your work desk.

The papers I have taken are far too sensitive to fall into the wrong hands, and I promise you they have not with me. You can curse me for not leaving the complete papers for you. I imagine you believe you are entitled to all his writings as his wife. The contents of these pages explain the unexplainable. The impossible. And they would place you in great danger once you possess their knowledge.

Cherish your ignorance when it comes to this.

I know you'll never forgive me for this. You always hated me. I also know you tried to find some common ground with me, and I love you for that.

You can take comfort in knowing I am pretty certain I'm not much longer for this world. But I will see this through.

No matter what.

Gloria

P.S. If some of the memoir is true, then all of it is true.

You already loathe me, so I'm just going to tell you that it's right and just that Stevie suffers like he does. It's right and just that J blew his face apart. It's right and just that Bobby and Chris are both moldering in their graves. And Davey is in denial, but I know he will suffer worst of all. I've seen the blood he coughs into rags. For months now…

Blood will have more blood.

PART TWO
WALK THE CRACKED SIDEWALK

"I honestly think it could all end tomorrow.
Not just the band either-I mean life."

-Marc Bolan

"I've got death inside of me. It's just a question of whether or not I can
outlive it."

-Don DeLillo

INTERLUDE (I)

From the Memoirs of Stevie Darius:

(1985)

The girl was little and the fight she put up surprised all of us. She lay beneath me, but her cries seemed to be coming from down the block. I felt the sturdiness of her throat in my hands, the burn of my palms against the skin of her neck produced this strange, macabre warmth as she twisted her head around and wriggled relentlessly. J. hovered around her flank, and he'd pulled out of her once she started to struggle. Chris Desmond wasn't there that night because he headed back to his mother's house to sleep after the gig and gather the rest of his things to move into our apartment. Lucky fuck! The other two guys gathered around me, J., and the girl. Davey took her by the right wrist, Bobby by the left. Securing her kicking legs fell to J., who kneeled around her flank because of the sexual position he'd taken with her moments before.

What started as a threesome involving myself, J. Germanian, and this girl called Lovebug, quickly turned into a mess of arms and legs and hands clamped over a mouth that nearly let loose a scream for the ages.

I started to strangle her.

This was a possession.

Because I'm not a killer.

Sometimes I think I'm remembering it all wrong. My mind has decided to finally show me what I couldn't handle in the moment. Couldn't fathom for years.

Sometimes, I remember it as J and Bobby slitting the girl's wrists with steak knives from our kitchen.

Other times, usually after nightfall, I remember it with more horrific significance. J and Bobby without steak knives at all. Both dipping their heads down to the girls left and right wrists respectively.

Chewing open jagged wounds. And a blackout without any alcohol in the mix.

Four-way blackout. Synced up.

A wild buzzing in the back of my neck where spine meets skull. Like a shaken bee's nest.

I have spots of memory where I check myself in the bathroom mirror and there is blood and bits of flesh on my mouth. Davey with his face between her legs, feeding-

No.

We are murderers. And our spree started that night.

With Lovebug the Runaway.

The other guys would all admit to experiencing that same buzzing in the backs of their brains as they were snuffing the girl's life.

It was only after the girl stopped struggling that the clarity, the crippling weight of what we did, came across.

Her blood was everywhere, like it rained from the ceiling.

One by one, we let go of Lovebug's arms and legs as recognition returned.

I let go of her throat.

J let go.

Then, Bobby.

Then Davey.

I looked at J, tears in my eyes. J seemed unable to focus on me, his gaze roving and empty. Bobby Royal stared helplessly down at his palms, gloved in red. Finally, J let out a shattered, desperate laugh and shook his head, wiping his own damning hands on the rear of his leather pants.

I turned to Davey.

Davey Grifter.

Cock-sure.

Shock glazed Davey's green eyes.

The dead girl lay partially clothed on the tangle of soiled tan sheets of J.'s queen-size bed. She had asked and, surprisingly, J. had let her keep her bra and black Misfits shirt on during our threesome. Shy. J. must have developed a soft spot for the girl. She was fresh off the bus from Minneapolis. Seventeen-year-old girl, running from a suffocatingly Christian household in Dearborn, Michigan.

One of the hundred or so girls we brought home after a gig.

She hated her real name (Prudence) and told us to call her Lovebug.

After she died, Bobby disappeared and returned with a couple bath towels. He tossed one to J, to me and to Davey. We

(wiped our mouths)

wiped off our hands.

A bad dream fueled by bad drugs. I wanted it to be true so bad.

Then, I wracked my brain to think of some way-any way-we could make it right. I was a twenty-four-year-old kid who still believed in miracles. That she would sit up and we would all have a good, long laugh about the whole thing.

The silence in the apartment, preceded by the raucous moans, was enough to drive me insane.

All hell broke loose.

All at once.

"I-I can't remember a bloody thing!" Bobby cries. "An inch in my brain and I couldn't scratch me. Vibration in our heads we can't get to. Blackness. I wanted to rip out of the back of my brain—"

That's how I knew they'd experienced the buzzing. "You felt that too? It felt like my skull was splitting open like a casaba melon."

Bobby looks at me, his eyes wide and fearful.

J says, "She was just a kid. I think eventually she would have gone back home."

Before I knew what I was saying, it just kind of came out:

"The Mountain. Fucking Mountain—"

Bobby punched the wall, denting the drywall. "The only thing that happened on The Mountain was that five fucking arseholes didn't last twenty-four hours at a rehab before they tossed us for doing the same shit they prob-

ably expected us to do. Nothing else. If you remember anything besides that? Then you were withdrawing harder than you all thought and your memories are bullshit."

"How could this happen then?" I turned to J. "I'm no killer."

"My head was buzzing, too. I …I was tagging her in the back and this-I dunno-this urge took a hold of me out of nowhere. A bit of kink. That's all it was, I thought. Not the first-time fucking gave me an impulse for violence. But I'm talking benign shit. A slap across the face. Spanked ass. This? Jesus … Christ …"

I was still in the dissociative throes of a heroin high. Still, the fear and shame of what I had done managed to wrench me nearly all the way clear of that oblivion. "I wasn't thinking anything. I swear to Christ, I left my body for a minute there. I watched myself doing it. And I couldn't stop myself. Something happened. And it sounds like it's the same for all of us."

One minute I was lost in the ecstasy of sex with a stranger. The next, I had my hands around her throat, and they had all crowded around this poor little thing with a sappy, self-imposed nickname, wringing her of all her blood in a shockingly systematic fashion.

Davey said, "Bad H?"

I said, "The heroin's from Manny. So, no chance."

"No point in parsing it out, lads," Bobby said, glumly, in his heavy Manchester accent. "We get our stories straight. Then we call it in."

Davey's face reddened, his cheeks fiery crimson and shuddering. "You serious?"

"We try to explain. We gotta try to set this right."

"How do we do that?" Davey said. "There is no fucking way out of this. We're dead. We're fucking done."

J opened his mouth, clamped it shut. Shut his eyes. Got it out. "We could dump her. Wetlands up north. Napa."

"Fuckhead," Bobby exploded. "You'll never sleep right again. You'll never get a moment's peace of mind. And it's right you don't."

Bobby Royal looked ten years older than the three years he had on the rest of us. We called him Papa Bear to rag on him. He was also the conscience of the band. He never touched women or ill-used them. Used cocaine with all the boring, rigid moderation of an accountant. His old man, Nolan Royal, is a millionaire many times over. Old money. The old man was our unofficial *manager in those days, bankrolling us for equipment and paying our rent by wiring money every month from abroad. And if you really want to get technical, we only landed on The Mountain because of Bobby's old man. Papa Royal was only trying to protect his investment like the savvy businessman he was. He bankrolled the visit to rehab, and he even stayed there with us for whatever reason. I love and loathe the old man to this day. He saw something in our band early on when we were still a cover band without one original song.*

I also think he knew more about the rehab and its eastern-European director, Stanislaw, than he came clean about.

Nefarious shit.

Sorcery-type shit.

Not to mention, the rehab director and his staff conducted themselves with all the glibness and flat affect of a cult.

"We can't turn ourselves in." J sagged down onto the edge of the mattress. He snuck a half-glance at Lovebug's body, and his eyes flinched away. "It's over if we do." He hesitated, hugged himself. "I can't go back home. There's no going back."

Strange. I think we all feared the death of our dream and the possibility of having to slog it back to our separate places of origin more than the justice system.

There was no home for me to go back to. Dad died of cirrhosis of the liver. Mom followed him shortly after. Friends of the family loved to romanticize both their deaths, claiming my mother died of a broken heart after losing her husband. I knew better. She would have gone on to travel in the wake of his death. Broaden her horizons. Dad wore her down so completely that there was little left to salvage of herself by the time he left her for good.

Bobby stomped out of the bedroom.

"Bobby!" I called after him. "We gotta talk about this!"

"Fuck all!" he called out. "I quit! This is Spahn Ranch shit!" We all heard the drummer wrenching at the broken closet door in the hall, then banging his suitcase all the way out and dumping it onto the floor.

Something in my gut seemed to shift.

"Listen," Davey said, "I came running from the other room when the girl started screaming. That much is true. But I was gonna pull you off her, Stevie. Then … I dunno."

"Man, don't even try it," J cried. "You're in it. With the rest of us."

"Fuck off, J!" Davey fired back. "What I'm trying to say is I-I had zero intention of opening her wrists. I remember … I-I grabbed for her right arm … then … don't fucking look at me like that, jerkoff!"

A girl appeared in the bedroom doorway. "I won't tell," she said in a low, confidential voice. She spoke in the sing-song, "baby-doll" way that had become a thing amongst groupies since Nancy Spungen, girlfriend of Sid Vicious from Sex Pistols, popularized it. The whole thing reeked of tragedy, of girls who'd been neglected or abused by their daddy.

"Glory," Davey said, waving her over, "come here. I forgot all about you, babe. Come sit next to me."

"What the fuck, Davey," I said. I asked her, "How long've you been standing there?"

The girl came a couple steps inside the room. She didn't seem to fit him. I always thought Davey gravitated only to blondes, usually with fake tits and non-existent asses. Vapid little Barbie doll clones. Glory was skin and bones, her limbs long. Her throat was thin and looked almost stretched beyond its original limits like I've seen African bush women do with their neck by using rows and rows of bamboo rings. Her big brown eyes confessed an amalgam of dark secrets. She was naked as the day is fucking long. Her hair hung down to her navel, a thick and slick mess of dyed black tucked behind one oddly large ear. Her skin gleamed the color of alabaster, with a texture made coarsened by drug use. Scatterings of pimples sat inside the divots of her cheeks, but this didn't detract from her rare, Mediterranean beauty. An Italian, my guess.

"She won't say anything. I believe her. Glory?" Davey stood, walked her inside. Slung an arm around her huddled shoulders. "Say hello to Grifters Anonymous." Any other girl would have wanted to cover up, but Glory (and I can only assume she was doped to the gills) swept her long hair off her chest.

She gave an extravagant wave. "Hel-lo, Grifters—"

"Get her the fuck outta here, Davey!" I said. "Are you kidding me?"

"She stays," Davey said. Wasn't even a question.

J stood up. Raked his poker-straight black hair back off his forehead. It hung down to his ass, and I can't remember having ever seen him with hair shorter than at least his shoulder blades. From what he'd told us, his parents were hippies, and they started growing their son's hair out at birth. They knew what he'd be before he did, or they'd made up his mind for him. "So …

what? We're talking a four-way possession? The buzzing and all that shit? Can it even happen that way?"

Bobby appeared in the doorway.

"I'll come right out and say it," Davey said. "We've all been fucked with. No reason to deny it. No call to ruin our lives over this. I mean, it stands to reason the girl was on a straight course to a bad end. You know it and I know it. This is just bad fucking luck for all of us."

"Bad luck?" I couldn't believe my ears.

"Chrissakes," Davey continued. "We're just a rock and roll band. Barely making it, no? But murderers?"

"What are you saying?"

"You know what I'm saying. And you know I'm right, Stevie."

"Alright," J said. "I think we can all agree something … something forced our hands. Maybe the drugs. Maybe something else we can't put a finger on. Anyone of us who can't live with that? Can't accept this for what it is? An accident? You can walk. No hard feelings, so long as you keep your mouth shut. And I mean you take this down into your fucking grave. Now's the time. Because after tonight, you try to leave, there will be hard feelings. You can count on that. This offer expires very shortly."

Yes. I kept silent. Said nothing. Did nothing

I want to die just thinking about it. That was the moment I could have saved my own soul of damnation.

I wanted to be famous.

More.

Bobby charged back into the room, shoulders squared and stance wide. He'd been a street brawler back in the UK. "You making threats now, mate?"

"No," J said, "Only laying it out. Stay or go. And if you go, I guess your pops will follow suit, so we're just gonna-y'know-have to regroup and figure some serious shit out."

I lifted my head, my cheeks red with shame. "We're going to have to explain all this to Chris at some point. Come clean."

J wheeled on me. "What would you have me say to him?"

"Offer him the same out you just offered us."

We voted on the question of telling Chris Desmond about the killing. To my surprise, I was the only one who voted yay

Ultimately, we decided to deny Chris any opportunity to get the hell away from us.

It was enough for us then to just swear to one another we'd never let this happen again.

Never again. We convinced ourselves what happened had nothing to do with The Mountain and everything to do with some bad drugs and temporary mania.

Lovebug's body. It would need to be disposed of. My stomach flipped over.

Davey said, "I'll take her away. I'll roll her up in the throw rug from the living room."

I shook my head. Covered my face with my hands. "Throw this poor kid out like trash?"

Davey sighed, reiterated. "Napa wetlands. Best bet."

Bobby sighed. "The swamp. She'll be picked apart by ... whatever the hell lives in there."

Davey was rocking on the bed, his girl crowded into him. "That's the idea," he said, just low enough to be misinterpreted."

"This is bloody fucked!"

"You ever been there?" Davey asked J and I, avoiding Bobby's searing gaze.

We shook our heads.

"It's perfect. I can make it in and out of there without a backward glance. I'll drive her there and I'll bury her. I'll even say a few words. I'm out of practice when it comes to prayer, but I'll try."

J kneaded his bloody palms. "I'll come. You can't do this by yourself."

"Nah, just help me wrap her and carry her down to the van. I'll move it into the back alley. Just gonna haul her on one of the amp handcarts when I get there. Otherwise ... I got this."

We all held our silence.

Davey said, "Guys ... you're welcome—"

"Fuck! You!" Bobby erupted. Launched himself at Davey and would've gotten him if J hadn't arm-barred him at the last minute and held him off until he calmed down.

Glory started humming an unrecognizable tune to herself that sounded more nursery rhyme than Top 40. Absently, she examined her nails, which were bitten to the quick.

It was decided.

And by the time we finished wrapping her in the rug and emptied a full roll of duct tape winding her up tight inside her death cocoon,

Then, something strange and obscene started to happen. I could tell the mood started to lighten among the other guys. I felt it too, God help me! J and Davey, hell even Bobby, by degrees exhibited an easiness of motion. J even cracked a joke I could have done without hearing. Yet, who the hell was I to take offense. I was complicit. In Davey's words, I was in it.

I was asleep not ten minutes after seeing Davey off. It would have been better if I'd suffered insomnia. Would have seemed just and right and well-deserved.

The dam would burst. I just didn't know when.

ELEVEN

The barkeep with shaved eyebrows and head to match slides the cassette tape back across the sticky countertop to Patrick "Paddy" Burnside. Eyes cold and mouth screwed up tight, done up in a heavy layering of black lipstick, she shakes her head in the negative at him.

"I gave the last two demos you dropped off to Harlan," she mutters. "Unless this is a new recording, the answers the same."

"He around?" Paddy asks.

"Harlan thinks your songs are ..."

"What?"

"They're *old hat*."

"Hm."

And he can only wonder if she's ever taken a punch from a man. He feels his right eye twitch, a tingling in his right hand as a fist closes in his pocket. He hauls himself up onto a barstool like he means to stay awhile, to order a shot or seven and drums his fingers playfully along the bar surface, which the bartender has just wiped clean with the cliched damp white rag.

"What do you like?" he asks her, splaying his hands in the air plaintively.

"What do I *like?*" She smiles to herself, a sign of discomfort or a prelude to flirting.

"Yeah, what kind of bands are you into?"

People are easy because they're all narcissists. They love to talk about themselves.

Unless, of course, you're putting the questions to someone with plenty to hide.

Then they usually demand some identification. When you tell them you're a PI, the exchange usually ends mid-sentence.

The barkeep straightens, looks at him. It's not even something she has to think about, and he knows this. Still, she pretends to consider his question. "Operation Ivy's my favorite. When I feel like channeling my inner demon, you can't go wrong with AIC—"

"Excuse me, AIC?"

"You serious?"

"I am."

"Alice in Chains?"

"Oh, those guys."

"Dude …"

Sucking wind, Paddy rubs the back of his neck and draws back to teeter on the edge of the stool. This is not his first rebuff, but he remembers the shame he experienced the first time a club owner belittled his songs. Kind of feels like flashing a family photograph featuring a slew of gap-toothed but cute and roly-poly children with pride in your gut, only to have someone glance at it and wrinkle their nose in disgust. In a painful shorthand of facial expressions, they reject your progeny and your genes and your wife's genes and your familial line and the looks of your offspring in one fail swoop. And while Paddy Burnside cannot exactly boast that he has been a singer and songwriter with his nose to the grindstone for any longer than two years, or that he's paid his dues tenfold at clubs just beyond the rock nucleus of the Sunset Strip, he is still of the belief that his is an untapped wellspring of genius. That someone will recognize the snatches and the stops-starts and the unfinished scraps of music and incomplete lyrics committed to a Memorex tape as nothing short of groundbreaking.

Then, there are the gatekeepers like the asshole who owns this shit dive.

The *Harlan Rigneys* of Los Angeles and the world who hide behind their sullen, underpaid bartenders.

But if there's one thing Paddy Burnside has learned since he first began networking around the Strip and hanging at sound studios while local acts rehearsed and lit the cigarettes of the handful of chick acts and mainlined the drugs alongside his heroes, it's that there is valuable capital in bullshit.

"What's your name?" Paddy asks.

The bartender rolls her eyes. "You never cared the other times you been in."

"I'm a shit, I know. But I'm asking now. And not to kiss your lovely ass. I want to *know* you."

"Yeah, you like cue-ball chicks, huh?"

"You got the skull shape for it. It suits you."

"Yeah," she laughs. And her eyes, a green the color of the Stroh's Beer light in her purview, deepens to an emerald when they land on him.

"Jeanie."

"As in *I Dream* of … or Bowie's *Jean* Jeanie?"

Even if I don't get a gig out of this, I'm still going to fuck her.

"As in grandma's name. Handed down."

"Oh," Paddy says. "Well, I'd change that around and make it's a nod to Bowie."

"Don't think I haven't."

She meets his gaze again. "Now, you answer my question."

"Anything, Jeanie."

"What's with the monkey-suit?"

Paddy has to have a look at himself. He is genuinely befuddled by the barkeeps question at first. Then he is reminded that he recently changed his daywear. More of a major overhaul. He's wearing a charcoal suitcoat and slacks that lost their pleat a long ago. Secondhand. He knows he looks like a market-district dweller who just got tossed. Even the white button-down, opened at the throat and yawning his head out of it, shows indentation in the polyester.

The illusion of professionalism is further undermined by the tattoo sleeves peeking out at either wrist, breaching the fabric sleeves which have been unbuttoned and rolled back.

From the throat up, Paddy is still maximum rock n' roll with his eyeliner and subtly applied foundation that barely conceal the acne scars salting his sunken cheekbones. His glacial, Nordic eyes still flash ice cold. His hair is driven and wound up into tight, dyed-white six-inch spiked wedges that could withstand torrential winds and quite possibly a hurricane due to the mixture of egg whites and rubber cement Paddy uses to hold them firmly in gravity-defying place.

This self-imposed professional makeover was inspired by the bitter realization if he wanted to grow his PI business and get that phone back at the office to ring more often than once every three weeks, Paddy ought to cut a sharper image. It's all about playing the part. By day, the professional dick. By night, the networking, leeching wannabe rock musician scouting for a band.

The result is just downright confusing to behold.

He knows what it looks like. Doesn't care.

"Everybody's gotta play the game during the daylight hours," he quips. "What else can I say?"

"And … what's your day job?"

"Private investigator."

Before the barkeep has time to shrug, he lays a business card on the bar. Slides it towards her. "For you? A reduced rate if you ever need my services."

Jeanie the Barkeep turns her back to reach for something on the higher shelf behind the register.

"Listen," Paddy says, leaning in again almost conspiratorially, "you should know-hell, *Harlan* should know—that there's some serious buzz around The Strip about this demo. I mean, I'm not just shopping it around to score a gig. No, I been passing them off. Passing them around and they've seen more hands in the last week than a blunt at a Dead show. I'm putting together a band around these songs."

"But they're … you know, they're not finished. They're bits and pieces, dude."

"They're crowning heads, Jeanie. And the big, beautiful baby is on the way. You just gotta believe."

Jeanie wrings out the rag in the sink.

"Tracii Guns is looking to exit L.A. Guns to come play with me. He founded that motherfucker and he's willing to jump ship." Pause. Nothing. "I ran into Bob Rock and slipped him a tape, and he's interested in producing once I get a lineup together."

A short squat man with grizzled gray hair and an American flag eyepatch sidles up to the bar a couple stools down and calls Jeanie by name in a whiskey-burned voice. Paddy is ready to get into it with him when he notices the leather vest and the Hell's Angels patches. Paddy holds his tongue. Jeanie greets the biker and proceeds to fawn all over him, smiling from ear to ear. Then she's downing a shot of Jose Cuervo with him, Paddy's mind is made up.

Paddy sits, seething.

He makes the demo tape disappear into his inside coat pocket, catches an unintended glimpse of himself in the fogged-out mirror behind the wall of bottles and tries to ignore the feeling of self-loathing. A man pushing forty, but still thankful he is blessed with a speedy metabolism and full head of hair.

The burst of laughter from the barkeep and the biker further down the bar sounds like it's right at his elbow.

In his head.

Paddy Burnside lowers himself down off the stool, raises a hand in farewell, and through gritted teeth calls for Barkeep Jeanie to "give my best to Harlan!" The biker and the bartender eye him without any spoken acknowledgement, which is the decider for Paddy as he bangs his way out the front door and blinks his way down the sidewalk against the blinding sunlight of Santa Monica Boulevard.

The chrome of passing cars twinkle in his purview as Paddy visors his eyes with his hand and makes an inventory of the dive bar's parking lot.

There you are.

He stalks towards it. Not even parked in a spot. This tickles his rage even more. The way the fat meatball biker parked his motorcycle parallel with the side of the building and right by the entrance for easy access. The fat shit could stand to walk a little bit to get to his ride, what with the extra Goodyear tires of fat he's wearing around his non-existent midsection.

Paddy dips his hand inside his suitcoat.

The wink of steel as he engages the thumb button.

Sucking his tongue with glee, he stabs the switchblade into the back tire.

Then, he's a ghost and back inside the warm confines of his very-used Dodge Ram Van, a black bull baking in the sun. The whole encounter took a lot longer than he expected. Now, it's back to the job. The one that has made his new-old wardrobe necessary. He's supposed to be tailing some oily defense attorney called Jackie Hanson, Paddy's services retained by his suspicious trophy wife. A platinum-blonde woman who suspects her sleazeball hubby has been screwing her younger sister. And supporting her drug habit, as well.

So, he's due in West Hollywood where he will stake out the law offices of Hanson and Toombs, LLC.

Now.

He drives and seeks to clear his mind.

But *The Man* always has a way of forcing his way in to Paddy's mind, like he must have forced his way into countless suspect homes and apartments, clutching a warrant in those sweaty meat fists of his.

When Paddy had told his father, *The Man*, he wanted to pursue music back in Junior year of high school, "Big" Billy Burnside Jr. threw him the mother of all beatings. It involved a belt with a buckle big as *The Man's* fist. Billy was lead homicide detective up in Reseda where Paddy was born and raised. Paddy's declaration for his future had stung his old man worse than if he'd slapped him cold across the face. Because Paddy had grown up with his father's mantra in his head ever since he could crawl: "You know I'll make sure there's a spot for you on the Force when the time comes."

That time never came.

See …

If Paddy had never heard "Strutter" off Kiss's first album, maybe there'd be a *Sergeant* in front of his name today.

Detective, even.

At Christmas dinner ten years ago, when Paddy announced he had opened his own detective agency in Los Angeles, he managed to silence everyone seated around the long table of food. His brother, Malcolm. Sister, Sinead. And parents, of course, bookends at either end of the dinner table. He added that he had already collected a rather impressive list of well-known clients who demand discretion. His father

The Man threw down his cutlery. The black look he'd set Paddy with across the table that long ago holiday could have blackened toast.

And Paddy had stood up right then and there, knocking the chair back. He winged a big turkey leg from off his plate at his father, striking the old man square in the face and painting it with sticky, shiny glaze like Billy Burnside had broken an intense sweat.

Two things happened simultaneously.

Billy Burnside Jr. never got to taste that Christmas turkey or any future holiday bird for that matter. He had tried to stand with the same outrage as his son.

Instead, Billy folded over onto the floor and stroked out.

And the sight of his father, twitching and dying on the floor, flipped a switch in Patrick "Paddy" Burnside.

It had always been simmering just below the surface, ever since puberty. The compulsions he sometimes suppressed and other times submitted to.

The remaining veneer of empathy within him fell away like a severed membrane.

Paddy had stepped over his dying father on the floor, fled his childhood home, and never looked back.

Now, banging a right onto Fairfax, heading west, he looks back not with regret or remorse but with wonder.

Enough with the memory lane bullshit.

Let's see what's on the radio.

He reaches for the small black box mounted to the top of his dashboard. Raises the volume and the van's interior is suddenly crackling with the sound of static and the occasional chirp of what sounds to be a female dispatcher.

"Didn't catch that last one, sweetheart," he says to the buzzing scanner, and thumbs the volume knob up louder.

"… 417A at the corner of 1st and North Fuller-white female-possible 10-50, possible 5150 … proceed with extreme caution …"

Crackle of static to open the channel for a responder.

White girl with a knife. Possible mental case. So, she's probably waving it around, freaking everyone out around her. On a street corner that's literally two minutes away.

Pass.

No units respond or accept the responsibility. At least, not as quickly as they ought to.

Apparently, they're as disinterested as Burnside, who is just now reaching to lower the volume knob on the side of the scanner so he can switch on the rock station.

"—dispatch, Car 4459 en route to scene now …"

The dispatcher confirms, adding the following: "… suspect is wearing a Grifters Anonymous t-shirt and torn black jeans—"

TWELVE

Burnside draws his hand back, lets the scanner sing the rest of its back-and-forth song to completion.

"10-4, dispatch."

A diehard fan of Grifters has become about as much a rarity to behold as a stripper who *really is* working their way through college. The tidal wave of grunge music, that fresh and new noise funneling down the west coast from a once-mediocre coastal enclave called Aberdeen and its adjacent Seattle, has rendered all glam and sleaze-rock acts the lamest of the lame and its makers misogynistic pigs.

By proxy, the fans were deemed losers. One step above the dweeb set.

In Paddy's experience, Grifters fans have gone underground to wait out this new era of punk-classic rock. For the pendulum to swing back around their way. When song lyrics are fun again, in celebration of fucking and tits and thongs and cocaine and Marshall stack insanity.

Not me, though. I won't go underground. I'll wear a Grifter tee. I'll blast Knives for the People *out of the van driving through any fucking neighborhood I feel like, and I'll do it with one middle finger flying out the driver's side window.*

Besides, Burnside is one of those musicians and music-lovers who can walk and chew gum at the same time when it comes to taste. He can appreciate the dark menace of Alice In Chains, the Aerosmith-Who mashup of Pearl Jam, and even the pure chaos of Mudhoney's loose musicianship.

But I love Grifters closest to my bloody beating heart.

I love The Crue.

Ratt.

The Cult.

Aerosmith.

Try to change my mind, motherfucker.

Burnside considers this mental case waving a knife around on a public street a *kindred spirit* for no other reason than the shallowest of all: *She's a Grifters fan. In distress.*

Time to swoop in.

There's also the great pleasure it will give him to scoop Car 08-4459 by somehow coaxing this crazy lady into his van and making off with her seconds before they roll up to investigate.

Anything to add to the egg on the LAPD's face.

The Man's face. One in the same

If only he knew where the responding unit was, how far away.

Paddy maneuvers his Ram van down an alleyway he knows will empty out onto 1st Street. He squeezes between the brickface side of a building and an ugly green dumpster puking up bulging torn, black garbage bags. Just when he thinks he's slipped through the narrow opening unscathed, Burnside hears the scree of metal on metal and the frame of his vehicle jostles ever so slightly.

Doesn't matter!

Nearly there. He pulls out onto 1st and hangs a sharp right that puts him on a fast track to the intersection with North Fuller. A red light hangs him up for a minute.

Green says go.

He punches the gas, brushing a rough-looking woman in an over-sized leather jacket and scuffed shades back up onto the sidewalk.

"Oh shit!"

An ever-thickening crowd of people have converged upon the street corner of 1st and North Fuller. Some mill about in the foreground while others deeper in writhe and exchange smiles or panicked glances with each other. Either way, he will not be able to get himself a good look at the knife-wielding maniac until he parts the sea of rubber-neckers and surges into the breach of spectacle.

He double-parks next to a Lincoln Town Car with the engine running and some guy dressed all in black leaning against the hood. The Johnny-Cash wannabe is already squawking at him.,

For the hell of it, he tosses the words "Police business!" in his wake.

The crowd splits like an overripened melon as Burnside pushes through. Faces angle around to get a load of him, but he surges through the gathering.

And he can hear the *crazed woman with the knife* before he sets eyes on her.

Burnside takes stock of the woman in the center of the circle. First impression is that the people have not surrounded a human being, but a raving animal escaped from the local zoo. The woman's heart is not in it. Her shoulders are slumped. Head down. Body turning around like she's dizzying herself up to hit a pinata. She does not so much wave the kitchen carving knife in her right hand as she rattles it. Dyed-blonde hair cut into a pixie style and standing up in tufts. A filthy black t-shirt hangs off her, the Grifters Anonymous logo writhing and contracting against a pair of deflated, braless breasts. Her jeans are cut off at the center of her calves, and her bare feet are covered by a moldy-green pair of gum rubber boots cut down to her lower ankles.

It looks like she's walked those boots through puddles of shit.

Then, Burnside realizes it is likely something else splashed up the sides of her boots.

Blood.

He lunges into center of the circle.

Within striking distance of the cutlery.

"Ma'am, they're coming to arrest you for drunken-disorderly," he says, hands up in supplication even as he has already figured out his Plan B, involving his subduing her and flashing the crowd a badge on his belt so quickly they won't even notice there is, in fact, nothing clipped there. "Let me get you out of here. You don't want to end up in lock-up. C'mon, honey."

The woman answers him by swiping gracelessly at him with the unwieldy blade. It comes within an inch of his person. They begin to circle one another within the makeshift public arena formed by hot-sweaty rubberneckers. Like two tigers sizing up the others' motions and reflexes. And Burnside likes his odds.

The woman lifts her chin in defiance, one lip curled up over her top teeth in an insane Elvis snarl. "Davey send you? I'll tell you what I told those crusty punks! The papers are ash! *I burned them, and you're too fucking late—*"

"Lady, right now I'm your getaway and times wasting. Come along, will ya'?"

Something buzzes in the back of Paddy's brain, the nagging of a eureka moment he can't quite bring forth.

Davey.

Grifters t-shirt.

Wait a minute—

A police siren sounds, its frantic shrieks close enough to make a few of the onlookers start at its sudden outburst.

It's gotta be three blocks down.

I know this woman.

Fuck-who are you!?

"What's your name, ma'am?"

She seizes her bottom lip between her teeth and chews at it. The carving knife does not falter. Does not drop an inch. The goal is to somehow distract her enough from the fact they have an audience, many of them rooting for the worst of all possible outcomes so they'll have a provocative story to tell their friends later that evening.

She's not gonna tell me so just skip this step—

"Glory ..." Her face reddens and her eyes glisten as her face crumples into a fit of weeping. "P-P-Please don't hurt me. Don't do it to me like they did it. No more Nasty Bits! They're ash! *Please!*"

Glory.

Davey.

Holy-SHIT! You're The Child Bride! Davey Grifter's kid wife!

Then, the last bit of what she said rings clear as a morning bell in his brain. Crisp and clear. *The Nasty Bits? You are* shitting me—

"Glory, honey, we got about five seconds to beat it out of here before that cop car you hear tearing up the road breaks up the party and hauls you in. Let me help you! I'll get you somewhere safe!"

"Why? Why would you do that?"

"Because I happen to know exactly what LA's finest will do with someone like you. What they'll do *to* you! And it sounds like you've already been down that dark road. Let me help you!"

A young voice pipes up amidst the crowd, spouting off snatches of a story no doubt involving their own experience with the LAPD and police brutality. Burnside hears only the word *"PREACH, MOTHER-FUCKER! FUCKIN' PIGS!"* Having always fancied himself a man of the people and an advocate of the youth, even if they were half his age, Burnside casts a sideways nod their way.

Paddy Burnside beckons to her. "Come with me. I'm a cop. One of the good ones. Cuz' I hate the rest of them."

This sends a ripple of dissent and agreement alike amongst the ranks of onlookers. Some of them even break away, crossing against the light or hurrying on down the sidewalk to their intended destination. The front door to a bakery which has borne the momentary misfortune of hosting this gaggle of folks and spectacle for long enough, bangs open. A swarthy, baldheaded man with full, oddly feminine lips and a rumpled white apron strung around his wide hips comes bounding out onto the sidewalk. He curses them in a language broken between English and Spanish.

From behind his back, the baker produces a Louisville Slugger, and he busts his way through the crowd as larger chunks of people break away. *"Puttanas!* How many times I gotta tell you fuckin' brats!"

Upon entering the center of the crowd, which has reverted to a mere street corner and nothing more of interest, the baker finds himself standing there with his baseball bat. And wanting for a head to slam it against.

Because he finds himself standing there with a police officer who's just pulled up, eyes covered in wraparound shades and jaw working at a stick of gum like his life depends on it. The cop has his night stick out, as if to match the baker's blunt instrument.

"What do you think you're doing with that bat, sir? Move back!"

"I don' unnerstand!"

"Yeah, me neither!" the cop answers. "Where's the disturbance?"

The baker scratches at the few black hairs standing up straight atop his tanned skull. The officer turns to one of the onlookers to question them, just as they show him their back and make to escape notice. It's no use and the cop's hand shoots out, seizing the fleeing man's flannel-shirt sleeve. Yanks until the man has no choice but to stop, but not without a gripe or two concerning his right to a lawyer.

"They're gone, asshole! Now I'm walking!"

"Who?" the cop growls. "Who's gone?"

Eyes burning with unfounded contempt and stitched in red borne of cheap hashish, he works his arm out of the officer's grasp and waves it about like a flustered chicken. "Th-the goddam girl with a knife and some guy!"

In the end, there is only the cop and the baker standing there staring at one another without seeing the other.

It's like the first line of a bad joke.

THIRTEEN

Once inside the van and cruising as the red dome light flashes in his rearview mirror, safely a quarter mile out, Paddy Burnside becomes aware of two things at once.

The girl reeks of urine and blood.

She is not only lying about the papers, the "Nasty Bits" as she referred to them. She has literally taken to wearing the papers like an additional set of panties. The Child Bride shifts and jerks in the passenger seat of Paddy's van like a child who needs to make most urgently. And if Burnside hadn't spied a flash of dirty white paper sticking out of her waistband, he would have thought her on the verge of incontinence also.

"You alright?" he asks her.

"Er … yeah."

"Because we can't stop anywhere. Too risky. The cops are probably looking for you, which means they're most definitely looking for this van and its driver. Best I can offer is a Big Gulp cup in the back. Behind your seat maybe."

Glory raises her shirt. She stuffs her hand down her pants. The flash of white paper is gone when she lowers her shirt again. And she doesn't bother to answer him about his offer to piss in a convenience store cup. Instead, she considers the steak knife in her left hand. Its serrated edge caked in what is decidedly old blood judging by its brown, crusted shade. "Where are going?"

But he's not ready to give up on disarming her. The Child Bride's question will have to wait until he has safely talked her into surrendering the knife to him. He'd tried once before and she'd shot him a dark look, hugged the knife to herself like a doll baby totem. And for the sake of getting clear of the street corner and the police presence on its way there, he'd let her hold onto the weapon.

Now, it is looking like this encounter could go south very quickly if she denies him again.

It doesn't matter who she is. Rock royalty. The most well-known groupie of the decade.

Paddy will disarm her. With sugar and honey in his voice.

After that, they'll ride the rest of the way home to his bungalow where he will start in on his next step towards laying hands on the Nasty Bits papers.

He wants to stick his dick where Davey Grifter's used to go. What a thrill! The childish side of him contemplates the possibility that he could contract some of the lead singer's genius by way of his wife's genitals.

A sexually-transmitted-inspiration.

"Look, er, Glory, is it?"

She nods, grabs at her short spiky hair, and realizes she can't pull it down to cover her face like she used to do in times of distress.

"You like steak?"

She doesn't answer. Her eyes are fixed upon the knife in her lap.

"Because, you know, I figured you do. You already got the cutlery to dig right in, after all."

No smile. No movement.

"Well, look, the reason I ask is I was on my way home to check my messages and cook a couple steaks out on the grill. Would you care to join me?"

Seconds pass and Glory lifts her eyes to stare blankly out the windshield. "Sure," she says, her voice toneless. Tired.

"Cool," he says. "That's cool. Then, if you want, you can tell me how you came to end up on that street corner waving a knife. But only if you want. Either way, I can put you up for the night or I can float you money for a couple nights in a motel of your choice. You decide. It's all up to you, Glory."

She lifts and drops her birdlike shoulders. Something like a shrug.

Ok, time to build my case for ignorance.

He glances at her shirt. The logo there.

Smiling with what looks like far too many teeth for a human to possess, Paddy says, "What is-or *who is*-Grifters Anonymous anyway? Are they a band or something?"

FOURTEEN

November 12, 1994

I TOLD *Doctor Garrity I'm not much for writing. But there was no getting out of this. I railed against her in our first session, the "Getting to Know You" portion of what the doctor insisted would turn out to be the first of no less than ten in total. I told my doctor her bedside manner was shit. She told me there is no such thing as* bedside manner *in the psychiatric field.*

"We deal in tough love, Gretchen," she'd said, sounding smarmy and cold.

I told her there's no reason for her to think I'll be here for any longer than the seventy-two hour minimum required by state law. I signed myself in and it's my understanding I can leave after that period, whether the good doctor deems me eligible for release in "good conscience" or "against medical advice".

I told her what she could do with her conscience. I'd be calling for Lori, my neighbor and only real friend, to come pick me up within an hour of that seventy-hour lapse.

She assigned me this morning journal writing. "Right after breakfast, I want you to request your notebook and a sharpened crayon from the staff. And

I want you to put down your first thoughts of the day. If you wait too long, the whole exercise will be pointless."

A crayon?

Yes, you may have noticed this is scribbled down in my Crayola color of choice.

Chartreuse. I like the name.

Doctor Garrity is not psychic, even if she turned out to be right about the length of my stay extending beyond the mandatory period. Otherwise, I never would have started these fucking pages. I would have waited out the clock and the realization that I'd jumped the gun in checking myself into The Grange Hall Mental Health Clinic five days ago.

Yes, you read that right. I'm still here. Nobody's decision but my own. The doctor did not pressure me.

This is my first entry after she threatened to send me packing herself if I continued to stonewall her about the journal.

I don't how it happened. But the threat of turning me back out into the street before I felt safe and collected enough to return home threw me into a nervous breakdown.

"I want to stay," I pleaded with the staff, as they'd escorted me back to my room after picking me up off the floor of the doctor's office. "Please, I'm not ready. I want to get well. Will you let me get well? Will you help me?*"*

I knew if I went back home before I got my head screwed back on right, I would have gone ahead with it. Pillow over Stevie's face. I would have suffocated the murdering ghoulish bastard, rather than rushing out of his bedroom in the dead of night.

He'll never know how close he came to oblivion that night.

I wonder if he would have welcomed it like he insists he would. Or put up a fight. It's my understanding he wants to die. That's not my responsibility. I'm no executioner. I simply had to find some way to make peace with what I'd learned when I did what to this day I wish I could somehow undo.

Somehow unwind the act of reading my husband's memoirs.

The pages Glory had left behind.

For what reason?

I'm convinced it was to shatter my world. My mind.

Well, mission accomplished.

Tired.

The meds do that, apparently. I'm gonna sleep this off until the anvil sitting on my head disappears.

NOVEMBER 13, 1994

THERAPY IS *like walking through a minefield. I have no choice. This is how it must be. Doctor Garrity is very good at what she does, and I think that's how she's able to lead me so fucking close to the explosive (personal revelation) before I manage to somehow backpedal and give her a non-answer to one of her leading questions.*

Yes, she walks me right up to that hole in the earth, the Abyss, and she does this hand-in-hand until I wrench mine out of her grasp.

I say, "I lost my train of thought."

I say, "I'm confused."

I say, "It's not important."

And my personal go-to: "I have to pee."

The first couple of times, Doctor Garrity let it slide. Then, as my non-answers snowballed into something burdensome and counterproductive, she would raise an eyebrow at me, and we'd lock eyes. Then, she'd abruptly break the line of sight and drop her gaze to the notepad in her lap where she'd scribble for what felt like eons.

While I waited.

Wondering how I'd be able to hold back everything I know for the length of my stay and somehow heal at the same time. I'm asking the doctor to assess a wound that I won't allow her to peel back the bandage from to have a look. I'm asking her to diagnose and treat without really knowing anything. The ignorance of all the crippling knowledge and the terrible realizations that have landed me here in the first place.

And put the pillow in my hands. Stood me there beside Stevie's sleeping body, ready to snuff him out.

So, today, I started to build a false narrative in therapy. The way I saw it, there's no reason I can't devise a series of lies that run closely enough and parallel to the truth that the doctor can treat me based on these. No one is ever going to get their hands on my journal. They will have to pry it from my cold, dead hands.

So, I can be candid, and I can lay it out.

The doctor likes neat and orderly in terms of her notes. Chronological, also. I began with what brought me to the hospital and made me check myself in. I told her about my brother Damon and his mental health challenges, but I was mindful to also include the fact that he was administered a vaccine while still an infant that has proven to have lasting cognitive and emotional effects on him. He displays certain savant-like, autistic traits like he has an unsettling eidetic memory. He even insisted he remembered his time in the womb and describes the experience to such a degree he was able to tell my mother about the bouts of bleeding she suffered and what food she favored most while he was in utero.

Doctor Garrity asked if I was ever worried that mental health would become an issue for me as it had revealed itself in my bloodline. It was more a passing trepidation that spiked soon after I had to have my own brother removed from my property and committed to a psychiatric facility indefinitely. Over time, I'd had little time to myself to contemplate let alone worry about whether I'd soon go crazy as well. The fear faded.

The parallel lie for my entering the hospital: a repressed memory of having been sexually abused by a neighbor after I'd agreed at a party to allow myself to be hypnotized. The memory of the assault came flooding back and crippled me.

The truth is far messier. Uglier, in my opinion. If Glory hadn't left the bulk of Stevie's memoirs behind that morning for me to read, I would not have suffered the mental breakdown after reading them. In a fit of mania, I can barely remember, I burned the papers in the firepit behind the house. I burned my right hand in the process, probably because I'd been so disconnected from myself, I wasn't paying careful enough attention.

I could have told Doctor Garrity the truth. It would not have harmed me in any way. I would not have incriminated myself. And this was not a decision I came to lightly.

To shield Stevie from the prosecution and the swift arm of justice.

It took hours of quiet time. Listening to my thoughts. My heart. Searching my morality and following its compass as best I could given the circumstances. And just as I'd stopped myself from smothering Stevie (and I'm certain I made the right decision there) I kept the reason for my wanting to kill him from Doctor Garrity.

Stevie is, in fact, a serial killer.

My husband.

And the memoirs are, *in fact, his confessions.*

It's as he said.

When I first started reading them, I made sure to pour myself four fingers of bourbon to have at the ready. I knew I was dipping my toes into boiling water. I grew sicker and more paralyzed with every turn of a page

I felt like I needed a long, hot bath.

By the time I was a quarter of the way through the memoirs, my pulse had quickened to such a degree I could hear the rush of blood between my ears. I downed the whiskey in one toss back. Poured another glass in a fog and sat down to finish reading. Hours went by.

I might have stepped away from the pages. Burned them without finishing.

I have no idea why I read on to the end.

Doctor Garrity asked a pointed question today involving Stevie. "You haven't mentioned him since you started here. He is your husband. Are you thinking of him? Do you miss him? What is happening there?"

The parallel lie: Dementia has almost completely wiped his mind. I don't see him in this situation at all, anywhere in the mix. Because he may as well be dead. That's not Stevie, at home in that hospital bed.

A part of me pities him. I can't help but to suspect maybe he was further along in his dementia than he knew when he started to write his memoirs down. Because there is no other explanation for the strange, surreal statements he makes. The events he describes. How he alludes to these events as the impetus for the killings to come.

I mean, he alludes to his "Time on the Mountain" like some rock and roll Moses. That he and the other Grifter members spent that time together.

That something happened to them on The Mountain. They were corrupted by some force or entity that resides inside the fucking Mountain! And it has given them no choice but to kill.

To sacrifice?

Stevie was clearly sick when he wrote these things.

What's the alternative?

Med and dinner time. Be back.

NOVEMBER *14, 1994*

HARD TIME GETTING *out of bed today and living.*

Flora called the hospital last night because Stevie tossed a fit and wanted to talk to me. She sounded wrung out. I've never heard her sound so beaten down. I asked her if she'd been sleeping okay. She's had to tranquilize Stevie the last couple of nights.

"Otherwise, I get no rest. He's still complaining his feet are on fire. I don't see anything when I take a look. He won't leave me be unless I bandage the foot, even though there's nothing to bandage."

It tears me in half when he gets on the phone. I tried to put this off, but I knew if I did I'd be putting her into an even tougher spot. I can't lose Flora. I don't know when the hell I'm getting out of here. Don't know when or if I'll ever be ready. Then thing about entering a mental health hospital is its sense of safety and the falling away of all adult responsibility and basic decision-making becomes quickly addictive.

You start to dread the real world. An avoidance impulse sets in.

I said very little to Stevie over the phone. I let him bark at me, then sob. I'd left him. I'd abandoned him. At one point, I could hear him cupping the receiver to hide what he was saying from Flora. Only to whisper into the phone that she is trying to poison him. That Flora is slowly killing him by filtering a toxin through the vents like the Joker or something.

I came dangerously close to mentioning The Mountain to him. I caught myself. Stevie is profoundly unpredictable with rapid mood swings. If the mention of The Mountain were to trigger something in him, like some violent impulse, and he hurt Flora, I'd never forgive myself. And there'd be no one there to save her if he somehow managed to overpower her or knock her uncon-scious in his rage. So, I held it back and rang off soon after.

This is wearing on me.

Not Stevie.

Having to lie for him.

Why am I doing this for him? Remind me, please!

I don't think I'm going to get any better until I come clean.

Tell the truth, not some parallel version of it to protect a killer.

Something is splitting inside of me. A schism. While I was on the phone with Stevie, I experienced something strange. For a couple seconds, I felt my body sag and then it was like something inside disconnected from the flesh. Suddenly, I was standing behind myself and watching my shoulders as they rose and fell. Tightened. It was the conversation. Stressing me out. The doctor on call told me that I was "disassociating", a byproduct of psychosis. Either the meds are not agreeing with me, or something else is at work here.

I'm regressing.

Because I'm lying.

To the doctor. To myself.

And I fear it's going to stunt my healing. I'm going to spiral.

All to shield a killer.

This can't go on.

I don't care if he's my husband and I don't want to believe it.

November 17, 1994

THE MEDS AREN'T WORKING. This is the third round of trials I've been on.

Antipsychotics.

SSRIs.

Opioids.

Mixing and matching. Tweaking.

And after roughly two and a half weeks, I am circling the drain faster than anyone could have possibly imagined. Even Doctor Garrity seems perplexed by my brain's resistance to pharmaceutical treatments. According to her, there is a very small portion of the population who shows biological immunity mental health meds. She wouldn't give me a number, and it's probably better that way. I think I'd heard anything from 1% to 5%, I'd probably want to send myself crashing headfirst through the second-floor window.

"I've been looking into another option for treatment, but we're going to treat it as a last resort. I want you to feel comfortable in knowing we've

exhausted every option. So, we're going to try — with a smaller dose of —, twice a day for three more days."

Am I going to say no? Of course not.

It is constantly on the tip of my tongue, a complete revelation of what the memoirs have revealed about my husband.

They are his dark deeds.

Not fucking mine!

If he was sick at the time of their writing, I imagine it will come out in the court proceedings. I wonder if professionals can trace the dementia back to its initial development.

Like a timestamp, maybe?

I wonder what prison will look like for Stevie if these same professionals fail to prove he was sick those years ago. Will they put him in a prison hospice or feed him to the wolves?

His writing is lucid. Clear. And it only tips into language that could be construed as disconnected from reality when he references The Mountain. And The Muse, whoever the fuck that is! Then, it is not only conceivable he was writing back then even as his mind was starting to deteriorate. There is no other explanation.

I asked the doctor a point-blank question. I knew full well such a random inquiry would spur her interest, and she'd want to know why I was asking. But I had to do it.

"Would you say its cruel and unusual to punish someone with brain damage for committing a violent crime?"

Doctor Garrity once more raised one dark, sculpted eyebrow. She adjusted herself in her seat, switching her crossed legs to the opposite arrangement. She retrieved her pen from behind an ear. She scribbled something on the pad in her lap. Said,

"Why do you ask?"

"Curiosity, I suppose."

The doctor holds my gaze for a beat longer than I'm comfortable with before dropping pen to paper once more to write something else. She tics her head slightly to the left, clicks her tongue off the roof of her mouth and lays a hand along the right side of her jaw.

"And ... what prompted *this* curiosity," *she said.* "I think even you would have to admit that this is a rather sharp turn you're taking here."*

I did not look away. "Nevertheless ..."

"A television program?" Doctor Garrity just wouldn't answer the questions without some frame of reference. Like a dog after a bone.

*I gave her what she wanted. "*Law & Order* episode. The other night."*

"Ah," the doctor breathed, nodding to herself and writing. "So, a hypothetical? Are you sure that's a wise course of action for us? We've only got twenty minutes together each afternoon. I think we ought to stay on task and stick with the issues and concerns that have led you here for help."

"So ... that's a —what—a no comment*?"*

Spreading her hands in the air, Doctor Garrity says, "I'd be happy to offer my opinion. But you'd have to do something for me."

My stomach started to flip. Was I about to paint myself into a corner I had been avoiding since I started therapy? "Like what?" I asked.

"I want to hear more about your husband, Stevie."

"I've said all there really is to say about him. He's dying. He's a stranger. He barely knows me. And he can't even talk anymore. What more could you be after?"

"Well, to be clear, I'm not after *anything. I'm simply trying to get a more complete picture of the people and the challenges that populate your life. You have said very little concerning him. He is your significant other. You've been married for five years. And yet, I am picking up on, well, a bitterness towards him. Typically, this is shared by spouses whose husband or wife has shown themselves to be dishonest. Unfaithful?"*

I felt the heat gathering in my cheeks. "Doctor, I want to be clear. I checked myself in here because I needed a rest *from my husband. I don't want to bring him here with me. I'm wrung out. It's not that I don't—" Tongue held firmly in cheek, "—love him. I only want to focus on myself and, yes, that would include leaving his name out of all this. I need a respite. Beyond that ... there is nothing else when it comes to Stevie."*

"Fair enough," Doctor Garrity acquiesced. She cleared her throat and pushed her glasses back up the thin, aquiline bridge of her nose. "There's a reason that convicted murderers are spared execution when it is proven they are clinically insane. Not guilty *is not merely a maneuver to get the guilty off. It is most certainly inhumane to punish the mentally ill for a crime, even something as heinous as murder, if it is evident from a psychological examination they have no concept of right and wrong. That the line between fantasy*

and reality has blurred so severely it's possible the patient thought they were witnessing the heinous act from a remove, or they were committing the act itself in some sort of alternate plain.

"In essence, to strap a mentally ill man or woman to a gurney for lethal injection or into the electric chair would be the equivalent of executing a small child with a brain that has not yet fully formed. Cruel. And, yes, unusual. By all means.

"Does that answer your question?"

I had no idea I was sobbing until she reached for the tissue box between us and held it out to me.

After pausing for the obligatory amount of time, the doctor sat up higher in her seat. "What was it that affected you in this way?"

If only I could tell her that sometimes there is nothing more crippling than an answered question you didn't really want an answer to after all. Any gray area I had been holding onto evaporated, leaving me to either adapt to the cold hard reality of what my life would be like once I return home. Or die. One or the other. And I knew all along I would not be getting the green light from Doctor Garrity to kill Stevie with impunity. That my psychiatrist would mandate such an act.

Hell, she wouldn't sanction such a thing even if I had come clean with her about all of it.

Stevie is the child with the "not yet fully formed" brain in the doctor's scenario. Only his brain had once been fully formed and then it had deteriorated. The question, which I now know I will never have a definitive answer to, of when exactly his mind started to fail is nothing now. The reasonable doubt, albeit a sliver, is what would keep Stevie alive. Even though he himself has asked to be killed, it is now all the more reason not to do so. Why give him what he wants?

This satisfies both mindsets. Covers both sides of the coin.

Okay. So, I'm going to have to find a way to live with the bastard.

I'm going to sleep.

NOVEMBER 18, 1994

. . .

TODAY IS THE DAY.

They are releasing me today. It would seem we have finally discovered a combination of antipsychotics and opioids that work well together in tamping down my intrusive thoughts and sense of doom. The fears are still there, but they've been driven underground, so to speak.

Now they linger there in the subconscious.

They are reduced. That's what matters.

I'm sleeping better. No more tears, like the baby shampoo bottle says.

I'm a little wary about reveling in this string of good luck. The proverbial shoe still hangs above, and it could drop at any given moment. Then, I worry I might find myself in-house once again, stuck in a state of limbo. No clear idea of when or how I will ever get out of here again.

Doctor Garrity has expressed to me she hopes I will continue to journal after I leave the hospital. I did tell her that this daily practice has been surprisingly cathartic. It's not like I'm going to just leave this notebook behind when I cut out, so I might as well fill the rest of its pages, at the very least. Why waste a handsome Moleskine journal like this one. They're not exactly cheap. And the doctor had gifted me her own. Whether or not she made this up to make me feel special or privileged in some way, I have no way of knowing.

The skeptic in me leans towards the former.

Time to make the round of goodbyes and complete my exit session with the oversight staff. Then, I will have the clothes I came there in returned to me after nearly a month-long stay. I can't remember what the ensemble was, but I'm certain I will not want to keep them once I leave. They're tainted now. A reminder of this time when I'd been at my lowest and most vulnerable. A gift for the backyard firepit.

The next time you hear from me, Mr. Moleskine, I'll be writing in bed or on my back patio, watching for ducks or slipping into a light doze while watching the waving redwood treetops.

NOVEMBER 22, 1994

I LOST FOUR DAYS.

That's what Mr. Moleskine says, anyhow.

Can I trust him, though?

Because I feel like I've been in the black for longer than that.

My bones ache.

My head hurts.

My tear ducts feel swollen.

And I've got a black eye.

Let's just say the mirror is not my friend right now.

They say I had a seizure. What they call a **gran mal**. *The mother of all seize-ups, apparently. One of the meds carries such a side-effect. It's rare, only occurring in about 10% of all patients who have taken it. Looks like my luck is running again. I fall within that slim margin of people who benefit from the — but will have to stop taking it or I'm going to seize and eventually my heart will follow suit, and it won't start back up again.*

I stand here, the drawing board before me.

Fuck my life!

I haven't been well enough to meet with Doctor Garrity until now. I have an appointment with her in a half-hour. She popped her head into my room briefly. I must have reeked of desperation when she'd laid eyes on me for the first time since I folded over before the front desk, smacked the side of my face on the lip of their countertop, and did the horizontal bop right there for all to see.

She thinks we've reached the point of last resort.

I don't disagree.

Even if the last resort is a euphemism for dragging my ass out back behind the building to shoot me in the back of the head. I will comply.

(LATER)

Came back to my room from dinner and who do I find standing there with a fucking shit-eating grin on his fat face but Howard S. Paranoid schizo Howard S. In. My. Room!? He's this twenty-something fuck with an eating disorder and the rankest body odor I've ever come across. And I've shared a tour bus with five sweaty, disgusting rock guys for months at a time! I don't know how he got in. I must have forgotten to lock my door. I thought it locked automatically, for God's sakes! The worst part was there it was! My journal-this goddam journal-just laying out on my bed where I'd carelessly left it. I'm shaking, I'm so fucking furious! Can't think straight. I'm going to hide it. Right now. In the air duct. Hopefully I can finger-loosen the screws. I'll find something. Gonna do this now. I've got a lot to say, but my thoughts are spinning. Circling. I need to sleep.

Let's just say I've got hope.

More to come, Mr. Moleskine.

FIFTEEN

Coming home for Gretch Solomon, after the odyssey of the mind she'd just experienced this past month, feels like she is re-entering the earth's atmosphere. Lori helped her get settled in, and Flora, Stevie's nurse, pitched in almost instantly so Gretch found very little required of her other than to reacclimate herself with her own home.

Lori Gallagher, Gretch's only real mainstay friend in the last five years, lives a quarter mile up the road from her. Ten years Gretch's thirty-six-year-old senior, Lori is a widower with grown twins, a boy and a girl, who hardly ever visit and never fully recovered from the excruciating experience of having to watch their own father waste away with pancreatic cancer.

The drive home was long enough Gretch discovered that while they'd been friends for half a decade, there was still a great deal she did not know about her only friend from down the lane.

Thankfully, Lori filled much of the silence with the radio (when the song was good) and her own prattling on about this or that. The ceaseless narrative of the lonely widower.

That was just fine with Gretch. She was grateful for this just as much as she was for Lori coming to pick her up at the hospital.

Gretch's headaches, while not endless, are still painful and perpetual.

The fits of nausea.

The bouts of fleeting blindness.

Doctor Garrity had explained all these side effects were to be expected as byproducts of the treatment. "They are scary. It will frighten you at first. But I want you to remember that this is temporary. And necessary. Remind yourself as often as you need to. Write it down."

The only treatment that had made it possible for Gretch to come home.

For much of the car ride, Gretch nodded in all the right places and faked her way through much of the conversation. Underneath this façade, she was struggling and straining to remember Lori's name. The effort shocked and consumed her all at once.

This is a nightmare!

Doctor Garrity called it *word-searching*. Temporarily clouded recall of names and places and circumstances. And then there was the inevitability that Gretch's extensive vocabulary and superior communication skills would also suffer a temporary setback. "You will experience something of a dumbing-down. This is perfectly normal. Your mind is busy with some heavy-duty sorting. Your abilities will come roaring back in time. Do not worry."

Still, it is hard for Gretch not to fear brain-damage.

A permanence.

She does not beeline to Stevie's room. This is not because she wishes to put off their reunion.

No, he has slipped her mind altogether.

Flora offers Lori a beverage. Lori sips at a Coca Cola can while helping Gretch place her clothing back in their respective drawers in the bedroom. The live-in nurse is in and out of the bedroom, but something has her preoccupied. And it is not until Gretch hears the ragged, extended groan of a man within her vicinity that she conjures his face in her mind. Only it is not the face of the man she married. The young lion with the full head of lush blonde hair streaked in black. Not the blue eyes that profess deeper understanding than his mouth could ever express.

The face she sees in her mind's eye is long and pale and cracked with wrinkles. A five o'clock shadow climbing his jawline on either side. A bald, liver-spotted head that is hairless except for tendrils of gray that sprout from the top of his head and shiver in the AC. The body is starved and barely there.

This is my husband? This is my Stevie?

I forgot him. Dear God!

Gretch follows the sound, which sounds increasingly inhuman the longer it holds.

It leads her into the room down the upstairs hall, last on the left.

The same wilted man she'd seen in her mind is sitting propped up in a hospital bed. The intermingling, overwhelming odors of Lysol and stale feces blows her hair back. She lingers under the threshold, the seeds of memory suddenly swelling with abundance as pieces of her life before the hospital sprout.

Behind her, Flora says, "I sorted some things in here. I hope you don't mind."

"Why ... why would I mind?"

Her eyes do not so much land on her husband, who is now reaching out his arms from the bed to fold her into an embrace, as they hover around him. She feels a wariness she can't understand.

And a sickness in her stomach that has formed out of nowhere.

Her hands fly to her belly.

She hugs herself tight. She cannot will her feet to carry her any further into the room.

But this is Stevie?

The man you loved above all other men enough to marry him.

Isn't that right?

On its face, yes, this is true.

This is correct.

But there's something more. Her mind tries to seize upon it. It is like grabbing at smoke. The notion shifts. Disperses.

Why is it the sight of her husband makes her want to vomit?

Gretch can only trust in what Doctor Garrity told her back at the hospital after her treatment concluded.

Names. Faces. Dates. Certain situations.

It will all come back to her.

Drip by drip by drip.

"Gretch? Honey?" Lori's hand touches the small of her back. "You okay?"

"Stevie," she says, approaching him now on knocking knees.

Flora stands just inside the room, allowing for their reunion to remain between the two of them. "He's gone nonverbal. The change took place overnight, literally. One morning, a week ago, he couldn't tell me what he wanted for breakfast. Couldn't communicate that he needed the toilet. A mess—"

"Please!" Gretch snaps. "Stop talking! This can wait!"

"Yes, ma'am."

Stiffly, Gretch slips into her husband's waiting arms and allows herself to be pulled in towards him. He smells like a grubby sweat sock. His labored breathing grazes the side of her neck, calling the little hairs there to attention. He mutters something unintelligible, a sound heavy on the *S's and R's*. Her hands hover just shy of his skin as her eyes had done moments before. It is like a there is a forcefield around him that she does not wish to breach for fear of

(remembering)

breaking into sobs.

As soon as Gretch senses the slightest loosening of his grasp, she slips from his arms and stands beside the bed.

Her body is vibrating with disgust.

Why? Why is this?

All of this is suddenly too much stimulation for her.

Her eyelids droop with new weight.

The meds have this effect on her. One is sedating while the other is regulating, which results in an onset of fatigue without warning.

"I'll be back in, Stevie," she says, fanning her finger at him in a loose wave and turning to the door. "I need to rest now. Flora?"

"I've got him, Gretchen," the live-in nurse says, changing places with the woman of the house.

Lori takes Gretch gently by the elbow.

Am I wobbly? Jesus.

After changing into a pair of flannel pajamas and winding a robe around herself like a cotton shroud, Gretch slips under the cold sheets. The contrast between warm and cool feels luxuriant. Lori lingers there in a rocking chair beside the king-size bed.

Gretch Solomon slips away.

She dreams of vampires, herself as the concubine.

SIXTEEN

The sound of a ringing phone rips her away from sleep.

The windows in her bedroom are dark. Black as a crypt. She can't remember the last time she's been able to close her bedroom door at night.

She remembers the *monitor*, which she faithfully carries with her from room to room and sets on her nightstand at bedtime.

This memory occurs to her as seamlessly as if she'd never lost it to begin with.

Will all the memories come back to me like this?

There is no Doctor Garrity there to confirm or deny. Although the ginger-haired psychiatrist had given Gretchen her card and told her to pick up the phone if she starts to feel hopeless or like the treatment has lost its effect.

The blue/black of her bedroom is wonderful.

Gretch remembers the night call from the hospital what seems like years ago, instead of weeks. It is the same heart-stopping feeling. Gretch checks her watch. It's only ten at night. Not nearly as late as the other call, but still as disconcerting.

Maybe not answer it?

She hauls herself out of bed, in no real hurry to pick up. Flora is still there. She will be staying on indefinitely. As she slips out of the bedroom, she hears the eighth ring cut off. Then, Flora's assertive, Hispanic voice talking to the caller on the kitchen phone.

The live-in nurse looks flustered, eyes wide and mouth set as she listens to the caller.

Flora cuts in and must fight to be heard." Excuse me! You tell me first why you call so late? Then if it's true emergency, I let you talk to the lady of the house." Pause. "No-no-*no-I*—"

Gretch motions for Flora to hand it off, which the nurse does with a pointed sigh.

"Who is this?"

The caller is male with a quick, motoring delivery like a coke fiend fresh from the mirror and the razor blade. "Gretchen Solomon? Like I said to your-was that your maid-I dunno-I'm sorry to be disturbing you at ten at night. I wouldn't have even thought of doing something like that if this weren't what I am certain you'll come to consider an emergency matter."

"Cal back in the morning. You've woken up the whole house. You abuse my husband's *nurse*. So please, if it's this important, I'm sure you'll remember to call back tomorrow. Goodbye—"

"Ma'am, if you'll just hear me out—"

"I'm hanging up now—"

"Okay, then I'm just going to shop these *nasty bits* to the highest bidder."

Gretch stops cold. "What the fuck are you even talking about, psycho? *Nasty bits?*"

"Oh, come on," the caller says, coyly. "You mean to tell me you've never heard of that?"

"Okay, you listen to me, you creepy fanboy. You ever call this house again and you will rue the fucking day—"

"It's not like you're going to involve the police. I mean, Gretch, these papers are *pret-ty* dark. Pretty damning for your husband. And in his own words, even. Talk about *Satanic Panic*, ma'am. This is some seriously depraved stuff he and the Grifter guys were into at the beginning."

Flora's eyes are wide, white orbs in the dark of the kitchen as she looks on with mounting concern. She motions as if to ask *What can I do to help?* To this, Gretch covers the receiver with her palm and cranes her neck away from the phone to answer her. "Go check to make sure the ringing didn't wake … S-Stevie? It's alright."

Gretch hears the nurse's footfalls up the stairwell. She uncovers the mouthpiece. "I want to know what the hell *nasty bits* are. What is that, some kind of sick code?"

"Oh, come on … geez, you really *did* quit the scene entirely," he says. "Alright-alright-*okay*. You should know that there has been a lot of underground rumbling since the Grifters breakup that there is supposedly a seedy little memoir written by one of the band members that has been hidden away and kept under wraps because of what it allegedly outlines. Words been passed on down the line until its existence passed off into something of myth. Until now. And people got to calling this memoir *The Nasty Bits*. I had no idea which one of the band members wrote it, well, until now. Your husband. Stevie Darius. I can confirm these papers do, in fact, exist. And I've got them in my possession."

When Gretch, stunned to silence, doesn't answer back, the caller dives back into the dead air.

"So … I'm sure you'd agree I have good reason to be calling you at ten o'clock on a weeknight. Do I have your attention now?"

Her shaky hands draw the phone away from her ear. "G-goodbye, asshole—"

The caller shouts to be heard as if he knows she's pulled the phone away. "Grifters Anonymous were moonlighting as serial killers all this time?"

"What the *fuck* did you say?" she cries, then remembers to lower her voice. She pushes the word out through her teeth as ripples of rage pulse through her. *"What the fuck did you say to me?"*

"Don't curse the messenger, Gretch," the caller says, his voice deepening just enough to shove an icicle into her heart. "You have any idea how many rabid fucking collectors are after this bit of rock memorabilia? Not to mention the unsolved murders littering The Strip and beyond the police could close the books on and give closure to the families. I came *to you*. Out of respect. You hang up the phone, and you leave me no choice but to go one of those alternative routes. After all, I gotta eat. I'm not living off that sweet Grifters royalty money, baby."

In the lowlight of the kitchen, she feels like someone about to strike a deal with the Devil. There's no other way to proceed. Stevie does not have it in him to take a life. If anyone, Chris Desmond, the rhythm guitarist, is reckless and spoiled enough to snuff someone and never think of it again.

But I know these boys and they're fucking bratty little pricks with no money sense or common sense for that matter. They're also one of the best goddam rock bands to come down the pike since Aerosmith and every heavy act that comes after them will owe them some debt of gratitude.

"What do you want out of this?" she says.

"I want what you want, Gretch. To get this garbage off the street and back where it belongs. With you. Under lock and key. It's sordid, scandalous garbage that can neither be proven nor disproven. And I'm well aware of Stevie's, er, downturn. Why pile this on him along with everything else the poor guy's got to contend with?"

"Mm … you sound like you've made the mistake of thinking this might make us friends. You're dreaming."

"I got plenty of friends, Gretch. Don't flatter yourself. I'm a fan. I'm *the* Grifters fan, of which all others aspire to be. So, I don't want anything. I *get* nothing out of this. Stand to gain jack shit. You understand?"

Her voice hoarse, she kicks her bare foot out at the wall, and says, "Fine. When and where?"

"You'll want to write this down. And you can call me … *The People's Knife.*"

Oh, how very clever. A play on words referencing Grifter's debut album, Knives for the People. *I can practically hear his gloating smile through the goddam phone. Christ!*

If she weren't so angry at having been called and angered at such an hour, Gretch would have laughed at the caller. And The People's Knife wastes no time diving back into the silence.

"The band is dead and gone, but their music is in the ether. It's everlasting. And see-I-I I couldn't care less about what they were getting into when the lights went down. Doesn't change a damned thing for me. From what I've read already, they did what they had to do. Can't help but commiserate with them because I know I would have done the same things they had to do to … you know … keep it going."

"People's Knife, huh?"

"Focus, Gretch. You're deep in it if these papers ever see the light of day and you know it."

"Fuck off, you opportunistic little sh—"

A quick knocking on the other end of the line and then a female's frantic voice fills Gretch's head.

It is like seeing a ghost down a dimly lit hallway.

"Gre-e-etch—"

"Glory!"

"Gre-e-e-e-etch—"

"Glory!" Gretch cries, grasping the phone with both hands so tight its plastic shell clicks. "Glory, f-for God's sakes—"

"Davey's Child Bride!" The People's Knife says, winsomely. "Not nearly as hot and spicy as I thought she'd be in the flesh. This junkie's been working my last nerve for a week now. She is one damaged chick. So yeah, I guess there is something I'm asking for in exchange. Take this bitch off my hands. I can't get rid of her, for Chrissakes! You leave her with me, and I'll probably have to mail pieces of this nutcase to you. Call her my incentive you'll show, since its sounds like you're still somewhat on the fence—"

"What did you do? Did you get her hooked again? You fucker, she was *clean!*"

"I didn't have to talk her into a damn thing. That's my point. Not when it came to what went up her nose, up her arm … up her ass."

"Sick fuck—"

"Financial District. Park on the street. *I'll* find *you.* 1p.m. tomorrow."

"I'll be there. Just … keep your hands off her. Please. I want her returned unharmed."

"That ship has sailed, Gretch. But I can promise to keep her alive from now until we make the exchange. The doctor bills and the therapy bills? They'll be your responsibility. She really tested me and

I'm afraid that I failed. But you've got the money to put her back together again. You'll step up."

Therapy? Doctors?

A nightmarish array of images bleed across her mind's eye. Visions of torture. Rape. Vile fetishes forced upon her, a captive and bound victim.

"I'll be there," Gretch seethes.

"Good … er … Grifters rule."

The line goes dead, but she doesn't replace the phone in its cradle.

Gretch smashes it against the wall.

Miraculously, this does not even rouse Stevie.

INTERLUDE (II)

INTERLUDE (ii)

From the Memoirs of Stevie Darius:

(1985)

The morning after we killed Lovebug broke earlier than any of us, aside from Davey, wanted. The rip-roaring thunderstorm from the night before carried over into the next day, a crippling reminder of what we'd done.

Davey was smart enough not to let the girl, Glory, accompany him to Napa. She fought to go with him, but it was halfhearted at best. I knew there was something in her system she needed to sleep off. Our band doesn't exactly attract teetotalers!

It was bad enough she saw what we did. Sure, she pledged in a drug-fog that she "wouldn't tell". It turned out that she was as good as her word with this.

Davey and J rolled Lovebug up in the living room rug, hiding away the dead girl's open eyes that seemed somehow still to search for meaning and answers. Her face and body rolled tight as a joint, we watched in detachment as Davey and J carried her out of the apartment. Then, one by one, Chris and Bobby slipped away into the bedroom. J slept in the bathtub for some reason, using only a floppy pillow for his head.

Glory went off somewhere to sleep but damned if I know where. Our two-bedroom apartment offered no place to hide let alone rest. I didn't see her again until morning.

I made a bed of the living room floor and called it my space when we first moved in. The carpet that had been repurposed as Lovebug's shroud used to soften what was a crusty rug underneath. I had to spread a fresh layering of garbage bags on the floor. I pulled the quilt from my mother's house over myself and tossed and turned until sleep came on.

I could have slept for days.

 Slept forever.

 But Davey and his piano.

 Forget it.

 The musical chords and individual notes were delicate.

 Heartbreaking.

 I opened my eyes to the sound of a sonic dirge unfolding across the keys of a piano. Seated there with his back to me and his shoulders hunched over the black upright piano, He'd brought it with him from his grandparents' house where he grew up. I always thought it looked like a battered black coffin.

 Half in and out of sleep, I saw myself opening the belly of the piano and finding the body of Lovebug stretched out across the hammers and strings. Her face black with the blood that gathered there, and her dead flesh brought back to hideous false life as Davey struck each piano key, and its hammer animated a piece of limbs—

Stop!

Davey picked out the song on the keys repeatedly. Main riff, repeated. He couldn't get past it, couldn't play his way into a verse riff or something like it. He wore only a pair of torn Levi's. His back muscles popped and writhed like snakes under the skin. Davey's back was smeared with dirt and grime, which brought me back to what he'd been doing the night before.

 Glory lay curled up on the floor next to his piano stool, a sleepy, loyal feline lulled into submission by the music.

 The sight of this turned my stomach.

Can't explain it.

I opened my mouth to fucking ream Davey out when his fingers found their way out of the repetition of the main riff and into a haunting verse-chord progression that literally hurt my heart to listen to. From there, the song unfolded quickly, fully formed and only just realized. Competence and authority over the melody crept into Davey's playing fingers until it sounded like he'd been playing the song for years.

Then Chris, who I hadn't heard come in an hour ago, and J were standing above me, each tuned in to the hypnotic song escaping Davey's mind. J picked up his guitar resting against the wall next to the piano. Davey offered him a slight nod, then returned his attention to his fingers. He stooped over even further until his angel wing's poked upward like jagged tentpoles. J slung the Telecaster's strap over his bare shoulders and set to searching out the root note of the song.

And when Davey played his way to what sounded like an obvious and perfect ending, J touched his shoulder.

"Start over man," he told Davey. "What was-oh dude-you smell like shit!""

J covered his nose, gagging.

That's when I smelled it too. How the hell could I have not from the moment I woke up? The song. It had muted all other senses but hearing.

Chris pulled the collar of his Ratt t-shirt up over the lower half of his face and crept over to the piano to stand behind Davey.

If I didn't know any better, I would have thought Davey shit his pants. I leaned in towards the brown smears lashed up his back. It wasn't shit. Mud.

Didn't explain the stench.

Chris gagged into his shirt. "Davey, go get a shower for Christ's sake-"

"No," J interrupted. He struck a chord and nodded. "Davey, start over. That was incredible. Where the hell did that come from?"

Davey straightened. His back snapped loudly. He stared down at the keyboard with wide greedy, eyes. "On the drive home." Mud had hardened to a crust along the ridge of his nose, along the divots of his high cheekbones. "It was squeezing my brain. I mean, it really wanted out. I must've done ninety all the way home. So I could, you know, transcribe it."

His fingers were covered in caked earth. It looked like he was wearing brown gloves. Flakes of dirt lay scattered across the piano keys.

"So … it's done?" I asked.

I jabbed a thumb at the slumbering girl at his feet. "What about her?"

Davey stooped even further over the keys until he looked more like Dr. Frankenstein laboring over his creation. "She won't say anything. Just put it out of your mind."

I blanched. "How do you expect me to do that?"

Davey sighed, like it exhausted him to explain something so obvious. "Because we're in love. We're … together."

We all laughed at him. At this. Fucking ridiculous.

"That doesn't make me feel any better about things, Dave," I said.

The least monogamous of all of us had just declared his eternal devotion to yet another groupie. Not the first time. Granted, Glory was a rare beauty among a sea of sixes. Mediterranean looking with alabaster skin, and a sculpted jaw that rounded into a lovely heart-shape. Big brown eyes. Italian? Greek, maybe? Very hot. But Davey's soulmate?

Get the fuck out of here!

Davey stooped his upper body over the keys once more and started again with the main riff. And I gotta say, I never heard him play so well before. This was a guy who bragged about the fact he brushed off Settlement Music School for piano in favor of learning the guitar. He thought piano would never get him laid. When we reminded him how well Billy Joel and Elton John made it with the ladies (and, for Elton, the gentlemen), Davey waved it off.

Still, there was a hidden fondness there.

The thing of it is, he sucked. We all suspected he was more of a dabbler on the keys. There was never any Settlement Music School. No NYU, like he'd also boasted.

That morning, Davey Grifter hadn't just learned piano.

The motherfucker mastered it.

Four and a half minutes later, the song wound down to a single note Davey plinked with his index finger before silence fell across the cramped apartment. I had played along, lending a shimmering chord progression and inserting inspired lead fills into the emptier spots of the song. I didn't know it until my breath came blowing out of me in a whoosh that I was holding my breath.

Arms crossed, Chris whistled. "Holy shit! You put some killer lyrics to it, and we got a hit!"

"I got lyrics," Davey said, talking to Chris over his shoulder. "It's done."

"No way, man," Chris said, exchanging disbelieving glances with J and I.

"I told you, man. I wrote it on my drive home. Then I laid it down."

I couldn't make sense of it. "Yeah, but …"

J looked at me. "But what?"

"Well, it's just that … that's never happened before … not with us."

"Alright, Stevie. But it's happening now. This is the beginning. You feel it?"

"I feel like I just pounded a fifth of Jack is what I feel like."

Davey said, "I'll take it."

Chris clapped his hands together. "Hold up, guys. Let me go grab my guitar." He strode out of the room, right past a haggard-looking Bobby Royal.

Bobby wore a pair of gray boxers and black tank top that hung off his bony frame like one of those off-the-shoulder numbers ladies wear on club night. His long blonde, feathered hair stood up in tufted and angry spikes. He rubbed viciously at his jaw, barely stifling a yawn.

"What's this then?" he asked, his voice ragged. "Was I dreaming or was I dreaming? That an original Davey Grifter number?"

"Bobby," I said, my smile so tight it hurt, "that was the sound of us turning a corner. No more cover songs. Well, maybe one or two. But that's it. Fuck it!"

Bobby blinked at me. "Oh, fuck off. You're winding me up."

J smirked. "This is only one song, boys. Let's not jinx it."

Davey shuddered, shifted on the piano seat. Something about the motion spooked me. "More will come. This song is … it's the first of many. We're … we've been touched. Our time on The Mountain wasn't a waste. It's just that this is more of a quid pro quo type of situation. It's going to require sacrifice. I put all the pieces together. Had nothing to do but think on the drive up and back. It came clear. Sacrifice on all our parts. If we want more of … more of this." He brandished a hand at the piano keys.

Bobby laughed. "That fucking Mountain is nothing more than a rock myth! A great story along the lines of Jimmy Page selling his soul at the Crossroads. Lore. Nothing more. I can't recall much. I know bad shit happened. That I suspect. Fuck. The. Mountain."

Chris held up his hands, questioning. "What am I missing? Sacrifice?"

"Later," J told him. "Soon."

J and Davey ran through the song again.

Bobby's tense shoulders started to sag and relax.

On the floor, Glory let out a soft murmur, wriggled her body a little, and pulled herself into a tighter fetal position.

With his Les Paul Gibson, Chris grabbed some sofa and set about finding his way into the mix of instruments. Little blues fills here. Accentuating notes there. And once Chris's guitar fell into a tuneful rhythm with the rest of the song, I looked over at Bobby, and he looked at me.

Then Davey Grifter started to sing in his scratchy second baritone voice.

The words. The melody.

Every bit of it was polished and pure poetry.

And it was all about how we'd lived in squalor for the last few years. Our circumstances. Our experience, told in a gritty narrative voice.

They all called us a "street band".

They called us a "gang", one that just so happened to play music.

And this song was our calling card.

When the song wound down, J asked Davey if he had a name for it.

In a low, uncharacteristically humble voice, Davey said, "'Knives for the People'."

Didn't make sense to me. "Yeah, but … it's a ballad. Power ballad. That's a title for a punk number. A two-minute."

Davey shrugged his pointed shoulders. "I didn't name it."

"You said you wrote it. Who named it then?"

Bobby dropped onto the sofa next to Chris.

In a deadened tone, Davey said the name "Calliope."

My confusion mounted. "Where have I heard that before?"

J shook his head. "Can't recall."

Davey shrugged. "Yeah, you do. It'll come to all of you when you're ready to remember."

Bobby leaned forward. "Jesus, Dave. What the hell happened to you in the swamps last night?"

Davey swiveled around on the piano seat and reached for J's Telecaster. "I got another one. Let me show it to you."

Mystified, J handed off the electric guitar to Davey Grifter.

I said, "Why don't we hit Mae's Diner down the road, get fed. Then we can come back and really dig in-"

They were having none of it, and I had never been told to "shut the fuck up" so quickly in my life.

It stunned me to silence.

We all listened to the next complete song as it rushed out of Davey's mind like sand through a sieve.

SEVENTEEN

Two blocks from the rendezvous point at 6th and Grand, home of the historic Pac Mutual building, Gretch finds herself trapped in a bottleneck of traffic that put the squeeze on her before she could so much as turn off or park. It would have been easier at this point to feed a meter and walk the rest of the way, although the duffel bag full of bound, unmarked blocks of cash slung over her shoulder would have done little to calm her already frazzled nerves. Stationary between a white Nissan Sentra in front of her and a van behind her, Gretch can only drum her fingers along the steering wheel, adjust the Dodgers baseball cap pulled down lower over her eyes with a red ponytail fished through the back hole, and lower her Wayfarer sunglasses to pick at a blot of mascara built up in the corner of her right eye.

Early this morning, The People's Knife had rung her phone a little before 8 a.m. to tell her where they would meet. She demanded he put Glory on. He'd laughed at her, a real full-throated guffaw that boiled her blood in her veins until she had no choice but to tell him she'd see him at noon at The Pac.

"Fuck around and find out!" she said before ringing off.

It felt good to say. Sent a ripple of pleasure through her thighs.

The light ahead goes green. There is a hopeful excretion of cars before red hits again. Gretch can see the Pac Mutual, which looks like it would be more at home in the heart of Havana, housing tourists inside its villa-esque architecture.

Almost there.

Then to put this short, trying chapter in her life to rest.

She had been lucky enough to get a hold of Lori so early in the morning. The part-time RN appeared on Gretch's doorstep at 7am with her medical bag and a smile on her face, even though worry lines had begun to encroach upon her forehead.

The walkways are bustling with pedestrians, clutching their purses and briefcases and overpriced coffees. This is what The People's Knife was counting on, a heavy flow of foot traffic. It would increase his anonymity.

It's strange. The feeling she has no way of effectively picturing what this extortionist looks like.

Maybe he's Glory's accomplice! Partner in extortion?

The traffic has frozen into gridlock.

"Oh, will you come the *hell on!* —"

The steering wheel rises to meet her face, striking her across the bridge of the nose. Gretch tastes a mixture of salty blood and mucous in her throat. She shrieks, disoriented. Her nose is uncorked. She looks down to find the front of her light blue cotton blouse is stained gleaming crimson.

She moves to unhook her seatbelt, setting off a painful twinge along her right rib cage, and realizes she's just been hit from behind.

With one hand she pinches her nostrils. Checks her rearview mirror.

A white van is stopped behind her.

"Fucking *idiot!*" she shouts, hammering the heel of her hand against the wheel.

The van's windshield is too dirty to see inside. But it's hard to miss the driver's hands waving around as if he's having the same kind of meltdown as her.

"*You* hit *me*, asshole! *You!*"

"You better have insurance or so fucking help me God …!"

Gretch checks the mirror again. It's a man, as far as she can determine. He's waving her off the road, telling her to pull over.

There are four metered spots sitting empty she can angle into with the van in tow.

Instinctually, Gretch fishes around under her seat for the tire iron she stowed there for the meeting this afternoon. The cold steel kisses her knuckles as if in reassurance. It imbues her with precarious confidence.

She angles her sedan alongside the sidewalk. She checks the rearview to verify he is doing the same.

"Come on, you sonofabitch."

She holds her breath until the van follows suit. Pulls behind her.

"Good. Boy."

Gretch shuts her eyes. Squeezes the tire iron.

She reaches to crank her door open when her passenger side swings open.

"Move," the man in the balaclava says, climbing inside and shutting the door behind him. "And be cool. Or I'll ventilate you, Gretch."

Gretch?

Her heart rides an elevator up to her head and its pounding in her ears. The muscles in her arms and legs tighten and spasm and jump as adrenaline floods them. She's never been carjacked before, only ever heard about it in the newspaper or the eleven o' clock news. And how she'd felt *for* those people. An empathetic dread. Now, it's her lungs locking up.

She can't breathe.

The carjacker is aiming a strange-looking gun at her. It looks like some space-age lunar laser weapon.

She puts her hands up. "Just take the car! I'll get out—"

"I don't want your car. Put your hands down."

"Look, I'm cooperating—"

By way of the briefest of glimpses in her rearview, Gretch sees the cab of the van behind her.

No one inside.

"You hit my *car*?"

The man in the balaclava spins the weird weapon around like it's a magic wand. It is a gesture of impatience in having to catch her up. "You got a space just there in between the Maserati and the Camry. Merge back into traffic. *NOW!*"

Gretch shoves the nose of her vehicle out in front of the oncoming Camry. The flow of traffic swallows her whole and moves her along like a guiding hand.

She can't hold her tongue. *"You don't understand! I have somewhere to be—"*

"You're not going anywhere. The People's Knife won't allow it."

"Are you … *him*?"

"Far as you know. The good news? You don't have to take possession of Glory. I've decided I'm gonna hold on to her. In the last twenty-four hours, she and I-we reached an understanding. And she told me everything. I mean, fucking *every-thing!* In short, I've decided Stevie's *Nasty Bits* are supposed to stay with me. This is how it's gotta be."

"Wha-what are you saying? Just take me to her. You can't. *Please—*"

"You're gonna want to take the next exit. Here! Coming up!"

"Why?" Gretch cries, her mouth tight and barely workable. "Where are we going?"

"Somewhere I can be my most convincing, and you'll be the most forthcoming with the answers to a great many questions. *This. Exit. Here.*"

EIGHTEEN

It is like being buried alive. Somehow clawing your way through the impossible weight of compacted dirt. Break the surface of a bald rectangular patch of earth.

Forcing a resurrection.

You are tempted to give in to death in favor of *something else*.

Anything but the pain of living and the menace that has lurked behind every corner of her life to the point every shadow boasts a threat. Promises violence.

But Gretch Solomon manages to open her eyes with the sensation of having been the rope in a tug of war between the *something else* and this world she's come back to. This was not her choice.

She would have gone the other way. Had wanted to run into the arms of the monolithic silhouette waiting and calling to her in the white-out blizzard blowing behind it. It could have been any number of people she would have given anything to reunite with.

The word on her lips when she comes to is not a flattering one.

"Fuck."

It made them laugh. Hell, they were just happy and relieved.

She'd been unresponsive when they collected her at a Texaco station twenty miles north of Los Angeles. According to the cashier, two crusty punks had pulled their Pinto up to the front door and dumped her out amidst a swirling dervish of dirt as they spun out and hit the road again.

Her heart stopped three times in the ambulance. Once more on the table. And Dr. Caterpillar Moustache nearly called it. He would have if the chest compression had not once more tugged on the rope harder than the celestial opposing forces of nature and the great beyond.

Fuck.

I'm back.

The nurse at her elbow touches Gretch's arm. It feels like five live wires animating the limb instead of five gloved fingertips. "Welcome back, Gretchen," the nurse tells her.

Gretch's eyelids flutter. She slips wordlessly into an unconsciousness that worries none of the attendants.

Her unconscious returns her to the oil-stained broken pavement of the abandoned textile building. She'd had the right side of her face in the dark, dry but ever pungent residue and she can still smell it now as she slips back into fogged memory. The phantom jolt of 40 volts coursing through her body, a dark figure digging some handheld contraption into her right side. Then it is like she's been struck by lightning.

His question.

Repeatedly.

The Mountain?

The Muse?

Who what where when why

Then—

Two sets of hands carrying her. Body throbs like a small glove forced onto a giant hand. The smell of weed and patchouli wafting off the two rescuers as they jostle her about and struggle at times and engage in a mildly heated exchange about some woman who they ought to have left where they found her.

I'm her she's me

Glacier grey eyes peering up close at her, through the openings of a black mask. The fury buzzing inside of them. The relentless inquiry—

Where is The Mountain?

Her mind still reeling from the electric shock from moments ago. A denial. *I don't know what you're talking about what do you want from me—*

The muscle memory of pain as the masked captor introduces a steel rod into the interrogation.

Then, sweet oblivion.

NINETEEN

"… fractured left orbital socket … multiple lacerations about the face and back of the skull … four broken ribs …"

It is starting to sound like there is no part of her body spared by her attacker. She is "healing nicely" according to Doctor Tremaine, who's taken something of a personal interest in helping and healing her. Nurse Stein told Gretch as much, that the doctor in question is typically more of a surrogate healer of sorts who will only meet with patients if its "absolutely imperative". The nurse, a born gossip who seems to be someone who simply cannot help herself, trades on information involving Doctor Tremaine's rather obvious reason for looking after Gretch so completely.

He had a daughter who was stabbed to death by her boyfriend when she'd tried to break it off.

In broad daylight, the murder.

TWENTY

Gretch held her tongue, much to the chagrin and impatience of the detectives who'd come to take her statement. It left the two of them, a man and woman, mystified and relieved in the same instance. Less workload for them.

But Nurse Stein? Why was it Gretch was more inclined to confide in someone who can only offer an ear and nothing of retribution or vengeance.

Well, because while I can't afford for the police to ever find The People's Knife and what he has, I still need to unburden myself to someone. Someone of no consequence when it comes to the memoirs.

Gretch convinces the nurse she had, in fact, wounded her attacker with a tire iron so viciously he is not likely to come back. That's if "he's even still alive". In a voice slurred by dope, she'd convinced the nurse the man had run off, trailing a delicious wail of agony behind him as he departed. "Disappeared … after I buried the business end of the iron in the side of his head."

And this series of lies allowed for Gretch to explain most of what had brought her attacker to her. What had enraged him so that he had beaten her within an inch of her life and left her for dead, in a dilapidated warehouse that was literally sinking into the earth.

"He was extorting my husband and I," she confessed. "For hundreds of thousands of dollars. I agreed to pay him. I had no choice. I met him at the designated location. He ambushed me. Stole my money. Made me drive somewhere remote so he could ... interrogate. To extract information I didn't have. Never had. He didn't believe me. At one point, I even tried to-I dunno-*invent* information just to get him to let me go. I couldn't think straight. That was just beyond my ability."

"This sounds like that Dustin Hoffman movie," Nurse Stein said. "With that famous line. He was being interrogated by this Nazi guy who kept asking him the same damned question repeatedly. Something like ... 'Is it safe?'"

The People's Knife: "Is the Mountain real?"

"Is the Muse real?"

Tell me about it! Tell me about it! Tell me more! You're lying you're lying you're lying

Moremoremoremore—

"It was nonsense," Gretch says. "What he tried to beat out of me. Just nonsense. And I think it dawned on him I had nothing to offer him after all. That's when he just ... snapped."

"Gretchen," Nurse Stein says, leaning in, "why won't you cooperate with the police. They say you've been ...'"

"Obstinate. Uncooperative. Bitchy." A smile flits across her face, and she winces. Her orbital socket wound lights up like a Christmas tree strung in radiating pain.

"Oh ... honey. I should have warned you about that."

"What's ... that?"

"Smiling will hurt." Nurse Stein motions for Gretch to press the morphine button for herself. "Sleep now."

The morphine drip works fast.

Gretch's eyes close.

It's the weighted and dreamless sleep of someone whose system is flooded with a narcotic. But the nightmares try to break through and get at her. There would be time for that.

A lifetime.

TWENTY-ONE

Five days after being admitted to Cedars-Sinai with multiple wounds and fractures and contusions, Gretch Solomon rides in a wheelchair with an orderly pushing her along until they reach the sliding exit doors. When she discovers Lori has sent her eldest son, a stuffy hedge-fund manager called Robert, to pick her up, she wishes she'd braved some form of public transport. Not that the hospital staff would have released her to a Greyhound bus driver.

She'd left a message on Lori's machine. The pick-up had been handed off to her son, who Gretch had met only once and taken an immediate dislike to for the way he constantly tried to infantilize Lori. Insisting she should come live with him and his wife in Portland. That she shouldn't live alone. Not healthy for her.

Now, Gretch feels a knot tie off in her stomach. Did something happen to Lori?

The severity of his expression as he helps her into the passenger seat of his Infiniti is a clear precursor to what will likely prove to be a long, uncomfortable ride.

Gretch can't help it. She must know, even if it sounds ungrateful. "Where's Lori?"

Through gritted teeth, Robert Gallagher chuckles drily. "Sorry to disappoint. But she's needed back home. Your home."

"Why? What's happened? —"

"Not yet," he stops her. "Let's get going. I promised my mother I'd be civil. To keep that promise, you're just going to have to give me time to dial down my temper. It's been a long drive here. I've done nothing but think. And stew."

She opens her mouth. It claps shut as she catches the red glare from her best friend's son.

The full weight of her circumstances and the isolated existence she has fallen into in the last couple of years is like a morning bell that sounds in her mind and sinks her.

Something is wrong with me. Has been for longer than I wanted to admit. I'm a recluse.

Once on the road, Gretch does not try for conversation.

The anger rises off Robert Gallagher like a musk.

Twenty minutes into the drive, Robert clears his throat and readjusts his hands on the wheel. Says, "Looks like you're in the market for a new nurse."

"What does that mean? Will you just tell me what happened?"

"Alright ... Gretch ... you want to know? Flora, is it? She's gone. She called Mom at four in the goddam morning. Tells her she's leaving. That *my mother* is going to have to come and take over and look after Stevie. *Your* husband! In the middle of the night! Oh, and the best part about this is that you were expected home three days ago, but you'd gone missing. No idea where you are. No phone check-in. Nothing."

"Whoa ... I mean, holy shit!" Gretch cries, raking her red hair back with fingers crooked as claws.

"What *holy shit*? What?"

"I was carjacked, Robert! And the sonofabitch beat the shit out of me before leaving me for dead in some abandoned warehouse! But—you know-I guess I should have *been more fucking careful riding around in my car. I guess I brought this on myself!*"

Robert looks at her, his jawline pulsing. Silence, except for the wipers he has just turned on to stave off the spitting rain that has just begun to fall. Eventually, he says, "You ... you never mentioned any of this in your phone message. I-I … thought you were having another one of your-I dunno—*Gretchen Crisis*. I—"

"Really? And what exactly is a *Gretchen Crisis?*"

"Hey look, I'm sorry this happened to you. Damn sorry! But you've got to admit … you've been needy and fragile these last couple of weeks. Mom's worried about you. You don't know what this does to her. She's a total empath. She feels *your* pain. Your … panic."

"Okay," Gretch says, laughing desperately, "so not only am I responsible for my own kidnapping and abuse. I'm also on the hook for having a nervous breakdown. Do you know anything about how mental illness works? Because maybe you ought to check a book out of the library and just *skim* the fucking thing before you go victim-blaming. I called for *Lori*, not for *you* to pick me up! And if you're that put off by me, you can just leave me off on the side of the road. I'm a big girl. I'm resourceful. Hell, I'll probably make it home before you."

Robert shakes his head and blows out a breath. "Don't be ridiculous. Don't be so dramatic—"

"Fuck you, Robert! This is my life and it's … fucking …"

(one big lie)

"… eroding."

The pinprick of tears presses at the corners of her eyes. Gretch rubs at them, and the pressure subsides. A dull throbbing starts up in her side where she has three taped-up ribs. It feels like three, long and sharpened talons pushing out at the taut skin there.

The rain turns to a filthy mist that hangs low along the highway. It spreads its gray tendrils across the fields on either side of the road, like they are rolling across the Moors of Europe.

Minutes dissolve before anyone speaks. Then Robert tosses up his hands, lays them back on the steering wheel. "Alright," he says. "Okay. I apologize for coming in hot like that."

Gretch stares blinklessly out the windshield.

"You should know … Stevie is not doing well. He's taken a turn for the worse."

It's a curious emotion these words stir inside of Gretch. It is a series of feelings at odds with each other. Relief. Solemnity. Regret. Rejuvenation. Hope. Emptiness. She must push the words out: "What happened?"

"Well, you can put two and two together. Flora … something happened in the middle of the night to send her packing. Mom wouldn't find out until she got there. She called me. Got me out of bed. Asked me to come. She's never done that before. Not ever. And I can confirm what Mom and I both saw with our own eyes. We've got questions, to say the least."

"His feet. Right?"

"Wha-you *knew about this?*"

"I did, but I took the necessary precautions as soon as I discovered he had taken to doing this to himself. I threw away every lighter and box of matches right then and there."

"Yeah, we didn't find anything like that. We looked. You understand, we had an obligation to do so."

Gretch waves this off. Her mind feels suddenly soft as putty. The lull of the car beneath her rocks her and she must pull herself up higher in the passenger to keep awake.

"Then I guess I *really* can't explain what we saw when we attended to Stevie, who was raving like a lunatic, peeled off his socks and … looked at the bottoms of his feet. They were burned. They were hamburger meat. You say he did this to himself before. How would he have done this to himself without any access to a flame?"

She shuts her eyes and drops her head back against the rest. "I have no idea. I … I … honestly, I've been exploring hospice care in the area. Even made an appointment for a tour of a place five miles north of the Hollywood Hills." She pauses, chews her bottom lip. "Flora up and quit for one of two reasons, only one of which I can fathom. She was afraid I'd suspect her of abusing him. Or Stevie just burned right through her. She couldn't take him anymore. There are times his rage is just so frightening. I thank God he's no longer mobile." A hitch rises in her throat. "I'm … I am—I'm frightened of my own husband."

Robert nods. "The last time he did this. When you saw it and you hid all the fire. How long did it take for his feet to heal?"

Gretch runs a quick mental inventory in search of the answer. She finds one of the many dark gaps in her recall, a crevasse with the answer lying dead at the bottom. *I'll have to lie. Can't exactly say I don't remember. Lori has no idea about the procedure I had done.* "A few days. I coated his feet in a burn salve every four hours. Kept them wrapped. I thought he could lose one or both."

"Mm … Mom ran to gather some creams and bandages. I hung back and looked after him. At least he'd stopped screaming. The pain just let him be. He tried to sit up, and I stepped up to help him lay back down. He didn't fight me. He let me guide him back down again. Told him to rest. And he just … he grinned up at me. But it wasn't a grin as in *hey I'm happy and I feel better*. I took it to mean the opposite of that. It was one of those rictus grins that accompanies desperation. Resignation. Something told me to check his foot again. When I went back to the foot of his bed and had another look … the flesh there was … pink. Smooth. Flawless, I tell you."

"I … just don't know." It's more than that, but Gretch can't explain. The mental word-searching. The sink holes in her brain where pieces of her life used to reside, now reduced to cavities like holes in a gum. "I'm going to have to place him in hospice if I don't find a replacement. I don't know that I can have him home any longer. I'm … I'm not mentally equipped. There was a time I was. But I'm slipping. And … the worst part is that his-his delusions … he harps on them so often and incessantly that I've started to question my own reality. I've been starting to wonder if he's right and *I'm the crazy one*."

"He's been coming out with the strangest things," Robert says. "Raving. I guess that's part of his illness."

"Doesn't make it any less distressing—"

"Please stop calling on my mother to look after your husband," Robert says, coldly. "She would never say this to you. So, it falls to me. Understood?"

The sting of his words stuns her to silence. Then, she finds her voice hiding in the back of her throat. "I understand. I won't bother her again."

"I thank you," he says. "But only when it comes to that. Otherwise, and I can't stress this enough, you are very important to Mom. She values your friendship."

They continue in silence, the wipers set to their highest speed as the rain turns from spit to a heavy spray. The view from her window provides Gretch with little solitude with its hard edges and industrialized landscape. No trees. Nothing of nature meets her eyes and she feels a deep sense of loneliness settle into her bones so completely she wonders if she will ever be able to get rid of it.

It is like marrow now.

She can't hold back any longer. "What kinds of things was he on about?"

"Who?"

"Stevie."

"Oh, well, a lot of non sequiturs. His weave of thoughts was wide, and it deepened with every word out of his mouth. Then there were times he'd fall silent and get to staring for hours. Not sleeping. Just, you know, staring off into space. There were times I felt the need to check him for a pulse."

"Nothing specific you can recall?"

"I didn't say that," Robert says. "Your husband has been asking to make a confession to someone, a Man of the Cloth-as he puts it- and he hasn't shut up about it for three straight days. He seems to think that is the only way his feet will stop … catching fire."

"My husband has dementia. He's got a lot of strange ideas about a great many things."

"I'll say," Robert quips, taking the exit off the Pacific Coast Highway. "He's a regular Lady Macbeth. Only instead of *Out, out, damned spot*, his mantra has been *Guilty, that's my plea, that's the plea!* Any idea what he could mean by that?"

Gretch's pulse quickens. Her chest tightens. "He's sick, Robert. I've heard all this many, *many* times before." She hesitates, says, "Can we put on the radio or something?"

"Oh, I don't know our tastes are comparable. I'm more of a Parrothead than Metalhead."

"Well," Gretch says, turning her attention out the window. "I'm in a lot of pain, so …"

"Fair enough. Just one more thing. You know, from the guy who drove an hour up and an hour back to pick up a woman who clearly loathes him."

Gretch bites her tongue.

Robert offers her an empathetic smile that brings tears to her eyes for a reason she does not immediately understand. "Promise Mom-since I know you won't promise me anything-that you'll seek out the help you need. I've got a therapist. Talk therapy has helped me to sort out a lot of my feelings. Chief among them, the trauma of my father's death."

Yeah, but see, Robert, the time for talking *is done and gone. It's time for answers and solutions. Time to start solving the problem instead of piling more on. Talking gets you nowhere.*

INTERLUDE (III)

INTERLUDE (iii)

From the Memoirs of Stevie Darius
   (1985)

Two months after the killing and we were still living in Fountainview Duplex. Nolan Royal, Bobby's dad, and our manager who started paying our rent there put the kybosh on moving without batting an eye. His reasoning? "Some of the best rock n' roll songs were no doubt written on an empty stomach." We wanted to move out after the murder to try and put it behind us somehow, like a change of address could get that done. And it wasn't just that.

   That morning when Davey and J pieced together nearly all the instrumentation and vocal melodies to three songs, fully formed and ready for the Hard Rock Top 40, the five of us never felt so connected. It was psychic. We all knew, though none of us dared say it out loud. We were bonded in blood.

   In murder.

   We played rock and roll together.

   And we killed together.

   We shared a bloodlust as unpredictable as it was overpowering.

   Increasingly, I'd been getting the buzzing where my spinal column connects with the brain and skull. I didn't have any health insurance back then, and this was not something I would have felt comfortable talking to Nolan Royal about.

Hey, Mr. Manager, would you front the bill for an MRI so I can make sure I don't have a fucking brain tumor?

Then J complained about something similar in the back of his head.

"A shaken wasp nest" was how he described it.

Eventually, the five of us confirmed with one another this was also a shared affliction. I took some comfort in this. What are the odds of five band members getting brain cancer at the same time?

Our hopes for transitioning into an original music band faded and reality stole over the whole situation. There was no way to pull that off with only three new tunes, unless we abandoned all rock convention and played the three songs three times each to fill a forty-minute set. Believe it or not, there were some acts out there on the Strip and beyond, over at the Country Club, that tried this. They never got the chance to pull such a pathetic plan again.

We didn't want to join the blacklist.

So we kept at it as a cover band with three originals sprinkled into the setlist. We kept up with the AC/DC, the Motley Crue, some tasty bits by The Misfits, UK Subs, and the obligatory Aerosmith classics. By the third performance of the new material, J nudged me in the middle of Davey's piano dirge, "Knives for the People", to draw attention to the fact the whole front row, all smoking-hot girls, were singing along to the lyrics. We hadn't recorded the songs yet, so that meant they must have come to every show since the song's first playthrough and the words had caught them without letting go.

They didn't know the other new song lyrics.

Not yet.

That came with the next show a couple nights later at The Troubadour.

I strode over to Davey during the guitar solo and told him to get the band to stop halfway through the chorus of another new song called "Dirty Starlight". I wanted to test a theory. He agreed and when he turned and swung his arm in a wide arc, silencing the band in one fail swoop, the five of us were treated to an audience sing-along. They knew the words, and they carried the tune for four bars before we cranked it back up again for the sped up, punk ending.

The killing of Lovebug did not-would not-leave any of us alone. Each of us wore it around our shoulders. I confronted it in the cracked bathroom mirror in the newly formed lines etched into my face. Bobby woke up four nights in a row following the death of Lovebug. Not screaming but cursing up a storm.

The second night, I wet myself in my sleep. Luckily, I slept on top of big Hefty trash bags and the piss beaded up on the plastic. Made for an easy clean up. And to my relief, none of the guys ever asked why it was I kept going through garbage bags so fast.

They're my brothers, but some things you just must hold close to the vest.

I got it into my head the best way to deal with it was to ignore it, to stuff it down with brown. I think we all thought if we turned our backs on it for long enough, the whole thing would cease to be.

We still threw parties at the apartment, which came to be called The Barracks by everyone on the Strip. Our army of fans started to swell in number, but we all knew it could become so much more. Instead of entertaining twenty-five or so hookers, druggies, waitresses, band guys, and the occasional straggler off the street, we wanted to cram our duplex full of fifty fuckups. We wanted Grifters Anonymous on the lips of every hot girl and dealer and promoter and club owner within a fifty-mile radius of Northern California.

We wanted all the drugs.

We wanted all the girls. None for the lesser knowns.

The problem was, we were still counted among those lesser knowns.

Bands like Ratt, Motley, Faster Pussycat, and Great White (guys we used to party with) were set on this upward trajectory we could only hope to hop onto. The guys of Motley blew the doors open, and seemingly overnight agents and managers and promoters were cramming their way through the mess of bodies to get at and sign up everyone with the look and the music to match.

Not to mention. Aqua Net stocks must have skyrocketed with all the necessity for high hair.

After three months, we were living like rock stars, but we felt like a bunch of frauds.

Frauds with three original songs, getting laid and hooked up because of the way J aped Joe Perry's solo for "Sweet Emotion" to perfection. We fucked our cocks raw because of the way Davey pulled off a spot-on imitation of Bon Scott during "Whole Lotta Rosie".

Fucking con artists.

One oddly quiet night at the apartment, four of the five of us too bummed and burnt to mingle out in the street in front of Rainbow or cram our way into a booth at the Troubadour to schmooze, Chris put it all too perfectly.

"We're just standing on the shoulders of giants, man."

If J were around at the time, I'm sure he would have argued against this. The fact is, Chris had no songwriting credits to his name, and the guy had been in three or four bands before ours. He didn't bring so much as a riff with him when he joined up with Grifters Anonymous. Yet, there he was calling out the one-half of our songwriting duo. I waited for Davey to rebuff Chris's indictment, but the singer lay on his back with his arms folded over his pale, bare chest. Snoring lightly.

Sleeping off a heroin ride. And that jailbait *hanger-on, Glory, crammed onto the sofa beside him. She clings to Davey for dear life. Dressed in a black silk nightie she has taken to living in.*

*J had warned our singer about having her around so much. Again, jail-*bait*! Glory wanted desperately to drop out of school. Davey was the one to convince her to stick out the last six months of her Senior year.*

It would turn out he had an ulterior motive for keeping her enrolled at Hollywood High, A marketing ploy for our music that would require her student ID to remain active.

So we had a girl haunting our apartment and tagging along on every jaunt without question or protest from the rest of us. She says little and needs less than that. Not exactly a parasite. Just a girl in need of a replacement family for the one she is trying to get away from.

On the TV, an old Mighty Mouse cartoon played, one moment dark and then twinkling white along the walls in a dizzying array.

Chris said, "You guys hear what I said?"

Bobby yawned, pulled hard on his private bottle of Ol'Granddad. "We heard you, Chrissy. We just don't give a fuck. So jog on!"

I shrugged my shoulders at Chris, who stood.

On the sofa, Davey grumbled in his sleep

I heard a key wriggling around in the lock of our apartment door.

Then it swung wide.

A waifish blonde with long, greasy black hair and wearing a red and black checked flannel burst through the door. J leaned on her, and she guided him inside, shouting at the top of her lungs for someone to help. For such a little girl, she carted our five-foot-ten guitarist into the room with the strength of three of us. Our eyes met and she directed her wrath towards me, as I was frozen in place. "I'm about to drop him! You wanna snap out of it and help me with him?"

I slung an arm around J. He sagged into me. Then his body stiffened. Up close, I could see the bruises on his face and an eye that seemed to turn from yellow to blue to black before my eyes. His layered dark hair lay flat against his skull, flattened by sweat and grime. I maneuvered J over to the sofa. Davey had already cleared out. He stood by, groggy from half-sleep.

J broke away from me and dropped into the cushions like a heavy stone.

"What happened?" I said.

The girl sat down next to J. His black frock coat was ripped along its seam in some spots. His Blondie t-shirt, its neck cut low enough to show a sprinkle of dark chest hair, rose and fell in jerky motions as J struggled to catch his breath.

Bobby lit a cigarette and handed it down to J who promptly tucked it between his lips and pulled.

The girl started to explain. Her voice was sexy as hell, ground down to a sultry near whisper. "Barfight. They come at him with bats and chains. A bad fucking scene. Four against one."

"Hold on," I said, turning to J. "What happened to Ragtag? You said you were going out with him?"

The girl tossed up her hands. "Who's Ragtag? -"

Irritated, Chris said, "Shut up for a second, bitch. Ragtag's our sometime-roadie."

"Hey, fuck you! He'd be dead if I didn't get him back here! I saved his life!" She turned to J, laying her palm against his fuzzy chest. "Tell em', baby."

J swallowed hard. "Rag rolled out early. His old lady was on his case. Wanted him home."

My face stung with anger. "Why didn't you roll out with him? He was your ride! How were you planning on getting home?"

"Fuck the third degree, Stevie! What are you, my mother? I always find a way home! When have you ever seen me stranded?" He dragged on the smoke long and hard and handed it off to his blonde savior. "And this is Anita, boys!

She ain't lying! I can't remember how, she got me clear of those redneck fucks and drove off! So don't be calling her anything other than a saint, Chris!"

"Sorry, man," Chris said. "Where were you?"

"O'Grady's."

Bobby sighed. "Oh, so you were looking for a thrashing? You forget about the last time you went there?"

O'Grady's was a trucker favorite on the outskirts of Reseda. J discovered the place on his own, while driving to visit his girlfriend of the hour. None of us could figure out why he'd ducked his head in there in the first place, since it was rumored to be a meeting place for some Aryan Brotherhood-type outfit. They don't like the long hair or the nose rings so much, see? The last time J went there, he barely escaped with his life, and there had been no Anita to rescue him.

J liked walking the razor's edge, tempting his own fate.

A part of him would welcome death if it ever came to smile on him.

He'd say Okay baby, it's time. It's good.

As for Anita, her look screamed lot lizard.

Yes, J. was most likely suicidal around that time.

But Anita was further proof he'd stick his dick in anything and anyone.

"I drink where I want," J said. "Fuck em'. They can call me faggot all they want! I'm buying a fucking gun tomorrow. I'm carrying from now on."

"Oh, that's bloody brilliant!" Bobby scoffed. "Very nice! I hope you shoot your rocks off—"

"Hey fuck you, Bob-"

The sudden motion winded him and he collapsed back into the battered sofa pillows.

Anita snuggled in closer, laid a hand on his inner thigh. "Don't do that, J. You'll only make it worse."

It was then I noticed how J was holding his right hand closer to his side than usual.

Nursing it.

"Holy shit!" I cried.

J's strumming hand was swollen to twice its size. Black dots ringed each knuckle, a sure sign of broken bones beneath. It was obvious he was too drugged out to even remember he was supposed to be writhing in pain and crying out.

"Oh baby," Anita said, "your hand."

J's brain must have lit up like a Christmas tree. He tried to lift the hand and screamed so loud we expected to see police dome lights washing across our windows in seconds. "My fucking hand! Goddammit!"

I went to the kitchen to get some ice in a ratty dishrag hanging on the oven handle. In the other room, I could hear Bobby talking to either Anita or J in a lowered voice. My hands shook as I readied the ice pack. It took longer than it needed to. I kept dropping cubes down the drain. As I balled the ice up in the crusty rag, the webbing between my index finger and thumb throbbed and itched.

I dropped the pack and sucked the membranous flesh between my lips.

The girl, Anita, shrieked. I heard something heavy hit the floor. Followed immediately by the sounds of male grunting.

The sounds you'd hear inside a cave inhabited by Cro-Mags gathered around a fire.

A primitive communication.

I understood it.

We could use an extra hand. Stevie.

I knew what I would find when I returned to the living room. I shut my eyes against it, trying to drive it from my mind's eye. But there's no blinding the third eye. No, sir. I braced myself along the lip of the countertop. Then, I felt a tug around my waist. A pair of invisible arms pulling me. And my hands betrayed me. They let go of the countertop as I begged for them to obey. To stay where they were. "I. Can't." There came the sensation of movement, my two bare feet tramping backwards out of the kitchen. I kept my eyes squinched shut, until some inner force overrode that command as well.

The grunting ceased.

I wished it hadn't.

Then I wouldn't have been able to hear the terrible noise of an airway closing.

Snorting.

Gasping.

Sighing.

We could use an extra hand—

My feet touched the living room rug. Davey, Chris, Bobby, and J encircled the girl on the floor.

Anita's fishnet-stockinged legs, torn at the knees, kicking out repeatedly.

Slowing.

Slowing.

Bobby and J assumed the same positions as before with Lovebug. They held Anita's arms. Slit her wrists. This time they grabbed a couple empty beer cans strewn about the room and held them under the wounds to catch the blood. Each can would overflow at once. They had another can in cue, waiting to be filled.

She died with her eyes stuck open in a widened, questioning glare.

I squeezed and pinched my hands until they turned to lumps of flesh, alive with pins and needles. I'd opened a wound in the webbing of my palm and soon I was pantomiming the washing of my hands in sticky, tacky crimson.

"Not again," I sighed, sunken. "Why?"

Then there was laughter.

Davey's trebly cackling mixed with J's lower chortling. And a third string of laughter that could've belonged to anyone. I didn't recognize it. A crescendo. Swelling to something far louder than anything four or five guys could have produced by themselves. No, it sounded like a live studio audience, hidden from our vision by a line of blinding spotlights. Belly-laughing at the dark spectacle before them.

Another murder.

Anita.

Lovebug and Anita.

Pain pulsed in my chest. It felt like a heart attack. My hand flew to the spot, massaged it absently as I slid down the wall.

Hit the floor. Lost time.

"Guys," I said, in a strained voice, coming to on my back. "Help …"

"Ho, he lives!" Davey cried, fucking joyfully.

The darkened shapes of my guitar player and singer sat across from each other on the rug. The TV on the tray stand was on with the sound off like always. Mighty Mouse had turned into an episode of Kojak, Telly Savales' shiny bald head gleaming orange in the shadows of the living room.

J held his Ibanez six-string acoustic across his lap. He was bare-chested, his Armenian skin a deep olive in comparison to Davey's bone-white body.

Davey sat cross-legged, hands clutching the knees of his jeans, held together by a patchwork of clashing swatches. Back straight as an arrow. He looked like the leader of some Buddhist cult.

J ignored me, rattling off a punky blues riff.

If I weren't so sure I was suffocating, I would have told him how good it sounded.

Wasn't his strumming hand broken last night?

I could've sworn …

Really good shit.

My chest hitched. "I think I'm … dying …"

Davey grabbed the tip of my boot and gave it a playful tug. "Contraire, motherfucker. You're dead and reborn! Rise and walk!"

I swallowed. My heart rhythm slowed. I let go of my chest.

J continued playing with his miraculously healed hand. I noticed a trickle of blood from his left nostril to his mouth. It looked old and dried. J always got nosebleeds when he banged too many rails of coke. He blamed it on the poor quality and even said something to his dealer about it. Said dealer gave him another bloody nose and deviated septum.

J's eyes were big and glassy.

Davey wore a lopsided grin. He was chemical-free.

Then I remembered what I'd heard and forgotten about.

"I could've sworn I heard laughing. An audience."

Neither one of them looked at me.

"Yeah?" Davey said, airily.

J's hand struck a sour note in the chord. He tried to pick back up where he left off, but his fretting hand went sloppy. I could hear him muting strings when he meant to let them ring. He shook his head, blew his overgrown black bangs up and out of his eyes. He stooped over, arching his back to an almost impossible angle. Eyes nearly an inch or so from the sound hole of the acoustic.

What's he see in there?

"Yo, Jay," Davey said, "circle back to the chorus. I want Stevie to hear."

"Where're Bobby and Chris?" I asked.

But I knew.

It was their turn to clean up.

. "Stevie!" Davey shouted. "Listen up!"

I rubbed at my eyes, as if it would drive the dread from my mind. It was palpable. When I was around seven or eight years old, I had this recurring nightmare. I was a grown man and locked away in a windowless cell. A solitary confinement type of situation. I knew I'd done something horrible, even though my little-kid mind couldn't really conjure the worst of the worst crimes. I remember the sheer terror of those nightmares. The isolation. Helplessness. There could be no rescue. No warm hugs from my mother. No Listerine-smelling breath on my neck when she sang me to sleep. And there I was, fresh into my twenties.

Prison an inevitability.

Death smiling.

There would be no waking up to find my mother in her nightgown, smoothing down my brow with a wet-warm rag.

"Stevie, you asshole!"

I snapped to. "Sorry, man."

"Where'd you go?"

"I'm right here, man. Right here. Go ahead."

Davey rocked back and forth on his ass. I counted off from four and the chorus started:

> *Trouble, baby, trouble is waiting on up the road*
> *Glory's got a rip in her stocking, head gonna explode*
> *Always Daddy on her heels, she's got the bad feeling*
> *What Mommy wonders, nobody knows*
> *She's bloody, got no money, but, oh, when she spins,*
> *Better hide away*
> *Better hide away*

The singer picked up a tambourine lying beside him and beat out a chiming rhythm. Eyes closed, Davey Grifter fell head over heels down into the darkness of the musical dirge.

Had I heard right?

Glory? A song about her?

There'd be no getting rid of her now.

"He wrote one for me, Stevie. I'm so fucking lucky!"

I nearly jumped out of my skin like a cartoon character when I heard her.

Glory sat down beside me, eyes closed and body writhing slowly like a serpent charmed by a flourish of flute.

In a moment of strange, unsettling kismet, we looked at each other and our eyes met.

Jesus Christ...

The girl's right eye was black and blue, swollen shut.

The sight of her pushed the song into the background. Davey was not a hitter, at least as far as I knew. If it turned out he had put his hands on this girl, I'd attack the scrawny shit. "Who did that to you?"

She shushed me.

Turned away to look at J and Davey as they worked their way through the rest of her song.

I could only stare at her profile. I felt the world I used to know turn onto its side.

I barely heard the bones of J's spine crack as he abruptly straightened back up from the compacted position he'd pulled himself into. He turned his face to the ceiling. Swaying back and forth as he kept natural time in his head and let loose with a rollicking breakdown that was intermittent rhythm and solo fills.

I watched him in awe.

All self-awareness stripped away.

I couldn't form a thought or speak.

I knew how J was dealing with the murders and what Grifters Anonymous had turned into. Cheap cocaine, cut with an overabundance of baby laxative. To numb his brain and mute the memories of our crime.

Davey? I'll never know, I suppose. The guy was always something of a mystery to solve at your own risk. When he showed up at our first gig with a peaked cap that looked too much like a Nazi lieutenant's hat with the insignia ripped off, we asked him where he'd gotten it. When he told us it was his grandfather's, we left it there. I still wonder if Davey was telling the truth about that or trying to be provocative.

The thing was, the peaked hat could have been a part of a 1950's police uniform just as much as it could have been a part of the Nazi captain ensemble.

I think the four of us leaned towards the former explanation.

J especially, being half-Jewish on his mother's side.

I vowed one day to ask him outright, Grifters be damned.

But today wasn't that day.

By the time the song wrapped up, my mood had slipped from the elation of hearing a great new song to a blacker disposition. And I repeated my question about Glory's shiner, this time to Davey and J. They didn't answer me right away. Didn't even acknowledge me. Not until I opened my mouth once more to demand an explanation did Davey answer me.

He spoke in a callus, removed way.

"Glory's dad smacks her around. Ever since she was little. Guy's a big greaseball asshole. Got connections to the Los Angeles Mafia though, so we gotta tread lightly with this. She's with us now."

"The fucking mob?" I gasped. "You know anything about Italian families? You mess with their kids and you-"

Glory bristled and spoke up. "It's handled, Stevie. Please, try not to be so uptight."

"She stays," J said. "She's cool. Has some pretty great ideas for a fan club. Figure we could make her president. Let her run the promotion at her high school. Get the kids into us."

"Again," I pressed, my head spinning at that point, "her dad finds out we've been hiding her from him? What's this Plan B you got?"

Davey shrugged. "Well, Stevie, we'll just have to work our asses off to make Grifters the biggest band in the land. We make that happen and no one's gonna fuck with us. Beyond that, you don't have to worry about anything else."

Glory crept away from me on her hands on knees, curled up beside Davey in her now trademark curled-up-cat position.

"Go grab your bass, Stevie," Davey said. "We can have this put together by the time Chris and Bobby roll back in."

"Give me a minute. I'm trying to wrap my head around all this shit." Then I realized something. "Wait … you just said Glory's been home and back here. How long have I been out for?"

"Six hours, my brother," J said, noodling absently with his acoustic

"Your bass, Stevie," Davey insisted. "We finish this, we'll be able to rehearse it tonight down the basement. Then we work it into our set this Friday night." Davey smiled, slyly. "Besides, we got two more besides this one."

"What?" I didn't believe him. I didn't want to believe him.

The murders.

The songs.

The connection.

I felt the heat rise inside. I wanted out and I couldn't contain it any longer.

"What the hell is wrong with you fucking guys?"

I saw Glory flinch. It only compounded my anger.

J looked blearily up at me, his hands slowing. His fretting hand fell away from the guitar neck and dropped to the rug. This was the least I had ever heard J say in a long time, and I worried he had snorted too much to silence him this completely. A sober J would have rocketed to his feet and screamed at me for "ruining his high" or "fucking up the process". He merely stared, his features frozen and waxlike.

I challenged him to say something, to say anything. "Don't you have an opinion about all this? You gonna tell me you're good with what we did? Cuz' I'm sick at heart, man! She was somebody's daughter! Somebody loved her, even if she had a hard time loving herself. And you!"

"We, motherfucker," Davey said, staring at J. He wouldn't look at me. The corners of his mouth had turned down, and I knew this look. He was stewing. I could not have given less of a shit. A confrontation with the arrogant, deceitful Davey Grifter would have been a long time coming. Hell, the guy wasn't even anybody yet and he carried himself like some younger version of Roger Daltrey

I seethed at him. "You know where these songs are coming from, man."

"Oh yeah?" Davey said, standing and taking a wavering step towards me. "Why don't you break it down for us, Stevie? Where are they coming from?"

"It's The Mountain. What we did. This is a punishment, not inspiration. Can't you see that? Something is taking away our free will. Shutting down our conscience. Turning us into fucking murderers."

"What did we do on The Mountain, Stevie? Huh? You keep talking about it like you have any idea. None of us know what the fuck you're talking about. Why don't you tell us what you think happened?"

I hated myself for the reaction that followed. My mouth worked but I couldn't find the words. My shoulders wilted. "You ... you know. You remember."

"Oh, fuck off!" Davey spat. "This is a fucking reward. Calliope must have

had a change of heart. Can't you just fucking ride this wave, you fucking killjoy?"

"That poor girl," I stammered. "Anita ..."

Davey crossed his arms. There was no denial. No scoff. No derision. I almost wish there had been. "So ... what? You think Anita had anything to give to the world? Or Lovebug even? Yeah, I feel downright shitty knowing I snuffed out the life of a future astronaut or astrophysicist! They. Were. Whores! Worth the sacrifice! They gave their piss-poor lives for something greater. We gave their existences purpose!"

"Who the hell are you to make that decision, asshole? I guarantee you there are plenty of people out there who could spin your death the same way if they wanted to. What are you giving back to society, huh?"

"We're writing shit right now that's gonna take the world by storm, Stevie. That's what we're gonna give back to them. Something sick and pure and ... and fucking timeless." Only then did he crack a smile. Laugh. He motioned towards J, still sitting there with his guitar across his lap and wearing a strained expression where before there had been befuddlement. "You think either of them had a shot at any kind of fucking legacy, man? Did you hear what we just played there right then? The other three tunes we got out of the last ... the last one?"

"So you see what I see?"

"And what's that, Stevie?"

"Every murder ... it ..." It felt crazy to say. I felt like I should have been wearing a tinfoil hat or lighting candles around a pentagram. My rational mind pumped the brakes, but I floored it because I needed to give voice to it. No matter how insane.

"It's like every time we spill blood. Every time we take a life. A door opens in our brains. Swings wide. And this music comes out. Fully formed. Finished. And all we have to do is-I dunno-excavate it. Like a fossil. It was always there. Always meant for us. But we had to ... offer up a ..."

"Blood sacrifice?" Davey said.

I didn't answer. Speaking it out loud made it real.

The deaths.

The shallow graves.

Hot Hell below us, ready to burn the soles of our feet off.

To eat us.

"Enough of this shit!" J said. "What's done is done. Moving on."

I looked at him. "J-"

"You're bringing me down, Steve. Change the record. Now."

Davey waved him off. J fell to noodling on the guitar again, but I could see his arm muscles were tight. Tendons jumped underneath the tight skin. His playing was amateurish and stilted, like a newbie around a campfire trying to impress a handful of friends.

"We're not Mayans, Stevie," Davey said. "And we never set out to hurt anyone. Hell, I brought Lovebug back here because you wanted her. And you know why just as much as I do why you wanted her. That girl was up for anything. She would have agreed to anything you asked. And if something went wrong or she tried to cry rape, well? Who would've believed her? Let me tell you something, man. You loved tag-teaming her just as much as I did because-"

"Shut up, Davey-"

"Poor little Lovebug treated us like the rockstars we aren't. Not yet anyhow."

"Shut the fuck up!" I screamed. "We're cursed, man. That's what I'm getting at here. I'm not trying to shift blame on anyone. But we gotta stop it. We can't ever do it again."

"Yeah, you think that's up to us? Still think we have a choice? It was never up to us. So why worry about shit we can't control. Why not fucking reap the benefits while we can? Before Calliope turns off the spigot?"

"No, man, I don't accept that."

"Tough shit, Stevie. This is all bigger than your fucking acceptance. This is a gift, bro. It's all in how you look at it."

"A gift?" I cried.

"Yeah," Davey said.

A cold finger touched the bottom button of my spine.

From the floor, J's voice sounded. It was still small, controlled and unassuming. "Guys ... moving on."

Without missing a beat, Davey waved J off like a gnat. "Start the next one. We're calling this one 'Run To Me, Run From Me'."

"Wait a goddam minute-"

I looked down to find J's eyes aimed upward at me. They were bleary and red. His jaw muscles clenched. Before I knew to brace myself, he leapt to his feet, wielding the guitar like a Louisville Slugger. J smashed the acoustic on the floor, smashing it down in eight downward-arcing strokes that sent splinters of finished wood all over the room. Left with just the stick of a fretboard, J drove the guitar neck into the drywall beside the tv. Breathing heavily, J made a quick search of the room for a shirt. He settled for Bobby's discarded Sweet tour shirt, lying on the back of a recliner. He made for the door without a word, angling into the tight tee.

He yanked the door open.

Bobby and Chris stood in the hall, both dirt-smeared and tired-looking. They took one look at J and made way for him to roll on by, down the stairs to the building's exit door. When the door banged shut downstairs, drummer and rhythm guitarist strolled in, shut the door slowly behind them.

I said my peace to them. Made my case. I wanted something that ought to have been obvious for all of us.

"This ends now. Right now. Are we clear?"

None of them said anything. I avoided Davey's eyes, the most headstrong and defiant of everyone.

They both shrugged and nodded halfheartedly before retiring to Bobby's bedroom for what I suspected would be sleep long enough to mute the memory of what they had just done.

Glory looked on, a small smile spread across her full lips.

TWENTY-TWO

Stevie is down for a midday nap when Gretch slips out onto the back porch with the sun highest in the sky. He will sleep for hours, soundly and without incident of late. Still, Gretch is mindful to bring the trusty monitor out with her.

Now, seated at the back patio table with the umbrella opened in its center, Gretch walks her fingers through her Rolodex. The black box is bursting with so many cards the lid doesn't close all the way. She flips through the contacts she has forged across the span of ten years in the music business. And it is like a trip down memory lane, at times regretful and other times sentimental. Longing, even. The experience shakes loose several memories from that time. It is as if someone else has lived them and she is relegated to that of an outsider looking in on another's life.

She can eliminate twenty-odd names and their contact numbers for various reasons. Mostly connections established by a younger and greener Gretch Solomon. People of little consequence or power or influence or, most importantly, insider information regarding the Sunset Strip of the early mid-80's and its key players. Outliers. Indie record labels that have since dissolved in the last decade. Recording engineers who were old when she was young and probably left the business or overdosed. They are people who at one time or another did Gretch a solid or somehow aided in her rise to the status she'd achieve a short time later as the premiere rock manager.

The temptation is there to call King Bo Tillotson for no other reason than she would love to talk to someone who could make her laugh or even crack a smile for that matter. King Bo was *the* DJ of the Los Angeles radio airwaves circa 1977 to the present. His heyday is well behind him, King Bo's downfall was set in motion when he'd made an off-color remark about Kurt Cobain's lack of musical prowess. This, of course, was heresy during the early 90's, as Kurt had been crowned (much to his chagrin) the reinventor of rock/ alternative. His morning drive gig was swiftly downgraded to an eight-p.m. time slot, right when people were turning *off* their radio in favor of their favorite tv show.

The King had dug in and refused to play so much alternative. He loved sleaze rock, and he was a huge early supporter of Grifter's Anonymous, playing their breakout hit "Knives for the People" on regular rotation. And he'd learned the hard way that you either evolve, or the world just paves right the hell over you. Not even his shock jock genius could save him from demotion, and his legion of fans fled from him the more he expressed his disdain for bands like Soundgarden and Pearl Jam. He especially loathed The Melvins, comparing their singer to a living Troll doll.

I could call King Bo.

Why shouldn't I?

Because she is on a clock, whether she wants to admit it or not. It is a race now to discover what, if anything, her husband had been involved in along with the rest of the band. Before The People's Knife grows bored with the memoir in his possession and decides ultimately to cash in with some publisher, spilling whatever allegedly dark secrets the pages contain.

There's no time for a smile or a laugh.

I need to find out what in the hell I'm dealing with.

Who I'm living with!

The treatment she'd signed on for at the mental health clinic had dug so many holes in her brain she imagines it must resemble a veritable honeycomb of dead spaces and fried synapses.

And now there is a moat encircling Stevie Darius in her long-term memory. Crocodiles snap at her if she dares to get too close. To seek all knowledge pertaining to the man dying a little bit more every day in the room next to hers.

Gretch glances across the rolling hills of her expansive yard. She looks without really seeing the flurry of wet activity unfolding in the duck pond. A winsome smile touches her lips. When she turns back to the Rolodex and the card pinched between her thumb and forefinger, Gretch is surprised by the flutter in her belly and the arousal between her legs at the sight of the name scribbled there.

The card reads:

HARRISON HART

310-785-9992

A LOT OF HISTORY THERE.

Pre Stevie ...

Before her husband and Grifters Anonymous, which would ultimately alter the trajectory of her life in every facet, there had been an intense, short-lived tryst with Harrison Hart. Harrison's band, Louder, had been Grifters' most direct competition in terms of marketing. It would have been Motley Crue, if they were not on their way down as Grifters and Louder were on the come-up as the fresh crop of sleazy hard-rock. The physical attraction between Gretch and Harrison had been so immediate and unfettered they nearly ruined each other's careers because they blew off more meetings and rehearsals for sex than either would admit to today.

As far as her husband knew, Stevie was Gretch's greatest lover.

But Harrison always lingered in the back of her mind. And all because she'd taken on Grifters as their manager. As Harrison saw it, this was the worst of betrayals, to represent Louder's rivals, albeit a friendly one. Still, she'd never taken on Louder.

In my defense, their management showed no signs of letting them go.

This is why she does not dial Harrison's number without some hesitation. She spends this lag staring at the name and the digits as if they have morphed into another language.

What if he's still holding a grudge?

I'm not about to abide an earful from him about ugliness that happened almost a decade ago.

Because Harrison had since changed in many ways since their last encounter.

He'd single-handedly blown up Louder by swindling the other guys into signing over rights to the band's name to him. He then replaced the other four members with studio musicians, claimed sole songwriter and steered the once-legendary band into the rocks. Harrison was coming unglued and in need of an intervention that never happened.

Last Gretch heard, he was scoring low-budget films and living off the band's royalties while the other former members pumped gas or sold cars or stocked shelves.

Always wondered just what the fuck they did to him to turn him into such a dark figure.

With stiff little fingers, Gretch punches the numbers into her cord-less phone.

Every ring tone clenches her chest muscles tighter until the anti-climactic moment when an answering machine answers her call. The voice of Harrison Hart, still crackling with the traces of the Southern drawl LA could not strip of him, invites her to leave a message.

Gretch leaves a brief message, asking for a call back and mentioning it's urgent before ringing off.

Okay, well, he's still alive. And he sounds, dare I say, contented? Happy, even?

Suddenly she wonders *who* it was that dodged the bullet.

Him or me?

Gretch dives back into the Rolodex and makes more calls. By the time she reaches the end of her contacts, she feels about ten years older and even more isolated than before. Out of all of them, four answer. Most are disconnected numbers, some of them once belonging to booking agents and club owners. A former producer, Richie Grouse, at Grifter's conglomerate record company, formerly Axis before it was swallowed up by Columbia Records, answered on the second ring as if he'd been sitting by the phone waiting for someone (anyone) to call him with a job or proposition. And Gretch had to do very little to get him talking, or rather, raging against the current music scene.

It's the same old tired, depressing take on everything she's heard echoed by every other remnant of the golden age of 80's metal.

"...Christ, Gretch, I mean, I been ringing in new year after new year and I'm becoming less certain with each goddam trip around the sun that this Grunge thing is gonna flame out soon ... no sign of it ... I read the trades, and they all turned on us ... the critics who'd suck *my* cock just to sit in on a Ratt recording session could give a shit who I'm in the studio with now ... and I just cut a Christmas song with Ace-fucking-Frehley ... *Kiss*, for Chrissakes!"

"I know it. Stevie still feels like the band got hit by a freight train out of nowhere."

"Yeah, *fuckin'* train called Nirvana. With a conductor called Eddie-goddam-Vedder. And Chris Cornell's riding the rails with Layne Staley."

I don't have the heart to slow his roll by telling him I do love Layne and Alice In Chains. They're the closest thing to early 80's metal, and they started on The Strip. Seattle can't lay claim to them entirely.

"I know it. Sucks. But—"

"We need another Aerosmith to bring it back to where it's supposed to be."

"Aerosmith? But they're still going strong. Didn't they just have a rebirth with *Pump*?"

"No-no-no ... *younger*! Young guys that sound like Aerosmith. Old heads can't compete with twentysomething guys. Not to mention, every front man in these Seattle bands could be on the cover of GQ. They all look like male models, for Chrissakes! How do you compete with that?"

Her temper flares, a quick flame up in her mind like a bit of fat or grease has been dropped into it. "Musical fads have always moved in cycles of ten-to-twelve-year turnovers."

"Uh-huh. Sounds like you got something going. Who'd you sign? Tell me it's fucking Zero-Sum—"

"They're just babies, man. C'mon. Didn't the drummer just turn seventeen?"

"And George Harrison joined The Beatles at sixteen! Irrelevant, Gretch!"

"It's too late in the game to find an original act. The new crop is already sounding like a copy of an imitation of Pearl Jam. The iron is already cooling."

Richie Grouse was tight with Grifters for an extended period when they were first laying down rough cuts for their debut album. They shared their drugs and, in some cases, their women with Richie, who at one point made the grave error of referring to himself as the Silent Grifter. The band cut ties with him soon after that unfortunate over-reaching remark made it to a prominent rock journalist.

She wets her lips, asks, "Any of the Grifter guys ever mention something about a … I dunno-a Mountain. They might have referred to it as *The* Mountain. They would have spent some time there?"

"A. Mountain. *The*. Mountain. What … like they hit the slopes or something?"

"Not a mountain resort. Jesus, can you imagine those five crazy bastards at Pocono Lodge? Terrorizing families. Lock up your daughters."

"Yeah, in their heyday, no self-respecting family establishment would have let guys like Grifters within a ten-mile radius of their front doors."

"They ever talk to you about someone, or something called Calliope?"

"Calligraphy? —"

"Ca-llio-pe. Someone. *Someone*."

Could be something?

A pause on the other end. She can practically hear him scratching his head in mounting confusion. "Uh … nah-ah. I'm a lot more lucid than I was back in those days. Ever since they dropped a pacemaker in me. And I'm nearly quit from alcohol. Don't tell my cardiologist."

"Did any of The Grifters say anything or confide in you about something, well, that would have freaked you out. Turned you off or … maybe you felt like you should reach out to …"

Pause.

How the hell do I phrase this? Christ, I really did not think this through.

Richie's tone turns over-curious. Suspicious, even. "Reach out to …? Who? You?"

"Sure. I mean, why not. I was their manager."

"If that were the case, you would have already heard from me. Especially something self-destructive."

"Right," Gretch seizes on this, looking to steer him away from these waters of inquiry again. *He knows nothing.* "You would have called. I'd already know."

"I mean, you remember I called when I worried about some of the things J was saying when we were splitting an H needle. I had no idea he was such a wounded soul. Such a rough exterior. Cocky as shit! And he was talking suicide that night. Talking OD. Opening his wrists in the bathtub—"

"And I thank you for that, Richie. We got him the help he needed. You saved his life."

"Shame that he couldn't —"

"Sorry, Richie. Stevie's calling me. Thanks for talking to me."

"Yeah, sure. You link up with a new act give a call."

She sets the phone down on the patio table. A murder of crows burst form the redwood treetops, spiraling towards the horizon like moving fingerprints.

The cordless phone rings.

"Yes-hello?"

"Holy shit, Peter Grant in fuckin' heels! Gretch Solomon!"

Lightheadedness. *What is wrong with me?*

"Harrison, thank you for calling me back so quickly!"

"Well, I tend to treat calls the caller labels *urgent* as, well, you know … urgent. Is Stevie okay?"

"Oh-oh-yes, he's doing well. There are good days and bad days, you know. Not to sound too cliché, but really that's the only way to describe it all."

"Is today a *good* day or—"

"Right, that would be today. I don't want to dwell too much on it. Don't want to jinx it."

"Fair enough. Just wanted to make sure."

"I appreciate that."

"So … that's not what was *urgent*. I can't imagine what else it could be. I mean, I haven't heard from you in-what's it been?"

"Four years."

"Shit, that sounds right. Glad to hear from you just the same. What do you need?"

While her explanation of what has happened with Stevie and his memoirs begins as a slow rollout of words, by the time she finds her stride they are not so much spoken as bled like blood from an arterial spray until she is breathless and overwhelmed by her own story. Laying it out plain for another person, Harrison being the first she trusts with her concerns about Stevie's ravings.

All the while, Harrison listened silently.

By the time she finishes with the backstory, Gretch regrets having told Harrison Hart anything.

"Mm … I never would've believed it," Harrison says.

"What?"

"The *Nasty Bits*. I had always just assumed they weren't real. I'd roll my eyes whenever someone'd even bring them up. I think too many Grifter fans *wanted* it to be real. They wanted their favorite band to be killers also. For some kind of street cred. The whole gang angle they played out. But these were all people who didn't know the guys. Never met them. Just knew their songs. Dave's lyrics."

"Some great fucking lyrics. You can't deny. And I hate that asshole—"

"I think we should meet."

"Oh … okay."

"Yeah, let's-let's not do this over the phone. It would feel-I dunno-seedy."

"Alright," Gretch says, feeling uneasy.

"Cantor's Deli? You name the day and time."

She says she will have to plan for Stevie. This makes the arrangement feel illicit, like the start of an affair. Still, she says she'll call him later with a time and day. She'll leave it on the machine if he's not around.

"But Harrison?"

"Mm?"

"I don't know that I can handle anymore suspense when it comes to this."

"Oh … right … then …"

She is suddenly struggling to work the warble out of her voice as tears have come to surprise her once again. *I'm not well. Not well at all.* "Nevermind," she stammers, now wanting nothing more than to get off the line and find her way under a hot shower spray. "I'll call you with the date and time."

TWENTY-THREE

Cantor's Deli stands a half mile from the fabled Sunset Strip and boasts its own myth largely because of this vicinity. Its quality food and twenty-four-hour operation has profoundly benefited the establishment since the days of Television City, only a block north, first cemented the deli's popularity among show business personalities in the 1960's. From there, the hippies, rock musicians, and other counter-cultural types have come to claim the spaces as their own, chasing out much of the previous buttoned-up clientele of yesteryear from the comfy, if not unforgiving red booths and counter seating. Still, its Jewish owners have not lost a meaningful connection to their early religious roots and faithfully close their doors for both Rosh Hoshana and Yom Kippur.

Gretch finds a parking spot right out front with ease. This both surprises and sinks her spirits, seeming to signal the passing of an era. The new crop of musicians, at least, gravitate more towards the mom-and-pop coffee shop than a deli to the stars. They are artists who forego a meal in favor of a double shot of espresso to go with their heroin habit or pair with their pills.

Cantor's wait staff mills haplessly about like zombies in search of brains rather than a tip tucked under a salt or pepper shaker. It's approaching twelve noon, a few minutes shy of the universal lunch hour. The deli may as well feature a tumbleweed or two rolling across its linoleum carpeting. Even as little as two years ago, your average tourist would have been hard-pressed to snag a table at such a peak hour.

The eyes of a few servers brighten at her entry, while others remain nonplussed.

A svelte blonde with an inch on Gretch sidles up to her at a sign reading *Please Wait to be Seated*.

"One?" Svelte Blonde, whose name tag reads Marybeth, slides a menu out from inside the greeter podium.

"I'm supposed to be meeting someone here—"

"Hey! Red!"

Harrison Hart is waving her over from across the deli, half-out of his seat.

Marybeth the Waitress does a half-turn, then comes to face Gretch again. "I'm assuming you're *Red*. You a natural ginger?"

"The bane of my existence."

"Oh, I'd kill for that shade!"

"Funny, I always wished I could have been a blonde."

"Well," Marybeth says, leading her towards Harrison's table, "we don't have all the fun. Don't believe the hype."

"Not all gingers love being gingers," Gretch says. "The amount of money I spend on conditioner annually. I ought to own stock in Pantene by now."

They share a superficial chuckle as Marybeth sets a menu down at Gretch's place, across from Harrison Hart. Sneaking a sideways glance at the undeniably handsome, movie-star attractive former rock star leaning back in his wooden chair, Sinead tells Gretch she will "give her a minute to decide".

Harrison Hart smiles thinly at the waitress then leans forward towards Gretch. "Well-well," he says, his deep blue eyes dancing, "and how is Gretchen Solomon today?"

Harrison Hart boasts a heroin-chic frame, even though he kicked the needle and spoon two years ago after a personal *come to Jesus* moment in a St. James motel room. It helps to stay so lean and lanky by standing a full six-two. During the heyday of Louder, Harrison would spray his wavy black hair up, teasing it five inches high. Now, his hair is dyed cherry-red and drawn up into heavily Pomaded wedged spikes. The sides and back are shaved down to the scalp.

He's also leaned more heavily into his motorcycle club roots. His father had been the head of the Los Angeles Chapter of a notoriously ruthless crew for decades, the Crazy 8's. It's rumored Harrison's father used this clout to get his son's band early booking at places they had no business playing so early on in their career, putting Louder on a faster track than most to stardom. Harrison wears a denim vest with the sleeves cut off at the shoulders. Under that, he sports a blue and grey-checked flannel and tight, faded jeans hug his stick-like legs. Chains and buckles jingle at his ankles as he rearranges his motorcycle boots under the table.

Gretch lowers her handbag down to the floor and slides the menu aside, having already decided on coffee and nothing more. Splaying her hands in the air, she raises an eyebrow at him.

"This look," she says, "It's—"

"My riding gear," he says, "and nothing more. I'm not following in daddy's footsteps. No need to worry."

"And—you know I must ask—your songwriting? Where are you with it?"

A shadow seems to pass over his gaze. He fingers the utensils of his place setting, absently. "It's not coming like it used to. The harder shit, I mean. I can't find a decent hook. Can't seem to write a decent lyric without some cliché finding its way into it and spoiling the whole fucking thing." He looks at her, momentary vulnerability sitting in his stare. Then, just like that, it is replaced by a brightening as he sits up straighter in his chair. Smiles. "You heard about my latest gig? Scoring movies? Now, there's no back-up when it comes to that endeavor. I was born to do it. And it is *so* lucrative. Not to mention satisfying."

"That sounds great. Really."

"Look, I know this doesn't compute, knowing me as well as you do. I knew Louder wasn't going to last forever, once I heard some of the shit coming out of Seattle. I'd already been tinkering in my home studio with synth and sampling. I just jumped in with both feet and before I knew it, I was matching music up to the love scene in *Coma Rose*. Composing 'Jackdaw's Theme' for that superhero movie, fucking blockbuster, last year. And the take is almost as good as the royalties for Louder music."

"You were always a forward-thinker. And smarter than you let on."

"Eh, dumb, dopey and rock n' roll like to hold hands a lot of the time. I played along."

"No groupies for John Williams, eh?"

"Something like that." An easy grin spreads across his face. "So. Not to rush things along. I got nothing planned after this. But you've still got my curiosity. What are you after?"

"That's a nice way of putting it." Gretch rolls her eyes.

"Is there any other way to put it? What is it exactly you suspect Stevie and the boys were into?"

"Oh, come the hell on, Harrison—"

"You know I love you and Stevie to death. Even when Louder had that whole unspoken rivalry going with Grifters."

"That's ancient history," Gretch says. She leans in conspiratorially. Laces her fingers together on the tabletop and suddenly finds it difficult to look at him. She is not someone used to shame. "Listen, I … I recently ran into some personal problems. I had a difficult time coping. Between Stevie's illness, and some things involving my brother's own mental health problems, everything just got to be too much to bear. It was sinking me. One day, I could shoulder it. Then, well, I just *couldn't*. So I checked myself into a hospital. Called a timeout from life."

Harrison leans forward, playfully mimics her interlaced fingers and somber, quietened tone. "Why are we whispering? Furthermore, why do you look like a dog who just had an accident in the corner? There is nothing—and I mean *nothing*—to be ashamed of when it comes to this. It's an illness like … like fucking MS or-or autism."

"I want to see it that way but—"

"But nothing," he says. "I want you to look at me. Will you please?"

Something about his approach makes her want to break down right then and there. She just barely staves off tears, nods and meets his gaze. She explains and chronicles what she can still remember.

Gretch tells him about Glory and her brief stay. How she and Stevie hit it off, much to her dismay given her history with the Child Bride. Glory stealing Stevie's memoirs right out of their house before fleeing in the middle of the night.

"A memoir I never even knew existed!"

Harrison doesn't say anything.

Gretch thinks she sees something in his eyes, a glimmer of recognition. "I believe you referred to them as The Nasty Bits?"

"Rumblings and rumors. Nothing I ever took seriously. Honestly, there's so much ridiculous mythology flying around the Strip it's more a joke than anything else. Booths left empty for the ghost of this rock star or some OD'd groupie. Hauntings. Lots of ghost stories. Something as salacious as a lost memoir written by the likes of Stevie Darius. That'd fit right in."

Gretch pushes back from the table. Tosses up her hands. "Christ, I've only been out of the business for four years. How is it I'm the last one to know about this? I'm married to the fucking guy, for God's sakes!"

"Maybe because it's bullshit and Glory's fucking with you? Ever think of that? The two of you were always like oil and water."

"No," Gretch says. "No, I wish that were possible. A bluff? No."

"How do you know? She could've fallen back in love with the H and decided to fuck with your head one more time."

"Because," she says. "It's been verified."

But her mind is suddenly awash in flashes of a man in a balaclava, the glacial eyes drawing in close and pulling away in a maddening intimidation. The sharp sting on her cheek. The back of his hand. A clunky metal ring on his middle finger that glances painfully off her cheek bone. Smoky, dragon breath fanning her square in the face as he touches noses with her. Out comes the cattle prod—

"Hey-*hey* Gretch! Where'd you go?"

Gretch snaps to. She finds her voice, craggy and frog-like. "I'm sorry, I … what was I saying?"

"You sure you're okay, Gretch?"

She says she's fine. Asks again what she was saying before her nightmare flashback.

"You said Stevie's memoirs were … verified?"

"Yes."

"How so?"

"Somebody claims to have them in his possession. That he stole them from Glory. He calls and says he's this big fucking superfan of Grifters and he has them. The ...the fucking Nasty Bits. Idiotic name for them!

"He says he wants to return them to me. That he shouldn't have them. He says they're incriminating. That Stevie and the Grifters were involved in terrible things. In the early years. I-I think he said the papers read like part-confession, and part like a ... what'd he say? A dark ritual. That was it."

Harrison's sits still and silent. Fully engrossed.

"I agreed to meet him. But ... I just dunno ... at some point between the phone call and our meet-up he changed his mind and decided he not only wanted to hold onto the memoirs. He also decided to pull a ruse. He kidnapped me. Made me drive to some an abandoned warehouse. There ... he ... he demanded to know if the contents of the memoirs were legitimate. He wanted me to verify all of it for him. And to point him in the direction of ... h-he kept talking about a-a Mountain. Mountain and Muse! I had no idea what the *fuck* he was on about. What the fuck he wanted. And when I couldn't give him anything, he ... he ... fuck ...."

Harrison reaches for her hands on the table. Takes them in his.

"Shit, I'm so sorry, sweetheart. So sorry."

For a moment, Gretch squeezes his hands and leeches some of his strength and warmth before pulling back.

"Gretch," he says, and his voice sounds suddenly guarded and laced with dread. "What did this guy call himself?"

Sniffling, Gretch says, "A stupid nod to Grifters. *The People's Knife.* Fucking childish."

Harrison straightens in his seat. And that shadow that had stolen across his face returns for one more crossing.

"What's wrong?" Gretch turns fully towards him. "What is it?"

"Shit, Gretchen," he says, looking stunned.

"What?"

"I've met this People's Knife psycho. Recently."

"What are you talking about?"

"There was this guy. He showed up on my doorstep. Not all that long ago. Flashes a badge. Literally flashes it and then it's gone again under his jacket. Not fast enough I could've missed the tattoo encircling his wrist. His sleeve hiked up his arm just long enough."

Gretch doesn't say anything.

Harrison rings his wrist with his thumb and forefinger to illustrate. "All the way around. *The People's Knife*. Ornate script."

"Oh my God."

"He didn't look like a cop, to tell you the truth. In fact, he *looked* like a musician bundled into a too small, secondhand suit. You know the way that rock stars look fucking silly in a three-piece when they show up in court for whatever reason? The long hair combined with the formal wear just turns these poor guys into walking contradictions. Yeah, it reminded me of that. Only this guy's hair was pulled up into these fucking chunky spikes that looked like he must have used rubber cement to get em' so sharp and-I dunno-lethal-looking. I swear he was wearing a bit of makeup, too. I shit you not."

"Makeup?" Gretch hears herself give voice to the word as if from a great distance.

"Like a light foundation? Thin bit of eye liner. Just enough to get noticed. And look, I called him on it. I did not let him in right off. And he tells me it's a part of his cover so he can blend in on Sunset. Says it's not his typical get-up. The suit is his *knocking-on-doors* attire. He tells me he's investigating a string of murders in the Hills. *Ritual killings*, that's what he called them. I asked him why I haven't seen anything on the news about this, and he had an answer for that too. *We're on the verge of making it public.* He said he didn't want to contaminate any info that comes through on the tip line. So, I roll the dice. I let him in.

"The guy-oh, and he introduced himself as Detective Robert Stiletto, like the heels—he tells me he has reason to believe the killer is a member of the music community. Somebody from The Strip. I ask him how he knows this, and this *detective* tells me he located a manifesto of sorts the killer left at one of the scenes, because he wanted it to be found. The book makes frequent reference to certain bands and rock stars and their own band and gigging and shit like that. He put it together. I dunno. I bought it. The guy had a way, I'm sorry to admit.

"Then he starts asking about—and I quote— 'Some real head scratchers maybe you can help to put into context'. He asks me if I knew anything about some Magic Mountain. And there's this old god, this … strap in, Gretch … this *ancient* Muse living inside the fucking mountain and that it's supposedly the best kept secret of creatives for centuries. Some shit like that." Harrison pauses, holding her gaze. "You mentioned a Mountain on the phone if I remember right? And … what else?"

Gretch's mouth is bone dry. "A Muse. Why didn't you tell me on the phone?"

"Honest to God, I didn't put it together until now."

Her eyes flash with ire. "If we're talking about the same maniac, then you let an unhinged *superfan* into *your* house. He—"

Don't.

Not now. Her mouth snaps shut with an audible click. She sits back, the rails of the wooden chair creaking. In a measured tone, Gretch says,

"Somehow he hooked up with Glory Tizione and they—"

"Wait a minute! Glory?"

"Yes."

"As in *Mrs. Davey Grifter?*"

"That's the one."

"And you think she turned Stevie's memoirs over to this … who the hell is this creepy fuck?"

"I can't prove the two of them are working together to-I dunno-extort me? He claims he's been trying to give her the slip, but she won't leave him alone. She always was a parasite."

"Dammit," Harrison says, hammering the table with a fist. "How could I have been so stupid?"

"You couldn't have known?"

"Still!"

"What did you tell him?"

"About what?"

"The Mountain. The-the Muse. Anything!"

Harrison throws up his hands. "What else could I say? I had no idea what the fuck the guy was talking about. I mean, why would I? I never believed in any of that *muse* horseshit. Songwriting comes from the gut. Nowhere else."

"And what did he do?"

"What'd he do? Only thing he could do. He stood up, shook my hand—although I could kind of tell he was a little strained and disappointed. He left. Haven't seen him since."

Gretch is about to flag down a waitress for a sesame seed bagel when someone back in the kitchen lets loose with a terrible shriek.

Gretch looks at Harrison wide-eyed.

"Holy. Shit. Gretch."

"What?" she cries. "What'd I miss?"

Harrison is looking past her. Something in the background He shoves back from the table and crumples over, staring down between his knees at the rug. "No-no-*no*. Shit."

"What!?"

Harrison's lips move in a whisper, almost prayerfully.

A waitress bursts through the swinging steel doors of the kitchen and, sobbing, slips into the waiting opened arms of her coworker.

They hold each other, shaking and sobbing.

Gretch notices another waitress standing a few feet away, her eyes shimmering with tears as she stares at something above Gretch's head.

A TV mounted to the wall above the countertop area.

It's tuned to MTV, a somber-looking Kurt Loder delivering sobering news with a set jaw and tired eyes.

The graphic beside his head shows a young man with greasy blonde hair that hangs just past his stubbly chin. Blue eyes committed to a thousand-yard stare that only now makes tragic sense. A pouting mouth, just above the simple but devastating headline that reads:

"Why?" the waitress from the kitchen moans, hands fingers pulling into and out of fists. "Why? *Why would he DO THIS*? Every-everybody *loved him!*"

"My God," Gretch says. "He killed himself?"

Harrison looks at her like she had suddenly become transparent.

The news conjures an image Gretch is not ready for, that of standing graveside at Stevie's funeral. Hollywood Forever Cemetery.

How she would wish for a small ceremony instead of the circus it could prove to be. Chris Desmond's funeral had been a circus of blinding flashbulbs, relentless paparazzi, fans crowding in like they were there for a Grifters reunion rather than to lay one of them to rest. Bobby had had his ashes scattered from a bluff in Scotland, where his family is from. He always did seem to be the smartest of the Grifters, as well as the most forward-thinking.

A haunting thought occurs to her. It will stay with her for the rest of that day.

Dementia patients are so far gone, there is a strong chance Stevie will never fully realize he's dead. He won't understand what's happening in his final moments. And I won't be able to explain it to him—

"Gretch."

She flinches, snapping to. "Yes. Sorry."

"Are you alright?"

By the subtle tremor in his voice, Gretch thinks she ought to be the one asking him that question.

"Fine. It's just … I -I don't know what to say."

Harrison's eyes are big and glassy with what looks like naked dread.

It doesn't quite gibe with Gretch's memory of how the 80's rockers had bagged on Nirvana and the other grunge acts when this new crop of brash, snotty young rockers put the old guard out of favor. It happened more quickly than any of the Sunset Strip boys expected, the equivalent of a sudden, bloody assault. Harrison himself had once been quoted in a *Rolling Stone* article to have said "Their music is just so fucking *depressing*. They hate everything. *Everything* sucks and the world's *just so unfair*. Every one of their songs are like a fucking suicide note. Who wants to listen to *that*? I'll spring for group therapy for all of them, and they can pay me back."

What if he's thinking of that interview right now and it's turning his stomach?

It was not uncommon for the sleaze rockers to wish the worst upon the Seattle bands.

Especially on Kurt Cobain.

"I'm sorry, Gretch," Harrison says, his eyes pleading now. "This … this news just knocked the fucking shit out of me. I can't think straight right now. I-I never thought he'd go through with …"

Gretch hauls her handbag up over her shoulder and stands. Her thoughts are awash in black thoughts. If he hadn't called it right then and there, she would have had to be the one. "So young. Only a boy."

And she will never forget Harrison's reaction to those words. They don't match up with what anyone would have expected of someone hit with tragic news.

He smirks at her. "Don't be so naïve, huh?"

"What does that mean?" Gretch's hands tighten on her purse strap.

"Nothing in this business is what it seems. And this is *no exception*, sorry to say. I thought you'd be wise to it after all these years. I thought it's why you got out."

"Harrison, I think we're talking over one another's heads right now. It's best that I go." She turns to walk out, half-turns and says, "It was good to see you."

"Gretch—"

"Goodbye, Harrison. I'll look for you in the movie credits."

He skirts the table and takes her by the arm, not roughly. She turns around to face him. Her cheeks are flush with resentment.

"Look. I'm sorry. I-I-I don't even know what I'm saying."

Gretch nods, solemnly. Silently.

The weeping of the wait staff has risen to a near fever-pitch. It threatens to drive Gretch clear out of her mind. She must get out.

"Gretchen, I'll call you. Tonight. Seven o'clock. Alright? I do have something to share with you."

"I have to go." She pulls her arm from his grasp.

"Can I call you?" Harrison asks, standing there looking like some high schooler asking his crush to prom.

Making for the door and the street where she will happily trade the buzz and drone of heavy traffic for weeping women, Gretch turns and says, "Seven o'clock."

TWENTY-FOUR

24.

ON THE WAY HOME, Gretch hangs a sharp left and pulls into the Tower Records parking lot. There is already a long line of people with the same idea, their hands grasping stacks of the band's CDs. Many of them still wear the red faces of recent tear shed, even the young men and smattering of middle-agers. The females weep openly and stand there shuddering as their boyfriend or their husband or even strangers in line fling their arms around them and hold them.

They cry together.

Twenty minutes later, she exits carrying a bag weighted down with all of Nirvana's studio recordings, along with their "Unplugged in New York" concert.

Try as she might, Gretch cannot even imagine the public being so moved had it been Davey Grifter's suicide, or any of his late 80's peers.

This collective emotional outpouring seems reserved for a relative few in the business. None of the Grifter boys, (or the Louder boys, for that matter) could ever dream of such a response to their passing.

Of course, it only adds to the mythos when the artist passes at that magical age of twenty-seven, itself a mystery and a touchstone for greatness.

Later, Gretch spreads herself out across the living room sofa. She's been losing weight without trying, a first in her thirty-six years. The flesh has been melting off her of late. With her feet covered in an Afghan blanket and two fingers of Kentucky bourbon shimmering in her glass as she holds it against her heart, Gretch listens to the Nirvana catalog in a meditative state. Kurt Cobain's throat-shredding pleas spiral above the tinny, signature guitar tones, thumping bass, and murderous drumbeats.

When the CD *Nevermind*, the band's breakthrough album, comes on, Gretch can't contain herself.

"Shit," she curses into the dim. "How does a power trio sound like a fucking five-piece band?"

Gretch decides to just let the words fly. No need for a listener. No response or retort required.

Her eyelids growing heavy.

"He's telling everybody what he was going to do," she laments, her voice airy with drunkenness.

The phone rings.

Gretch doesn't hear it at first.

The first raucous, minimally-mixed track opening the next album, *In Utero*, drowns it out.

By some dumb luck, the caller does not give up after seven rings. They hang in there for a few minutes, and it extends into the break between the first and second tracks. Gretch's thick and lazing mind doesn't register who could be calling after ten at night. Then, just as the guitar intro for "Heart-Shaped Box" creeps across the floor, she remembers.

Harrison!

Fuck!

She pounces on the phone resting on the end table, knocking the glass of bourbon onto the rug in the process. But the rug is the same color as the alcohol so it can wait. Gretch hollers into the receiver, struggling to be heard above the stereo. "I'm here! Hold on-hold-on! Don't hang up!"

Gretch seizes the stereo remote and lowers the volume. Still, she decides to take the call in another room.

If it does turn out to be Harrison calling, I don't want Stevie to overhear anything. He may be all the way in his bedroom, but you never can be sure.

And yes … I still need to be able to hear him.

Gretch rushes up the shallow flight of stairs leading up into the kitchen. She heads for the music room, where a turntable is flanked by endlessly overflowing shelves of vinyl records. It is a soundproof inside, the walls padded with gray foam insulation. The floor is a black and white checkerboard tile pattern with an oversized orange shag rug spread across its center.

She shuts the door a crack to listen for her husband and sits cross-legged on the rug. Her fingers absently pluck and pull at the long carpet fibers.

"Hello."

"Red? It's me."

"Hi."

"For the record, I'm one record ahead of you. I'm listening to *Unplugged in New York* now."

"Full disclosure," Gretch says. "I'm a poseur and I know it."

"No more than me."

"Oh, I don't know." She tells him about her buying spree at Tower Records.

He laughs. "Sorry to run out on you back there. I don't know what happened. It just—I dunno—it paralyzed me."

"I have to ask. You said I was being naive about Cobain's death. What did you mean by that?"

"I meant nothing by it. I was distraught and fucking pissed. Just a range of emotions and I punched out at you because you were there. No other reason than that. I have no excuse. Sorry, Red."

"Got that. Only … it sounded like you knew more about this than you were letting on."

Silence.

"You there?" she says.

"Too soon, Gretch. Ask me about this a year-maybe even two years-from now. I'll tell you everything. Right now, let's just say I wish I wasn't within earshot of a particular conversation at a dive bar I hadn't been to in years. A nefarious one. Nothing I would have given a second thought to if not for today. Back at Cantor's, it came back to haunt me. I thought I was gonna be sick all over the table. Another reason I had to get outta there."

"Jesus, Harrison, are you saying—"

"That's not why I called. Let's just leave it."

Now it is Gretch's turn to pause, for want of what to say next. She pushes a breath of air out of her lungs, the word "Alright" barely audible.

"Now … I wanna preface this by saying what I'm about to tell you is secondhand info. And the source is a groupie from the old days. For all I know, the girl could have made the whole thing up. The only reason I would even think of sharing this story with you is … well, because … there have always been whispers."

"Whispers?"

"You know. Rumors. Don't tell me this is news to you!"

"Well, no. Not exactly. The record company was pretty keen on playing up Grifter's dangerous reputation. Now, whether that comes from any incident or more of a perception because of how the guys carried themselves-always looking to brawl over the smallest thing-I can't speak on that with confidence. I was hired on as their manager after they were already infamous. Nobody wanted to represent them. Grifters made people nervous. That was their aura. Do I think it was put-on? Some of it. I will say it's hard to imagine my Stevie striking fear in the heart of anyone. Ever. Davey and J? Especially, those two? I can see it when it comes to them."

"You still haven't told me what *crime* Stevie thinks they've committed."

Gretch chews her upper lip. "I'm not sure it matters."

"Sounds to me like it's everything."

"Well, Harrison, I guess it would be my turn now to ask *you* to *leave it.*"

Harrison sighs deeply. "Alright. I'll just tell you.

"This was before your time with the band, I'm guessing. The Grifter boys were never short on groupies to have a time with. Back even before they started writing and performing their own songs, they just had this draw-this magnetism-where the girls would just line up for them outside the dressing room. To put this in perspective, they were only a cover band back then, and still—"

"I get it," Gretch interrupts, an edge to her voice. "They're a bunch of hunky rock guys. Check!"

"Right. I'm backstage at this poorly attended Great White show at The Cathouse. Just shooting the shit with the usual suspects. Body-guards. Dealers. Band Aids. Couple techs. And there's this girl sitting with us. In the mix. Apparently, she hooked up with Chris Desmond after a show. They went back to the apartment where all the guys lived together. By the way, I still can't fathom how the hell all five of those fuckers squeezed themselves into that little bedroom-and-den. Must've been like a clown car in there."

"The way she explained it, she was only into Chris. She was supposed to be Chris' girl. And she thought he was really into her, more in, like, an almost *romantic 'this girl could be The One'* kind of thing. And, of course, the girl made sure we all understood she doesn't just fuck just any rock star."

"Mm, standards," Gretch says, drily. "How quaint."

"I know. She never stood a chance. Chris was into monogamy like The Pope's into Greek mythology. But we all let her talk.

"Then she says something like *'Things just took this turn and the whole arrangement got real dark, real fast'.*"

Gretch feels her cheeks start to sting with a new heat. "I'm listening."

"She pulled us all the way back in when she said that," Harrison says. "According to her, one minute she's in the bedroom with Chris. Just the two of them. Door locked. Lights out. Pitch black room on account of the fact the boys liked to live like vampires, and they blacked out all the windows in the apartment like a bunch of psychos. Just kidding! As a matter of fact, I don't know if you were around for this, but they blacked out the windows in their band van too."

Her stomach flips and she tastes bile and acid. The music room feels suddenly as if the walls are closing in. "Weird was always their forte. It was also their shared persona."

Who are you trying to convince of their harmlessness?
Harrison or yourself?

"The girl said one minute there was one pair of hands on her body. Then, she felt hands kneading and pinching and massaging her all over. Someone bit her in the darkness. She couldn't tell who. Then, well, she says someone-could've been Chris-flipped her onto her back and she found herself looking up into five sets of red eyes glowing in the darkness. *Like rubies*, she said. With a black fleck in the center of them. She swore she never heard anyone come into the room. No one made a sound at the door, one of them slipping inside, let alone the other four guys. She never saw their faces, but the girl knew it was the Grifter guys. *'It was their apartment, and they weren't having a party, so it had to be them.'*

"Then she says she felt a couple fingers penetrate her. And she screamed because she thought she was going to be gang raped. She felt Chris come off the bed and then he started arguing with the others. She tried to climb up off the bed. She wanted to get the fuck out of there. Someone took her by the wrist and yanked her backward. She says she felt something like wet lips sucking at her wrist. Then ... again ... this is what she said ... someone took hold of her other wrist. Two of them started to graze her wrists with their teeth. She said Chris saved her, but we didn't see it as being exactly that.

"She said he was screaming *'Not this one! You can have the next one, alright!'*"

"*What!* The hell! Wha-what the fuck does *that mean?*"

"I ... I honestly don't know, Red."

Gretch can barely think.

"Red?"

"Yeah, I'm here. Just ... wait a minute. You said she was a groupie whore. Not credible? That's what you were implying."

"Gut?"

"Gut."

"She wasn't bullshitting."

"Yeah, but what makes you say that—"

"Because she excused herself and we all listened to her lose her fucking lunch in the backstage bathroom. She was crying. Never saw her again. I heard she went underground, though. More grapevine, bullshit. She's one of those Mole People now, lives down in the LA sewer system with the rest of the ghouls. But she got away with her life."

Gotaway.

The word leaps into her mind, misspelling and all. She feels a significant pull to get off the phone.

The fact she is in the exact room of her home where she needs to be in that moment is not lost on her.

It's downright spooky.

The records are shelved along the far wall with the turntable arranged in the center of the collection like a god nestled amidst a shrine of worshippers. An eclectic mix of vinyl. From Gregorian Chant to Sex Pistols.

Still, Gretch can't help herself.

She must push back.

"*Red eyes*? What is this? A Poe story?"

"Hey, I'm only telling you what the girl told us. You can toss this story out if you want to. But you called me, remember? You were the one fishing for anything about Grifters that raises an eyebrow. That's what I got. Do I honestly believe your guys are-what? -serial killers? Jesus, Red."

"One more thing," Gretch says.

"Yeah, sure."

"What was the girl's name?"

"Er … *Cassandra*? Yeah. Cassandra."

The conversation has run its course and practically ends itself with a murmuring between the two to get together under happier circumstances.

Gretch switches on the lights, opens the door, and listens to the purr of Nirvana at a lowered volume.

Lots of broken hearts and bad poetry getting written tonight.

She listens for any stirring from Stevie's room, then gently shuts the door.

TWENTY-FIVE

Gretch crosses the room and searches the narrow, barely legible spines of the vinyl slipcovers. Thankfully, the Gs are at eye level, and she doesn't have to stoop or drop onto all fours. She slides a white-spined vinyl 7-inch slipcover out from the stack and holds it out before her. It's an all-white layout with what appears to be the top of a shaved head pushing upward at a white membrane holding it down. Centered above the graphic:

Grifters Anonymous

A) Walk the Cracked Sidewalk (Radio Edit)
B) Gotaway Girl (B-side)

A RARE SINGLE. Pressed in Japan.

Hungrily, her fingers ease the liner notes insert out of the slipcover and holds it up to the light.

Gretch sets it down on the furry shag, slides the 7-inch record out and arranges it on the turntable. A pair of headphones are already plugged in, and she claps them over her ears.

B-side plays. It's a song she barely remembers. A throwaway or filler, with the rhythm of a wheezing, speeding locomotive. Davey delivers the words in a machine-gun staccato. The guitars are an assault on the senses.

She reads along with the lyrics to "Gotaway Girl", whispering the words to herself and tasting their sting on the tip of her tongue:

POOR LITTLE RICH GIRL COULDA' been a part of something
    bigger than herself
    But he chose her life, she's not right
    in the head
    His Gotaway Girl
    Running in an incredible shrinking world
    Needle missed your vein
    for now,
    Love is a starting gun
    run, rabbit, run!

THE CONNECTION IS tenuous at best. Something of a relief for Gretch. A "gotaway girl" could very well be one of the many girls the Grifter guys let slip through their fingers.

Or discarded.

The song has grown on her by the time the fade-out comes at the end.

Gretch hears something in her headphones at the tail-end of the fade-out that gives her pause.

Casual back and forth conversation.

Then laughter.

Left in by the sound engineer. But there is no way it would have if Davey and J, who oversaw every recording of their music, hadn't wanted it.

She swears she heard something specific. Must verify it.

Lifts the turntable dome up, runs the vinyl backward to the start of the fade-out again.

Plays it again.

Reaches for the volume. Turns it all the way up in her headphones once the music is low enough not to blow out her eardrums.

A microphone in the foreground picked it up:

DAVEY: *Fuck, yeah! That one'll blow out your —*
J: Run, Cassie, run!
(Laughter)

"WAIT," she says, and plays it back again:
"Run, Cassie, run!"
"No."
Twice more.
"Run, Cassie, run!"
"Run, Cassie, run!"
Cassandra,
A sacrifice?
To be someone bigger than herself.

WHEN SLEEP FINALLY FINDS her just after 3 a.m., Gretch dreams of reds eyes in the dark.

Five sets of them.

TWENTY-SIX

26.

THE LITTLE BOY, no older than six or seven, is wearing a Spider-Man costume and clutching the mask with one sweat-soaked hand. His father is with him, a white-collar guy who looks like he stepped out of the pages of LL Bean.

Burnside stands before the Men's Room door. Barring entry. He wears a red pleather jacket. Dad's eyes snag on Burnside's ragged yellow t-shirt underneath that reads *TAKE IT SLEAZY!* and features a cartoon dog underneath with its overlong tongue wagging. The studded leather belt hanging on his bony thighs and leather pants tucked into jangly motorcycle boots inspire Dad's hand to close tighter around his son's shoulder blade.

"Hey, big guy!" Dad says. "What gives? My son's got to go."

"Can't let you do that, kid," Burnside says.

He watches Dad's eyes, calculating the odds he will be able to handle this situation as opposed to losing face in front of young Spidey.

And a decision is made.

"Please … we don't want any trouble, guy," Dad says, his eyes just shy of imploring. "Just played some Frisbee Golf and my boy needs to pee. You know how it is." He smiles thinly, his lips bloodless and taut. "I-I don't have my wallet on me, but—"

"I just called maintenance," Burnside says, angling his chin in the direction of what he wants them to perceive is the maintenance shed nearby, when in fact, there is none. "Toilets are backed up. The floors are all —" he checks himself, remembering Spider Man is standing there staring up at him "—dirty." Had it been the dad alone, he would have said *shitty*.

Dad wrinkles his nose, casting a woeful glance towards the door to the supposedly soiled Men's Room. The only one in the park. "Seriously?"

"Seriously. Check the Ladies Room on the other side of the building. Poor kid looks like he's about to spill the lemonade, Dad."

Young Spidey finds this hysterical.

Kid, if you knew what was waiting for you behind this door, it'd wipe the smile off your face faster than the back of your dad's hand. Inside, there be Tygers! The comfortably dumb child will live to stay that way for another day. A year. God-willing, maybe through puberty. Had Burnside not had business with the *monster* inside the Men's Room, he would have no reason to be there, and the worst would have happened.

Another child destroyed.

Double zeros in the kid's eyes for a lifetime.

Because Burnside knows (he doesn't know *how*) the dad is the antithesis of street-smart and would have sent Young Spidey in there by himself without scoping out the inside for any lurkers.

"Dammit, they really should hang a sign," Dad says, exasperated. His grip on his kid loosens some. Turning this way and that, Dad sighs and seizes his son's hand. "Can you hold it? Couple more minutes?"

Sure he can. Spidey would be doing the pee-pee hop otherwise.

"Just thought I'd save you the trouble. You know."

"Right," Dad mutters, leading Young Spidey around to the other side of the building.

They're headed for the Women's Room.

Paddy Burnside bashes the Men's Room door open and is greeted by a stench of shit-on-bleach-on-*what is that, cologne?* His boots stick to the tiles as he charges over to the row of stalls along the back wall. It's just as well he sent the kid and his dad packing. They would have been hard-pressed to find a working urinal. Both are flagged as *Out of Order* and taped off.

A pair of brown moccasins showing in the opening at the bottom of the stall all the way to right become an upside-down face.

The bathroom *lurker* sputters like a Tourette's patient. This turns into a laugh, a cackle. "Why are you *following* me?"

"Are your pants up, Garry?" Burnside stops just outside the occupied stall.

"Wha-what kind of fucking question is tha—"

Burnside spreads his hands along the top of the stall door. He rattles it violently.

The latch snaps. Door swings wide.

And Garry Gravity is sitting on the toilet with his threadbare jeans around his knees and his shockingly huge member in his hands. Throbbing with anticipation.

The impulse to choke the life out of the molester paralyzes Burnside in its vividness. His hands shake with wanting.

Kill him after you get what you want from him.

Gravity grabs for his pants and stands to yank them back up around his non-existent thighs. Half-formed phrases and strange noises sputter from his lips as he notches his belt buckle and yanks his black, wrinkled t-shirt up and out.

The sight of the Grifters Anonymous logo running across Garry Gravity's sunken chest stings Burnside's eyes. He sees red. He thinks he could beat this informant of his, going on three years, to death right there in this national park rest room.

But Garry Gravity's notorious obsession with that Grifters is the reason Burnside has been tailing him all morning in the first place. Not to nail him with his pants down. Not to save some kid in a dumb superhero costume.

Certainly not to mingle with the likes of Gravity out of any kind of kinship.

Everybody who is anybody on The Strip or the rock world knows of Garry Gravity, sickening flaws and all. He's a walking encyclopedia of insider knowledge when it comes to bands born on The Strip, chief among them, its most notorious and brightest burning flame, Grifters Anonymous. When it comes to them, Gravity's knowledge hedges a near-savant level of knowledge.

Burnside grabs him by the scruff of his shirt and hurries him out of the stall. "I don't want to see you in this shirt ever again, you hear me? You fucking ghoul!"

"Jesus, Burnside, where's this coming from? You know they're my fav—"

"You're bad for their brand! I swear to Christ! Wear a Poison shirt next time you feel like putting this one on!"

"Ah, Poison's pussy!"

Burnside shoves him up against the wall.

"You've been hiding from me. We agreed you'd always make yourself available for me when I send word through your little pipeline of tweakers and rejects. You went further underground. Like the fucking worm you are. You want I should drop my end of the bargain? Haul your ass into the precinct and take the top prize for hand-delivering a disgusting pedophile to them? Because I'd be happy to end our relationship and get you off the streets!"

"Hey, fuck you, Paddy—"

"Fuck *me*?"

Anyone who would have walked in right then would have thought these were two men waltzing across the grimy, piss-stained tiles. Round and round they waltzed. But once Burnside's face spun into view, anyone could clearly see the bigger of the two men looks like he is not only capable of bloody murder but practiced in it.

Burnside throws Gravity to the floor and kicks him in the ribs repeatedly with the unforgiving steel-toed tip of one of his motorcycle boots.

Struggling to make himself somehow smaller, Gravity pulls his knees up into his stomach, only for Burnside to kick out at his kneecaps. Then, Gravity's midsection exposed once more, Burnside sends one more righteous and powerful boot tip into the molester's stomach that forces a ragged rush of wind out of him. Gravity makes a sound like a beaten dog, cowering before its master and lifelong torturer.

"I. Own. You." Burnside, partially winded, backs off and leans over him. "Get up!"

"For God's sake, I can't—"

Burnside lunges towards him. Gravity scrambles to his feet. His eyes are resigned, twin X's. There is no fear. And Burnside sees a suicidal impulse in them that wasn't there before.

Suicide by PI.

No, I don't think I'll be doing that for him today.

"Come on, you sick fuck," Burnside says, and seizes Gravity's arm. "You don't know it, but I just saved you from yourself. Again. Let's go!"

"What do you want from me?"

He drives Gravity towards the door. The molester drags his right foot like a petulant child. Burnside wrenches the door and shoves Gravity out into the cloudy afternoon.

Sometimes it takes a dirtbag, bred and produced by the streets of LA, to tell the seedier stories of the men and women who would much rather not have told. Garry Gravity is the flubbing, arrhythmic beating heart of the city and to kill him would be to sever an invaluable direct line to the evil that lurks behind every garbage bin and darkened alleyway.

One of these days, though, Burnside knows in his heart he will find Gravity in the middle of *something*, and he will finally put the bad dog down.

Threading through the tall redwood trees by way of a narrow walking trail, Burnside leads Garry Gravity along by the arm.

"Hurry it up!"

"Not supposed to go off the path," Gravity whines. "Park ranger gonna fine both of us."

"Well," Burnside says, pulling Gravity on a hard left towards something he has just now spotted, "we get stopped and cited, I'm gonna hand you over to them. Lickety-split."

"Ohhhh, why? *Why-why-why?*"

"Shut up!"

"But-but … what'd I do?"

"I already told you."

Gravity pulls back. "I was trying to get clean. Trying to figure out how to suppress the urge. To-I-I-dunno-drive it out! I'm possessed, Paddy! I see it now! An unclean spirit. I was trying to get it out and it-it-*will you stop for a second? I was trying to—"

Burnside stops, gives Gravity a quick and violent jostling. "Don't ever hide from me again, or I'll leave you wherever I find you."

"Why are we stopped?"

"There." Burnside shoves him towards a wide stump, one that must have belonged to a tree predating the indigenous, judging by its astonishing number of rings. "Sit."

The woods are still and silent.

Gravity doesn't sit.

"What do you want from me, Paddy?"

"I want you to tell me a story. Believe me, I want to puke every time I gotta come to you for *anything*. But somehow your knowledge seems to know no limits and it's the only reason you're not in gen pop taking a shiv up the ass for all the kid-touching you've done. Please understand, that could all change—" He snaps his fingers— "like that!"

Gravity tosses up his hands and lowers himself down onto the stump with a self-pitying groan. Head down and hands steepled in his lap, he presents himself as a false penitent. "Just do it. Do what you're itching to do. Our little arrangement has run its course."

"I disagree."

"Well … I'm tapped. I been laying low."

"Not from the looks of it back there at the Men's Room."

Gravity slaps the back of his neck, smashing a bothersome mosquito. "God-god*dammit*- I mean I been keeping myself low. Far and away from my usual bad company."

"Lucky for you I need to tap into your favorite subject-well, *besides* young boy ass—"

"Fuck you, Paddy! You can take a knee and suck my crank! I ain't giving you shit!"

Paddy's hand disappears inside his jacket. Gravity's whole body cringes, his bottom lip quivering. "Don't-just-please-*don't*—"

Burnside's hand comes out holding a fan of hundreds, crisp and clean. A crooked grin touches Paddy's lips as he watches the pedo slowly rise with a slack-jawed look on his face. "I want you to know something. I'm on retainer with a certain VIP who has authorized me to pay whatever fees necessary to loosen lips and crack consciences. He's not someone I'd want to disappoint. Now, I assured him there'd be no need for it, but he insisted. So I figured I'd come see you first, hook you up with more cash than you'll probably ever see all at once in your whole fucked life."

Inching closer, hands still up to ward off any surprise blow. "That … that's a real kindness, Paddy. It'll buy me some more time with my landlord because—"

Paddy smirks and the money disappears inside his jacket with such an adeptness the pedo wonders if he hallucinated it.

"Then it dawned on me that I may as well hold onto the cash. At least when it comes to squeezing *you* for intel. And that was a cool three grand easy. I've been blackmailing you for years as it is. You're only free for as long as I choose *not* to turn you in. No need for a fee with you, Garry. So, I guess I kind of owe you a small debt of gratitude for your being such a ghoul that a good ol' fashioned threat ought to get you talking until I say to stop. You have inadvertently padded my wallet with some serious green."

"Yeah?" Gravity says, seething. "Well, I reiterate my previous *fuck you*! You think I can't take you down with me? You think I can't *get at you* before you know what the fuck is happening?"

"Now … let's get down to it before we're interrupted. Because if I don't get what I need from you, that is *verifiable* knowledge about Grifter Anonymous, by the time we're discovered off the beaten path, I'm gonna turn you over. Just like I said."

Gravity's face brightens like someone has come and shined a flashlight there. His eyes widen. "Grifters? Seriously? Fuuuuck, why didn't you say so."

"What do you know about their early days?"

"How far back you want to go? You want to know what kind of

grades Davey Grifter got in grammar school? Did you know he's dyslexic?"

"I'm talking back when they were still just a cover band. That period."

Gravity's eyes twitch. Then he launches into what sounds like a memorized book report for some unforgiving English teacher. "Three of the five original members lived in a shitty two-bedroom apartment they called The Barracks. Davey and J. founded things and before Chris Desmond this guy called Johnny Kalodner did a short stint on rhythm guitar. He ended up finding Buddha, then Buddha showed him where to find Jesus and last I heard he's pastor at some out of the way Christian church in flyover country. And he likes reminiscing about his time in the band about as much as you like talking about *your* even shorter time at the academy—"

"Watch it, fuckhead!"

"I kid. Anyways. Spring of '85, the band was still playing other people's shit. They were within a cunt hair of calling it quits because none of them could put together a decent song of their own. As a matter of fact, they're something of a miracle for no other reason than none of them really knew how to play their instruments. They passed, but as far as applying, like, musical theory or bringing any God-given talent to the fold, the closest any of them came to that was Davey. He had charisma, and seven years of piano lessons. Beyond that, these guys really are the prime example of *fake it until you make it*. They faked it for a long time. And somehow, they got as much pussy as the boys on The Strip with the talent *and* the presence. They're pretty. Those Grifter boys. They really rode that for all it was worth.

"I say this with love and awe, Paddy," Gravity insists, wryly. "They were five guys who had no business becoming the legends they are today. They *should* have busted up and gone five different ways. Gotten jobs slinging fries or mopping up puke or dealing. And that's what makes them such a fucking *goddam* anomaly.

"Not to mention, they were five less-than-talented guys barely covering AC/DC and Aerosmith properly and shooting smack and swallowing pills and drinking and partying like they already made it. They really put the fucking cart before the horse in those early days.

And they wouldn't have been able to do any of it if it weren't for Bobby Royal's daddy. Bobby comes from old British money. Daddy's daddy made a shrewd investment into British Rail back when it was still a speculative venture. I don't think he knew his son was feeding his and the other guy's drug habits. Now … it is possible if they'd buckled down and quit the drugs they might have made something of themselves *before* rehab but—"

"Wait! Did you say *rehab*?" Burnside feels his heart clench.

"I'm getting to that, but yeah, not many people know about it, but Grifters went into rehab for their drug problems *before* they wrote one note of *Knives for the People*. Again, they did the drugs and excess thing *before* the fame and that's strange. But they did *rehab* before the fame, also. They did all the fucking things bands do after they sign. And again … Bobby dad funded all of it. Nolan Royal got wise to his son's addiction. The other guys' problems too.

"The old man decided to manage them. Some say he did it to save his son's life. Some think he saw the band as a *diamond in the rough* and a guy like him, savvy and shit, knew he ought to get in on the ground floor.

"Again. They sucked back then. So, I don't know how Bobby's old man could have possibly seen anything other than a shitty cover band. But … I'm not the millionaire investor. What the fuck do I know?"

Burnside blanched. "Well, I was just gonna ask how the hell these guys could afford a drug rehab for all five of them with cover band money. But I think I know how now."

"Nolan Royal funded the whole excursion. Looking for a return on his investment, no doubt."

"Mm … you mind?" Burnside produces a crumpled pack of clove cigarettes from virtual thin air. With a flick of his thumb and forefinger, he performs a similar sleight of hand and a matchbook leaps into his grasp. He shakes one of the brown-papered, aromatic cigarettes out and pops it into his mouth. "Oh wait, I could give a shit if you mind," he talks around it. He stands there, smoking and spitting. Staring off into the distance as the scented tendrils of smoke crawl up the sides of his head.

"Can I get one?" Gravity asks.

Burnside shakes his head once in the negative. Then, his head swivels back around and he pulls hard on the clove. The burning end flares and weakens.

Stevie Darius had written about *The Mountain*, but he mentions it in passing. His stream-of-consciousness style of writing flinches away from the topic like mere reference of it will sting like a bee. This is how the memoir begins, but Burnside read it all the way through, and Darius eventually comes to explore and elaborate upon *The Mountain* and what he firmly believes are its unspeakable powers and-*what was it?* -an old god trapped inside The Mountain itself. An old god who doles out access to these powers in exchange for sacrifice.

Of course, Paddy Burnside had done his due diligence and cross-referenced the name of this old god (Stevie Darius called it *Calliope*). Several resources, chief among them a Greek God index, gives considerable attention to The Greek God of Muse, Calliope.

Yeah, and The Greek God of Muse's page is sandwiched between the God of War, Athena, and The God of The Underworld, Pluto. Doesn't mean they're real.

Then again, Paddy Burnside wants to believe. Otherwise, what is he doing there questioning a pedophiliac ghoul in the middle of the woods.

Because you want it to be true. All of it.

The Magic Mountain of The Muse—

"What was that?" Gravity says, leaning forward and planting his hands on his knobby knees.

"What was *what?*"

"You were talking to yourself," Gravity says, his bright with awareness. "Something about a Magic Mountain?"

"No, I wasn't."

"C'mon, dude. We all talk to ourselves. Most of us do it when we think we're alone. Nothing to be ashamed about—"

"Look at my face! Do I look ashamed?"

"Christ! You stupid … I mean, you're the one should be … so what a mountain? Go on."

Gravity chews his bottom lip, folds his arms and kicks out at a small lump of leaves and buried detritus. "The rehab they went to? Grifters?"

"Go. On."

"Nolan Royal spared zero expense when it came to where they went to dry out and get clean. From what I hear, this place was no exception to that rule."

"What does that mean?"

"Their new *manager* paid for them to rehab in the mountains. Part ski resort, part clinic."

A shudder passes through Paddy Burnside. He swears it stops his heart in its tracks for longer than it has any business stopping. "What's the name of the place?"

"See …" Gravity smiles thinly, wags a finger at Burnside. "That's where you got me stumped. I can't remember. And that's if I ever even knew it." He presses a finger to his lips, thoughtfully. "The place is somewhere up north. Pacific Northwest. Close to the coast. Lots of elevation around there."

"And where'd you hear about all this?"

Another finger-wag. Burnside wants to break it off at the bottom knuckle. "Organic-like, man. Word of mouth. But I have it on good authority. I don't feed you shit. I got top-notch, quality intel. I mean, let's not forget how I helped lead you to that councilman with his pants down in Luxury Motels and that weird dude wearing a baby bonnet and a diaper slobbing his knob. Don't ask me how I know this shit. Only that its good shit. It's good."

"Yeah, well, it better check out because you send me on a goose chase, I'll rip your head off."

"You mean, *you'll turn me in.*"

"Is that what I just said."

Gravity looks up at Burnside, morosely.

"I mean what I say. You hear me?"

Defeated, Gravity gives his slumping shoulders a subtle jerk to express agreement.

"Now, this place up in Oregon. What else can you give me? You don't remember the name of the place. I don't entirely believe you, but I'm sure you've got your reasons for holding out on me. Just hope it doesn't come back to bite you, because it will if it stalls my investigation in any way. Is this rehab still up and running"

"Last I heard, they had to shut their doors. Maybe a year ago."

"Fuck! Seriously?"

"Yeah," Gravity says. A bit of satisfaction in having disappointed the PI sits inside his small, pinched eyes. "Happens when there are allegations of abuse and the use of unorthodox therapeutic drugs."

"I don't get that. It's a rehab. They're usually highly-regulated. They don't have the carte blanche of operation all those mental hospitals had before Reagan shut them all down with one stroke of a pen. There's more to this."

"Word has it the remoteness of the place and the fact that a lot of the staff spent much of their employment there snowbound or living there-and I'm talking leaving their families for months at a time and not because they had to but because they *wanted* to-resulted in the development of strange, dangerous practices. I heard a cult started to form within the rehab's walls shortly before they shut their doors for good. Devil worship. Collective madness. Not quite on the level of Jonestown, but not far off either"

"Bullshit."

"Bull-*true!* You don't trust my intel now?"

It's not that Burnside believes this last bit of information to be horseshit. It is quite the opposite. The more Gravity talks, the more the bastard is proving the validity of the pages and its dark claims.

I'm closing in on the truth. And it's fucking messy.

Gravity says,

"They came back, and they weren't exactly altar boys. They never did stop cold turkey. They just learned how to hide their addictions better. And a few of them did learn *some* moderation. But drugs and drink would always be cooked into the Grifters sauce.

"What *did* change is what matters when it comes right down to it. They started churning out originals. They started getting better on their instruments. Musicianship started to matter more to them. Up until this time, they were all about the punk ideal. *Carry the tune just enough that it could all fall apart any second.* There's a danger in that."

"This is around the time you say you linked up with them. Became part of their regular entourage. Yes?"

"Yeah," Gravity says, fixing his gaze on something intangible. The memory of that time years ago. "I was their pussy wrangler. I was good at it. When things started to get serious and they wanted their women served to them. No more hunting. No more flirting. Skip the work. Go right to the fucking."

"They ever find out what *you're into*?"

Gravity fixes him with a stung expression. "No. But I don't know it would have even hit their radar."

"So, you're saying they would have been okay with your raping kids?"

Gravity winces. "Why do you always gotta put things in such disgusting terms?"

"There's another way to put it?"

"Paddy, you fucking—"

"Hey! What're you two doing here? You're supposed to stick to the path!"

Both wonder how the park ranger managed to get the jump on them like this. They never heard a thing. Not a twig or branch crunching under the ranger's boots or the clomp of those same boots thrashing through dead leaves. The ranger stands ten meters from them. He has removed his hat to scratch at a dark Jewish afro trimmed down to an inch all around. His easy posture clashes with his hard, fast eyes as they size up Burnside's back.

The PI does not turn around and holds Gravity in his obsessive sights.

Gravity peeks around Burnside to offer him an *aw shucks!* wave that goes unacknowledged.

The ranger starts to walk towards them. Now, ironically, the sounds of his tromping footfalls are so loud they echo throughout the forest.

In a low, affectless tone, Burnside utters, "What are you not telling me, Garry?"

Mouthing his response, Gravity says, "I don't want to give you the wrong idea about those guys. They saved my life. Their music-it—"

Burnside hisses, an uncoiling snake. "Give me the wrong idea."

"Hey! *Hey! Turn around! TURN! AROUND!*"

Now, the park ranger is close enough to them they can hear him breathing.

Burnside's eyes flash.

Gravity knows what this means.

Tell me now or we're done and I'm burning you to Ranger Rick back there about everything you've been doing!

"They wrote all of *Knives for the People*," Gravity mutters, "and they turned mean. They were a bunch of rabid dogs. Punching fans for no reason. Cutting themselves on stage. Fist-fighting with the cops. And … everyone was afraid of them. But from fear comes love. Danger is sexy as fuck in rock and roll. They ate it up, and the thought never once crossed their mind."

"What?" Burnside pushes.

"*Turn around, you two!*" the ranger barks. "*NOW!*"

A CB burps up an unintelligible string of words on the ranger's hip.

"Their entourage They never thought the Grifter boys would ever hurt them. But I did. Started carrying a Leatherman whenever I knew I'd be hanging with them. Just to be safe. I loved them. And I feared them."

Shit! Oh shit!

By this time, the ranger is seething, and it is rising off him like a musk. "Turn. The Hell. Around—"

"Oh, my apologies!" Burnside pretends to startle and turns an about face to look right at the ranger, who has his hand on his gurgling CB like it possesses any lethal quality. "Hard of hearing. Legally deaf, sir. My friend here was feeling nauseous. Had to blow chunks so I led him back here. Figured you'd be put out if I let him upchuck where people gotta walk. My apologies."

The deep, relieved sigh he hears from Gravity as he comes up alongside Burnside sickens him to his core. And he is now certain the next time he sees this destroyer of lives and worlds, he will make it slow and agonizing.

INTERLUDE (IV)

From the Memoirs of Stevie Darius

1987

We called them the Massengills, or, rather, they called themselves the Massengills and the name stuck. No, they weren't an all-girl punk band. They were high school girls who went to Hollywood High, pulled in stellar grades by day, and snuck into clubs on Sunset Strip by night after mom put her curlers in and dad passed out on the sofa with some Gore Vidal novel splayed across his belly. The Massengills were the best word of mouth we could have asked for. They wore Grifters Anonymous t-shirts to school every day with our faces on them in black and blue silkscreen. They walked the halls with Walkmans stuffed into their purses and headphones on, blasting our demo tape so loud everyone within a five-foot radius could hear the opening licks to "Walk the Cracked Sidewalk" or the flute-like final guitar notes of "Run to Me, Run from Me".

Glory, Davey's girl who'd stuck and who he announced he intended to marry, was promptly installed as the leader of this Grifter fan club. We didn't protest. The girl's enthusiasm for the band knew no bounds and her loyalty had already been tested. After all, she'd been there for the first two murders *and Glory never ratted us out. She kept our secrets. So we let her assume the role of President and she took the job very seriously.*

She gave the high school girls their marching orders in terms of promotion and strategic merch placement. Glory had dropped out of high school her Junior year, but she still had her identification card. This allowed her entry into the school and free reign of its hallways and various wings. Glory put this to use for the Grifter cause. She had taken it upon herself to sneak into the little booth in the high school' s main office where they made the morning announcements, set up a tape player in front of the microphone, and she blasted our song "Bury Me" to the entire school for a good minute before the principal located his keys to the booth and put an end to it. She had locked the door from the inside and somehow slipped out.

You can't buy this kind of devotion.

We thought nothing of it when Davey told us he had not only met Glory's father but asked for her hand in marriage. It should have given some of us pause. After all, Glory Tizione was six months shy of her eighteenth birthday. She was jailbait. I think we dismissed it because of guys like Jimmy Page and Elvis Presley, both of whom kept underage girls very well.

He told us the father was raging at first. That's an understatement according to Davey (and this is what worried us more than the whole jailbait angle). Glory's father was a connected guy, an enforcer for the Los Angeles Mob. And he nearly put two in the back of Davey's head when they met for the first time. Somehow, Davey was able not only to calm the guy but also to gain his blessing to marry his youngest daughter.

None of us ever pressed him about how he accomplished this with a scary motherfucker like Peter Tizione. We were just glad he didn't kill our lead singer, chief songwriter, and bury Davey somewhere in the Vegas desert.

If only we had asked more questions.

The Massengills were our PR people, and we never touched any of them. They were sixteen and seventeen-year-old girls who would have freely granted us any sexual favor we wanted. But J had a little sister back home and he put the rule in place that the girls were off-limits. His sister was their age and the thought of defiling them sickened him. So, we held off and loaded them up every Wednesday with homemade fliers advertising our shows that weekend.

Troubadour.

Rainbow.

Whiskey.

Country Club.

*Once we cut that demo at The Orange Glo Studio in Burbank and circu-
lated it on The Strip, things started to happen faster than we could have imagined. It was four songs. That was all we could afford. It cost a little more than
five-hundred bucks fronted by Bobby's dad, our surrogate manager over in the
UK we met one time to play a couple songs for him.*

*It paid for itself a million times over when we became the house band at
The Country Club, then headliners at Cathouse, co-owned by Riki Rachtman
and Faster Pussycat's singer, Taime Down.*

We broke through at the last possible second.

We were an unemployable bunch for the most part.

I mopped floors at a peep show. Briefly.

Chris sold vacuums door-to-door. Briefly.

And Bobby dug graves, if you can dig that. Very briefly.

. The Massengills, bless their hearts!

And Davey Grifter.

*I'd have to take my shoes off if you asked me to count how many other
bands in LA tried to steal him away from us early on. A couple sleazy agents
tried to lure him away from us with promises of solo stardom and legendary
status. To Davey's credit, he never stepped out on his old lady, so to speak. We
knew how lucky we were to have him.*

Part of the problem was so did he.

*Before Grifters came together, Davey was once quiet and painfully shy. I
know he was raised by his grandmother and lived with her in a South Philly
rowhome until he lit off for the LA territory like some pierced Huck Finn. He
brought a girl with him and lost her to Ace Frehley a week in. That's a sore
subject for Davey and if you were to so much as mention Kiss to him, he'd hit
you with a petty devastating roundhouse. I heard he had a hard go of it for the
first year. No band would have him, and he almost left the scene with his tail
between his legs. Then, he struck up a friendship with his drug dealer, our
very own J, or John Germanian, which was the name given to him by a strict
Armenian grocer and his wife.*

*Davey crashed on the floor of J's little apartment just outside Compton
and they started what would be the first incarnation of Grifters. A power-trio
called Blood Runner, a play on words from the movie Blade Runner. They*

were god-awful, two chord punk. But for how bad the one-minute-and-thirty-second songs were, Blood Runner was the band that brought Davey out of his shell. From there, he hopped into and out of the bands Jumpin'Jerry, Magic Pie, The Paper Souls, and touched down for an extended stay in Louder, one of the bands who sent the punks packing on The Strip and ushered in the era of sleaze rock along with the beloved Motley Crue.

In '84, someone in Louder came up with the profoundly stupid idea of shaking up the lineup for the band. They sent one of their chief songwriters packing, not realizing Davey had a strong allegiance to the guy and had developed a brilliant writing bond with him as well. Davey would later be replaced by a guy called Harrison Hart, too good-looking for rock and roll.

Davey cut out of Louder along with a guy called Johnny Kalodner, someone who'd quit before we even moved into that apartment together years ago and killed for the first time. Quitters deserve to go unnoticed and to stay unnoticed.

Anyway, J was Johnny Kalodner's dealer too.

And mine.

And Bobby's.

I was in a going-nowhere outfit called Cum On, a cover band with a balding lead-singer. That's a deal-breaker in rock and roll, genetic or not. Bobby was the only one not in a band when we snagged him up. He auditioned and left all of us wondering how the fuck he'd flown under the radar and never landed a gig. He was thunder and lightning out of the gate. And his Brit accent made us feel like we had found our own personal John Bonham.

Try to understand, none of us wanted to be a cover band. I don't know what drew me into Grifters, leaving one cover band for another. There was just something about this group of guys that was addictive. We learned how to gel by playing other band's shit! Looking back, I don't know it could have worked any other way. There were so many false starts when it came to original songs. It was like a five-way creative block, and still something held us together.

Friendship?

Maybe.

For me, it was Davey Grifter, although I would never tell the other guys that.

The motherfucker was a star. Kills me to say that.

You'll understand why soon enough.

Something happened to Davey while he was in Louder, something trans-formative. I don't know that word even does justice to what seemed to turn an anxious, soft-spoken Philly kid into the front man who came walking in the door to J's shitty apartment one rainy afternoon like he'd just inked a deal with Geffen. Sunglasses on to hide his deep green eyes. A chiseled chin that jutted out in constant obstinance. Dressed in a cheetah print vest, Cathouse t-shirt, and skintight leather pants buckled with a stud belt and packed with a codpiece, which we all would come to wear for one gig and later abandon out of embarrassment. His cowboy boots were scratched up and written on, black marker that had faded to indecipherable graffiti. Davey walked like his dick was a roll-out and he had to move his legs around it. His speaking voice was deep and thick.

He talked like a street kid with a library card.

Before we moved into the apartment, The Barracks, we already managed to secure a rehearsal space in the basement of the building. We found Chris Desmond to replace Johnny Kalodner on rhythm guitar. The maintenance guy for our duplex was another customer of J's, so you can see the pattern clear as day. J opened a lot of doors of opportunity that would have otherwise been bolted shut to us. That day, Davey followed us over in Chris' ugly orange Pinto and they auditioned together, sending the clear message to J and I they were a package deal.

I swear to Christ when Davey started singing over Aerosmith's "Rats in the Cellar", he nearly blew my bass amp he was running through. The guy sang like his fucking very existence depended on it. In many ways, it did. Everything we'd heard about the guy from the huddled masses and rejects and freaks and band guys and half-naked girls and hangers-on milling about Sunset every Saturday night had been a half-truth.

They'd said he was "decent"

J and I understood Davey Grifter was The Guy. The Only Guy.

Davey used to do this type of dance on stage that was a weird hybrid of a cowboy and a male stripper. He would raise his free hand, the one not holding the microphone, and he'd twirl it in the air like he's swinging a lasso above his head. And he would buck his hips in a circle at the same time, in rhythm with the song. That's usually when the girls' shirts went up. The girls on their boyfriends' shoulders. The girls in the rafters holding a banner made from a *dirty white sheet that said things like "**TAKE ME THERE, DAVEY!! XOXO** -------------- (insert name of fan". "Take Me There" was the last song we wrote and added to our setlist, officially trimming any unwanted cover song fat from the repertoire. We kept our version of Aerosmith's "Rats in the Cellar" in there, because the crowd loved how we sped it up to a punkier version of what it already was.*

By Spring of '87, we had fifteen songs written, including "Take Me There".

All the while, among the five of us, we murdered eleven people to keep the juices flowing. We learned by sheer accident the five of us did not necessarily need to take the life together to reap its reward. So long as we each pulled our respective weight in it all, the songs kept coming and their hooks sounded more addictive and, dare I say it, radio friendly. But don't get me wrong, we didn't pussify our music to get on the airwaves. If anything, the radio stations tailored their standards to play our music, and in many cases, they lowered those standards in terms of censorship and (ha ha!) good taste.

Another strange and darkly humorous thing started to happen.

It got so that we started to directly attribute each new song or songs to the human sacrifice we made to bring those songs to life.

"Knives for the People" and "Bigger Badder Faster More" was Lovebug.

"Run To Me, Run From Me" and "Bury Me" were Anita the Lot Lizard.

And on and on and on.

People who gave their lives for our legacy.

Without any say in the matter …

Last night, my dreams touched on a primal fear I have not experienced since My Time on the Mountain. I dreamt of a vibrating mountainside, alive like a tuning fork is alive after you've tapped it against the bone of your knee. And there is something inside that mountain sending such tremors through the valley at its base. Not quite an earthquake. And yet somehow more terrifying in its implication.

The something inside the mountain is wrapped in an endless, profoundly furious anger.

I'm running. The snow drifts are nearly waist high and my legs ache from the strain of lifting them and plunging them back down. Repeatedly.

And my brothers are there. With me. They're behind me. And I don't have to look to make sure they're there. I just know. One of them confirms this by letting loose with a shriek that sounds like his flesh is being flayed from his bones bit by bit.

It's J. I know it's J. He took it the hardest. It changed him more than the rest of us.

The vibration entered each of us through the soles of our boots. A Conqueror Worm riding our bloodstreams upward, blackening each vein and capillary as it rides the red tide up into our brains. As we follow and submit to new and perverse impulses, it is killing each of us. It is rewarding us with fame and riches. It is also sucking the fucking life out of us, in its own way.

Then again, maybe not.

I don't trust my own memory. I can't fully commit to any of this. Stop reading here if that's a deal breaker for you. I'm trying to tell the truth, while seeking to remember what the truth is. I'm learning right beside you. I am the audience and the storyteller in one.

Make of that whatever the hell you want.

TWENTY-SEVEN

Harrison Hart laughs, a slow and low sound that always seems to coincide with waxing nostalgic.

"You wouldn't believe how fucking hard it was just for Louder to agree on the names in our *Thank You* liner notes," he says, scratching at his salt-and-pepper speckled jawline. "Scott would take issue with a name. They pissed him off or they failed to adequately kiss his ass. Max was no better, but he really had it in for me towards the end there and he wanted to nix every other person I put in there. At one point, Maxxie and me almost slugged it out over whether to include this belly dancer we both had a thing for who worked at the Seventh Veil. Connor tried to play mediator, but it's never been in his nature to over-rule anyone. Too meek and mild. All about peace and love to the nth power! "

Gretch sits cross-legged across from him with the cardboard sleeve for Grifter's debut album, *Knives for the People*, opened in her lap. She makes no apology for having to use a magnifying glass to read the small print liner notes on the dust sleeve in her hands.

Harrison got his good-natured ribbing in already and didn't belabor the point. "We're all getting old in one way or another, Gretch."

Poring over the notes, the magnifying glass in her hand pauses in its travel back and forth over the small print. "Wait a minute. Oh … goddammit! How do I not know this? Christ!"

"What?" Harrison scoots over next to her, eyes searching.

Gretch stabs a finger down on the name *Dale Monahan*, prominently listed towards the beginning of the *Thank You* list on the record sleeve. "I *know* I *should* know who he is but …" Her words trail off. She gnaws at her bottom lip, the only thing she can think to do in lieu of words.

"Why that's …" He blinks down at the name on the sleeve, switches his eyes to Gretch. Then back down to the name. "You really don't know who this is? Or are you—"

"No, I am *not* fucking with you," Gretch says, jaw clenching. "I … Jesus, will you just tell me who he is and quit looking at me like I'm some kind of fucking oddity!"

"That's Grifter's Anonymous' producer." He opens his mouth to elaborate and stops himself when he sees her eyes welling up. "Hey … now we've been poring through every liner note for every B-side and international pressing and collector's domestic pressing of every recording Grifters ever committed to vinyl. I'm still not clear on what it is I'm supposed to be doing to help. Or what this is even for?"

"I told you," Gretch says, swabbing her eyes. "My memory's not what it was, and I wanted you to help me with some of these names. I'm looking to create a master list and reach out to them."

"About Stevie's memoir?"

She nods, tracing the small words with her fingertip.

"And how would any of these people, these *contacts*, know any more than you do about the band you managed for five years. Traveled thousands of miles with. Crossed five continents. Wiped their snotty noses. Wiped their asses, for all I know. Who's got you beat when it comes to knowing the band inside and out. Let alone your husband—"

Gretch looks at him, her green eyes narrowing. "I. Know. My husband. Well enough."

"See, now what does that even mean? What are you not telling me?" He lays a hand on her shoulder.

"Would you please just …?"

"Look, I'm not trying to be an asshole here, but there's something I suspect is *pretty fucking* important you're not telling me. What are you after? You said this People's Knife psycho claims he's got Stevie's bootleg memoirs. That they're allegedly incriminating for all the Grifter guys. Then, you just clam up. Like you don't trust me enough with the whole story."

Sullenly, Gretch lays the record sleeve off to the side. Casts her eyes to the ceiling, shuts her eyes. Looks at him with watery eyes. "I don't know any more than what I've told you. And ... it's because ... oh Christ, I made a big mistake. I never should have done it. I wasn't thinking of anything other than just easing the pain. A piece of memory that was going to rip me apart if I didn't ... you know ..." She pantomimes plucking something out of her right ear, like a swimmer's plug. "I told you I checked myself into a mental health clinic. I was there for a little over a month. And the day I was cleared for discharge, I suffered a ... a setback. A breakdown. So ... the resident psychiatrist there ... and I don't blame her ... she did not push me into doing anything ... I jumped at her suggestion. I was desperate for relief. I thought the only way I could ever function normally again was if I could just live out the rest of my life comfortably oblivious to a terrible truth."

"So ..." Harrison scratches his jaw, looking thoughtful. "They wiped part of your memory. The part that was—I don't know—giving you so much grief?"

Gretch nods, stiffly.

"Shit. I had no idea that could be done."

"Mm-hmm. It's called Electro-convulsive therapy. Targeted. Very effective, as you can see."

Looking dumbfounded, Harrison rubs pensively at his jaw. "I never would've believed it. So ... you're telling me that they have a way of just-I dunno-zapping parts of your memory that are trou-blesome?"

Gretch nods, squaring her shoulders and drawing in a deep breath as she reclaims control of her emotions.

They sit together in silence. It should have been uncomfortable. The fact it's not confuses Gretch.

Gretch feels a sudden stirring of butterflies in her belly.

A hint of lust pressing at her inner thighs. A sensation she barely recognizes.

She stiffens, thinking she's heard Stevie let out one of his quick, startling shrieks from across the house. A signal that he has begun his ascent out of the dark, wet folds of narcotic sleep and will break the surface of his slumber very soon.

This is not cheating. Calm yourself! You needed a friend, and you damn well know it.

You needed the company of someone who doesn't fill you with instant nausea and weaken your limbs—

"—and they're gone forever or … what happens?"

Snapping out of her thoughts, Gretch looks vacantly at him. "I'm sorry. I zoned out for a minute there. I'm not sleeping so well these nights."

"The bad memories."

"What about them?"

"They're just *gone*. Never to return."

"Not exactly," Gretch explains. "My psychiatrist says that the electric shocks damaged certain synapses associated with those memories, but the brain has a way of regenerating those connections. They'll grow back."

"How long?"

"I think she said something like … six to eight months." She pauses, chews her bottom lip. "So, when I tell you I can't remember the people I used to work shoulder-to-shoulder with when I was *in the business*, and I was—what did they call me?"

A smile crosses Harrison's face, perhaps too wide for the occasion. "*Peter Grant in Heels.*"

"That I remember," she says. "I'm telling you the fucking truth. Alright?"

"Hey … I'm here to help. I'll be your memory. Wherever you need me to be."

Before another round of tears can encroach on the arrangement, Gretch pats his knee and smiles. "Alright," she says, snatching up the record sleeve she'd been studying with her trusty if not geriatric-looking magnifying glass. "There's this." She hands it. To him. "Help."

He looks down at the glossy sleeve, brow furrowing. "Okay. Who do you—"

"None of them. I don't recognize any of those names. Just help me to figure out who would be useful to reach out to about the early years of the band. The *undocumented* years all bands have when no one knows or cares who the hell they are. Yet."

It is slow work, what one might call a slog. Yet, Harrison doesn't seem to mind it one bit. He identifies one name after another, moving through the surprisingly bursting catalog for a band who'd flamed out after only one full length album and an EP of B-sides and acoustic versions. Different pressings. Alternate artwork. The slightest tweak of the information contained on the sleeves or color change of any portion of the inner or outer art warranted yet another pressing and labeling it as a *rarity*. Therefore, a collector's item with a hefty price tag attached to it.

This is how it went for the better part of an hour, Gretch and Harrison slipping back into the years together or following tangents that led to branching off conversation and the slow-burn of sexual tension warming between them as they worked side-by-side. He identified, helped her to gauge whether they could possibly possess the information she was after.

Gretch added them to her trusty Yellow Legal Pad.

On the sleeve for a rare pressing of the band's EP, *Gods of Swine*, J thanked a slew of women and even rated their level of sexual prowess after each name. How she ever let this slip through, along with Axis Records' team of lawyers, Gretch can't know.

How have none of them sued for libel?

The highest-rated name is Gabby Fellman: *"Could suck the chrome off an exhaust pipe! -10"*.

That name sets off some bells in her head.

Gretch speaks the name out loud.

"Dead end." Harrison says, shaking his head. "Literally and figuratively, I'm afraid."

"Really? She's—?"

"She's a *he*. And *he* jumped from the Golden Gate a while back."

"Wait-wait-wait," Gretch says. "Are you saying J was …"

Harrison leans in closer to Gretch, conspiratorially. "Between you and me?"

"Of course."

"It's one of the best-kept secrets on The Strip. I don't know how he kept it under wraps the way he did. I suspect he made some threats. Gathered some dirt on the big mouths and saved it all up for the day any one of them dared spill it. Hell, I always suspected he had something on me, since he knew that *I* knew. Damned if I know what he's got that'd bring me down, but what can you do?"

Chewing on this bit of information, Gretch quickly realizes she couldn't care less.

They continue to work together, Harrison feeding her names and context and Gretch either adding the name to her list of potential contacts or leaving them out.

When she finally lifts her eyes and lowers her pen, Gretch is both pleased and overwhelmed to find she and Harrison have compiled twenty-three people to reach out to. There is no guarantee most of them, or any of them really, can be indexed in the Los Angeles Yellow Pages. For all Gretch knows, the lot of them could be scattered across the nation.

The globe, even.

Harrison rubs his hands together. "I'm gonna make a run for some food. You feeling some Thai? There's this place—"

Distractedly staring down at the list of names, Gretch says, "The Drunken Noodle. That would be awesome. You mind buying and I'll pay you back when you return?"

"Your money's no good with me, Red," Harrison says, flashing a wry grin before standing and stretching his legs.

He is gone.

Gretch does not even hear him go, hyper-focused on the list.

Straining her brain to remember them.

One. Just one.

Something about them.

Please, God, just let me have that.

It is like trying to swim upstream against a furious current.

TWENTY-EIGHT

Gretch finds Stevie lying on his back, eyes staring at the ceiling in the dimness of his room with all the shades drawn against the setting sun.

A shard of memory breaks off and reminds her that she was not so much afraid of him before as she was *overwhelmed* by his needs and the breath of his inevitable death constantly on the nape of her neck.

She speaks into the shadows. "Stevie? Can I get you something? Are you alright?"

The oscillating fan beside his bed is the only sound, a slurring whir. Its motor is close to burning out. It is always running. It animates the white wisps of cottony hair atop his head.

More often, Gretch has had to remind herself of what Stevie used to look like with photographs. She even listened a couple times to an interview CD with the band. Stevie does not say much, clearly the quiet one. But his somewhat scratchy, whip smart delivery tells the story of who he used to be.

This is not the man in the hospital bed, wearing a thousand-yard stare and mute to her questions.

Then, a cold shard of ice slips into her heart. *What if he heard Harrison when he was here? Is he angry? Is he capable of anger? Jealousy?*

"I can make you tomato soup and grilled cheese."

His favorite, when his appetite revived here and there.

He turns his head towards her on the pillow. His mouth opens.

Closes.

Opens.

Claps shut.

A fish drowning out of water.

They lock eyes. And Gretch feels her skin crawl as she watches the knowing in his eyes, like a little sentient being sitting just behind his pupils, retreat into the recesses of his darkening brain.

She finds herself staring into the eyes of a living corpse's eyes.

Filmy. Milky. Sightless.

Gretch can't back out of the room and shut the door fast enough.

It is just quick enough she misses Stevie's hissing plea for help, as the soles of his feet burst into flames.

TWENTY-NINE

What seems at first like a more bearable task, that of calling eight instead of twenty-three, becomes something quite time-consuming.

There is three Gage Samples listed in the directory. No answer at any of them.

A whopping eighteen Jerry Cardinales.

Five deep into her list, she thinks she's hit paydirt when she hears the pause that follows the question "Do you know a Stevie Darius?" But *the* Jerry Cardinale's pause is followed by a scoff and then a dial-tone. Both are listed in Chris Desmond's "thank-you" section.

Davey's three LA "thank-you's" are women. This surprises Gretch. He always seemed so wrapped up in Glory and her every move there seemed no room for other female connections of any kind.

Laina "Viper" Melrose takes Gretch's call at a tattoo parlor on Melrose. She did Davey's lower back work, a cluster of overgrown vines slipping into and out of a mess of barbed wire with the gored, bloody faces of an unidentified male and female breaching the treacherous clusterfuck. Davey never did tell anyone who the two are. Gretch comes close to asking the tattoo artist who they are but holds back. Just as the conversation is wrapping, Laina "Viper" Melrose halts the farewell with a seemingly random interjection:

"You were their manager, so you'd know …"

"I'll do my best," Gretch says. *Lately, I'm finding I don't know shit about Grifter Anonymous.*

"Who did the bloody lyre at the base of Davey's spine?"

"Oh … well …I wouldn't know. Davey and me. We weren't close. No idea."

"You ever see it?"

"No."

"A lyre-you know, like a harp-only his was dripping blood."

"Mm … sounds hack."

"Really fucking hack," Laina says. "And dangerous. You can paralyze somebody working over that area. One false move, you know? I only ask because if you gave me a name, I'd find them and light them up for their carelessness. It makes the rest of us look like shitty amateurs. That's why I don't tattoo faces. I send them packing they want *anything* done to their face."

Lyre.

A harp.

It seems like a piece of work that would stand out like a sore thumb among the rest of Davey's rather extensive ink.

She files that away in her mind under *random weird shit I did not know* and continues her calls.

The second woman, *Slade Baker*, has one listing in the directory. Honestly, could there be more than one Slade Baker within a hundred-mile radius, if not anywhere else on the planet. Slade (or whoever is with her or taken over her number) picks up the phone, says nothing and gets to loud fucking that unnerves Gretch and awakens something in her she thought she'd lost forever.

Where the hell is Harrison? Did he get lost?

Why would that suddenly matter to you. Right this moment?

Her inner voice falls silent, pleading the fifth.

She hangs up, her mind fixing on just how long it's been since she and Stevie made love.

The length of time is too much to bear. She shoves the figure down deep.

And Gretch Solomon doesn't know just how much this has affected her until she lifts the heft of Yellow Pages and heaves it across the kitchen.

"Hey-hey!"

Harrison appears in the archway adjacent to the stainless-steel fridge, his hands loaded with a pair of big brown bags. He's already dipped into the food, his mouth frozen in mid-chew and eyes wide with a mixture of shock and amusement at the flare-up of Gretch's anger. Had the hefty phone directory flown a mere six inches more to the left, it would have caught him right in the balls.

"Maybe take a break? Eh?"

The tangy, enticing smell of Thai chicken and rice makes her stomach growl as Harrison sets down the bags on the kitchen table. She waves her hand at him, mouths the word "Sorry", and agrees to hit pause for the meal. "I could eat."

Even as her mind screams *What are you doing?*

Stevie could wake at any given moment.

Harrison skirts around the table and moves to take her hands in his, Gretch is reminded of one of the few things that worked between the two of them when they'd been an item. Such a short list of positives when it came to their romantic involvement that it is not hard to remember it. The electricity in his touch. Years ago, in the bedroom, it had brought her to climax enough times to be more than mere fluke. Now, it weakens her knees, and she must hold herself back from moving in towards him with her lips.

"Old times sake," he breathes, their faces barely an inch apart.

Her eyes shut.

His lips graze hers.

The shouting starts upstairs. "Lub-ba! Lub-ba! Make stop, *Lub-ba!*"

Gretch and Harrison separate.

He cocks his head in the direction of the shouting, looking confounded. It's not hard for Gretch to identify what it is he's feeling in hearing the unhinged ravings coming from a man Harrison used to jam with.

"Is that … is that really *your* Stevie?" Harrison asks, his face a white sheet. "Shit—"

Gretch shoves past him. Arranges herself before the kitchen sink with her head bent. Bracing herself along the lip of the marble counter-top. Shoulders shuddering. Gagging sounds coming from her.

"Gretch? You okay?"

"Lub ... ba! God-dammit ... lemme die or lemme be-Lub-ba—"

Gretch claps one hand over her mouth. With the other, she waves him back towards the kitchen archway. It takes him a moment to catch her drift. She is trying desperately not to vomit.

Harrison moves to gather the food then thinks better of it. He leaves it for her and circles back around to squeeze her shoulders. "Who is Lubba?"

She makes an awkward grab for his wrist over her left shoulder, pinches his wrist just enough to shut him up and send him off.

Lately, Stevie had taken to calling Gretch by that strange, babbling-baby-talk name. It sounds too nonsensical to mean anything of significance. When he pronounces it, his jaw is loose. Tongue wagging.

Harrison exits the house without a word. He leaves the food.

The sick rides up her throat and it is all she can do to stop it from bursting from her lips and splashing the steel basin before her. Five minutes later, when her stomach has settled, Gretch straightens and does not so much surge up the stairs to come to Stevie's aide as she creeps up the stairwell with back stooped and eyes stitched in red from the strain of holding back her stomach's contents.

All at once, the last thing on her mind is Harrison Hart.

Or his feelings.

THIRTY

Half-listening to the tail-end of a storm grumbling in the distance as it rolls towards the Pacific, Gretch practices slow, deep breathing. It clears the fog from her brain. Much as she would have liked to get back to dialing the remaining contacts on her list, she finds her well of energy is dry. Meditation has proven a good friend in these moments, which have become more frequent since she became lone caregiver for Stevie.

There is also the fact she feels defeated, her efforts beginning to reek of hopelessness. A mad scrambling and grasping at straws, her mind offering little to no help. Here and there, shards of memory surface to offer her a glimpse of something or some event. But they are mostly details of an insignificant nature.

Like Stevie's favorite midnight snack. *Pistachio ice cream.*

That Davey had once tried to sleep with her early on, a ham-handed attempt at best. *Some men are still boys who can't handle rejection.*

She showered after finishing up with Stevie's feeding, change of clothes, and ablutions. The needles of water spraying the crown of her skull as she hangs her head, Gretch has a flash of something she cannot make sense of. A full moon partially obscured by rolling mist. And something pale white funneling upward to pierce a black velvet sky.

What is it? Makes no sense.

She tried to will the mist to part.

It only thickened, a clear refusal of her mind to be rushed into any revelations before their time.

Now, she sits cross-legged on the floor of her bedroom in the dark, eyes lidded and mind free-floating.

And the white-something from her shower time appears to her again. Clear of the obscuring mist swirling about.

The tip of the white-something is capped with an unmistakable crucifix.

A church steeple.

A tumbler in her brain slips into its proper place, setting off a chain of recall that sends her downstairs to the kitchen. The table is littered with scribbled notes, her open Legal pad, record sleeves, and a half-empty tumbler of whiskey.

The cordless phone lies on its side amidst the scattered items.

Before she realizes it, Gretch is dialing the operator, who comes on the line and sounds how everybody remembers their grandmother sounding during their earliest years.

"Yes, I need the number for The First Church of Michael the Archangel in … in Lincoln, Nebraska."

"Hold for that number, please."

An automated voice reads her the phone number with area code.

Gretch scribbles it down under the list of contacts.

"Dammit," she sighs, frustrated at this late development. "He would have been there for it. He was Chris's predecessor. The best witness hiding in plain sight."

There was never a need to reach out to John Kalodner until now. He had been an early member of Grifters, back when they were still a hack cover band with a serious handicap for writing original material, or as one journalist called it Grifters' *Purple Period*. The color of sexual frustration applied to the creative impulse.

While she can't remember where she'd heard the name of Kalodner's church, Gretch can only assume the band or Stevie, or *someone* had referenced it in passing. Probably making light of it. Mocking the rocker-turned-minister.

Kalodner, in an obvious act of misguided penance, has spoken out to anyone who'd print his words about the perils of heavy metal music for young people. He even aligned himself with the PMRC, (Parents' Music Resource Center), Tipper Gore's now infamous campaign to sticker even the remotely offensive musical release with a "Parental Caution" label.

He leverages the whole "I used to be one of them" angle to bolster his credibility.

Stickering tapes and CDs now the law of the land, she holds the former Grifters rhythm guitar player responsible. And she considers him something of an ingrate and a Judas for the way he did not just flee the band but then came to betray them and compromise their livelihood.

John Kalodner is a small man.

An afterthought, Gretch checks the clock over the stove. Quarter to five in the evening.

Shit. Don't holy rollers have a thing for turning in around this time? Nobody's gonna an—

An elderly woman answers on the fourth ring at the church in Nebraska. "St. Michael's. How may I direct your call?"

Come on. How many extensions could you possibly have at your little backwoods church?

She plays along. "Reverend Kalodner, please?"

"May I ask who's calling?"

"Gretchen Solomon … I'm new to Lincoln."

"And you're looking to join our family of parishioners?"

Sigh. "Exactly."

"That's good, ma'am. I was about to remind you of the hour. But the reverend will want to take your call. Mustn't leave any of the flock to stray. He's who you'll need to speak with."

You don't fucking say …

"Please hold." The old woman's doting voice is replaced with stilted organ music.

It is not a long wait and Reverend Kalodner's warm-molasses voice fills her ear with a greeting.

"Reverend, my name is Gretchen Solomon. I'm Stevie Darius' wife.

I was the manager for Grifters Anonymous. Do you have a couple minutes to talk to me?"

A guardedness chills his tone of voice. "What's this about, Ms. Solomon? I'm with someone and the matter is urgent."

You wouldn't have taken my call if that were true.

"I promise I'll keep this very brief and I'm sorry to disturb you."

"You-hmm-you're certainly not disturbing me. It's just I can't imagine what you think I could help you with. You're referencing a time in my life I barely remember. Are you writing a book?"

This is as good an angle as any to get him talking.

"As a matter of fact, I am in the research phase of an autobiography about the band. I'll be writing it from my angle, but for the sake of a comprehensive story, I've been making the rounds with the people who were there early on. You know, the ones who knew the band members before they hit it big. That era is a big blind spot for me, obviously, since I didn't come on board with them until they were known and really catching fire. You've got firsthand knowledge of this period. You were there back when they were still a burgeoning cover band."

At first Gretch fears he's hung up on her. The other end has gone quiet. Then, in a more subdued and wistful voice, John Kalodner says, "It was enough for them ... until it wasn't. I remember them as something of a leviathan, never satiated and just devouring everything and everyone in their path. Sucking the life out of anyone stupid enough to attach to them. But that way is not exclusive to the rock star. It is also the way of the addict, and that was nearly me. Only, I had a *come to Jesus* moment and I've never turned aside from my Lord since." Pause. "You married Stevie? Did I hear right?"

"Yes. It will be four years this May."

"Stevie was the one who put the spike in my arm for the first time. Did you know that?"

"No ... no I didn't know that—"

"As it happens, I've come to equate your husband with Satan himself. They are one in the same in my mind. I can only hope he's mended his ways."

One more shred of proof she never really knew her husband at all.

"Oh, if Stevie could tell you himself, I'm certain he would ask for your forgiveness."

"And I would give it to him. Only penance could make his apology mean anything."

"Well, Reverend, he is dying from dementia. Does that satisfy you?" An edge has crept into her voice.

A sigh on the other end. "Of course not. No. I'm sorry."

"The band's struggles with drugs and alcohol are no secret. I imagine you've made sure to avoid any news concerning them. There was a time they were all over the television and you'd be hard-pressed to turn on MTV without seeing one of their videos in heavy rotation that first year. But you were there during their formative years. Like you've said, you were there with them during their private stumbles."

"Nothing to be proud of in those days. We were frauds. The drugs clouded our inferiority. That's why we went at them with such … enthusiasm. To dull the sense of fakery."

"Every band has to start somewhere. It's different for every act."

"Yes, well, if you think I have any regrets for jumping ship before they became famous, you're sorely mistaken."

"I never thought that at all. You were destined for a different path."

"That's correct. Praise God."

"If you don't mind my asking," Gretch inquires, "how did you come to get clean?"

"Rock bottom, Ms. Solomon. I woke up in a motel room I didn't recognize. The others weren't with me. I had taken to doing my own thing. Carving my own path of recklessness. Godlessness. Debauchery. If you were to ask the others who was the most-er-incorrigible of the five, they'd come to agree I was the worst of all. The harder they fall, I suppose. The veins in my left arm were in such poor condition when I finally submitted to getting clean-I wasn't very good at finding them with the needle-I required a bit of reconstruction. They did what they could. To this day, I deal with a numbness in my forearm that sets in just as the sun starts to set. I like to think of that sensation as a reminder from my Lord and Savior to never look back.

"My memory of that fateful evening is spotty. Right up until the I found myself surrounded by a circle of ten bushes, all of them flaming.

The motel had been situated in the middle of the Vegas desert outskirts. I must have gone to the casinos with a pair of whores I had spent my time with earlier that night. They fleeced me while I slept off a terrible high. They were long gone when I had come to in the middle of the night. I must have thought I could still catch up with them. Get my money back. I became lost. Wandering in the desert."

Gretch bites her tongue. Otherwise, she might have laughed out loud. *How very Old Testament. Lost in the desert. Burning bushes. Paging Moses?*

"They found me huddled in a ball. Shivering. Naked. And the bushes were mere husks. Burned all away. Eventually, I would come to discover I'd been out there for three days. Nothing of sustenance. My body was cleansed. My mind was sharper than ever before. They told me I would have died within an hour of their finding me. *One. Hour.* Do you understand what I'm saying, Ms. Solomon?"

"A miracle," Gretch says, tongue firmly in cheek. "Thank God they reached you in time."

"Precisely. Thank *God.*" Another pause. "As soon as I was physically able to do so, I contacted the other members and told them they would never see me again and not to try to contact me under any circumstances. No, not unless they too were ready to accept Jesus as their Lord and Savior. I knew that call would never come. But, as it happens, they were given a chance of their own to clean up and get right. They took it."

"Is that so?" Gretch shoves back from the kitchen table and comes up out of her chair. She starts to pace the kitchen tiles, back and forth.

"Wait," Gretch says, kneading her forehead. "Are we … talking rehab?"

"The entire band went in together. And as far as I know, the only other band before them to do that was Aerosmith right before they put out *Pump,* their comeback album."

"How? They were dirt poor. Who would've funded a stint in rehab for a no-name cover band?"

"Well, see, Bobby was born with a silver spoon in his mouth. He played it down, no doubt. The starving artist is far more appealing to the press than a story involving a shitty band being put through rehab by the drummer's billionaire mogul father. That's who Nolan Royal was. Don't know if he still is. What I do know is they never could have done it without his help. From what I heard—and I can assure you, I happened upon this last bit of information purely by accident—they were so unruly and disruptive the moment they arrived that they were asked to leave the next morning. The addictions lingered. Persisted, I can imagine. Maybe they found some other way to *lessen* their dependence. The next thing I knew, they were rock royalty. Quite literally, an overnight sensation. And …"

Kalodners voice trails off as if he's run out of steam or lost his train of thought.

"Reverend? Are you there?"

"No … no, I'm still here. Only, I'm measuring my words very carefully. I want to speak as delicately as I can. I'm not interested in offending you. You seem like an innocent bystander."

"A bystander? How so?"

"Well, you said you came to them *after* this period. That would make you a bystander."

"Still not following."

"They were compromised at some point between when they tried rehab and signed their record contract. In between, they ran afoul of wickedness. Temptation. I've had visions. I've seen things behind the eyelids."

"Wait … wait-wait-*wait* … you've had visions? What kind of visions?"

"God loves me. And He has seen fit to show me what coming to Him has saved me from."

"And what is that?"

"How many of them are left?"

"Of the band members? I don't—"

"Three, Ms. Solomon. All of them are my age. Early thirties. Two are gone. Suicides. Which will have placed them completely clear of God's reach, if He were not already alienated by the lives they'd led and things they'd done."

"I thought you steered clear of that world. Seems to me you know more than a holy man ought to."

"Fair enough," Kalodner acquiesces, a patience in his voice that comes across as patronizing. "I've dipped my toe into that world here and there. Only for the sake of strengthening my own resolve in the face of extreme doubt or a lapse in faith. We do suffer such things from time to time."

"You … faith leaders?"

"Yes."

"Uh-huh," Gretch says, seething, "so what you're saying is that the band members—my Stevie included—are suffering or are gone too soon because of something they've done or … I dunno … some karmic wheel retribution."

"No karma. God *is* karma."

"Fine. Whatever. So, my husband is losing his mind and wasting away because of his sins? What drinking? Drugging? Fucking some strange here and there?" Speaking about her husband in this way makes her feel like she'll need a bath immediately after she hangs up the phone but so be it. "Did you know that Davey's some bigamist, small-time cult leader up in Oregon? Do all you faith healers keep in contact with each other?"

"Please *do not* equate what I do with *anything* that sinner is involved with."

"Is this retribution, Reverend? Be clear!"

"I think I have been, Ms. Solomon," Kalodner says, flatly. "All members of Grifters Anonymous are cursed. I cannot offer you any sort of specifics for what may have brought them to this point of no return, only that they arrived there freely and willingly. God's message is never literal or linear because that is not what He knows. It is up to us sinners to make sense of what He is trying to tell us. That is *your* charge, I gather. Ms. Solomon. And if you're really interested in the hidden truth, you'd do well to ask *your husband —*"

"You know, I never thought of that, *Reverend.* Wait! I can't on account of the fact he is losing his mind!"

Silence.

Then:

"I suggest you track down Davey … the false prophet, as you've described him. Or … sit down with John Germanian and ask him your questions. Although, I don't know how fruitful even that would be."

Now, it is Gretch's turn to pause, her tongue frozen in dread at the prospect of what the reverend has proposed. "So, you know what happened to J, too?"

Of all the things I'm doomed *to remember, when I've lost so much else.*

"Yes, I do. I can't say I'm surprised he'd be the one to pay the most punishing price of them all. When I left Grifters Anonymous, J took up my mantle of outrageous, godless behavior and, competitive man that he is, he took what I'd been doing before my spiritual rebirth and ramped it up to a greater extreme."

All this time, Gretch had considered J to be the cool head of the band, especially when Davey did or said something to set one of the others off or things came to blows, which was more often towards the bitter end.

"J and Davey," Reverend Kalodner says, in a dusty voice, "have placed themselves out of reach. They cannot be saved. There is no point in mourning them. They are the dead. They just don't know it yet."

Yeah, tell that to J. Germanian.

"I am sorry about Stevie. I've got to go. I had to step out of my office, and I've got a pair of newlyweds waiting. I don't know it's appropriate to say I hope you find what you're looking for. It could prove to be something you would have been better off distancing your-self from, forgetting altogether if you can. I *will* pray for you. I will say a Mass for you, this coming Sunday. I hope you feel the Holy Spirit beside you for that hour. I will ask that He watch over you and guide your hand and your mind."

She only heard half of what was said but manages to thank him for his time.

Her thoughts have already moved on to the inevitable next step she had thought she'd be able to avoid.

The mere thought of it turns her blood cold and calls goosebumps across her forearms.

It's only when the recorded operator comes on the line to ask her in an exasperated tone if she'd like to make a call that Gretch realizes she had simply gone somewhere else in her mind.

Why not see if you can reach Bobby Royal's rich daddy, Nolan Royal, first? If he can provide you with enough information, you may not have to see … J …

The thought of having to sit across from J. Germanian as he exists now frightens her. It calls the hairs of her arms to full attention.

It would have to be a face-to-face, after all.

A live meeting.

Not a phone call.

J Germanian has lost the ability to speak.

For want of lips and a tongue.

Dear God …

THIRTY-ONE

Gretch crosses the kitchen to replace the cordless in its charging station on the countertop when it rings in her hands.

She jumps, unaware of just how tightly wound she is. Answers the call:

"Gretch, Christ! Are you alright? I got my keys in my hand. I was all ready to drive back there!"

"Wha-why would you do that?" Gretch says, her mouth suddenly gone dry. "I'm fine. Stevie woke up. I had to see to him."

"Yeah, but … I tried calling you. I mean, shit, the last I saw you had your head in the kitchen sink ready to be sick."

Am I a terrible person to feel like I just don't need this shit right now? This third-degree like we're-I dunno-dating or something?

"I'm *fine*, Harrison," she says, flatly. "He went down a little over an hour ago. I've been keeping busy with you-know-what."

Silence on the other end.

Every second he prolongs this, Gretch finds her distaste for him burgeoning. "You still there? Because I'm fine. Like I said."

"I thought … you're gonna think I'm crazy but …"

"What? What did you think?"

Pause. "I-I thought Stevie … that he—"

"You thought he-what? -that he hurt me?"

"I know-*I know!*" Harrison says, voice sizzling with an underlying chuckle that never quite breaks through. "It's my fucking overactive imagination. When I couldn't get you, I dunno—I pictured you dead on the floor. Stevie standing over you. And he clubbed you over the head. You're all bloodied up—"

"Jesus, Harrison!"

"I know," he says. "I don't know what's wrong with me. Sorry. I just … I worry about you."

Gretch grabs absently at the back of her hair, gathers it into her hand, and lets it drop down her back again. "It's alright. I guess I'm being a bit sensitive. Thank you for caring, Harr." Blowing out a breath, she hits mental reset. "So, I've made some progress. I don't know if you knew anything of Grifter's *first*-first guitarist. Before anything on *Knives*. He left before they really hit to become a minister in the Midwest. I found him and we had a conversation."

"No shit," Harrison says. "How was he?"

"He's a pompous ass. And it's clear that while he eschews the lime-light, he's never missed an opportunity to find his way back to it. He's aligned with the whole Tipper Gore censorship movement."

"*Real*-ly. So, he went full-on pussy?"

"Methinks he doth protest too much when it comes to his distaste for all thing heavy metal."

"So, no help, it sounds like?"

"Quite the contrary," Gretch says. "Ever hear any whisperings in your circles about Grifter's *first* manager? Because I gotta plead igno-rance. This information has been in my blind spot all this time. I had no idea there was anyone before I came along. I mean, Davey and J told me they were always the ones steering the ship. That no one would have them."

A pause. She hears him make a sound like a tongue-click or his top and bottom teeth coming roughly together. "Shit … yeah. Now that I think about it, there was some mention of a rich guy bankrolling them before they were anything. But I could've told you that Davey and J are not self-made men by any stretch. They got a lot of help. Not to mention, they manufactured a lot of the *dangerous-to-know* reputation that brought you to them. Well, that and the music. You did say their gang-like presentation was a major selling point."

"I stand by that. Rock and roll is ten times more interesting and lucrative when the people making the music come across like they pose a threat to everyone around them."

She can't help the next thought that crosses her mind. It blindsides her. \

Something that Louder never possessed. You were practically a bunch of Boy Scouts in comparison to Grifters.

"Gretch," Harrison says, with a hint of unease, "last I heard this benefactor-Bobby's pop, right?"

"Right. So, you have heard of this?"

"Yeah, I have. It's coming back. I also seem to recall the guy only ceased to be their manager because he had no choice."

"What does that mean?"

"I'm sorry to say you've hit a dead-end when it comes to Daddy Warbucks. Bobby's pop is dead. Ten years now."

"You're kidding. Please tell me that's only what you *heard.*"

"My tattoo guy—you know Merlin—he seemed damned certain that's what happened. And he's J's guy, also. Christ, I think he's done more work on rock stars than all the plastic surgeons in Beverly Hills."

"Goddammit, a second ago you sounded just as in the dark about their *first* manager as I was. Now you say you've got *solid* fucking *intel?* Jesus, Harrison are you blowing smoke?"

"Whoa-whoa-shit! Where is this coming from? I'm on your side, Gretch!"

Her heart is hammering between her ears. Her arms are glazed in sweat. She wonders if she might be having a heart attack. A deep breath suddenly escapes her. Bracing herself on the lip of the marble countertop. She cups the mouthpiece with her hand, shuts her eyes. Calls her lungs back into a normal rhythm. All the while, Harrison is shouting into her ear.

Finally, she answers him. "Fine. I'm fine. I'm here."

"What happened? You don't sound right?"

"No, I'm okay."

"I can be there in forty if you need me to come—"

"No!" she says, more forcefully than she meant to sound. "I'm sorry. It's just …"

"What? Talk to me."

"No, it's just now I've got to talk to someone I've been trying to avoid altogether. I don't have a choice now."

"I don't understand. Who?"

Gretch rests her forehead against the wall and wets her chapped lips. "Listen, I-I'm sorry, Harrison. I'll be out of town for the next couple of weeks. I'll call you when I get back."

"Gretch, wait—"

"Thanks for your help. I mean it."

"I could go with you—"

She ends the call and turns in at the ridiculous hour of eight in the evening. There is nothing humorous about the glass of wine and two anti-anxiety pills she mixes before slipping between the sheets and hauling the nest of weighty quilts up over her side-sleeping form. The combination is no joke, especially as it drops her deeper into the blackest, bleakest hole her subconscious can provide for her. There is no bottom, and Gretch won't remember it in the morning.

What her final thought was before deep sleep.

A wish for death.

THIRTY-TWO

Paddy Burnside has a hell of a time adjusting to his rental car. Every mechanism, from the brakes to the adjustable seats, feels sticky. Driving on the left side of the road has been in perpetual conflict with his spatial orientation. As for his body, he'd heard Brit food was garbage, so he'd gone with something safe and familiar. Bangers and mash. Now, as he pulls up to the security station set off to the left before the grand wrought iron gates, Burnside feels the rumbling in his gut that proves his mind *and body* both are struggling to acclimate themselves to this other way of life.

He remembers one of his buddy's descriptions of the Scottish Isles. He'd done a European tour and crossed through the region. *America is Scotland observed through a film-layered lens.*

You forgot the thick, damp air. The foreboding coal-colored clouds rolling ceaselessly by without ever breaking for some blue.

Sunlight a rare commodity.

A barrel-chested guard emerges from the Security station and comes to stand in Paddy's path before the PI can even achieve a full stop. The guard is dressed in black fatigues and boots brought to a high shine. Black half-gloves and a black knitted cap screwed down onto his head so he could easily pass for a longshoreman lifer.

That comparison is quickly shattered when he unslings the AK-47 on his shoulder and aims down its sights at Paddy's windshield.

"You lost then?" the guard shouts, grey eyes offering no quarter should Burnside's answer prove insufficient.

Burnside is quickly reminded he is in the middle of nowhere. The last main thoroughfare was five miles back. He'd followed a series of winding backroads to reach the heavily guarded compound. What's to stop the guard from gunning him down? Spidering his windshield and punching him full of holes.

You are not safe.

The old man is expecting you.

But it's clear he gave no notice to his security staff to roll out the red carpet, or at the very least, refrain from holding a machine gun on me like this.

The bangers and mash stir in his gut. He fears he will soil himself. His mouth is a desert, but he puts up his hands. Holds them up, then motions to the driver's side door. "I'm just gonna roll down the window. I ... fuck."

The guard nods once, giving him the green light to do so. And little else.

Paddy has the window down, its button sticking. His finger comes away with a substance like pancake syrup rubbed into its tip. "I ... can I lean out the win—"

"Hold." The guard stalks over to the driver's side.

Does not relax the machine gun. It is now trained on Paddy's jackhammering heart.

Hands up, Paddy flashes his shark teeth smile and thanks his lucky stars he wore his suit to this meeting instead of his street wear. The latter ensemble would have no doubt gotten him barred from entry, if not shot on sight. Still, even his perfect dental work cannot cancel out the hint of foundation he powdered onto his cheeks, the hint of eyeliner, or the white-blonde dyed spikes that stand three inches off his head and shine with dried rubber cement.

He vanquishes his smile, clears his throat. "I-er-I'm here to interview Mr. Royal," he says. "I spoke with him three days prior. He said he'd-how did he put it-he'd *give me an audience?* Sounds like him, right?"

Stop. Fucking. Smiling. You. Look. Feeble.

Before Paddy can even disappear his smile for the second time, the guard reaches for the talkie clipped to his hip. He holds Paddy in his gaze, initiates a back and forth. "Visitor here to see Black Hat."

It's unclear to Paddy whether the guard called Old Man Royal Black Hat or *Black Cat.* Neither one makes a lick of sense, either way. But why the code names? Why the thick and swirling air of confidentiality surrounding the old man and his sprawling estate deep enough in the woods to qualify as a house in a fairy tale.

The talkie squawks: "You like the look of him?" The voice on the other end is a thick Manchester accent. *Ya loik da look o' im?*

The guard says, "I can take him or leave him. You nearby Black Hat?"

Squawk: "Bring him up. Black Hat approves."

Bring um' oop'. Block Hot appreeves.

The guard tells him to put it in park and step out. Once Burnside emerges halfway, the guard drags him the rest of the way out and jacks him up against the car. Burnside flinches at the sudden groping of what feel like many hands. *Pat down. Makes sense.*

So why did I fucking flinch like a bitch?

When he is cleared and allowed to re-enter his vehicle, the guard steps back two paces.

His arm is a blur as he clips the talkie back in place. "I'll be right behind you. Don't stop moving. You ken?"

"Yeah. Sure."

"You'll wait until I pull the cart up behind you and the gate swings wide. Then, you'll drive no faster than five miles an hour up the drive. Exceed that speed and I will ventilate you at once."

THIRTY-THREE

The estate is called Blacketer House.

Listed among the most expensive properties in Edinburgh, Scotland, it boasts thirty-four acres of *Sound of Music* plateaus and a spacious mansion refined in the Tudor-Gothic style. Every edge looks lethal to the touch. Dark stains have burrowed into various nooks, never to be extracted with a power wash or a steady, determined hand. The four chimneys marking the corners of the rooftop are highly decorated. Various crenellations mark the top wall of the mansion, although the building never endured a siege during war time where it would have needed to be protected or held down with firepower or the like.

The mansion was, in fact, built according to Old Man Royal's specifications. And Blacketer House does not boast a welcoming air to Paddy Burnside. It could well have served as a mental hospital or a prison. Twenty-five barred windows, tall and slim eyelets, do not even seem to take notice of him as he surrenders his vehicle to another guard waiting to receive him.

Blind windows.

This is what they look like to Burnside. Devoid of any spark. Like dead, rheumy eyes. *And that's a cool name for a song.*

An LP, even.

No time to write it down.

You take the look of this place and combine it with the staff of fucking mercenaries roaming the grounds with machine guns and you have a bunker.

A bunker implies there is a threat to be staved off.

Burnside casts a wide look around himself.

Suddenly, he feels watched. It's not the guard, who is already on his way back down the drive in his golf cart to the front gate and the shoebox security station.

A shudder climbs Burnside's spine.

"Come along," the second guard commands. A tall and slightly stooped man in black fatigues sans the knitted cap so he can show off a full head of blonde, close-cropped hair. His blue eyes twinkle with mischief. Want of a scuffle to break up the monotony of guarding an eccentric billionaire recluse. "You're cutting into Black Hat's sculpting hour."

"Sculpting hour—"

"Come along, lad!"

Before Burnside realizes it, the guard is suddenly standing alongside him. Nudging the nose of his Ruger pistol into the small of the PI's back.

Corralling him.

"Christ," he sighs, raising his hands once more.

The thirteen-feet high doors open inward. A sweeping, shadowy main hall yawns before him. Two stairwells wind upward to a second story landing that looks like it could host the giver of an especially grandiose speech to an assembly of party goers. The risers are covered in a rich and royal mauve carpeting. The floor is of a distressed dark oak. Burnside tests this the moment he steps foot on its surface and notes its solid resistance to the heel of his boot. Gold railings and fixtures wink at him from countless points.

A grand chandelier chitters twenty feet above his head.

It feels as if he has just taken a trip back in time to when bards walked the boards of a circular, open-air theater or lanky, bearded men of consequence with expressive eyes tapped their canes down the winding lanes of London.

The guard grounds the nose of his handgun deeper into Burnside's back.

Two more guards stand beside both stairwell entrances, machine guns slung over their shoulders as they make a serious study of this visitor. Black fatigues. A uniform. The longshoreman cap, optional, judging by the fact one of them dons it and the other sports a beret instead.

"Walk," the guard at his back says, screwing the gun into his back. "Or we will cease to trust you, and you will die."

Laughing now, Burnside says, "Lead the way, friend. Just taking it all in."

"You are here to have a conversation, no?"

"Yeah, that's right," says Burnside, reaching the foot of the stairwell.

"Not to *take it all in*. Remember."

There is a handoff of sorts.

The two guards take symbolic possession of Burnside. They walk him up the stairs, flanking him on either side. They leave barely enough room between him and them for a ray of sunlight to shine through. And Burnside can practically feel the two of them vibrating lethality like a pair of tuning forks.

I've got to ask.

They shoot me-well, then they shoot me.

The one on his right hacks and sneezes, clearly cold or flu ridden.

Burnside says:

"Why's the old man feel he needs the protection of a small army anyway?"

The sick guard honks his nose into a handkerchief in response before stuffing it back into his pants pocket.

The stairwell ends in the center and runs off to the left and right. The high, arched windows are muted with thick, heavy red draperies that puddle on the floor like pools of blood. But the walkways are lined in what at first seems like an impressive number of unframed paintings and quickly hints at something odd or threatening afoot. The paintings vary in size and style, from oil to acrylic to watercolor. Burnside tries to make a tally of them all and realizes this is a fruitless effort given how quickly the two guards usher him along.

Paintings are stacked against the railing, four or five deep and arranged into ten leaning stacks. They do not come out further than the mauve runner which maintains a walkway amidst the splendid, unsettling chaos of artwork. The right side of the runner boasts a similar arrangement of rows of stacked paintings. *Is this where Nolan Royal lives, or where he stores his paintings? The guy's quite the collector!*

Then he notices hands and feet and heads, all extremities of a dark torso, piled up amidst the stacks to his right.

Holy shit, body parts?

"Sculptures," the guard mutters, jabbing a thumb at one of the piles of renderings. "Mr. Royal has a hard time finishing them. They end up discarded out here in the hallway. He's never completed a full body rendering. That's his goal."

"Wait a minute … Nolan Royal sculpted all those … pieces?"

"The paintings also. And this only a small portion of what he's accomplished—"

"Bullshit!"

A hand stays him. Burnside turns to the guard, whose eyes are suddenly flashing with a mixture of reverence and dread. "How much do you know about Mr. Royal?"

"A baseline knowledge," Burnside blurts. "That's why I'm here to interview him. I'm writing a biography of Grifter's Anonymous. I was steered his way."

"Fuck Grifters Anonymous," the guard blanches, annoyed for some reason. Insulted, even. "That's small. That's nothing. You should know you are about to enter the studio of a true genius. Unrivalled. Driven, often to the point of borderline madness. And he just celebrated his eightieth birthday. It hasn't slowed him. His productivity surpasses those creatives a quarter of his age." The guard pauses, his eyes never leaving Burnside's face. Blinkless. "Still, if you are here with any designs on ill-using Mr. Royal, you should also know he is not to be trifled with. He is as dangerous as he is brilliant."

Dangerous?

Murderous … maybe?

This is all connected.

Fuck.

There's no question the guard is expecting Burnside to shudder, to shake in his boots at this revelation. To perhaps even cancel the interview for fear of his own safety.

Burnside is practically ready to jump out of his skin with anticipation.

He has never wanted to speak with someone more in his entire life.

Still, no harm in threading the needle: "Dangerous *how*?"

The guard looks at Burnside like a hopeless parent looks upon a dimwitted child. "Come along."

For a moment, Burnside is surprised at his physiological response to the guard's sudden caginess. His heart speeds up. It fills him with a sick feeling, like how the Romans must have felt at the coliseum just moments before the Christians went into the lions' mouths.

They start to walk again, approaching a closed door framed in a threshold darkened by a jutting, ornate canopy jutting out from the high ceiling. As they make their way, the door itself seems to recede by small degrees. Lengthening the distance. Eluding him. Playing with them. Or is it a trick of the eye?

A residual effect of the jetlag Burnside is till in the throes of?

The stacks of paintings gradually shed their organization with every forward step.

By the time the Talkative Guard moves in front of Burnside to unlock the door, the paintings litter the floor in a hodge-podge that hints at a *giving-up* at some point. The abandonment of order. Burnside at one point must mind his footfalls for fear of stepping on a few of the canvases.

He does not even notice the sickly guard who had been bringing up his left side is gone until he gathers a quick glance all about.

Then, he realizes something that deepens his confusion.

The door to Old Man Royal's rooms locks from the outside.

He is caged.

At his request.

Burnside's last thought before following the guard into Royal's room is whether the guards are there to protect the old man from any bad actors or to protect the public at large from the old man.

"Both, my lad."

Nolan Royal is eighty years old, according to Burnside's notes. The mogul leans precariously upon a fat, black cane with one hand, gnarled as a tree knot, curled around the walking implement's capped top. The old billionaire's appearance does not defy his age but rather surpasses it by what seems to be decades. His bald pate is liver-spotted. White hair, shot through with blonde, rings his skull and hangs long and neglected and wispy over a pair of two oversized ears like satellite dishes. The left side of his face droops off the bones of his face like they'll slip away at any given moment. If this is the result of a stroke, somehow it has failed to affect his speech which rings clear if not sodden with fatigue. His eyes are big, watery reflecting pools over a nose that looks razor-sharpened in an extreme aquiline formation. His lips have curled inward towards teeth that have gone to black as they extend further back into his mouth.

He looks like he's closing in on a century of living.

Holy Christ. Once a titan of British industry. Now …

Openly astonished, despite his best efforts to appear unaffected, Burnside eyes the metal collar fitted around the old man's turkey throat. He can't wrap his head around the distinct possibility it is a shock collar. And the old mogul has submitted to wearing it voluntarily.

His meager frame is wrapped in an ankle-length sheet. Judging by the countless smears of various paint shades and a handprint or finger mark here and there, Nolan Royal wears this as a smock. Something tells Burnside the old man lives in his smock for fear of being struck with inspiration and not wanting to have it slip through his fingers before he can get the damned thing tied on again.

The artist stands like a canting tree, flanked by a dizzying assortment of paintings on various easels set up around the expansive quarters. In different stages of completion. Some barely begun, showing the ghostly imprint of a pencil outline. No toilet, but it could be in an adjoining bathroom. No bed, at least none that he can readily view from where he stands. The floor is completely covered in drop cloths, stained and mottled in dripped and spilled paint hardened to a thick, impenetrable crust. Towards the rear of the luxury-sized room, the top of a dark marble sculpted head stands just above the colony of loaded easels.

Burnside recalls how the guard had said Nolan Royal was still trying to achieve a sculpture worthy of display. Judging by how the artist has set it far enough back that it cannot be readily viewed tells Burnside Nolan Royal is still at an impasse with this particular art form.

Not so with the paintings.

They are genius works.

They steal Paddy Burnside's breath. If asked, he couldn't for the life of him explain why or what it was about them. Only that they are special.

That they are to be adored.

"I'm afraid we are on a clock, of sorts, young man," Royal declares. Stiltedly, he turns himself around and makes his way towards what turns out to be a crème-colored wingback chair tucked away in a small nook formed by a cluster of loaded easels.

The old man stumbles, the cane slipping his hand for a moment.

Burnside lunges towards him.

Just about to brace the old man and assist.

He is suddenly looking into the old man's yellow, cataracted eyes.

He feels himself swiftly shoved backward by two solid objects on the right and left sides of his chest.

The PI stumbles and sits down hard on his tail bone.

Nolan Royal stands over him, now perfectly balanced upon the cap of his cane with both hands. His expression is both regretful and severe.

"You are to stand clear of me," the old man says. "If you value your life, you won't make that mistake a second time."

The door to the room flies open. Nolan's eyes cross the room and briefly light on the guard now standing just inside. Sternly, he tells him to leave and that *it is handled*. "Isn't that right, Mr. Burnside?" he puts the question to the PI, who is now standing and dusting himself off. Paddy offers a nod. And the two of them are alone once more.

"Please ..." Nolan Royal waves him over.

Burnside claims the wingback, twin to the other where Royal lowers himself down. His smock slips off his legs as he crosses them, revealing a tattered bathrobe of earthtones woven into a dizzying, decidedly confused pattern. "My apologies," he says, perched on the edge of the seat. He steeples his hands across the knobs of his knees, partly to still them from knocking.

Royal waves this away like a bad smell and settles deeper into the sharp folds of the chair.

Close enough now to get a better look at the mogul's true and actual physical state, Burnside wishes he'd somehow been permitted to pull his chair back a bit.

The mogul's eyes are horrid looking. The pupils looked like holes punched out of a piece of brown paper. Red stitches the corneas like bloody electrical conductors reaching back behind the old man's eyes to light up his brain.

"I'm not blind by legal standards. More of an impairment. Nothing I can't work around. As you can probably ascertain when you had a look around."

"I had no idea."

"How could you know?"

"I did my due diligence before coming to speak with you."

"As have I, Patrick Burnside. Born 1958 just outside Los Angeles. Father is a highly decorated detective who served longer than his full pension required. Thirty-four years. He must have been quite taken by the blood-stained streets of that demonic city. The whores on their knees next to a dumpster down every other alleyway. The cold cases that by now have gone the frozen route. So, so many bodies. The count for this year alone of homicides would turn your hair white, if it were not already such a shade. Although, you're a young-ish man. What is your natural shade?"

"I don't remember," Burnside says, batting the benign question aside. "Listen, I've come a long way. And I'm not looking to wander into the weeds when I've already been informed I'm cutting into your creative time."

Not that I'm incurious about what the fuck happened to your eyes, old man.

"Yankee manners," Royal muses. "They never cease to ring false in my well-attuned ears. You need not pretend you respect my time. Americans couldn't give a fart what someone else's schedule looks like." His left leg falls to the floor soundlessly, muted by the overworn slipper on the bare foot. "If you're looking to show some respect to your elder, you could drop the ruse."

"I don't follow."

"You're not writing a bloody *book*. About Grifters?"

"Well, I—"

"Fuck off with you or tell the truth. Why are you really here?"

"All due respect, Mr. Royal but—"

"There's that word again, and yet I could not feel *more* disrespected by you. In my own home. You tell me what you're after. Because if it is what I suspect ..."

The mogul pauses, those hole-punch eyes boring into Burnside.

Burnside shrugs. "If you suspect ... then ... what?"

"If I'm right about your true motivation, then you and I are going to agree to some very specific, non-negotiable terms before I begin."

"Alright. Name them."

"In due time," Royal says. "Ask your questions. I've got to get back to it."

The PI doesn't even have to think about him. Burnside puts forth his questions with recovered confidence. Back on the plane, he 'd studied his notes for hours at ten-thousand feet. They were written out long-hand back on the ground in LA. Now, they are as ingrained as the names of a mother's children, and it sets off a rhythm of back and forth that seems at first to be off-putting for the old man.

Then, Nolan Royal settles into this quick volleying.

Burnside: "What's with the security detail?"

"A private firm. Mercenaries, many of them veterans of the Royal Guard. They'd become disenchanted with the lack of steady combat.

Threat of death. The rush of it. That's how one of them explained it to me. I knew right then I'd hired the best group to guard the estate. The Caelid Group. That's the name of their outfit. They have earned the reputation for being the most brutal and unscrupulous security groups in the world."

Burnside leans forward. "Well, from the looks of that ... *steel collar* ... you're wearing, you're the one I should be more wary of."

"So, you understand the security detail works *both ways* then?"

"Yeah. Doesn't mean I understand it."

Royal tries to raise himself up higher in his wingback. Something in his back cracks. A wince of pain registers in his face. He loses it at once, covering it over with a winsome smile. And he settles back into the leather upholstery. Burnside suspects arthritis or sciatica, even.

The abundance of art choking the gallery/ bedroom/ study had distracted Burnside form the reality of Nolan Royal's advanced age, as had the quick and powerful shove he'd doled out to the PI that put him on his ass.

"Look around you, Mr. Burnside."

"Oh, I saw—"

"Look a second time. Indulge an old man."

Burnside does a half turn. He's already been enthralled by the dizzying array of artwork. "Yeah," he says, "it's astonishing. I'm awe-struck. And not just by the quality, but the *quantity* This is the output of a-well-a much *younger man*. Wouldn't you agree?"

"Would it surprise you to know there was never a time I showed a hint of aptitude or potential for any of this. I appreciated the form as well as anyone. That's not to say I ever thought of myself as *having an eye* for any of it. I never once considered trying my hand at the form." The old man's eyes close. "Ten years ago, my *hand* was *forced*. Every-thing changed."

"Ten years, eh? What do you attribute it to?"

"My separation form Grifters Anonymous," Nolan Royal says.

Burnside must think about this for a second. *It checks out. The memoir pages confirm this.*

He holds this back and keeps silent.

"I was *not* looking for any such blessing as this," he says, sweeping his arm towards the army of loaded easels in their midst. "But The

Muse … does not discriminate. She didn't gift me with the same talents as my son and the other members of his band. I don't know why She chose to saddle me with this bloody albatross. Miles and *miles* of fuckin' canvas. Until I die."

The old man's rheumy-looking eyes shimmer with tears that quickly seep back under his eyelids. "I don't know how they were made aware of these pursuits of mine. I'd kept all this very much under wraps. And still, there came agents and dealers and investors to darken my doorstep. Begging to view my works. Escorted through my gallery. They'd heard *great things*. To this day, I don't know how. I suspect I've got a guard with loose lips on board this ship. And I *will* have him out." He pauses, perhaps considering a few names of the guards he suspects presently. "Had I not rejected them all and banned them from my property for fear of swift and violent retribution, I would have begun the twilight chapters of my life a world-renowned artist counted among the ranks of your Dali. Picasso. Basquiat, even."

Leaving space for the mogul to continue to fill the silence, Burnside holds his tongue. And it is the right thing.

"The more I rejected the fame and pushed back against the blessings of The Muse of The Mountain, Bobby's band gave themselves over completely to their *blessings*. It is why you and every other inhabitant of the goddam planet knows all five of their names. I've been told their debut album is one of the top three rock albums counted consistently among people's private vinyl collections. Third only to The Beatles "Rubber Soul" and The Rolling Stone's "Beggars Banquet"."

It takes Burnside by surprise, the smile that spreads across Royal's thin lips.

A series of tumblers fall into place for the PI. He sighs, feeling as if he is now seeing the old man for the first time.

A businessman first. Manipulator second. Opportunist third—

"The rehab. You made them all enter *that one* in particular. In the middle of nowhere because … you'd done your research."

"I've never made it a habit of going into any situation with blinders on. I'm not a Clydesdale pulling a coach down Madison Avenue."

"Right, of course. You're all about securing a valuable dividend in every situation. Even if it endangers the welfare of your only son, Bobby."

"That is right. Those young men were less than nothing. I only agreed to manage them-to fund them-to keep abreast of my son's dealings. Bobby was getting deep into the drugs. I felt it necessary to inject myself back into his life. Bobby's mother had a similar addictive personality. She died with a bellyful of barbiturates. It only made sense our boy would fall victim to addiction in the same way. I wasn't going to lose him without a fight. So, I used my reach and my influence and my wealth to steer their ship for them. Away from the cliffs."

And you ended up losing your son anyhow.

"In that I failed him as well. Gone into the earth some two years ago. This June."

But that's not the only reason you would have insisted on a no-name cover band enter drug rehab, is it? It's never made sense to me until now.

Until that small smile of yours a second ago.

The old man knew of The Muse and the reputation of the rehab for *blessing* its patients with certain legendary, profoundly rare creative impulses. And Nolan Royal had them go there because they could quite possibly leave the remote, snowbound rehab in the Pacific Northwest as five future legends of rock and roll.

A return on the business mogul's investment.

Christ.

"Now, I mean no disrespect when I ask this. But would it be fair to say you knew what you were getting into when you insisted they enter that *specific* rehab? And they did not."

"Of course they didn't know," Royal says, testily. "They griped for a little while when they were informed them they would be getting clean at an out-of-the-way sky-resort type location. Chris was impossible. He complained the loudest and most frequently, as I recall. He couldn't understand why they couldn't get clean on the west coast at one of those fancy, new-age places. He was under the impression he was entitled to rehabilitate where his heroes had done their stints. The guys from Aerosmith. He really wanted to check in to where the whole band got clean together. And it wasn't that I couldn't afford it.

"I believed they would benefit from Endsley Hall. No distractions.

No …well … no escape. For all intents and purposes, they would have had no choice but to work the program."

"Now you sound like you were dead certain the band *would benefit*. From Endsley. Specifically. What was it about Endsley?"

Burnside vaguely recalled his informant, the disgraceful Garry Glitter, who had spilled his knowledge in that public forest hundreds of miles away like a gutted deer whose steaming entrails splash across the leaf-choked ground. The pervert had, in fact, said the band did not last at the rehab. *Not even twenty-four hours; and still, they were not the same when they came back to Los Angeles. Someone worked on them during that short period of time.*

Or something.

A Muse, for instance.

Nolan Royal leans forward, employing the same jolt of speed as before (and completely at odds with his aged appearance and advanced age). Hands curled around his knobby knees, he raises his chin and shows Burnside a recalcitrant sneer. "Here we are. We've come to why you're really here."

"Mr. Royal, my book. I'd rather not leave here with an incomplete account of—"

"Do you know who Juan Ponce de Leon was, Mr. Burnside?"

"No fucking idea."

"He was an explorer. Credited with having been the first to explore the Florida coast."

The old man's eyes flash.

"Alright," Burnside says, exasperated. "An explorer."

"He had heard tell of a mythical fountain from the Taino Indians. Located in a river that cuts through the Sunshine State proper. His motivation was not merely to lay claim to yet another slice of the New World in the name of Spain. No, Juan had taken the stories and the directives of the Taino quite literally. He became obsessed with finding what we know today as The Fountain of Youth."

The old man sets Burnside with a severe gaze. His brow is knitted. "Now, what if I told you his ultimate goal was *not* to swim in the fountain. *Not* to take advantage of its blessings, but to *fucking* sit down beside the *bloody* fountain, break out the parchment and pen, and set to *writing an account of his journey and a detailed description of the damn foun-tain itself.* Never once intending to dip so much as a toe in that magical healing water."

"Alright, Royal, I get it—"

"Would you believe that bullshit story? Would you?"

Mindful not to raise his voice any louder for fear it will draw the attention of the mercenaries and their guns, Paddy Burnside backs down. "Alright. You got me. I mean, *shit!* Can you blame me? If what the memoirs claim is true-and a great deal of it requires an even *greater* suspension of disbelief—and there is an old god trapped inside a mountain range and she exchanges a divine spark of creation for sacri-fice, you bet your ass I'm gonna track the fucking place down. I'm going to put my detective skills to work, only this time, they're for *my* direct benefit. For *me!* Not some wife who suspects her husband of banging his secretary. Or some private insurer looking to prove fraud with one of their clients. *This is for me!*"

"Mr. Burnside—"

"No, you wanted to know *what I'm after,* so I'll tell you."

Splaying his old hands wide, Nolan Royal motions for him to proceed.

"I … I know this is the one … the push I need to launch my rocket out of the atmosphere. I've been trying at this rock and roll dream for so long. I know I'm probably fucking aged out by now. All the more reason I need this … this *edge.* Because I've seen the competition. And even though I know in my bones I'm fucking ten times better than all those motherfuckers, it's my age that turns people off. Shuts down their attention. They fucking laugh at me. They. Fucking. *Laugh!*

"But if I disappear. For a month or so. I visit with The Muse and maybe even bring a preemptive sacrifice to lay at Her feet. And She *blesses* me? I come back and I hit the Strip again. Only now, I'm armed with a demo of the fucking best rock and roll songs to hit anyone's ears since-well-since *Grifters.*

"Tell me how to find it," Burnside says, his face flushed. "Or don't. I'll find my way there. To the rehab and that *fucking* mountain. One way or another. I will not back down. I will not give up."

Nolan looks down his long, aquiline nose at Burnside. "And what is that exactly? Just so we're clear."

"I want to be the next *Plant*. Fucking Tyler! Nikki *Sixx! Jagger*-I want it all! Times fucking ten!"

The two men have become locked into a silent standoff.

Burnside shatters the silence, his muscles flooded with adrenaline now. "I'm not gonna change my mind. If you're sitting back, you know, waiting for me to come to my senses? To pack it in and give up? You'll be waiting the rest of your life. What's left of it."

Nolan folds his gnarled hands in his lap. Clears his throat. "I can only tell you what I remember. My memories of our check-in at the rehab are intact. Then, after Chris Desmond ultimately comes to *doom the lot of us* with his bloody revolting temper, it all turns to something like an x-ray with a series of dark spots. They are suspicious. They could prove cancerous. Deadly. Much like the dark places in my mind where I just cannot seem to get the light to shine."

THIRTY-FOUR

(1985, One Month Before Lovebug)

ENDSLEY HALL HOLISTIC RETREAT *stands at the base of The Cascades, a mountain range belonging to both Oregon and Washington State respectively. Nolan Royal's private plane lands in a frozen field coated in an inch of undisturbed snow. The clinic is self-sustaining, set apart from a scattering of the hundred or so clapboard houses, three farmsteads, a pair of mom-and-pop stores and a small strip mall, comprising the adjacent town of Guthrie.*

The five Grifters gripe and groan at first sight of the retreat, which sits at an elevation of 2500 feet above sea-level...

"Why here? Why?"

"Christ, Nikki Sixx got to dry out in Cali! Steven Tyler lost his monkey at an island retreat twenty yards from the fucking Pacific! And here we are, kicking our habit in avalanche country!"

Nolan Royal put down what nearly turned into a mutiny of sorts?

By not mincing words nor sparing their feelings.

"You're nothing yet. This is the way to get there. You can only get there through *here! Through me!*"

An architectural symphony of concrete and a heavy-timbered wood frame with white trim brands the retreat with something of a ski-resort resemblance. The elevated windows, twenty-some blind eyes that stare sightlessly out upon the white-blanketed clearing, reveal two stories within. A brick chimney juts into the overcast sky, spewing smoke that instantly thins into the elevated air currents.

The back half of the building stands on raised bulky slabs of that same dark wood that is set into the cement structure itself.

"Wait," Stevie Darius exclaims, surveying the back end of the building that at first glance seems only to sit snugly against the base of the mountain. "I don't … get it."

He blinks his eyes to try and drive any obstruction that could be fucking with his vision.

The building does not merely hunker snugly up against the side of the mountain range.

This place looks like it continues right into the side of the mountain.

"Dope sick," Stevie says, trying to shove the obvious hallucination aside.

But it won't budge.

Not even when Nolan Royal calls to Stevie. The manager is standing there holding the big wooden slab of an entry door open.

"Alright there, lad?"

Stevie nods and hurries along. He brushes past him, mutters something unintelligible.

The first thing they notice upon entry is the blast of heat that blows their hair back like they'd walked inside a glowing furnace.

"Shit, man," J groans, lowering the zipper of his bomber jacket away from his throat...

Bobby nudges his father. "It's boiling in here, Pop."

Royal shrugs. "Once you boys realize you've all been standing in your own damned way all this time, the better off you'll all be. This spot comes highly recommended. And you're lucky to be here. You can now count yourselves among the likes of some of your heroes, past and present."

"What's that, Pop?" Bobby says.

"Let's just say many an artist, from visual arts to literature to rock and roll, have walked these halls and dried out within these walls."

J sighs. "Bullshit. Never heard of this place."

Royal, never one to be flustered, pushes the side of his cheek out and shrugs. "I'll give you names. After you've gotten a couple nights here under your belt. I have no doubt something will have shifted inside the lot of you by then. And you won't care as much." He pauses, touches an index finger to his lips. His blue eyes glint with knowing. "I have it on good authority ... you will be changed."

And although all five of the Grifters do not acknowledge it to one another, it is like a shadow crosses their path in an instant before shuffling along and burrowing into the adjacent darkened corners of the reception area.

From the door, Endsley yawns widely before them. A hush falls over the band. Mr. Royal stands by with his arms crossed over his chest, as he surveys the vast expanse of the Main Room. The walls are varnished oak that climb fifty feet to a vaulted ceiling that has enjoyed the touch of a skilled artist's brush and brain. The manager knew he would have to ask someone who was behind it. It is so reminiscent of the ceiling of Shakespeare's Globe Theater, Mr. Royal makes a mental note to inquire if that is what the artist was going for. When viewing a play at The Globe, spectators' imaginations were coaxed into believing the ceiling was, in fact, The Heavens, and adversely, the space beneath the raised stage represented Hell and all bad things that animated The Bard's most famous plays. A yellow sun and pale, burnished moon swims amongst stars and swirling mists of the cosmos. All set against the deepest navy blue.

When Royal's eyes find the painted Heavens above, he finds he can't tear his attention away. The likeness, at least from fifty feet below, seems spot-on.

Bobby snaps him out of it, the drummer having noticed the ceiling.

"Whaddya' know about that! When's the next Hamlet performance, eh?" He waves his hand at the ceiling, and the other band members follow it.

J clutches his midsection, his face gone the color of cottage cheese. "The hell is that supposed to be?"

"What's tha-you uncultured buffoon!" Bobby said. He tries to explain its significance, only to abandon the attempt when J and the others drift away towards the Welcome desk set into the right wall, in a recessed alcove.

"Look at the size of that fucker," Davey says, temporarily confounding the other guys. "No wonder we're melting!"

Then they notice it as well.

Set into the south wall, a walk-in fireplace houses hulking, oversized flames that crack and whip about like a ten-headed monster.

It dazzles Davey's eyes.

He is staring, then descending into them, it would appear.

Fraught with a sudden regret in the pit of his stomach, Royal watches the singer from afar. He doesn't like what he sees.

A hand falls on his shoulder and Royal turns to find himself staring into the most piercing green eyes he's ever seen.

"Mr. Royal?" the man asks.

This is Karl Stanislaw, director of Endsley. The guy is a celebrity "without a face", as Mr. Royal thinks of him. A paradox of notoriety. His photograph does not appear on any of the book sleeves he's written, and Stanislaw has written five self-help and New Age national bestsellers, topics ranging from the creative intelligence of the Universe to the healing power of stillness. He is a spirituality rock star who shuns any representation of his physical appearance, viewing it as a distraction from the true purpose and intent of his ideas.

Nolan Royal reads a tightness about Stanislaw's eyes that forms as Chris Desmond can be heard to say to the woman behind the intake desk, "Look up my room so you'll know where to find me after hours."

Stanislaw blinks his eyes slowly, opens them wide and holds out a hand to shake with Royal.

He cocks his head in Chris's direction, attuned to the potential problem unfolding only a few feet from them.

"If you wouldn't mind nipping that in the bud before we start?"

"My apologies," Nolan says, unused to acquiescing to anyone. He turns around. "Chris! Come along!"

Chris Desmond takes his time turning around. The others have come around sooner, J wearing a curious lopsided grin like a bad boy whose been caught out.

"Oi, Chrissy!" Nolan barks. "Behave yourself! Come and meet our host—"

Chris rubs the back of his neck and winces like he's just been slapped. Then, as if he's gone deaf to Nolan Royal, Chris turns his attention back to the intake coordinator. "As I was saying, sweetheart ..."

Stanislaw and Royal lock eyes.

Something about the director's cold, unflinching stare causes Royal to break the line of sight first.

This has never happened to Nolan Royal before. Not with any mortal man of stature or title or power, anyhow.

"Excuse me," Stanislaw says, smoothing the front of his beige turtleneck flat against a long, lithe upper torso. His shorn head, bulbous and dented along its crown, is slick with perspiration as he stalks past Royal.

Towards the reception desk.

Chris speaks to the intake coordinator behind the desk in hushed tones, but the rash of embarrassment is evident in the young woman's reaction, a redness that rises past her starched white collar. She smiles thinly, her fingers flying over her keyboard as she enters their names, seeking their room numbers.

Stanislaw comes to stand directly behind Chris Desmond, rolling his head around on his neck. Squaring his shoulders. He stands a full five inches above Chris, who is no slouching littlun' himself.

Royal realizes what is about to happen. He tries to pump the brakes, but his chance to do so has come and gone.

"Daphne," Stanislaw says to the girl, "why don't you take your lunch, love. I'll check this group in and show them to their rooms."

The girl meets Stanislaw's stern gaze with the same set of piercing green eyes.

"Yes, Father," Daphne Stanislaw murmurs, and disappears through a door behind the welcome station.

Stanislaw claps his oversized hands onto Chris' shoulders. "You will show every member of Endsley's staff respect. Yes? After all, they are here at your *service in getting well."*

Chris slips Stanislaw's hand, wheels around, his eyes red with ire. "Who the fuck are you, dude? You got a death wish?"

Stanislaw folds his hands together, a patient and somewhat doting smile spread across his face. "On the contrary, Mr. Desmond," he says. "I wish quite the opposite for you and for your friends. That's why you've come to us. You want to live? You must learn the right way. *Yes?"*

When Chris rubs the right side of his jaw, a tell Royal has come to recognize as a tic that precedes a violent first-strike, the manager finally remembers something from the man's bio in the back of his books. Karl Stanislaw is a master in jiu-jitsu and hand-to-hand combat. The big man has won awards in competition and holds several records.

So when the rhythm guitar player throws a sloppy haymaker at Stanislaw's chin, Royal watches it unfold in a sort of slow-motion.

Stanislaw dips back to the right, dodging the strike. He seizes Chris' shoulder with one hand and bicep with the other. Spins the guitar player around like a top. Drives Chris' arm up his back and pins it between the guitarist's now writhing angel wings. An embarrassingly high-pitched squeal rips its way out of Chris Desmond's throat.

Stanislaw hisses in Chris' left ear. "Control yourself, Christopher."

Bobby Royal looks on, about to pounce. "You're gonna break his bloody arm!"

Stanislaw leans in close enough to Chris' right ear to nibble it like a lover. He speaks into the guitarist's ear.

And Chris's eyes widen.

"-alright-alright-alright-alright-sorry-"

Stanislaw releases him, takes a step back.

Chris Desmond hugs his strumming arm to his chest, rubbing the feeling back into it with his head down and eyes on the rug. This time, Stanislaw lays the same bear-like paw of his on the guitar player's shoulder, asks him if he's alright, and there is no recoil. Chris even nods he's okay and that's enough out of him for the remainder of the check-in process.

Of course, Royal knows he should offer some kind of protest to show good faith to the band.

He decides not to, though.

He cannot afford to alienate Karl Stanislaw. There is too much at stake.

Royal realizes they are a man short. "Now where the hell has Davey gotten off to?"

The Grifters cast their eyes about until J calls, "Yo, Davey?" then turns to Royal. "He's standing over by the fireplace."

Royal looks across the breathtaking, open expanse of a main hall.

Davey is a black silhouette backlit by the writhing, restless flames inside the oversized hearth. The singer stands there, stock still with arms flat at his sides and head cocked slightly as if he's reading something inside the fire like a seer reads tea leaves.

And Royal asks to use the phone behind the desk, where he makes a long-

distance call to Liverpool and his assistant, Rhea. He had planned on flying back after seeing the Grifter boys settled into rehab. How stupid to have assumed they would simply fall in line like your run-of-the-mill addicts.

They're rockstars in their own minds. And this has poisoned them against any sort of self-improvement. So, he tells Rhea he won't be flying back and plans on staying through to tomorrow afternoon at the very latest.

By then, by Christ, they had better have gotten with the program.

Or he'll be cutting them loose and relinquishing his managerial duties.

Cutting off the money, in short.

Just past midnight, *the main hall is empty except for J and Bobby. This is where Nolan Royal, bleary-eyed and too tired to sleep, finds the two of them. The lancet windows, set high along the raised and darkly varnished oak ceiling disclose nothing but that same inscrutable white.*

Snow falls thick and frenzied outside

The main hall is still a hot box. Sweltering.

"Hey there, Pop! Don't trust us on our own, eh?"

Bobby waves his father over to an empty spot beside him on one of the leather sofas.

Both Bobby and J are dressed for the heat. J wears black cargo cutoff shorts and sleeveless Fender t-shirt. Bobby is in blue basketball trunks paired with a gray tank top emblazoned with the words I Fucked the Law and … I Won. *Their clothes look vacuum-sealed to their bodies. Royal is surprised the heat hasn't chased the two of them back to their rooms, but then he remembers his own room drove him out as well.*

There are no smiles.

"Davey?" Royal says.

"Sedative put him down for the count," J said.

"And … Chris?"

Bobby says, "Nursing a bad case o' wounded pride."

"No surprise there," J says. "Turtleneck Man really humbled his ass. You see his face when it looked like his arm was gonna snap?"

Royal leans forward. "Either of you catch what Stanislaw whispered in Chris's ear?"

They shrug.

J says, "Whatever it was, it turned Chris white as a sheet. Just like that!"

Bobby shakes his head. "That doctor knew anything about the Chrissy I know, he woulda' kept his hands to himself. Now, he's gonna find out one way or another. Bloke is not gonna let it slide."

"Hell it's not over with." Royal says. "You lads better rein him in. This is too important."

"Easier said than done. He's like a bull in a China shop. It's gonna be messy. The challenge will be in stopping it before it's too late. Chris won't just come out and thrash the guy next time they cross paths. No, it's a game for Chrissy."

"Now hang on … did you not hear what I just said to you?" Royal says, irritated. He waits for J to nod in agreement. "They'll throw the lot of us out and then what? Police your boy!"

Bobby shrugs. "I know how to tamp down Chrissy when he gets his blood up."

Royal doesn't completely buy it, but he lets it lie and moves on to something that has always confounded him about Chris Desmond.

"Chrissy. He a private guy?"

A slow smile floods across J's lips. "Yeah. And he—"

"Leave off with Chris, huh?" Bobby says.

J looks at him. "Just passing the time. Distracting myself from … the fuckin' inevitable."

Sullenly, Bobby folds his arms and settles sullenly back into the leather sofa upholstery. "Feeling something coming on. Something that's really gonna fuck me up. You know, like right before you wake up with the flu. Feeling … off."

"Yeah," J says. "I can feel it coming on too. I got the shakes. Trying to ignore the spots in front of my eyes. I went in to get clean a couple months before I founded Grifters with Davey. Not a place like this, of course. A real shithole. State-run. And I wasn't into it like I should've been. Hitchhiked out of there. Went off the grid for a week or so. Came back to the H slowly but surely in Grifters." He paused. "This time, though. This time. I've got my head in this. All the way. And no one better even think of leaving until we're done our thirty days."

Bobby shakes his head. "I'm staying. I'm going to work the program. No bullshit."

Yes, you bloody will, my boy, *Royal thinks.*

J and Bobby both turn to the fire. The main hall lapses into a thin, uncomfortable silence.

Having heard enough to give him a headache, Royal stands, arches his back until an audible crack issues from his spinal column. He notices the white, engraved placard set into the stonework beside the roaring walk-in hearth. The lettering is too small for his seventy-year-old eyes to read from where he's standing.

He gestures towards it. "What's that say? My eyes are shite without my specs."

"What?" *J says.*

"Placard here."

"Oh," *J says, an uneasy snicker sizzling out of him,* "Bobby and I were admiring that earlier. Apparently, the staff's weird about anyone fucking with the fire."

Bobby says, "And it would seem every bloody fuck in this place is obeying that directive. Doesn't make a lick of sense. I'm sweating my bollocks off! Why the fuck don't they let it die down. Just for a couple hours so the place can cool off some."

"Strange thing," *J says.* "I don't know that anyone's tending to it. Not the staff. No one's been by to throw another log on. And it's still just roaring away."

Royal has a look at the grate from which the fire blooms with a great rage. "Mm, lads, I got news for ya'." *He stoops and is puzzled by what he sees.* "Oy, there's no ash on the hearth floor! What's keeping this fire going? There's not one bit of log lying on the grate."

J is unmoved. His stomach is starting to spasm. "Fucking fire had Davey in a catatonic state for a good ten minutes earlier."

"Maybe he was seeing what I'm seeing," *Royal says.*

"Maybe," *J says.* "Davey tends to see what he wants to see. Who the fuck knows."

Bobby scratches at the tuft of ash-blonde hairs rising and out of the loose neck of his t-shirt. "Who fuckin' … who cares?"

J and Royal trade looks. It would seem Bobby Royal is starting to feel the first serious twinges of withdrawal. His temper is up. Bobby rarely has a bad day if you were to go by the lopsided smile on his face that never seemed to soften. At least, not in public. Royal fears Bobby, happy-go-lucky, is going to prove the hardest hit by withdrawal. He knows his son, and his history of living under the thumb of various governesses after his mother took her life. His boy, always chipper and cheery, is bottling and burying a well of rage that has been waiting for some time to burst.

The musk of discomfort is coming off the drummer. A sour odor, like rotten apples. Stuffing down his parental regrets, Royal moves closer to the hearth to read the placard inlaid there:

STAFF <u>ONLY</u> TENDS THE HEARTH!
ANYONE CAUGHT TAMPERING WITH THE FIREPLACE WILL BE
IMMEDIATELY ESCORTED OFF THE PREMISES
AND PROSECUTED TO THE FULLEST EXTENT OF THE LAW…

ENJOY THE "FAMOUS" ENDSLEY FIREPLACE!

Royal smirks.

Who the fuck could if they wanted to? My knickers are soaked through!

Behind him, J says, "Fifty bucks if you snuff it out, Poppa Royal!"

Bobby says, "Like Pop needs your fifty quid! You'd have to borrow it off him only to give it back, stupid!"

The hearth spits a fleck of cinder at Nolan Royal. It lands between his slippered feet. Hisses! And his largely logical mind suddenly entertains an alien train of thought. Is it telling me to keep back? Trying to protect itself? *He laughs despite the unease the thought brings and turns his back on the fire.* "The signage? A bit much, eh?"

Both Bobby and J glower at Royal.

It's coming over them now.

"Regardless, I'm going to need the both of you to police your own while we're here. Don't let Chris retaliate. Save him from himself, lads."

"Chrissy was out of line," J says, wryly. "Johnny Kalodner would have known better."

"Again, leave off with Chrissy. And Johnny's a wank. There's a lad who don't know moderation. Makes us look like a bunch of Mormons."

"Bobby—"

"Whaddya' got going against Chrissy all the sudden? He's our guy now!"

"Seriously, Bobby?" J's features start to pinch. "You got a fuckin' hour, man?"

"That's bullshit, J. You're still sour Johnny K. lit out. You're not gonna like anyone takes your boy's place."

J drops his head back against the sofa's cushion. He lets out a long groan, claps his hands over his eyes.

"You're right, Bobby," he says. "This ain't the time. Or the place. And I gotta get back ... to my room."

J stands in place and immediately loses his balance. He grabs for the sofa arm and barely grasps it.

"I got you, J!"

Bobby rushes to aid the guitarist, even as he stands unsteady on his own feet. He manages to slip his arm under the guitar player's arm and buoys him upward. J's legs are shaking now as Bobby walks him away from the sofa and clear of the circle of black leather upholstery and burnished glow of Tiffany lamps.

A minute later, Bobby reappears in the hall. He looks befuddled. "Uh, Pop! He's asking for you to sit with him."

Wordlessly, Royal nods and makes his way to J's room.

Upon entering, the creeping sensation of feeling watched touches Royal's shoulder blades.

J is not too proud to ask for help in stripping down to full nakedness, although Royal nearly balks.

I'd wager this boy is fatherless. Has been his whole life.

"Hot ..." J moans.

Royal yanks the quilt back to the end of the queen bed so it doesn't cover any of his legs. J shoves the sheet down just below his navel, sighs. He turns his head on the pillow. His cheeks are huffing and puffing as he pants like a dog.

"All settled then?" Royal croaks, eyes fixed on the wall behind the bed.

It surprises him when J rolls his head in the negative along the plush pillow and waves his hand towards the chair behind the manager. "Pull up ..."

"Pull what?"

Sweat shines up J's face. His lips pull into a sneer as he points at the chair behind Royal. "Pull—"

"Oh, pull up a chair? Course, lad."

Royal wheels around, sees the fine, hunter-green upholstered desk chair and hauls it closer. Arranges it beside J's bed.

J's condition has rapidly deteriorated in a matter of moments.

He's not dying.

It only looks that way.

J hauls himself up onto his side, groaning and wincing with every muscle called into motion. The pull of his eyes draws Royal's attention to them and does not let go. They are tractor-beams, brimming with tears of pain. At least, that's what Royal assumes them to be.

"Royal ..."

"What can I do?"

"Came on ... quick. Never felt like this. Bad ..."

"And you're all in for it, sorry to say. But only one time. Nobody in their right mind wants to take a walk-through Hell more than once."

"Heart ... feels like it's gonna beat right out of my chest." J rakes his fingernails across the lift of his left pec.

Royal drops his chin into his chest.

Someone rushes past J's door, bare feet slapping at the low carpeting. They are retching so loudly Royal waits for something wet and thick to slap the wall or splash onto the floor. A female voice, low and doting, sounds in between the horrid sounds of a stomach overriding its body. Must be Bobby. Thank God an attendant got to him in time. Their words are indecipherable but comforting and almost angelic.

"Just try to relax," Royal soothes, his words tasting hollow. "It's going to be ... alright." He swallows a bitter dollop of mucus. It burns all the way down his throat.

"Blankets," J begs, making a feeble grab for the comforter. A second ago, J was breaking a serious sweat. Now, it's a cold drip against his skin.

Royal pulls them up, tucks them under the guitar player's chin. J pins it in place by burrowing his chin down into the small of his throat. A terrible *tremor rushes through his blanketed body. He bites his bottom lip so hard Royal expects blood to pool between J's lips.*

A mournful, high-pitched cry echoes down the corridor.

Male.

Royal can see J's roving, twitching eyeballs beneath the closed lids. J is not sleeping, no matter how much he looks like he is. His mind is still very much at work. Watching a mind reel projected against the thin membranous skin of the lids, a captive audience to God knows what! J will wake up feeling like he never went to sleep. This poor excuse for slumber is merely a placeholder for the pain to come.

When Royal finally makes it back to his room, he finds the feeling of being observed has only gotten stronger.

His room has now climbed to sauna temperatures.

"Bollocks on this!" Royal cries. "Fucking fireplace! Enough already!"

I've got half a mind to stomp that fucking fire out myself.

With weariness settling into his bones, Royal begrudgingly lays down on his bed without pulling the blankets back. He stares up at the stucco ceiling; his old spine is not used to such spare accommodations. When a shallow doze washes over him, he is stuck in the presence of his wildest nightmares.

THE NOISE *that rouses him from a deep sleep is something he has never quite been able to pinpoint. But he knows one thing and that is if he were to hear it again, Nolan Royal's heart would fail.*

At once.

THIRTY-FIVE

Nolan Royal's hole-punch eyes land squarely on Burnside. They are accusatory.

"Have you ever heard of *locked-in syndrome*?"

"Tell me," Burnside presses, expectantly.

"You must understand there are a great many blind spots in my memory of that night. What I'm going to explain to you is nothing short of a patchwork of flash images I've been able to stitch together to make some sense of things. And even now, I cannot make any reasonable sense of it. My fear. My dread. It is for a phenomenon I do not completely understand, but my lizard brain knows that it needs to be afraid. That is the stuff of nightmares, and I should *run* from it. *Not towards* it.

"Locked-in syndrome is just what it sounds like," Royal explains, clinical and removed in his tone. "I have since been put through numerous diagnostic tests by a battery of specialists seeking to tie this sudden paralysis to some underlying illness. We traced my family lineage and its medical history. All that surfaced was a prevalent history of heart murmurs. One specialist inquired about any history of mental illness in my line. You see, after this happened, I feared insanity. This was not the case.

"

"I couldn't get out of bed that night at the rehab. I could only listen. A captive audience. I opened my eyes to this—this nerve-shredding cacophony of sounds outside my room. Down the hall to be exact. The main hall, where I'd just been sitting with the J and Bobby what felt at first like moments ago. Time had slipped since I laid my head down. Hours. I willed my body to rise but I could not make it happen … not at first. Then, I found myself walking—more wobbling from side to side— and before I knew it, I had reclaimed my seat before the fire. The very seat I'd been in earlier.

"It was as if I'd wandered blindly into a carnival in Hell. So … so hot. I remember liking it.

"The moment I sat down, the locked-in syndrome took hold of me once more. This time, it did not let go. I was made to pay perfect attention to things no human being can or should be made to endure without eventually praying for a psychotic break.

"I would have broken completely if not for the fact my eyelids had stopped lubricating my eyes. They were stuck open like a pair of old, broken shades. Helpless, I was made witness to the chaos unfolding around me without rhyme or reason. When it all ended, my eyes simply dried up, and I could no longer see. They had held on to their function until there was nothing more to see."

A pause. "Wait," Burnside said, horror fluttering through him. "Are you telling me—"

"There was nothing even the finest and most expensive surgeons could do to restore it."

"You … you're blind?"

Royal nodded, tucking his chin down into the wattled pocket of his throat. "You're wondering how I paint. Sculpt. And how I was able to track you and throw you down earlier."

"Heightened senses to compensate for your sight."

"There is another component I'm going to explain. Are you familiar with Caligula, Mr. Burnside?"

Burnside laughs uneasily. "How much did you see when you were managing Grifters?"

"Nothing would compare."

"Well, let me just tell you. Fucking Sunset! That single stretch of road? Caligula would have gladly presided over the things I've seen there. Alleyways. Back rooms. VIP wings. Dressing rooms. I'd say he gave birth to the excess and depravity of the early 80's. He'd be proud."

"The main hall," Royal says, solemnly as if fearful of being heard by anyone other than the PI. "Caligula blushed."

They look at one another, sharing in a loss for words that is fleeting but noteworthy.

"If only I'd flown back to London that night. I'd have nothing to tell you. There'd be no art gallery in my home. No private security, at least not at the level of lethality this current detail boasts.

"I had no intention of staying the night—I managed them from afar. Across the pond. Through wire transfers. Surrogates. Oddly enough, my entire staff of advisors and assistants begged off from accompanying the band to the rehab. Understand, they freely and willingly put their jobs in potential jeopardy by denying me. They did not fear the bread line. Not as much as they seemed to fear that ... place."

"Well, how would they have known—"

"A feeling in the pit of one's stomach," Royal says. "Not to be ignored. The reptilian portion of their brains did not fail to warn them. Mine failed me on a seismic level."

Burnside moves to the edge of his wingback chair. "Tell me."

"The fire in the hearth. Someone stomped it out. Chris Desmond. He had been looking for some way to even the score with the moderator, Stanislaw, after their altercation. The fool had even tried to remove the silver placard set into the wall beside the hearth warning against his actions. It was bolted into the granite.

"And ... it was as if all culminations of depravity and blackness had been unleashed upon the main hall by way of the dormant hearth. That the fire had been holding it all at bay, this hidden chaos that offends the eye and disheartens the spirit.

"There were cries of pleasure and torture blending into one another until there could be no differentiation. By moonlight. A white band shining through the elevated windows. Illuminating it all in the faintest, ethereal glow. Strange, misshapen shadows cast along the walls. Writhing and twitching and heaving and sighing and screaming things. The smell in the room—don't ask me how I remember it more vividly than other things—but the *smell* could only be compared to that of a room where a thousand human beings had taken their lives in the bloodiest fashion and then vacated their bowels. Copper and excrement. And the thinnest scent of sex and secretions threaded through it.

"A mingling of humans and oddities. Abominable couplings. An orgy. The hall was crowded—choking on it." Royal pauses, collecting himself. "So … so strange. I'll never look at the creative impulse in the same way again. Some of the people—and I can only assume the ones I did not recognize were the rehab staff—were defiling and being defiled by these vaporous black shadowy creatures. Others … they had taken to marking up the walls. They'd opened themselves up and they were painting with their own blood. Using their wounds as a fount like an artist uses a pallet to mix and take colors onto their brushes. And the renderings? Understand … they were not mere child-like smears. They were … works of a high standard. Vivid and alive with detail and appeal and the rarest spark of artistic genius.

"Others, perhaps thirty or so men and women I failed to recognize, had taken to writing on the walls, their handwriting too cramped and stilted to be read.

"I saw other artistic impulses acted upon … only in more terrible ways. One of the humans had slaughtered and opened another one's chest cavity and taken to p-plucking the entrails like one does with a guitar string. And … the note they coax from it? The musical note? I don't know how. But even amidst the insanity and the cries and the screams. I could hear the note, and it was … heartbreaking."

The old man's bottom lip quivers.

With hooded eyes, Royal continues.

"The depravity. It left trails of gray and white and pale green on the air. And I don't know how it … it parted like a dizzying, electric curtain." Royal's eyes adopt a fogged, thousand-yard stare. "There they were. All five of them. The Grifter lads. My son. Lined up on their knees. S-Stanislaw hovered—no—he towered over them. Lording.

They were all naked. The band. Stanislaw, also. They were covered in sweat, even as the hearth loomed dark and dormant behind the tall, sinewy rehab director who I'd once admired. His books. His wisdom.

"This was not that man.

"No, this was a cheat of the original Stanislaw. That's what I'd thought. It's what I believed.

"Stanislaw's shaved head showed more dents than before. His skull looked like wet clay someone had pressed their fingertips into. His eyes were black. The way the moon struck him in profile, he appeared somehow larger in stature. The tendons in his neck bulged. He appeared under extreme strain and agitation. I had thought he assembled the five lads to reprimand them. To extract a confession regarding who had fiddled with the fireplace. My logical mind simply worked around the deeply upsetting fact that they were all nude together and one had made the other five subservient to him.

"Stanislaw stepped forward to loom large over J. The first one, all the way to the left. He had his head down. Just like the rest of them. I don't know how Stanislaw turned them docile. These were five rowdy, unscrupulous twentysomethings. It seemed nothing short of miraculous. Then again, fear is a powerful motivator.

"When Stanislaw laid his right hand on the crown of J's head, I reconciled myself to the possibility of a strange sort of benediction. A gesture of forgiveness for breaking the cardinal rule of the rehab.

"I watched—and I swear to you on this—*I watched* the man's hand pass through the hair and the skull. It entered J's brain. I can't remember if I screamed. I must have. How could I not have? Stanislaw extracted his hand from the inside of J's brain and held it out before him with a look of repulsion and fury on his face as he beheld his own appendage. J ... the poor boy started to convulse at once. He went down on his side. A seizure that shook his whole body. And I swear it also wrung a musical note from the rattling of his bones like he'd been transformed into a human tuning fork.

"Sometimes, in the quieter hours of night, I can still hear that very same note in the air. A D sharp.

"The other four did not react to J's seizure. I don't know how they could have just carried on as if nothing happened. Then, I discovered they had been stripped of their sense of hearing and sight. Blindfolded. Their ears fitted with plugs. They would have had no idea of what was happening until, well … Stanislaw moved to the next in line. Stevie Darius. Then, Stevie suddenly knew all too well when the big man laid hands *on* his brain.

"The damned ghoul moved wordlessly among them. When he shattered his own silence, how I had wanted him to shut his damned mouth again."

Royal was wound up. There was no denying this. He might have benefited from a brief respite, had Burnside offered him none. A kind, gentle soul would have done so. Burnside was no such soul and waited on the old man with nothing short of manic anticipation. "What were Stanislaw's words, Royal?"

"'I claim you as … as a vessel for Calliope's free use.' The bitch." He pauses, his eyes flying to the window, then crossing the ceiling. "That's right! You. Dirty. Bitch! I said your name! Now come and put an end to it, once and for all—"

"Mr. Royal," Burnside interjects, "finish it!"

"Stanislaw, son of a demon whore he is, he went on with this rite: 'To be blessed … and cursed. You will create and you will … destroy. A-And there will be no … no distinction between the two.' When he came to stand before my son, I remember how I strained and struggled to free my body from whatever chains of goddam sorcery the bastard had imposed on me. I needed to protect my boy. The last of my bloodline. My hopes hung on him. But … see … I couldn't. Fucking. *Move!*" The old man's dead eyes shut, tears slipping the eyelids to go skating down his sunken cheeks. I could only sit there and watch in mounting horror as this-this *minion-this small man who thought himself ocean-size*— he laid hands on my son's head. Then he reached in. Inside his poor brain. My boy. My God, I swear it made a sound I still hear in my wildest nightmares. A tearing, gelatinous sound. As he altered—no, *destroyed*—my boy for all time."

Burnside nods, soberly. When Royal does not stir, having slipped into yet another trance-like state, Burnside fills in the blank:

"The daughter. Stanislaw's daughter."

Slowly, a new light enters the old man's eyes. The light of knowing and realization. "It would seem you're more familiar with all of this than you initially let on, Mr. Burn—"

"Nevermind that. Tell me what happened to the girl."

The old man's eyes land on Burnside, then turn aside. He begins to haul himself up and out of the chair. "I'll have one of my men see you out—"

Before the old man can finish his sentence, Burnside is upon him.

His hands wrapped around Nolan Royal's turkey throat.

Bearing down on him, flecks of red dancing in his eyes. Burnside breathes on the old man.

"You're not the only danger in this room, you old fuck. It seems Stevie was the only one of the band members who remembered enough to write it all down. He thought it'd save his soul if he made a full confession. But that's not how it works. Even I know that. And his confession is full of holes. It's maddening to read. It's non-linear. Coded in spots. And I've come a long way for you to bring it all into proper focus. I am fucking *sick* of obsessing and losing sleep trying to make sense of it all. You *will* do this."

"I—won't—"

"You *will* or I'm going to saw your mummy head off!"

Royal's tongue lolls out the side of his mouth.

"The girl!"

"*G-gaaaahhhh-hoo-geh …*"

The nod, shallow as it is, still registers as an answer of compliance for the old man.

Burnside's hands fall away. He doesn't sit back down. He hovers over the old man, hands balled into fists at his sides.

Royal's voice is raspy from the assault. Massaging his throat with precarious fingertips, he continues:

"After the five of them fell into convulsions, each of them experienced the same exact response to Stanislaw's sickening laying on of his hands."

Royal pauses, wets his lips. "I must have slipped into the black. Not for very long. The bastard wouldn't have allowed it. Before I came to again. I could hear this guttural, demonic shouting in another language. A man's hollering. When I came to the rest of the way, I saw Stanislaw was *that* man. Tearing into one of the revelers nearby, entangled in the jungle of writing bodies. Human and other. He surged into their midst. A girl started shrieking. A horrid haunting sound. Like a sexual assault.

"He emerged from the tangle of bodies with the girl in tow. He was pulling her along by the wrists. She pulled back and he dragged her across the floor. She screamed. He kicked out at her ribs—"

"His *daughter*?" Burnside says, his face a mask of confusion. "Th-that doesn't make sense. It doesn't fit."

"You said you already know the story—"

"Yeah, but I'm telling you *that doesn't fit!*"

"The girl was not his daughter," Royal says. "She was his wife. One of many. I'd come to find out. And that is, by far, the *very fucking least* of his dark secrets.

"And they—"

Royal slashes him with a look of hatred. "You know it already! What is this? Is this pleasurable for you? I will *not* indulge you any further."

"Yeah?" Burnside says, his glacial eyes flashing. "How about I hand-deliver Darius' memoir to Scotland Yard on the way back to Heathrow airport. They can read all about how the five Grifter guys held an innocent young woman down while her—father or *husband* or whatever the fuck this Stanislaw was—put a plastic bag over her head and suffocated her with it. And that you beat her to death when she held on longer than Stanislaw expected. How long until they storm this fucking fortress of yours, take out your little team of mercenaries, and haul your ancient ass out of here dead or alive?"

At the mention of his part in the killing of the young girl, Nolan Royal moans and covers his face with his hands like he'd done so many times before.

"Yeah, when I said this was a confession, I mean *this was a confession*. Implicating every one of you. Cry more, motherfucker," Burnside hisses at him, holding his voice down so as not to rouse any merc attention.

"*Ohhhhhh … God save me,*" the old man gasps, daring to roll his eyes upward in search of some reprieve from the Almighty. "I relive it every day. And whether I like it or not … all that you see around you … these *fucking* pieces of art … they flow through me like I'm nothing more than a conduit. All that you see! That bitch Calliope thought I *deserved* this gift in exchange for the brutality I showed … in sacrifice to her. I never wanted this!" He weeps softly, his slight body quaking with every sob.

Paddy Burnside stands before the old man. He squares his shoulders. He clears his throat and rubs at his eyes. Regains focus. Stares down his nose at the once unscrupulous King of British Steel. The PI can hardly believe it. A week ago, he never could have imagined he could have broken the spirit and the mind of such a man. Or, at least, the rest of the way.

Nolan Royal? No way. Not me. Nolan Royal breaks other people down to the sum of their parts.

Not the other way around.

"Thank you, Mr. Royal," he says, mockingly. "The memoirs are legitimate. You just validated them. Now, I've got my mandate from the fucking universe to go forth and stake my claim there. I've got a date with an old god, it would seem."

Slowly, the old man raises his head. Slides his hands down so only his hole-punch eyes are visible. "You still seek The Mountain? *Still?*"

"You better fucking believe it." Burnside casts a look around. Finding what he is looking for tucked beneath a long wooden work bench littered with all manner of sculpting tools and half-formed, aborted formations of hardened clay. He navigates the labyrinth of easels to retrieve it. He snatches something out of one of the easel's storage wells and returns to Nolan Royal.

The old man's complexion has gone the color of old cheese.

The defeated look of the Nolan Royal does little to slow Burnside's roll or stir up sympathy for him. *He bashed a girl's head in. Let him stew in it!*

Burnside thrusts a coil of sketch paper and nub of charcoal into the old man's lap. "Where is the rehab?"

"*Still? —*"

"Draw me a map. Put that gift of yours to actual use for the first time in your miserable fucking life."

THE SHADOWS FALL longer and deeper across the main hall as Paddy Burnside emerges from Nolan Royal's godforsaken art studio. A thick piece of sketch paper folded eight ways rides his crotch on the inside of his pants.

It's strange, this lightness of being and sureness of step he experiences as the two guards that had brought him to the mogul escort him back down the stairwell.

The verbal of the two speaks to his back. "You look like a man who just got laid. Old Man Royal put out for you, eh?"

Burnside scoffs. Shakes his head. Rolls with it. There's no need to answer the man. *He's got no idea what's coming for him and the old man once I'm safely off the property.*

No loose ends. He can't snuff out Nolan Royal. He'd never make it out of there alive.

They would ventilate him before he even noted the sudden breeze blowing through his organs.

Once down the long flight of stairs, Burnside turns to Mr. Verbal. "Maybe you can help me?"

Mr. Verbal produces an unfiltered cigarette form his cargo pants pocket. With a sleight of hand, he lights it behind a cupped palm. "Yes?" the merc says, a strange smile in his eyes.

"How the hell do I get back to the thoroughfare? I had a helluva time finding my way here and I know damn well I'm gonna get myself impossibly lost."

Mr. Verbal pulls on his cigarette. Gesticulates with it like he's drawing something in the air. "Ha, you got no fucking idea where the fuck you are?"

"I … don't."

"Idiot. American."

"Huh?"

"Oh, no—no*! I mean no offense!* Just … this is perfect."

"What's perfect?"

"Time for lights out," Mr. Verbal says.

"Wha—"

Burnside does not realize the other guard has slipped his periphery until something blunt and flat strikes him in the back of his head.

Blackness.

THIRTY-SIX

"Mrs. Darius?"

"Yes?"

"I'm here about the live-in nurse position?"

Gretch's mouth opens and shuts, making a *clop* sound.

This girl.

Here?

Now?

I haven't even posted the position yet.

The girl's cornsilk hair catches the light of a trademark Cali sunny day. She stands out on the front step with a colorful, patchwork duffel bag slung over her narrow, birdlike shoulders. She Barely comes up to Gretch's chin. For a moment, Gretch can't help but muse about what her own daughter might have looked like and if this girl standing before her with an expectant expression and easy optimism comes close to what she would have looked like. Her sunbaked skin amplifies the electricity of her blue eyes. Make-up free.

She wears a thin, stitched yellow sweater with the white collars of a button down underneath clawing their way up and out like two shark's teeth folded across her shoulders. A plain charcoal-colored skirt skims her ankles. Gretch realizes she has not seen a skirt of such length since the nun's used to measure her own uniform skirt, terrorizing the girls of Cabrini High School with dark glee.

Had the girl not opened her mouth and stated her business at once, Gretch would have taken her for a door-to-door Bible thumper.

"I'm a little confused—"

Cornsilk Girl's smile widens. "Your neighbor? Lori? She recommended I come and speak with you. I'm a friend of their family. Fresh out of nursing school. She said she was going to call ahead for me."

Maybe you should hold her in the foyer and call Lori to verify—

"She. Didn't. I—come in."

Gretch steps aside, waves her inside. The girl murmurs her thanks. Comes along. Gretch leads her into the kitchen. Something spins out in her stomach. A queer sort of feeling like she is trying to digest a live goldfish.

The moody murk of the poorly lit foyer gives way to a somewhat brighter, if not steely, kitchen area as they climb the shallow stairwell. She pulls a chair out for her at the kitchen table.

The bay window casts a blinding ray of sunshine across the scarred wood of the table. It obscures the facial features of Gretch's guest so the blonde girl's skin shimmers. Eyes flash with fire. Lips could be parted. Could be closed.

"Too bright? I can close the curtains," Gretch moves to do just that.

"No," the girl says, a smile in her voice. "Please. It reminds me of home."

Gretch shrugs.

She takes a drink order.

Cornsilk Girl asks for lemonade. Gretch must think whether she can oblige and remembers she has a lone, slim carton of Minute Maid stowed towards the rear of the fridge's top shelf. She fills a tall glass for her visitor then tops off her mug of coffee she'd let sit on the counter to answer the door.

"So, have you come a long way?"

"Yes," Cornsilk Girl admits. "But I couldn't pass up the opportunity. I hopped on the first flight here."

"And where's home?" Gretch asks, setting the lemonade before her guest and slipping into the seat across from her with a steaming mug of Folgers clasped in one tight fist.

Christ, you haven't even asked her name yet. How about we establish that first, eh?

"Flyover country. Corn country."

Cornsilk.

It's not funny.

"I'm sorry," Gretch says. "I never caught your name."

The girl holds out a hand to shake, fingers turned downward primly. "Pru. Pru Garland. Thank you for seeing me."

Gretch shakes Pru's hand. She can't help but note how spindly and fragile the bones of the girl's hand feels. Like Gretch could roll the hand across her palm, folding it up like a mini accordion. "Thank *you* for making the trip … Pru. Hmm … a unique name. Is it shortened?"

"No, it's not," the girl says, flatly. "Just Pru. It's a family name."

Pru Garland traces her full upper lip with a small, darting tongue. Her gaze dips to the tabletop. It looks as if she has embarrassed herself into silence by speaking so abruptly. Her small hands fall to her hips and smooth her skirt down to her knees. Then, she straightens, and her smile refreshes itself. "Sorry," she utters. "Jetlag, I think?"

"Oh, I'm no stranger to that. I think I've become permanently pinned between two time zones. Very Twilight Zone. I don't miss those days. You start to-I dunno-lose yourself after years of it. Your sense of time and place."

"And time starts to feel like more of a mental construct than trusted reality."

Said the farm girl! Talk about smashing the hick stereotypes!

Pru Garland continues.

"You'll find … well, time is an illusion. It will eventually come to mean little to nothing at all. In the end."

"Nursing degree?" Gretch says, steering the interview out of this unsettling turn of topic.

"Yes."

"Where from?"

Pridefully, Pru's shoulders broaden. "William and Mary."

"Mmm," Gretch muses, wondering to herself if she should skip the due diligence of checking on this claim when the girl comes across as someone who would rather die than lie. "Where is William and Mary?"

"Oh, this is Williamsburg."

"Right, right. I've always had a fondness for Virginia. My father's family is from there. I grew up in southern Arkansas."

"Oh, wow." This seems to genuinely impress the farm girl.

Gretch pauses to hit her mental reset. Lightness and banter aside, she does have questions. The problem is, she hasn't taken time yet to commit them to paper for reference.

Again, I haven't posted the job yet.

And then there's the small matter of verification, Gretchen, you fool—

"I hope you don't mind," Pru Garland says. "I left the folder with my resume in it on the plane. I haven't been able to print a new one. I meant to, but I didn't want to sleep on this opportunity, so I just came—"

"That's fine," Gretch said. "We'll just talk. Is that alright?"

"I'm so embarrassed—"

"Don't be. Please."

Pru nods.

No need for the formal approach. I'm going to wing it. It'll be fine.

After all, Gretch has always prided herself on being able to read people within the first couple minutes of having made their acquaintance.

"Tell me about yourself," Gretch says.

"What would you like to know?"

"Well … what made you choose nursing? Um … tell me about a situation you found challenging and how you overcame this."

Boilerplate interview questions Gretch Solomon has been on both sides of before she broke into the music business.

It goes better than Gretch Solomon could have predicted based on the awkwardness at the front door. Perhaps most surprising for herself, Gretch does not give it a second thought about putting off hiring Pru Garland so she can at least talk to a few more applicants.

Shouldn't I exhaust all options?

No.

No, just ... no. Leave it.

The waifish girl ("with a heart of gold") shrinks with a whimsical bashfulness, confessing she is "secretly a rock and roll fanatic". She had to hide her taste in music from her stereotypically-narrowminded mother and father, but Pru Garland states with a pride that is amusing to Gretch "Louder is my favorite band of all time".

It's silly and Gretch knows it, but she can't help it. When Pru Garland professes her love for Grifters Anonymous's biggest musical rival, she feels a sense of having been slighted on a personal level. *Grifters has always had the edge on Louder. Everyone knows that.*

Still, she can't resist. "What do you think of Grifters Anonymous?"

And this seemingly harmless question sparks the only awkward and decidedly confounding moment of the entire interview.

The best way Gretch can describe it to herself for later consideration would be *a cloud seemed to suddenly come to obstruct her sunny complexion*. A cloud that somehow manages to silence her and stamp her smallish features with an expression of disorientation. The sort of confusion found in the face of a newborn seconds before they utter their first cry.

Pru Garland traces the rim of her empty lemonade glass as this new expression tugs the corners of her eyes and mouth downward.

A deep sadness.

The brooding gaze of a mourner.

"Not a fan," Pru Garland mutters, like one would reveal a childhood molestation. "No."

She knows who I am. Who Stevie is.

Poor kid was probably hoping I wouldn't put her on the spot and ask her.

Pru asks, "How advanced is your husband's illness?"

Contemplating her hands, the roped blue veins and liver spots Gretch swore were not there a season ago, she sighs from the depths. The anti-anxiety pill currently dissolving into her bloodstream dulls her, even at its lowest clinical dose.

"Stevie is in the end-stages now. I refuse to put him in hospice care. Call it stubborn resolve. You can even read a little selfishness in this decision. Lord knows Stevie's doctors have hinted at it. I want him to die at home. It's as simple as that. I don't see why it's so hard for them to understand."

Pru Garland looks on, her face washed out and blank.

"I'm sure your—aunt, is it? —I'm sure she explained how she's been helping me when I needed to step out for errands or just decompress. Lori has been an absolute saint." A pause. "I know we're close to the end. He's practically non-verbal now. The wheelchair is no longer of use to him. He's bedridden.

"His inability to express himself beyond that of moans and groans … it's become a guessing game. I had someone before you who must have been better at translating for him."

"You don't have to explain anything," Pru says, hands folded before her and shoulders squared as if she recognizes she now has the upper hand in the conversation.

"Right," Gretch says in a gasping croak. *"Right-right-*right." She pushes out from the table, reclaims some semblance of a grin, and stands. "Well … that's good. That's fine. You are aware this is a live-in position. You'd have your own room. Unpredictable hours, I'm afraid. But I'll try my best to keep them within reason. I'll be going away for a few days—"

"When will that be?" Pru asks, slinging her bag back over her shoulder and standing.

"As soon as your settled in, Ms. Garland."

"Call me Pru."

"Oh … I—"

"It's just I—I'm relieved. Would that mean I could stay?"

"Stay? As in starting now?

"I don't mean to be presumptuous. If … you'll have me?"

"How about you meet Stevie. And we'll go from there. How would that be?"

Pru Garland says that would be just fine.

When Gretch turns her back on the little blonde, a pair of greenhead flies that had followed the visitor inside earlier rejoin her.

One lands on her right eyeball. Pru opens her mouth wide enough to allow for the other to zip down her throat.

THIRTY-SEVEN

The Pickford House of San Jose, where John "J" Germanian now resides and has for the last year, is one of two residential houses situated on the sprawling hundred-acre estate of Heathwood Mental Hospital. Pickford and its "twin", Hulmeville House, stand side-by-side with one another in the southwestern-most corner of the hospital grounds and seem at such a remove from the main buildings that if Gretch were to have come upon them by themselves she could have very easily mistaken them for historic structures housing members of the wealthiest 1% and their families instead of the psychologically challenged.

The hopeless, and some scattering of hopefuls.

In J's case, the low brought to their lowest point because of repeated suicide attempts.

The Collegiate-Gothic style building, an impressive if not stoic and dated-looking edifice constructed of granite that enfolds two-stories with three white-trimmed gables bursting from the A-framed roof like flinty eyes, does not welcome her. If anything, it's very appearance is a caution in and of itself. Even the quaint carriage house extending from the left-hand side of the residence doesn't warm her like a hearth. The flowerbeds, bursting with all manner of colorful perennials, do not cheer her.

Because her business there is dark.

Gretch is terrified of what J will look like.

None of the rock magazines or newspapers had run a photograph of the horrifically disfigured John Germanian alongside reports of his final and tragically most "successful" suicide attempt. By all reports, made public and privately gathered by Gretch from those in the know, the legendary half of the songwriting duo that included Davey Grifter (and dubbed by the press as the *Twisted Two)*, had slipped into a rapid and seemingly self-orchestrated downward spiral spanning the year and a half following the break-up of Grifters Anonymous.

The music community had expected him to press on, to assemble another band to back him for a solo stint. J himself could carry a tune almost as well as Davey, his voice a higher screech that critics have compared to a manic Stephen Tyler. But the last time the public saw J in a public setting, he'd been busy burning the last remaining bridges that would have allowed for a continuation of his legend and career.

He crashed the '88 Grammys and managed to get onstage during an acceptance speech delivered by a one-hit wonder R & B artist. J turned an otherwise mediocre and forgettable ramble into one of the most infamous self-sabotages in entertainment history. When the smoke cleared and the security had hauled a very drunk and drugged-out J from the stage, it was not before he'd managed to take a proverbial blowtorch to every single record CEO and executive (not excluding their wives) in the audience. He even managed to whip his cock out and piss all over the front row, where Roger Kemmerer of Arista Records and his wife were sitting, staring up at him one minute with widening eyes and the next dodging his yellow stream. He insulted some spouses and propositioned others from the stage to the gasps and behest of the who's who members of the audience.

It is said that security had to treat one of the older record moguls for a heart attack shortly after the tirade.

For all intents and purposes, John Germanian had committed social suicide. An agent who Gretch had once been close with before Stevie's illness went full-blown had told her so: "Not only is his name mud for all fucking time in the record business … he also better watch his ass because there are so many people in cue who want to beat him—some who've actually looked into putting a hit out on the poor bastard—and the guy will never know peace."

Of course, the same brass who cursed the name of J. Germanian raked it in hand over fist when Grifters debut masterpiece *Knives for the People*, enjoyed another 72 weeks in the Billboard Top 10 following the incident.

From there, John Germanian took himself off the street permanently. All dealings, business and otherwise, was conducted by his agent, who'd surprisingly remained even after the Grammy debacle. Gretch suspected the woman hung on because they had been fucking for the latter part of two years and the poor thing had fallen in love with J. This was not impossible to fathom. J was slated to be the first "rock star" to be crowned Sexiest Man Alive by People Magazine.

Until he rendered himself *persona non grata* at the Grammys

This is not common knowledge. The rest of America knows John F. Kennedy Jr. as the Sexiest Man of 1988. The last-minute change had been made from J. to JFK Jr. roughly twenty-four hours after the Grammy incident.

J couldn't have cared less, had he even known he'd been nixed.

Everything after that happened very quickly.

J Germanian slipped into seclusion soon after the incident, broken up only by sporadic statements sent to the press (which consisted mostly of rock and guitar magazines). These statements were the equivalent of alien transmissions from another planet, showing proof of life and at the same time confounding its audience. They were long and rambling. If anyone else had written them they never would have been printed for fear of the publication losing face. They touched upon a myriad of topics, each of them tied to some level and element of the supernatural and the bizarre. They were vague in their wording and syntax, clearly by design.

Not quite press releases.

More like warnings akin to the homeless man pacing a street in Times Square with a sandwich board strapped to him reading THE END IS NEAR. J's loyal and unwavering fan base ate it up. His paranoia was contagious for the few who needed merely a push into insanity.

Warnings:

The state of California will break off and sink into the ocean sooner than anyone thinks. J contends he knows where the start of the tectonic shift and subsequent break will start. A mountain range he does not name but alludes to, along with a possible reason for such a devastating disaster: a failure to recognize and worship the Old Gods.

The Legitimates, as he calls them in these releases.

A sudden sweeping mass aphasia where every human being is stripped of the ability to form coherent, logical words or sentences. And this other plague of sorts is tied to the same cause as the eventual sinking of California into the Pacific Ocean.

The Legitimates demand recognition and allegiance.

In one of his more-unhinged rants, published as part of an op-ed in *Rolling Stone* magazine, J. Germanian railed against all the "creative, unwashed leeches" who live and work in the Golden State. *Who tuck themselves away up high in their mansions and their houses on the fucking bluff, believing they are out of reach. No one is out of reach. Not from the Old Gods. And I'm not either. None of my Grifter brothers. One way or another, we pay.*

Gretch imagines that was around the time J lost his professional reputation, his pretty young agent/ girlfriend fleeing his madness and his own mansion on the hill in Laurel Canyon.

And Gretch wondered if this was not the same condition plaguing J. Germanian as the one that impaired Stevie. The unforgiving, unyielding and sadistic Alzheimer's dementia. And if they shared such a diagnosis, what are the odds it would have affected the other Grifters. If it did, Gretch hadn't heard much.

Then again, she'd also unplugged herself from a good portion of her once bursting social pipeline. She had only been kept abreast of J's downfall because she had struck up an unlikely friendship with his stepmother during a leg of the band's tour, and it held.

Adele Germanian, a soft-spoken and highly intellectual woman who taught elementary school, had seen fit to notify Gretch of the first four suicide attempts her poor son had tried. And Gretch, who had liked J as much as her husband because he'd backed her up in many band votes, felt her heart break a little more each time she heard from Adele. The reports also explained that he'd *turned mean*. "Like a kicked dog," his mother had said, her voice a conspiratorial whisper. "I never hurt John. His father never hurt John. And yet, John insists—and he's threatened to cut us both out of his life—that I molested him and his father safeguarded the abuse. My God, Gretchen, I felt like I'd been punched in the stomach."

Again, this further sold Gretch on the dementia suspicion.

Finally, J was convinced through an intervention to seek in-house help with his crippling delusions and all-consuming depression.

The guitar god lasted twenty-four hours there before quite literally *going over the wall*. He simply could not abide by the mandatory seventy-two-hour rule for those who have gone in for voluntary help. They must remain for that period.

Germanian had other plans. He hitched it back home to his house in Laurel Canyon, tasted the oily gunmetal at the end of a shotgun barrel, and fired it into the roof of his mouth.

It did not kill him, as if by some dark trick effected by a cruel, malicious God. Not unlike the gods he warned everyone about in his press releases, which had all been turned into tongue-in-cheek columns by *Hit Parader* magazine and dubbed "J's Sound Board". They treated these crazy statements as novelties. J was too far gone to realize the magazine that had once hailed him as a Legend Among Legends was making monthly fun of him for all the rock world to see.

The jokes and the mockery ceased for a good month following this last attempt.

After all, the listening public at-large and the brass comprising the recording world were not savages.

No, they waited five weeks.

He hadn't died after all.

Now, the round, motherly black woman in nursing scrubs who greets Gretch at the reception desk to Pickford House sounds like her first-grade elementary school teacher.

"Here to visit, honey?"

Yanking her handbag back up over her shoulder, Gretch is struck by both the gorgeous interior and the smell of varnish mixed with some pungent pasta dish that signals lunch is in-progress. The high shine of the nearby banister adjacent to the front desk bewitches and dazzles Gretch's tired eyes. The floors are hardwood with various tapestry rugs spread across them in strategic spots of high-traffic areas. Runners climb the rises, a rich navy blue. The premonition of a skylight above the stairwell that hovers just clear of her view illuminates the stairwell and digs out the shadows.

"I am," Gretch says, "but I don't have an appointment."

"Is that so?"

"I called the main building. They tried to transfer me three times and hung up on me three times. I had to get to work so I couldn't—"

"That's fine, honey," the nurse, whose name plate reads Lidia, assures her. It almost makes Gretch feel bad in having sold the nurse this lie so well. "What's your name?"

"It's Gretchen Solomon."

"That's fine. Okay, Miss Gretchen. Who are you here to visit with, and we'll take it from there."

Leaning forward conspiratorially without meaning to, Gretch says, "John. Germanian."

The nurse is in the middle of shuffling some papers, searching for sign-in paperwork when she hears the name. It stops her cold. Her eyes land on Gretch, a pair of pinched raisins narrowed with what could read as either suspicion or a wariness. Then it's her turn to lean in like the two of them are now sharing a deliciously depraved secret.

"Alright," Lidia says lacing her hands together primly. "Have you been here to … visit with Johnny before?"

Johnny?

"This would be my first time."

"How do you know Johnny?"

"Er …" Gretch wonders how she had come to not expect these types of questions. Still, she can't help but to wonder if every visitor is required to "state their business" before gaining access to one of the residents there. "We're old friends." She holds back, then decides it's alright to share more. "You know John's history? He was in the band Grifter's—"

Lidia holds up a hand. "I know all about Johnny's celebrity. His fans been flocking to these grounds like it's his final resting place. They want to leave gifts for him. Cigarettes. Bottles of Jack Daniels. Sketches they done of him, some of them very good. One young man wanted to have Johnny sign his prosthetic arm. He kept on about how he was going to be the next Johnny Germanian and all he needed was a *magic signature* on his strumming arm to make it happen. Unfortunately, we couldn't accommodate his request. Johnny is … well, let's just say he has his triggers. And mention of his history with that band … it sets him off.

"And there is also the fact he is very insecure about his appearance."

"Of course," Gretch says, turning her eyes down. She can feel her pulse quicken. "I know about the, um, the attempt."

"*Attempts*, unfortunately."

"Right. I was the band's manager. I married their bass player."

"Honey, you'll have to forgive me. I'm not really one for the rock and roll. Gospel's more my speed."

"Oh, no need to explain."

"I got no doubt Johnny's talented. But that's over now. He's in his end-stages. His injuries have cut down his life-expectancy significantly. We look only to keep him comfortable." The nurse pauses, continues with a smirk. "Of course, Johnny seems to have no problem with giving us daily stress. I've taken the time to talk with him. Try to understand him, so I can ingratiate myself towards him. But Johnny abuses the staff on the regular. The only reason he's been allowed to stay on here until the end of his life is because money talks. And the bill gets paid every month without fail."

"Now, you said you took time to understand him. What do you mean?"

Nurse Lidia raises an eyebrow. Hesitates. "Mm … you sound like a reporter sniffing around."

"No, no. That is most certainly not the case."

"Because I'm not going to dish on Johnny to a damned reporter—"

"I only wanted to see him and to speak to him before he passes. I know about his condition."

"Honey, you *can't know* his condition until you lay eyes on him."

"I know."

"It'll break your heart. Make you wonder just what in the hell drove him to it. He seems to believe he's done horrendous things, and he deserves to die. He suspects—and I don't condone this kind of thinking—that some power out there actually *drove the bullet* in such a way that it *would not kill him*. Says this is part of his punishment. *This. Life.*"

The two women slip into a precarious silence that is ended with one of the residents sidling up beside Gretch at the front desk with a broad smile and her chin in her hands like they are slipping up along-side her at a bar. The woman is small and smiley and reminds Gretch instantly of home and a girl with cornsilk hair and an aversion to Grifters Anonymous.

Lidia pushes out from her desk and stands. She is short, her body tightly compacted inside a set of navy-blue scrubs. The girl at Gretch's elbow skirts around the welcome desk and flings her seemingly over-long arms around Lidia with such excitement one would have mistaken them for long lost friends.

"All right, Inga," Lidia says, wincing and trying to conceal it. "I have to escort this nice young lady to visit with a friend upstairs. You go get back to crafts. I'm sure Nurse Holly'll be missing you. Alright now?"

Her brow creased with patience and an infinite grace, Lidia grace-fully peels the girl off, who goes skipping off into the next room.

Lidia moves towards the stairwell. "There goes the president of my fan club," she says. "Shall we?"

No. No. Turn back around.

Run.

But Gretch's mouth says, "Lead the way."

J GERMANIAN IS NOT PREPARED FOR visitors just yet.

"He's sleeping," Lidia reports, after ducking her head into the dark-ened room. "I'll hurry him along. He sleeps too damn much."

She waves Gretch over to a nearby upholstered bench.

Behind the closed door, Gretch thinks she hears a grumbling animal rather than a human being. She hears Lidia engaging in conversation (or what passes for such) with Germanian. Lidia seems to understand everything he is saying in his slushy, vowel-heavy drawl.

J's voice kicks Gretch's imagination into overdrive.

What must he look like to have now been reduced to such grunts and growls.

Specifically, his mouth—

Stop!

Just.

Stop!

It will be hard to mask her shock.

At one point, J. let's loose with a part-panicked, part-irritated shriek that calls the fine hairs on Gretch's arms to attention.

Lidia's voice cuts through J.'s cries, her tone patient but pointed. "You got to wear your pants, too. There's a lady here to visit with you. Bad enough I got to see all of you every day. I'm a married woman, Johnny. You know?"

And there is a strong compulsion to abort this mission. Gretch can feel her calves jumping under the skin. Trying to lift her into a standing position. To move her down the hall. Down the stairs. Out the front door, biting back a scream that presses at the seal of her lips.

Winded, Lidia emerges. "He's decent. Come along."

"Was that … him I heard?"

"Yes, honey. He's non-verbal, for the most part. I force him to talk. To challenge him so he doesn't turn completely mute. But he won't talk to you. He won't even try. You'll be communicating with him using a notepad. Got one right in there we use. Tacked to the footboard of his bed." She pauses, studies Gretch with narrowing eyes. "You gonna be alright, Miss Gretchen?"

"Yes, it's just … I have memories of John. I remember him a certain way."

"You gotta let go of that. He's not that man anymore."

"Who is he now?"

"He's turned mean, Miss Gretchen," Nurse Lidia admits, tossing up her hands. "And something tells me he was not always this way.

Otherwise, I don't know that you'd be here to see him. You're the only proof I seen that he used to be anything *but* mean."

"I'm the only visitor he's ever had?"

"You are."

Lidia opens the door and leads Gretch in. A single bedside lamp glows softly and casts a shallow ring. A larger spill of natural light filters through a square of window sheers. It casts the wheelchair-bound figure parked there into a bulky silhouette of combined hard and soft edges.

John Germanian's knobby shoulder blades stick up above the back of the chair's seat like tent poles. His long hair is either gone or thread-bare enough to escape immediate detection. His posture cants to the left arm rail where he lays his head into an upturned palm like he's trying to sleep sitting up. Something Gretch imagines he's probably had to do once or twice since his *accident*.

He shifts ever so slightly in the chair and the shadows shift. The light finds the top of his skull, and it shows Gretch something she is not ready for.

A thin patch of gray, moss-like hair is combed across what is clearly a bowled-out portion in the top of his skull. The thin strands cover the hole in his skull like a set trap of leaves spread across a dug-out hole in the middle of the forest.

Oh. God.

"Oh … no …" Gretch gasps. She turns to find Lidia standing beside her, a look of commiseration in her big brown eyes.

"Would you like me to stay?" Lidia whispers.

It is like the nurse has lapsed into a foreign language. It takes some time for Gretch to understand.

When she finally does, it feels like the hardest question she's ever had to answer in a long time.

She touches Lidia's shoulder, says,

"No. No, I'll be fine. Thank you."

Lidia tells her she'll be right outside if there is any problem and slips out.

Get.

It.

Together.

Gretch squares her shoulders; her breaths are slow and deep. She moves deeper into the room. It's evident the nurse has just spritzed Germanian with some kind of aftershave. The strong, pleasing scent hangs in the air and tickles her nostrils. As Gretch moves closer, the body odor that Nurse Lidia had tried to mask with the spray overrides the pleasant scent and nearly nullifies its effect.

"Hello, John," she says.

THIRTY-EIGHT

A chair has been pulled back from a simple round table. A small house of cards stands amidst a scattering of other player cards. The remnants of other attempted houses that have collapsed. One remains like a tenement in the rubble of a Bicycle card apocalypse. And a dreadful thought traipses through Gretch's mind as she lowers herself down onto the chair arranged a few feet from the wheelchair-bound figure with his head in his hands.

What will he do if the last house of cards collapses while I'm here?

Will he hurt me?

Stop.

"It's Gretch."

Nothing.

"Solomon."

In profile now, the disfigurement is made plain enough to steal her breath. He lifts his head and considers the sheers before him, fuzzing his view of the miniature labyrinth of bushes in the courtyard below. Lidia has already given him the notepad he will use to communicate with her.

He is dressed in a long-sleeved Great White band t-shirt, showing a pretty blonde's face with a backdrop that features a shark fin slicing through a body of water like a razor blade. This single, solitary touch of the familiar, as Great White has always been one of Gretch's favorite sleaze rock acts, is muted by the rest of John Germanian.

Gretch tries to spot the previous in the present.

Impossible.

The young guitar player she once shared a bottle of Jameson with and laughed for twenty straight minutes with when Bobby had not only split his leather pants down the middle backstage, but that he'd also shit himself.

"John?"

Angry red scars wind around the crown of his skull. Ghosts of the seemingly endless string of stitches that had been sewn into his ruined scalp to hold it together after whatever reconstructive efforts had been made. His face is almost entirely man-made. There is none of the gentle slope of his brow or the divots of his high Armenian cheekbones. The crudeness of man's attempts to ape God's brilliant design are made plain in his face. His brow and the lower half of his face look like a pair of glazed donuts piled on top of one another and pinned together. They hold a sickening shine as if to betray the plastic they are made of. No eyebrows. Eyes that used to hold a woman's stare without much effort at all. Once green as emeralds. Now, they are black raisins that look as if they've been pressed into dough. His nose is serpentine, reduced to twin holes that look like watermelon seeds. And his mouth is a sickening, twisted mound of flesh with a scattering of teeth stuck into it in no discernible pattern.

"Can I speak with you? I've come a long way."

He cranes his neck in her direction. Somehow this turns his deformity into something far worse.

His upper body shudders like a car that won't start in the middle of winter.

Then his body, like the car, starts up and fires on all cylinders as his hands jump into manic, twitchy motion. He positions the clipboard containing the notepad across his lap. His writing hand skids back and forth across the page, scrawling out a message with a fat Sharpie.

His breathing quickens.

He flings the clipboard at her.

He mutters something that is more a grunt than a word. His tongue, a thin sliver of flesh, traces a wet line across his slanted, too-fleshy bottom lip.

He wrote: *"You came a long way just to rubberneck! What did you expect to see?"*

"I-I don't know what I expected. I mean, I heard you tried to … to end your life … but you didn't …"

He snaps his fingers at her. It takes her a moment to realize he needs the clipboard back. She returns it to him.

His hand falls to writing at once. All the while, Germanian's mangled tongue and palate and spare teeth sound out every word. The sound is horrid and slushy.

"Not allowed to die. She pulled his strings. He stuck those long white fucking fingers of his into our brains and he fiddled and fucked around so we'd only get to remember just scraps of what we did on The Mountain. Things went all to shit when we broke the terms. He must've done something to my brain to make me suicidal. Installed some kind of self-destruct switch in all of us. Poppa Royal knew-knew-knew we'd get ourselves in trouble. And he brought us there anyway. Wanted a return on his investment."

Germanian's burst of words paralyze her. She hasn't even started asking her questions yet. The answers seem to have been waiting on the tip of the rock god's fleshy, roving tongue. All this time.

"I don't understand, John. Help me to understand. Please!"

Germanian sits there with the clipboard in his lap, suddenly stalled out. His slivery lips mesh. When they separate, it is with a suctioning sound that causes Gretch's stomach to lurch.

Then, J stabs the Sharpie down with such force Gretch hears the paper rip.

"The rehab a front for a cult. They worship the God of the Mountain. The Muse. Calliope. That's Her. Through Stanislaw, the leader, She infuses the 'worthy' with this fucking divine inspiration. Turns even the most mediocre artists__which is all Grifters ever really was—into what we became. Royal knew this. Let us believe he was taking us somewhere to get clean. He must

have gotten so sick of fronting us for money. We were a drag on him. I know he did it for his son. Guy would do anything for Bobby. But at the end of the day, Nolan Royal's still a businessman. He needed us to show some kind of value. Some progress. A return—"

"On the bastard's investment," Gretch says, seeing red. "I get it. You said you—one of you or all of you, for all I know—got into trouble?"

-

"Take a wild fucking guess. You already know."
She does. "Chris. *Asshole* Chris Desmond."

...

"He got into it with the leader. Chrissy just couldn't control that libido of his. Thinks the rules don't apply. He hit on the intake coordinator there, who turned out to be someone important to the leader-guy. Stanislaw. Thought she was his daughter. Come to find out he was one of the fucker's sister wives. So, he and Chris got physical and the guy bested Chris. Embarrassed him. Chris couldn't let this go.

"There was this walk-in hearth in the main hall. Place was built like a ski resort. Probably was before it was repurposed by the cult. They had a strict policy in force that only the staff—staff, yeah right, more like followers— could tend to the fire. There was a posted sign and everything. Hands off. Chris saw this as a challenge and his chance to stick it up Stanislaw's ass. After we all went down for the night, he snuck to the main hall, and he put out the fire. Then, he pissed all over the inside of the hearth.

Gretch's brow furrowed. "That's it? Christ, that's what started all this goddam *madness?*"

...

"No, but it's what turned what would have been a gift into both a blessing and a curse. See, Royal arranged with Stanislaw to impart his gift of inspiration onto the five of us. Nothing beyond that. Poppa Royal padded the cult's money source to keep the leader honest. But when Chrissy did what he did— not knowing what in the fuck he was doing when he fucked with that fire— the terms changed. They were turned on their head. Perverted. Chris had incensed the Muse. The worst insult. And She pushed Stanislaw into doing what he did to us.

"And we were blessed, as promised. It all happened very fast for us when

we got back from that place. Stanislaw, he fucked with our wiring. I swear to you I can remember it now. How it felt to have his hand *inside my fucking my brain. Changing it. Every poke and prod and manipulation. He cursed us. The trick. The underside of the Faustian Bargain."*

A door inside of Gretch's mind swings wide on rusted hinges. She wonders how long it has been shut to her, then realizes what should have been obvious. The shock therapy had targeted this portion of her memory. It had welded this door shut. And this is what it had taken to pry it open again.

You're here because Stevie wrote a memoir. Confessing to serial murder alongside the other Grifter guys.

"Oh … God," she gasps, hand flying to her mouth.

J flips to the next clean page and drops the Sharpie down once more, the marker squeaking against the paper now as it starts to run dry.

"That fire. The hearth? It was a barrier. To temper the power of The Muse in the Mountain. The power She wields is so intense and powerful it is too much for the human mind to handle without some sort of padding. Muting. The fire did that. It also protected The Muse from the outside world. Any interlopers looking to enter The Mountain. To petition Her personally. The fire was symbolic of a truce between The Muse and Stanislaw and his follow- ers. When Chris did what he did, he threw it all into a flux. He touched off a war. And we paid the price.

"You see the price I've paid for Chris's revenge?"

J's writing hand stops.

Gretch's mind is suddenly awash in several different thoughts and emotions, many at odds with one another.

He's a murderer. It's just, he should suffer.

Don't give J Germanian any sense of commiseration.

"Bobby's father brought all of you into this with his eyes wide open. He knew the risks."

Before she even finishes talking, J falls to his pad with the marker:

"We all watched the way that motherfucker fawned over Stanislaw when we first got there. It was the kind of hero worship you see between an eight- year-old and a ball player. You stand him in front of me right now and I'd rip

his flesh from the bones. It'd be the only spilled blood that wouldn't haunt me!"

"I was informed Nolan Royal is dead."

…

"I haven't seen him since The Mountain. He cut ties with us soon after. There is one thing I never really understood. He was there when we really started to catch on. Not in body, of course. He kept across the pond. But he was still our manager when a crowd of a hundred people crammed into the Roxy started to sing along to our songs. Our songs. He knew things were starting to happen and he was about to reap.

"He still cut us loose. Gretch, you don't want him. He's a small fish when it comes to this. What are you after?"

She'd never had any dealings with Bobby Royal's father. Never knew he was their manager before she came along. The Grifter guys never mentioned him. Nothing. Now, it all makes perfect sense to her how and why they would have chosen to excise him entirely from their backstory.

"I want to put an end to it all," Gretch says. "If Nolan Royal knew about this place. What Stanislaw could do for any artist who found their way to his rehab? Then God knows how many more there are like the five of you. Out there. Cursed. Blessed? Whatever you want to call it. Everybody dreams of being a rock star and living that life at least once in their life. I'm right, aren't I? You're not the first artists to visit Stanislaw in the hopes of being *blessed*."

J's black, raisin eyes disclose nothing. He hesitates, then starts to write.

She sees he is writing a list.

When he hands it over to her, Gretch Solomon can't help but feel like the earth has shift beneath her. The world as she has come to understand it now defies all expectations.

The names J Germanian has written down in his cramped handwriting is a who's who of fifteen visual artists, writers, and musicians she had grown up worshipping along with the rest of civilization:

Wyeth; Hendrix; Warhol; London; Basquiat; Hemingway; Morrison; Rockwell—

"John," she says, eyes wide and jaw stiff, "what the *fuck* is this?"

Adamantly, the doomed rockstar reaches out and jabs his index finger down upon the page, nearly knocking it out of her lap. She reads it as a *doubling-down* on what he's just revealed to her.

"They've all been to see Stanislaw?"

J grunts, his bottom lip pulling upward to overlap the upper.

"Their lives are spread across an entire century, John. There's no way this is true. Not unless Stanislaw has been around for a *very* long time—"

J doesn't go for the tablet. His mouth working and eyes suddenly darting this way and that, he manages, *"Wunninnaline-wunninna ..."*

"John, I-I want to understand," Gretch says, stuffing her revulsion down at having to watch him produce a wet slew of mashed-together words.

He starts to rock back and forth in his chair. *"Wunninnaline-ennaline-ennaline—"*

"Alright, alright, John. If you could just slow down the words. I've almost got it."

J snorts, derisively.

"Wunn ...inna ... line."

"One ... one? Inna. In. A. In a line? One in a line? Is that right?"

He grunts and stops rocking in his chair.

The bedroom door swings open, and Lidia pokes her head in. Her big brown eyes land on Gretch with the weight of accusation. "Everything alright in here, Johnny? Miss Gretch?"

Before Gretch realizes what she's doing, she reaches out and covers his hand in hers. She smiles at Lidia, but it is a winsome grin like one brought about amidst great pain. "Yes, he got a little excited. But I was able to calm him down."

Lidia transfers her gaze to the back of J's head. "Johnny? You good?"

Another grunt, along with a stilted forward nod.

Lidia retreats and closes the door.

"So, you said 'one in a line'," Gretch continues, without removing her hand from his. The tightness of his overhand, stitched in a webwork of jutting veins, feels as strong and toned as it had been when he'd exercised the hell out of it on a nightly basis for shows that reached three-hundred-sixty in a row the first year. "Do you mean Stanislaw? He's the *one in a line.*"

A nod.

A question bubbles to the surface of her consciousness. It shocks her. A shard of memory returning to her. A jagged memory. It steals her breath.

Ask him.

Only then can we move from there.

"You and the other Grifters … were you … killing people? Was that the *underside of the Faustian bargain?*"

J Germanian turns to look at her head-on. The destruction of what had once been, by all accounts, one of the most perfect faces in the history of rock and roll, is so offensive to her eyes she wishes a dagger were handy so she could scoop out her eyes.

Gretch flinches when his hands swallow her own.

Squeeze.

Once for *Yes.*

For a few minutes, they sit silently in one another's company. She is still reeling from the piece of memory that has come back to roost in her mind. *In the memoir, Stevie made his confession. They murdered close to twenty-two people as a band before flaming out. That's what triggered your breakdown and landed you in the hospital. It was just too fucking much!*

The doctor from the hospital who'd suggested the electric-shock treatment had told her the memories she had had expunged from her long-term memory would not stay gone, They would occur to her again over time. He'd described her memories as birds who'd fled a power line for fear of a passing truck, only to light back on the hanging wire-one, then another, and another- until they had all come back.

She chose to see them as shards breaking away from various frozen and dormant portions of her memory. Returning to her.

Now you know. So, what the fuck are you going to do about it?

Gretch feels a heat rising in her blood.

"I'm going to put an end to it, John."

She hesitates, then remembers he's non-verbal and this is not something Lidia will ever take seriously anyhow should he share the contents of their conversation with her.

"You've got your pad there. I need to you point me in the right direction. Where is The Mountain? The rehab. What state? Landmarks? Nearest town? Anything. You get me there, John, and I'll do my very best to find Stanislaw. And if he's still breathing, I'll kill him."

J IS bent to the act of weeping. The jagged sticks of his shoulder blades jump with every stilted sob.

"Your Nurse Lidia won't wait outside much longer. She worries about you. Protective of you."

Gretch rises, turns to the window. She peers through the sheers. A little old woman in a sun hat moves among a humble but lovely garden of stone landscaping and thriving flowers. She pushes a small, empty wheelbarrow, maneuvering it through the simple labyrinth formed by the stonework.

A small smile touches Gretch's lips at the sound of a Sharpie marker scribbling on a Legal pad.

Wonderful.

The door to J. Germanian's bedroom opens.

Nurse Lidia slips inside.

J shoves a folded piece of paper into Gretch's hand. Folds her fingers over it.

Gretch shoves it deep down into her pants pocket.

"We should probably wrap it up, Miss Gretchen? They're missing J at supper."

"Of course," Gretch says. "Goodbye, John."

She touches his arm.

Heart thumping between her ears, Gretch follows Lidia out.

By the time she is shown her way out the front door to The Pickford House of San Jose, Gretch can contain herself no longer.

Slipping into the shadow of a nearby elm tree, she retrieves the folded piece of paper.

Two words in the center of the page and pressed so hard into the paper every letter is not so much written as engraved.

GIVE UP

She's just about to curse J Germanian seven ways to Sunday when Gretch flips the page over.

Sees the entire page is filled from top to bottom margin with drawings and bullet pointed words.

Coordinates.

Mini maps.

"Atta' boy, J."

INTERLUDE (V)

(From the Memoirs of Stevie Darius)

1987

Our first record, Knives for the People, *almost didn't happen.*

We brought twenty-one songs to the table for evaluation by the time Grifters sat down with Gretch Solomon, our manager/ producer, and a coke-nose-face-numbed genius named Jam Taggart. Jam had this thing about everyone in the band being in studio, whether it was time to lay down their part or not yet. Gretch corralled us into the control booth like drunken cats at 6 every morning, to oblige the engineer. Taggart never said why, and we never complained (at least, not to him). We were just happy to have found the fucking guy.

Him and Gretch Solomon both.

Because nobody wanted to work with us.

We were who we were, but that didn't mean other folks in the business had to put up with it. Starting fights with strangers. Springing cruel and unusual stunts on the competition of The Strip. Nothing was taboo when it came to our sexual exploits either, and we delved into everything from gang bangs to triplet cum parties.

Chris even came up with the idea to float a rumor out into the circuit that we killed someone, if you can digest that dark irony.

The way he explained it, if we were cursed and doomed to murder, we may as well make it work for our image. The rest of us were so taken aback by such a dangerous, reckless suggestion that J shut it down without even putting it to a band vote. He must've known we were with him on that.

Then, as it became more evident no one was coming to arrest or even question us, we started to warm to Chris' suggestion. To this day, I have no idea how we got away with it all. It started to feel like we were under some kind of supernatural umbrella of protection, shielding us from accountability of any kind.

It was exhilarating as much as it was unsettling.

Was it Stanislaw?

The Muse?

No way of knowing.

So we parsed out bits and pieces of the rumor until it founds its own legs and made the rounds.

It became the most notorious unanswered question ever to float around The Strip since Syd Vicious murdered his junkie girlfriend, Nancy. Did he or didn't he?

The record companies had no idea what to make of us once this rumor hit their ears.

*Rather than put themselves into the position of ever having to ask the mother of all uncomfortable questions (*Are you guys ... or no?*), they shunned Grifters.*

No one wanted to touch us.

Until one brave soul just fucking stepped forward and pulled the sword from the stone.

Gretch Solomon started out booking bands at The Continental House, then graduated to The Strip at large as a talent scout for all the major clubs. She pushed the bands she believed in most (a meager sum of acts) to the reps that showed up to tap their loafers on the beer-stained floor of the clubs and check their Rolexes every two minutes.

Gretch was and continues to be a force of nature.

We made inroads with her right before Atlas Records snatched her up, put her in a big corner office, and appointed her chief talent scout for the label.

She eats, sleeps, and dreams of rock and roll. Her instincts are prophetic and mystifying, like someone skilled in the art of reading tea leaves. Gretch wanted to be the female Clive Davis, aging guru of raw talent who headed up RCA Records.

She might have done it if things had gone differently. I'm not just saying that because I'm the one that ended up putting a ring on it and marrying the self-professed "perpetual bachelorette".

I'm clearly biased when it comes to Gretch. She's my blind spot.

Still, I stand by this bold claim; she could have unseated King Clive.

Grifters was one of the bands Gretch Solomon championed over the other hundreds of other acts in LA. Word of our difficulties in securing management had gotten back to her. Gretch was never one to shy away from a challenge, to dodge pending calamity or wait for the net to appear before diving off that cliff. If anything, Gretch preferred all these elements well in place before she even picked up the phone on behalf of a band. Call it sadomasochism? Visionary?

So, we took a meeting with Gretch at Rainbow. A lunch that consisted of free-flowing alcohol and fried food spun into the liquid mix.

We proceeded to conduct ourselves like the gang we'd been painted as. We embraced the degradation. The band with the wheels that can come off at any given moment. But it's important you understand we were just being ourselves. There was no affect to be had. There was no need for it. We liked to fucking fight. We liked to argue. We liked to intimidate and philander and use and lady-lay and mainline and put our boots up on the table in a five-star restaurant. We liked our sunglasses because our eyes were impossibly and perpetually bloodshot, our pupils either dilated or fucking pinned. And it all started happening around us.

Without changing us.

Were we insufferable assholes?

A thousand times yes.

Gretch knew her way in. At that lunch, she led with the following, which I'll never forget. Sticks in my mind like a filthy joke your uncle told you when you were five:

"The five of you are so full of shit. Don't think I don't know that, boys. You're a bunch of pussycats. Great gimmick, though. You've done a bang-up job marketing yourselves ... and managing to creep out every rep working in

the industry. But I don't scare so easily. And my bullshit detector is well-calibrated."

It was Chris who tried to counter Gretch, unaware he was well out of his league. "We can, you know, neither confirm nor deny-"

"Are you dangerous?" Gretch continued, neutering poor Chris. "Depends on who you ask. If you ask me? I'd say no. In fact, I think I could take any one of you if I had to. So, J? Take your boots off the table so the waitress can bring us some onion rings and has somewhere to set them down. Chris? Wake up. This is the only lunch we're going to have together, and I'm only going to say my thing once, so you don't want to sleep through it. And Davey? Don't bother looking at me like that. It's not going to work. My panties are just as dry as they were when I walked in. I'm not going to fuck you. Not any of you. I don't buy what you're selling, but that doesn't mean I don't fucking love the hell out of it. And all that matters, really, is the Atlas Records brass? They fucking love the ruse. They believe you guys are dangerous."

"You don't get it," J said, after taking his boots off the table like a good boy. "What you see is what you get with us. The rumors? They're not from us. The Strip draws its own conclusions."

"You do anything to discourage that kind of word-of-mouth, John?"

Gretch is the only one outside of J's mother who has ever gotten away with calling him John. He never called her on it.

J smiled. "What do you think?"

"Good," Gretch said. "Because you'd be a genuine dipshit to do so. You rode that wave of speculation all the way to this table. This moment." She paused. "And I know what you're going to say, Davey. What about the music? I think your songs are the equivalent of holding a switchblade to the audience's throats. Your slower numbers? First time I heard "Run to Me, Run from Me", I could barely catch my breath. Make no mistake, guys. I'm a fan, first and foremost. I'll pull out all the stops. I'll call in all the favors. I'll put you onstage all over The Big Apple until either the east coast or the west comes through with the right numbers and accommodations. Now, you gotta let me know right now. Are you ready to be managed? And I don't mean mothered. Managed."

Bobby gargled his scotch. It ran out the sides of his mouth. Chris hammered him on the back. "Gonna need another couple fingers in my glass ... Mama."

We all fully expected Gretch to get up and walk out in a huff. What Bobby had done was a test. A push back. A small example of the power struggles to come, no matter what promises we made at that booth in The Rainbow.

The push-back wouldn't come from Bobby, though. Not for the long haul. No, that would come almost exclusively from Davey. He was the lone holdout when it came to take a band vote about whether to sign with her.

As far as we all knew, this obstinance was borne of the fact Gretch Solomon called Davey out for bringing Glory there that day.

To a business meeting.

"Honey," she'd said to the President of our fan club and Davey's wife-or property-depending on how you chose to see their relationship, "you can better serve all of us if you just went and stood out front. Kept the meter fed so nobody gets a ticket."

Davey had opened his mouth to protest and slammed the flat of his palm down on the table. "Who the fuck do you —"

Right then, J laid his hand on Davey's shoulder, staying the impending tongue-lashing.

Gretch didn't miss a beat. She called a waitress over and ordered another round of whatever the five of us were drinking. And that inscrutable look on her face never dampened or faded in the slightest.

From then on, the blood was bad and black between Davey Grifter and Gretch Solomon, immoveable object and unstoppable force, respectively.

That wasn't the moment I fell for Gretchen Solomon, but it was the thing that made me sit up and take closer notice of her.

The moment of perfect clarity about Gretch would come a year later while we were in Japan touring for Knives for the People. *The big promoter there is called Mr. Sato. It's rumored he used the influence of Yakuza muscle to climb so high so quickly. You don't ask questions when it comes to some things. Even Grifters know that. Gretch had laid down the law before we even got on the plane bound for Tokyo:*

"You do not fuck around in Sato country. He'll start out as your best friend the moment you get off the plane. From there, you'll either turn him into a dangerous force of nature or your greatest international ally."

I think Davey might have scoffed at the words "Sato Country", and I nudged him. You don't nudge Davey. He feels a certain way, there's no changing it. Unless you're Gretch. There was a time J could have knocked

Davey down a few notches when he got too big for his britches. Then, it was what we all paid Gretch to handle. And handle she did. She stepped up to him, and it was nearly a battle royale right there on the tarmac.

Gretchen Solomon is half Swede, half Jewish. Straight long, ginger hair parted down the middle. Big green eyes that look almost too big for her face and full lips that barely hide the sexiest overbite. Gretchen stands five-eight. She did her time on the beauty pageant circuit as a kid in the Bible Belt until the first time she had her first listen to Led Zeppelin's "Physical Graffiti". From that moment on, it was goodbye tiaras and hello bell bottoms, a Business Degree at Southern Arkansas University (financed by her extensive winnings from those damned competitions), and a fanatical passion for rock and roll with all its trappings. Men learned quickly not to take Gretch at face-value, or to mistake her for a vapid groupie to be taken advantage of.

I almost felt sorry for Davey whenever he got into it with her. It was like he always seemed to hope against all hope he'd leverage with his celebrity and the rapidly burgeoning attitude that he was the guy, you know? The flight crew must have been on standby for a half hour while Davey and Gretchen traded barbs and threats. He wanted to cut her out right then and there. He wanted to quit. Pulled out all the predictable stops, but Gretchen called his bluff on all of them. Brushed him back until finally Davey stormed off to board the plane, a mist of profanities hanging in the air behind him.

None of us said it. We never needed to. But every one of us were thankful to have finally found somebody to humble Davey Grifter.

Later, I'd come to find out Davey had tried to fuck her a handful of times and she'd laughed at him. One time, and this is coming from J, she even patted him on the head like a dog.

We'd racked up several bodies by this time. Sure, we'd disposed of them as well as we could. We got better at this step, come to think of it. And, yes, we chose a specific, seemingly expendable portion of the population.

The Grifter Code.

Every murder a Grifter committed had to be sanctioned by the rest of the band or it was a no go. We weighed the risk against the need. If our career was going well and the songs were coming at a rapid pace and the demo was selling and there was a steady parade of cooze to fill our laps, we left off with the bloodshed. Life-taking was employed only as necessity seemed to dictate. If the Grifters felt a slump in creativity or we suffered a string of bad shows or we botched an interview and turned some influential rock journalist against us and our cause, we'd have a meeting behind closed (and bolted) doors. And we'd vote yay or nay on a new "hunt".

We held firmly to the practice of hunting runaways, junkies, and the homeless. The disposable wads of society with no connection to family or lifelines of any kind. Disgusting, I know. And it was just as well.

The palsy in our hands that preceded the murders before had faded to nothing.

We had become conditioned.

We injected democratic rule into the vilest of human endeavors.

And somehow, we had convinced ourselves what we were doing was less sinister because of this fucking ideological set of standards and code of conduct.

It was Davey and Chris' bloodlust that made the sanctioning of every murder necessary.

It was the look that stole across their eyes at certain times when the band would be out and about. Circulating around the Strip. Holding court in a booth at one of the clubs.

Their expressions changed. Like a shadow on the sun.

Their faces darkened, eyes blinkless and hyper-focused. On some prey in their midst.

I noticed it first. He knew exactly what it was. Maybe he'd experienced it too but managed to tamp it down.

Davey and Chris are not disciplined when it comes to impulse control.

I believe the two of them were born without that part of their brains.

As well as the portion that houses empathy.

That day, on the tarmac, with Gretch and Davey? I swear I saw that shadow move across his face while he was arguing with her.

I knew I'd kill him before he'd ever lay a hand on her.

Grifters be damned.

That was the moment I knew I loved her.

When I knew I wanted Gretchen. Needed Gretchen.

Love.

Love's what did it.

My interests broke from those of the band.

My motivation turned selfish and self-serving.

I was as mystified by this sudden shift as I was relieved.

Gretchen was smart and in-charge. She didn't invite me into her bed when the band was thrown out of The Burroughs, a posh neighborhood five miles north of San Fran. Atlas Records had put us up there while we recorded the Knives LP at Studio Hive which was only a few miles away. If we were too drunk to drive there, we could walk. Atlas and Gretch and Jam Taggart, the engineer, mutually agreed this was the best arrangement for a band as unpredictable (and undependable) as Grifters. What they didn't plan on or take into consideration was that we got bored faster than your average group. And too much boredom always led to bad behavior, sadly.

The rented baby grand Davey had to have. The baby grand Bobby set on fire in the middle of the night just to see if piano wire was flammable. We awoke to the living room in flames and Bobby and Chris struggling to open the floor-to-ceiling glass doors wide enough so they could roll the flaming piano out onto the back porch. Into the waiting in-ground pool. It turned into a group effort. We were fuckups. But when it came down to survival, somehow Grifters united in a common cause and just barely avoided total annihilation. Three of us wrestled the doors opened wide as we could and dumped the piano in the drink. The other two managed to put the fire out, but not before three of the four walls and a good bit of the hardwood floor in the living room was scorched and stained with livid black scars.

We got three things out of the incident:

First, a steep bill to cover the damage to the house, which Atlas made us split five ways.

Second, a song Davey and J composed in an hour called "Brain on Fire". Originally titled "Baby on Fire", until I had to explain the implications of such an on-the-nose title. It would bump off the B-side crowd favorite "Grain" from the final track listing for Knives at the last minute. J sulked about this for a little bit because "Grain" was his baby, a testament song to his love for grain alcohol and moonshine.

Third, Gretchen had no choice but to take the five of us in for the remainder of the Knives sessions.

Three months.

She put up with five fucking sloppy assholes without killing one of us or herself. Her apartment was not nearly big enough to house six people. Not to mention, the steady flow of visitors in and out of Gretchen's place at all hours of the day and night plagued her with a vicious bout of insomnia.

She couldn't sleep soundly because the people in and out of her home were admittedly the scum of the earth. Drug buddies. Prostitutes. Dealers. Enablers. Obsessive fans. Mental patients. The kind of people who usually made it into our dead pool so to speak. And, unfortunately, the same type of people who'd rob Gretchen blind in the night if she dared try for a good a night's sleep.

I still feel like a shit for what we put her through for the three months we crashed there.

Atlas Records had it with us.

We finished mixing and mastering Knives for the People *on June 26, 1987.*
Twelve songs.
Confessions, a couple of them.
No one listened. Really heard. You know what I mean?
Don't misunderstand.
The liner notes tell a story no one wanted to acknowledge for some reason:

Knives for the People, 1987
    1) Walk the Cracked Sidewalk
    2) Dusty Starlight
    3) So Sick at Heart
    4) Run to Me, Run from Me
    5) L/A
    6) Bigger Badder Faster More
    7) Bury Your Dead
    8) Good Girl Blues
    9) Take Me There
    10) Hollywood ('s) High
    11) Brain on Fire
    12) Knives for the People

Track 1, "Walk the Cracked Sidewalk". A blistering, furious rock number in the vein of Sex Pistol's "Holidays in the Sun", only more nuanced by guitar riff shades of light and dark. The title comes from something Glory, the leader of the Massengill Army, once told Davey. It was something to the effect that she hates her mother so much she always makes sure to walk on the cracked parts of the sidewalk in downtown LA in the hopes of breaking her back. "Thing is," she said, "the sidewalks are in such shitty shape, I could break my mother's back and then some. I could break everyone's backs in the whole wide world if I wanted to. The sidewalks are in such shitty condition all over the city."

Track 3, "So Sick at Heart". A mantra for our dearly departed Lovebug, who said it so often in the short time she spent with us we thought it was a tic or something. Turns out, it's a line from Shakespeare's "Macbeth". It's a sick feeling of guilt and regret and isolation. No doubt Lovebug was damaged by the time we got to her. But she was also a creative force, a lover of the arts if she picked up such an obscure quote from a Shakespeare play she probably read Sophomore year of high school.

Track 4, "Run to Me, Run from Me" ought to be the anthem for people with Borderline Personality. The theme of it is "I hate you, don't leave me". Davey was undiagnosed at the time the song was born, but eventually he was, and a psychotherapist would even come on tour with us to provide him with daily therapy and breathing techniques to curb his anxiety attacks. Davey never showed any signs of anxiety or depression until we were five bodies in as a band. Dead bodies.

Track 5, "L/A" is not what everyone thinks it is in terms of symbolism. There's no symbolism to it, as a matter of fact. Has nothing to do with the City of Angels. "L" stands

for "Lovebug" and "A" stands for "Anita", our first two sacrificial lambs who put us on the track to stardom and success. It's an homage, and a confession hidden in plain sight.

Track 10, "Hollywood ('s) High" is a punky, sped up middle-finger of a song to the high school where a couple of us went. There's something to be said for the fact it graduated so many famous musicians and artists and actors through the years. It also put a lot of schlock and bullshit out there. It emboldened a lot of mediocre creative people and that's why we would flip the school off if given the chance. Not to mention, Hollywood must be high. Perpetually, eternally stoned. We believe the smog that hangs over LA has got nothing to do with air pollution, and everything to do with a giant pot cloud that has fucked everyone's head up.

Track 11, "Brain on Fire" is a love song about obsession that cools into something that won't scare the girl off. Davey had a really hard time writing for this one, but when the floodgates of creativity opened for him, there was little he could do to close them when the lyrics were finally written. He says this is the song that "almost killed him" because he wrote and wrote and revised and revised for four nights straight without any sleep. That's how he developed what became a nasty habit with sleeping pills. Black beauties. Then he'd chase that with a few rails of cocaine and come to practice rearing to go. So, I guess what I'm trying to say is this is the song that almost killed him and still might in the end. To think, a flaming baby grand in a swimming pool was the inspiration.

Track 12, "Knives for the People" is the first song we wrote, and coincidentally, it would be the last song that all five original members of Grifters would share a song credit for. Davey brought the piano skeleton of the song to the band that infamous morning two years ago. J paired this with a Drop D riff that drives most of the song like a locomotive that barrels right into a second part that turns into a ballad of loss and regret for the ghost we'd made of Lovebug. It was an attempt for the five of us to wash the blood off our hands, or at least, to get most of it off. But we all knew the killing was not finished and there was no telling when or if we'd ever be able to quit it.

By the time we were ready to embark on a tour that would last two years and span 150,000 miles globally, I was carrying on a love affair with vodka and various fruit juices. I would get the DT's after only a few hours away from the bottle and made sure our tour rider carried four bottles of Stoli chilled backstage.

J and Chris were using H on the regular by then. Back in our apartment days, they were both careful to avoid the way of the needle. They snorted and thought that was somehow better and less pathetic. I don't know when or where J and Chris decided to just say "Fuck it" and start shooting, but before we knew it, they were disappearing from mixing sessions or radio interviews to go tap a vein in whatever bathroom they could hole up in for a half-hour. J was careful about it, and he never left a trail. Only a series of questions and raised eyebrows from those close to him. But Chris was sloppy and not all that skilled when it came to shooting it. He had a bad habit of drawing the needle out of his arm too quickly and spraying blood on the wall. We laughed about it until Gretch found the spray in a bathroom at WNEW and read us the riot act.

To this day, she never did find out whose blood it was, only that it was Grifter blood.

Bobby was more a dabbler in H back then and preferred cocaine and Black Beauties. Where J and Chris got off on the ritual of shooting H, Bobby took more of a utilitarian approach to it. He snorted it and never strayed from this delivery method because he wanted it done so he could get right down to all the feels. Like I said before, Bobby did drugs like an accountant crunches numbers. Methodically.

Davey.

Davey.

He'll never admit it, but it's always been my belief he sustained himself solely on the blood of our hunts. The guy stopped using with the rest of us once we moved out of the apartment. Just like that. There was no struggle. Other than the sleeping pills, Davey lived a clean lifestyle.

When he wasn't writing for the band, he was engrossed in his artwork. Davey should have gone to art school, and we all told him so. He always resented it, thinking we were trying to push him out of the band into something else. Of course, this is a guy whose mother tried to sell him to her dealer-pimp. He nearly ended up in the system of foster homes. His dear, sainted grandmother materialized at the eleventh hour like "some fairy godmother" to take him home to live. It would make sense he took refuge in his sketches and music, but the money and opportunity to go to school for his art wasn't there like a pipeline into a rock band and the scene would have been. The guy's incredibly gifted and we cheered him on.

Then we discovered what he'd started sketching and filling his pads with.

Ten of them by the time J snuck a peek at one of them while Davey was in the bathroom.

We couldn't believe it.

Scenes of graphic rape. Animal torture. Hangings. Disembowelment drawings that made us wonder when the hell Davey had gotten his medical degree. That's how fucking detailed they were, down to the shiny liver and crinkled-looking pancreas sliding out of a slit belly.

As if that weren't fucking bad enough, some of the pages depicted the hunts we'd been on. The faces of the victims. The strangulation. The group effort. J may as well have happened upon a written confession or ghoulish diary admitting to and outlining the murders.

Lovebug's pale, sweet face with its shocked expression peeked out at us and J flipped past her, fast as he could.

Anita the Lot Lizard was in there.

Grizzly, a big-boned street kid who took up with the band, to his own detriment.

The faces of our victims swam up from the pages, real as life. Encircled by their killers. Grifters all.

Faced with our sins and the ill-gotten gains we'd scored from them, I felt like I'd just been slapped awake after two years of coma.

I don't know what it did to the other guys.

I'm pretty sure Davey got off on the sketches. The memories and the new renderings of evil and torture were his stepped-on H.

Yet, he never said a word or raised a question when that sketch pad went missing. J said he was going to take it and burn asap.

I imagine Davey must not have cared because he needed only to draw it all over again. I have no doubt another sketchpad will show the same confessional renderings of the Grifter murders. And if they were to see the light of day, I take solace in the fact the authorities will find me out of reach, so to speak.

Instead of insisting Davey talk to somebody about his morbid fascinations, that he purges all the negativity swirling around inside him before we started the biggest tour of our lives, Grifters Anonymous made one more in a long line of regretful decisions.

We stuffed down all knowledge of Davey's psychopathic ideations and hit the road to make Knives for the People *the fastest-selling debut album in history.*

THIRTY-NINE

The cold kiss of burnished hardwood along the side of his face and his eyes fly open like a pair of spastic window shades.

Burnside catches the tail end of the shriek that rips its way out of him as he comes to on the ground. His head throbs. A vicious pain breathes behind his right eye. He is lying on his side. When he tries to raise himself up into a sitting position, it sets off a series of fireworks across his chest and down the sides of his rib cage. But he can breathe without any real difficulty. None of the ribs are broken. Otherwise, every breath would make him wish for death.

He settles back down onto the floor, digs deep into his constitution, and with teeth bared hauls himself up into a sitting position. It's too painful to remain this way. He swivels his body ever so gingerly and swings his legs around with the momentum of molasses.

And Burnside sees the bottom of the grand staircase that divides to either side of a second-floor landing. A hop and a skip away from where he had fallen. His last memory is that of something striking him from behind, a blunt object against the rear of his skull. Then nothing. The additional injuries that have begun to announce themselves in rapid succession, must have been visited on him while he was unconscious.

I'm still here.

Nolan Royal's compound.

The walls are bare.

The interior is stripped to its simplest components.

Burnside's stomach clenches as fresh fear takes a hold of him.

How long have I been out? Long enough for them to peel the flesh off the carcass. Lots of flesh. Hour's worth of work, if not a full day.

He yearns to climb the stairs and revisit Nolan Royal's studio. To see if the man has been left behind. Left for dead. His art hauled away with the rest? Are they worth more than he or Royal had estimated?

Why now? What touched this off?

My arrival?

My hands around his throat?

The forbidden knowledge from the old man—

Burnside searches himself for the thick, folded scrap of sketch paper Royal had used to draw him a map. The jerky movements set off jolts of pain that encircle his upper torso. But he can't let it stop him. Not yet. Not until he knows for sure. He pushes through the pain. What if they took it from him? What if it is the reason for beating him and knocking him out? What if they oversee everything their supposed "employer" does to make sure he does not make a grave error, like leading someone to a forbidden landmark.

Like a secret Mountain that supposedly houses an age-old god.

He slips the folded sketch paper out from inside the front of his pants, opens it. His tired eyes rake over its contents. There will be time later to examine the map and its supplementary prompts more closely once he's settled into his seat, in-flight, and on the way back to LAX.

Dirty martini in hand, if possible.

Burnside climbs the right banister, hauls himself up onto his feet.

He is stripped of his suit jacket. His once white dress shirt is torn open, the buttons popped. The cotton fabric is stained a rich red. Blood. He raises the shirt and the tee underneath. With stilted movement, he examines himself for bullet wounds. Any holes in the flesh.

Ultraviolet-colored bruises form a slightly raised patchwork across his chest. Their mingled shading scares him a little. He thinks of internal bleeding. An invisible killer on a clock he can't stop.

No hospitals. That could rouse the police.

And time is not on his side.

Burnside lowers both shirts.

Suddenly, they feel more constricting and oppressive than ever before.

The façade it presents to the public for the sake of looking more the part of a private investigator now feels more on par with a children's Halloween costume. Concealing the true self.

Disrespecting it.

Selling himself out so he can enjoy the "privilege" of chasing cheating spouses, locating runaways, or simply verifying injury fraud for some small insurance company who cannot afford to hire an in-house investigator.

All to keep the lights on and the rent paid on his bungalow/ office.

The trade-off is no longer bearable.

Time to become.

A random factoid traipses across his mind, both taunting and urging him on.

Did you know all human beings completely shed their skin every twenty days?

Burnside rips the dress shirt off, the remaining buttons popping like BB pellets.

The sight of the Blondie t-shirt underneath, featuring the iconic blonde herself winking her eye precociously, fills Burnside with some semblance of comfort. The familiar will do that.

"Fuck it all," he says, patting the subtle bulge for good measure. "The old fucker gave it all up. Let's go."

He tests his step and finding it bearable, staggers across the main hall for the huge bronze doors, opened outward into the great wide open.

They've either taken his rental car with them or dumped it in the woods in haste, thereby erasing his visit to the palatial estate alto-gether. For now, at least. And he wasn't just making conversation when he'd confessed casually to the merc that he had no idea how to get back to London and would be needing some direction.

That was and remains the truth.

Only now, Burnside has no mode of transportation to get back to the airport.

To the nonstop flight.

To the dirty martini, which now seems more like an oasis in the desert of his clouded mind.

Think, Burnside. Focus.

Through the pain.

Keeping staring at the fog until you see through it.

It'll come.

Ten minutes later, Paddy Burnside is making his stilted way across the rolling field of dead, gray grass.

His forehead burning with fever and brain on fire with a plan.

FORTY

Gretchen Solomon's younger brother, Damon, has exhibited strange behavior since he was a toddler. He had been diagnosed as autistic and that is what her parents adjusted their lives to, until another specialist deemed him as having what is today called Asperger's Syndrome. They saw fit to test his IQ once he reached an age it could be administered. And Damon Solomon scored a staggering 160, leaving Siobhan and Gavin, mother and father respectively, both daunted and mystified at the same time.

Big sister Gretch watched as her little brother grew into a teenager, his affectless way of speaking translating into the sort of sullenness attributed to most young people. During this period, the oddity of his nature was camouflaged, and he escaped adolescence unscathed by any social ridicule. Then, the true nature of his awkward demeanor was once again obvious to those around him as those same school peers went on to higher level educations and developed aspects of young adulthood like maturity and drive and measured emotions.

His grades never dipped below a 98, despite his stilted personality. Damon Solomon had a photographic memory, and his cognitive ability edged into savant levels. His toneless voice spoke of things seemingly incomprehensible to your average intellectual. He had no idea what to do with praise of any kind from his teachers, let alone his parents.

The praise is not what drove him to function on such an advanced level.

He did it because he had no choice in the matter.

The drive was built in.

A brilliant shell.

A vessel of genius.

Gretch's parents died within a few months of each other. Broken heart syndrome, according to those who knew them. Both had died not knowing what would become of their only son. Who would care for him? How long would he last if left to his own devices? Initially, Gretch had been living hand to mouth, still making her name in the proving grounds of the A & R field. She'd brought him into her one-bedroom flat and cared for him as best she could.

The presence of Damon in her life and under her roof delayed a great many goals she might have achieved earlier solo.

He subsisted in a halfway house in the San Fernando Valley for years. She'd gotten him in, settled, and set him up with a job at a local grocer stacking fruit and bagging. Assuming no news about her little brother was good news, she'd settled into this new freedom from fearing for his welfare. She believed he'd found his footing in the world.

This was not the case.

Gretch took Damon in for a second time, this time on the sprawling farmhouse property she and Stevie call home today. She needed help with Stevie, whose condition had already begun to deteriorate. Damon Solomon needed a place to stay after rendering himself *persona non grata* in yet another town for preaching on a public street.

Without a permit.

Resisting police.

Jail time.

It occurred to Gretch his next step would be prison or Potter's Field. He used his one phone call to contact his big sis, and she opened her house to him, all the while drawing the strength to do so by calling up the faces of her mother and father and certain promises made.

Ultimately, he ended up spending more time out in the garden shed then in the house. As Gretch would casually come to understand, Damon was feverishly at work and beyond obsessed over a manuscript of sorts he'd started on a roll of toilet paper during his two-day stint in the county jail.

He still held up his end of the arrangement, assisting her with Stevie as needed. This was before the days of Flora. Gretch supplied him with a walkie talkie to summon Damon out in the shed when she required his help to turn Stevie in his bed, to turn the mattress, to bathe him, or merely to calm him. Damon's abilities proved even to surpass those of Gretch when it came to easing the dying rock star's mind.

Theirs was a singular, direct line telepathy of feelings and emotions from the start.

Their connection mystifies her to this day.

Gretch had harbored no illusions about her brother's wild ideas and theories stemming from an overactive and untapped beautiful mind. Even when Damon set up a cot in the shed, moved all his belongings in there among the rakes and tarps and the mower and the volleyball net, opting to live there, she thought it odd. She had offered him the guest room. He'd balked at the suggestion. She knew enough not to push.

So, the backyard shed that smelled strongly of motor oil and grass clippings.

Damon made his way independently, relying on public transportation and a second-hand bike Gretch picked up for him. He returned often under cover of night, coming and going undetected.

Until one day when Stevie experienced something of a miraculous lucidity and prompted Gretch to check the back yard shed to "make sure everything's in order". Stevie rarely gave sound advice any longer, but Gretch knew he'd grown close to Damon. One mentally ill and the other mentally impaired. Potato-*po-tah-toe?* Looking back on this rare moment, Gretch thinks if ever there were proof of a higher power, He or She was behind this warning from a man plagued with dementia.

What she discovered nearly sent her into hysterics.

Dirty bombs and other explosive devices, all stockpiled alongside a simple cot with a ratty army blanket thrown over it, a poster of George Orwell pinned to the wall above the bed, and various hand-drawn blueprints spread across a small card table he'd brought into the shed.

A small but lethal collection of books is piled up on the table against the far wall.

Mein Kampf.

The Anarchist's Cookbook.

Rules for Radicals.

Standing there amidst the implements of destruction, the tools of the domestic terrorist, she faced a crossroads. One that would determine the trajectory not just of Damon's life, but that of her own and Stevie's as well.

Am I for country or family?

She chose family. No regrets.

GRETCH LOATHES the filthy feeling the memory elicits. How she'd leveraged Damon into disarming and hiding every explosive before the ambulance came to transport him to an ER for a psych evaluation. If they had found the shed furnished as it had been when Gretch first came upon it, the paramedics would have wasted little time in calling the police.

The bomb squad.

The FBI.

EMTs arrived within five minutes of her call in which she worked herself into tears.

And the question which sealed Damon Solomon's fate: *Do you believe your brother to be a threat to himself or to those around him?*

"Yes," she'd said. "Yes, I do. Yes to both."

It had felt like a lie. Tasted like a lie, similar to a dirty penny on the tip of your tongue. But it was not. When it came to the bombs and the manifesto (which she'd thought of as a harmless journal of self-reflection), Damon most certainly posed a threat to those around him. The only unknown was *who* would have been in danger exactly. And where?

The worst thing about it was that Damon made no denial. He accepted this new development without any resistance and went along quietly. For the last two years, Gretch has financed his indefinite stay at the Overview Hospital for the Mentally Ill. No prison. No Potter's Field. No public infamy.

Now, Gretch Solomon finds herself in a strange circumstance.

She is grateful her brother was up to the bad business he was when she had seen him committed.

FORTY-ONE

Whoever said you can't go home again, well, they meant you can, but you should avoid checking in on Stevie and Pru.

This is not a check-in visit.

Circling back home was not planned for.

Now, considering all she's learned about the Mountain and the Muse, Gretch's return home is inevitable as it is required. She can only hope and pray her gut is to be trusted.

Otherwise, she's come back to her ranch home estate for naught.

Crouching low as her body will allow without pitching her forward into a faceplant, Gretch trots through the neglected lawn. Her lawn. Her black JanSport backpack jostles almost playfully around her right shoulder where it is slung. Its new and uncreased, the tag still affixed to the front pouch's zipper. She straightens some, shifting her weight to descend the downward slope just beyond her inground pool choked with all manner of uncollected debris and detritus. Dead, red leaves from the adjacent woods. Thankful she still has not found a groundskeeper to mow the property in months. The overgrown grass hides her well. The waves of green stand as tall as her waist in some spots.

The ground levels out again. She lowers herself down and duck-walks past the duck pond.

A small cluster of mallards, mixing with a handful of yellow bills, are gathered around the pond's hairy, green edge.

She is forced to circumvent that area entirely. Gretch crosses all the way to the northernmost perimeter of the yard, overshooting the pond and keeping her wary distance so as not to scare up their attention and squawks.

Holding her breath, she picks up her feet while still running stooped over.

I'm sneaking around my own property. Fucking surreal.

All it would take is one audible, squishy footfall in the muddy terrain to raise the alert among the gathering of ducks and mallards. They would voice their displeasure in a cacophony of squawks and quacks, but that's not what worries Gretch. They will also break from the pond's edge in a cloud of flapping wing chaos, fleeing the yard in favor of the treetops and the horizon beyond.

Such a sudden flurry of motion in the yard could get the attention of someone in the house up the hill. Some twenty yards south of her present position.

One of the yellow bills takes notice of the woman scrabbling through the tall grass a little ways away. The duck stiffens. Stops. Quacks twice in rapid succession.

And continues meandering in its seemingly confused concentric circles.

Gretch casts a wary glance up the hill where the stone farmhouse she calls home hunkers. No one standing in any of the rear-facing windows.

As Gretch understands it (and, really, she is the only one who need *understand* it), she is avoiding her house and her dying husband and the nurse left to care for him is that she does not want to disrupt their routine.

Yes, that is what her rational mind wants her to believe.

While the darker recesses of her mind know full well she does not want to disrupt something very specific.

An event she believes to be an inevitability.

The back yard shed that had housed her brother Damon for six months doesn't look so hot, slouching in the evening shade. As she draws closer, Gretch thinks it looks like the shed had been swept up in the eye of a tornado, lifted skyward with a terrible ferocity, and then dumped back in its original location as a fractured, precarious assembly of parts. A condemned structure, now. A whitewashed structure no larger than a freshman dorm room, butted up against the redwood forest that forms a natural border for the property itself.

The two entry doors, designed to slide to the right and left respectively, appear mangled and out of alignment with the track that runs above and below them. The right door looks especially abused, the aluminum wrinkled like a neglected dress shirt. Gretch tries to drive the left aside. It groans in response. Stepping back, Gretch plants her feet in a wider stance, lays her hands along the side seam of the right door. Heaves. It's too an awkward an angle to be successful.

A little winded from struggling against the stubborn door, Gretch realizes her patience is not what it used to be.

The *fuck it* approach seems to suit her better now. She wears it well. And Gretch aims a well-aimed kicked out at the center of the damaged left door. The weaker of the two. The door shrieks ss it falls inward. Reminding her of a drunken ghost. The strike stamps the aluminum with a near-perfect print of her boot print.

Well, if she wasn't aware of my presence on the property, Pru is aware now.

Let her come…

She steps over the collapsed left door and enters the shed where her brother had gone the rest of the way mad.

Gretch is met with an altogether new and revolting smell that has taken up big, broad resident within.

It is the smell of rot and ruin.

Something, an animal, must have gotten trapped inside and died in there.

The contents of her stomach, a spare breakfast of yogurt and coffee, churns in her gut. Threatening revolt and expulsion. She claps a hand over her mouth. Squeezes her watering eyes shut.

She stands still and waits it out. The nausea evaporates and Gretch hauls her shirt up over her nose just to be safe.

Unvarnished wooden beams comprise the floor. She expects them to have come loose, judging by how the exterior looks like a war-torn building. They hold, surprisingly. There is nothing left inside. Gretch remembers it like yesterday. Not just the harrowing discovery of what her brother had been up to right under her nose, but the aftermath. The disposal of the materials he had collected to build his explosive devices. All manner of shrapnel pieces, many repurposed as such (forks, knives, piano/ picture frame wire). He would have packed all of it into a series of pressure cookers, like witches tossing frog's legs and firstborn blood samples into their bubbling cauldron.

He'd built seven dirty bombs by the time Gretch made her discovery. Items locked inside of a series of footlockers amassed around his simple sleeping cot and threadbare army blanket. Damon had even built a workbench of down redwood branches he collected during his many walks through the crimson forest.

His workbench had a blue tarp thrown over it, secured by stones placed at its corners. Where she'd discovered the bulk of lethal implements and tools. Precursors to what could have culminated in a terrifying attack upon some government building or, worse, an elected official home. She had only dipped her toe into the contents of his unearthed manifesto. A black college-ruled spiral notebook, brimming with rants and veiled allusions to possible targets. Threadbare arguments explaining the *why's* and the *how's* of Damon Solomon's new endeavor. His hatred for capitalism and the constitutional republic under which he lived.

Her brother's voice blooms in her ear, like a ghost flanking her.

"I left you something," Damon had told her during a phone call shortly after his entry into Overview Hospital. "A thank-you for letting me stay. Consider it a *break glass in case of emergency* sort of leave-behind."

Gretch remembers what she'd said in response: "You left an explosive on the property? Is that what you're telling me, Damon?"

"Is that what I'm telling you?' he'd said, cagey as ever. "If so, no need to worry. They are nothing until you arm them."

"Where are they, damn you!"

"Look for a slight discoloration along one of the wooden floor planks. It will stand out in a vague but detectable contrast to the rest of the flooring. I applied a small enough amount of weather stain for it to stand out. Pull that section of plank up. It is not nailed into place. Just lift it up and out. Et voila.

And yet you never did get around to getting rid of the explosives.

Why is that?

She doesn't have an answer.

Doesn't matter now. Damon was always a forward thinker.

Sometimes it scared her.

Gretch turns to the right wall. The section of wall where she had dismantled his workbench, dragging it out and dismantling it with swings of a pickaxe. Her muscles were still jumping along her upper arms like live wires long after that. The aluminum wall is wrinkled like the left entry door, but she had done that while taking his bench apart. Knocking part of it into the wall and creating the crease.

The flooring looks uniform from her vantage point.

The floorboards lie side-by-side in perfect smoothness.

It would seem.

Gretch plants her right boot near the far-right corner, on the verge of turning an about-face to make another pass in search of the imperfect cut of wood Damon has sent her to find. The plank of wood jostles ever so slightly beneath her sole. It is not nailed in, but it does not jump up either. Still, it's enough for Gretch to fall to her knees and pry it up with her overgrown fingernails.

Damon had indeed stained the cut of wood to stand out among the rest of the flooring. It was no longer discolored and had strangely adapted to its surrounding shade. Blending right in. If she hadn't stepped where she did, it's possible Gretch never would have found what takes her breath away once she pries it up and lays eyes on the small lockbox in the ground.

The lock box is *not*, in fact, locked. Damon told her it would not be. It is impressive, however. Temperature-controlled, insuring the C4 blocks remain no less than ten degrees below 84 degrees. She finds a snub-nosed revolver nestled inside as well. Loaded. No safety. Gretch knows her way around firearms enough to empty out the cylinder into her hands, along with the one in the chamber.

There is also a grainy black and white photograph sealed in a sandwich bag, tucked in among the other mildly chilled contents of the box.

With palsied hands, Gretch slips the photograph out of its plastic sheath and stares down at it with eyes that fill with tears.

It is a picture of a little red-haired girl and a two-year-old boy. They are posed atop what looks like a wool blanket. She is just old enough to hold her toddler brother in her lap, propping him up as he stares goggle-eyed into the camera with one stubby index finger prying at his lips.

She flips it over. Finds the month and date scribbled there in her mother's shaky writing. The unconfident script of the immigrant.

Gretchen and Damon-Fall, 1959

There is no sense in trying to make sense of Damon's reasoning for pairing their childhood photograph with a stockpile of homemade explosives. In the earth. Unless he always anticipated it being discovered by Gretch at some point. He'd wanted to sweeten the discovery somehow by including the photograph? She cannot be sure. She had grown up thinking him incapable of displaying, much less entertaining, any sort of sentimental feeling.

She kisses the photograph and tucks it away in the inner pocket of her jacket.

Gretch Solomon gingerly hoists the lockbox of explosives out of the hole, hastily replaces the cut of wood, and steals back across her yard. She pauses briefly before exiting the yard by way of the cattle fence that separates it from the country road out front. She swore she would not, but Gretch cannot resist.

She makes a quick study of her home across the yard.

Has it happened yet?

Doesn't matter. Whatever will be.

Will be.

Gretch Solomon leaves her property as silently and stealthily as she came.

Only now, she holds a box full of death and destruction close to her bosom.

PART THREE
RUN TO ME, RUN FROM ME

*"The gifts of the gods are not to be rejected, as you no doubt
know, since you have heard it from one of the devotees of
Kalliope (Calliope)."*

-Philostratus the Younger (Greek rhetorititian C3rd A.D)
Imagines 13

"Muses had a way of killing those they inspired."
-Katherine Neville

INTERLUDE (VI)

(From the Memoirs of Stevie Darius)

1990

The Mud Festival.

We were the headliners.

Knives for the People *was enjoying a revival of record sales on the back of our half-live, half-acoustic EP titled* Bloody / Serrated. *Atlas Records demanded we put something out in lieu of a new album. They were aware of the tension within in the band. How rank and file in Grifters had fallen off.* Bloody / Serrated *proved to be just the shot in the arm Knives needed to land back on Billboard at #2. Bear in mind, our debut record had already broken records. The EP ended up being the fastest-selling extended-play release ever.*

The festival was the first time we saw Davey since he'd headed home to see to his grandmother's funeral, the woman who'd raised him to manhood and rescued him from the foster care system. He'd been called away from the studio during the EP recordings with the news of eighty-five-year-old Ilsa Crocker's death. Davey's vocals were already tracked. It was no great loss, and frankly, the rest of us all breathed a secret sigh of relief to be free of him for a week or so.

The rest of us had chartered a jet to Mud.

Davey arrived in an RV.

He'd cut his long mane of wavy brown hair into a pencil thin black mohawk running down the center of his shaved head. It stunned us to silence.

If only our collective shock ended there.

There was another girl who exited the RV behind Glory. Young. Baby-faced! Built like a bird. Tweety Bird. Her head looked too big for her slight build to hold upright. A buxom chest heaved beneath a pink rubber tube top that looked downright obscene on one clearly just shy of fifteen or sixteen. Her eyeliner was thick and clotted. She required a steadying hand from Glory just to walk across the fenced-in blacktop behind the venue where an army of tour buses and trailers were parked.

Davey introduced his new child *as Allure.*

Gretch took the appearance of this young girl called Allure especially hard. It threw her off her game. She was flustered. This quickly gave way to barely tempered rage.

"How old is this girl?" she'd growled at me in private. "She's a fucking *child! Has he completely lost his mind?"*

Gretch wanted to get into it with Davey right off. Somehow, I managed to convince her to hold her anger at bay.

But her claws were out for him.

Then there was the matter of separating Davey from his two-girl entourage for the pre-show meeting. Glory knew the ropes when it came to this and made herself scarce. But Allure was not so easily put off, carrying herself like a petulant fucking child with J, who tried his best to coax her to clear out with Glory. J is not one to be trifled with. Once this Allure girl realized she had come up against the human equivalent of an abutment, she became teary-eyed and exhibited this weird "separation anxiety". It made me sick to my stomach to stand by and watch as Glory silently slung an arm around the young girl and led her out sobbing and crumpled over.

Somehow, and in a short period of time, she must have developed a connection to our singer more akin to father-daughter than rock star-groupie.

The irony was not lost on any one of us how Allure was just the type of victim we hunted and sacrificed for the past two years. No doubt she checked all the boxes to qualify.

An absent father (enter Davey-all twenty-six-years-old of him).

Drug-addicted mother or quite possibly a woman who'd been young herself when she'd given birth to Allure.

Molested?

Raped?

It wasn't like we interviewed our victims before cutting their wrists and bleeding them dry.

Often, we needed only to look in their eyes.

All the hurt and trauma live inside the eyes.

I watched Glory and this little girl wrapped in her embrace file past, her narrow and bowed shoulders shaking. And I am certain if Allure had turned and met my eyes, I would have lost my temper in an ugly way.

Just a backward glance from her and I know there would be no need for these memoirs. Because when you boil all these pages down, they are an elaborate confession to vile and terrible crimes, wrapped inside the less damning bow of the rock bio.

I'm also in a race with my pen. This increasing forgetfulness has been grabbing at my legs the whole way, trying to trip me up.

I will win this race, though.

I have to.

See, I know what's waiting for me on the other side. Increasingly, there is a burning sensation on the soles of my feet. Not as benign as pins and needles.

I know what it is.

So I write faster.

I write until my hand cramps up. Then, I somehow manage to force myself to write through the goddam cramp, so

STOP

FOCUS

...the Davey who exuded confidence weeks before was not the same guy perched on the edge of one of the crushed velvet loveseats we required backstage at every Grifters show. Of the five of us, Davey took to the drugs and drink with the least enthusiasm, yet he looked like a man going cold turkey and stuck in withdrawal. He'd also developed something of a tic that had forced J to pause more than once to ask Davey if he was alright.

Our singer's right eye twitched and crinkled every so often, followed by a quick, hunted glance over his shoulder.

I almost asked him outright if he'd gotten into a car accident or taken a fall in the shower or something and hit his head. This was a neurological problem. The whole damn presentation.

Per usual, we left it to J to handle much of the conversation and field Davey's clipped, stand-offish responses.

We all knew something else was going on.

I wished I'd told J what I suspected. I could've saved Grifter Anonymous from utter ruin.

That Davey Grifter wanted to blow up the band.

For whatever reason.

It was only after our now notorious performance at The Mud Festival my suspicions were verified in the form of one of the worst concert tragedies since The Stones at Altamont.

Afterward, Chris would blame Gretch for "fucking with Davey" right before we took the stage:

"You could have waited to give him shit about his new girl until after *we played the biggest show of our lives! Would it have fucking killed you to just wait? You fucked his head up! You tipped him into this fucking dangerous psychosis, Gretch! You! Did! This!"*

I was within earshot of his tirade.

The next thing I knew the concert promoter and a beefy security guy were dragging me off Chris Desmond.

His nose was laid to the side and broken. His face was a dripping red mask of rage.

And Grifters Anonymous was dead.

Grifters got bumped from the headliners spot at the last minute. Davey was raging. The promoter, a big Danish guy dressed in a white tee and white slacks that looked painted on, nearly took our singer's head off after ten minutes of back and forth. Gretch, preoccupied with trying to get to the bottom of the situation with Allure, neglected to rein Davey in.

She couldn't have his back, knowing in her gut this Allure was a "kept girl", even after Gretch had plied her for something concrete to hang her suspicions on and the girl stonewalled her.

Black and gray clouds had been boiling above seventy-five-thousand people's heads all afternoon. People were climbing the sound towers and hopping off into what they could only pray were a sea of upturned palms to buoy and float them.

I caught Louder's set. They seemed at odds with one another for the entire set. Turns out that wasn't just my imagination. They broke up two months after that show and proceeded to badmouth each other all over West LA. I would have gone back to our dressing room sooner, rather than to stand by and rubberneck stage-left for Louder's swan song, but I knew it was a bad scene back there.

And after Davey's tantrum had almost gotten us thrown off the bill altogether, I didn't even want to see him.

The rolling clouds slowed to a simmer as I stood there watching the sound towers start to sway. The winds kicked up. An alien chill swept across the grounds.

The rollicking sea of sweaty faces with grime stamped into their faces.

The feel of the bass drum inside my body.

Punching me in the chest. Louder's drummer liked his drums miked to the max and every bass kick literally blew the hair back off the other band members' foreheads. Irritating them even more.

Really stirring the shit.

The audience hung in there for as long as they could, patiently waiting on some glimmer of

Louder's former greatness to show itself. The third song in, they turned on my old friends

from the Strip. They pelted the guys with water bottles. One bottle exploded all over Mick Bevan and his bass. "Piss! Fuckin' piss!?" I never would have known what was in it if ol' Mick hadn't stopped playing, smashed his bass to splinters, and peeled off his Guiness t-shirt, now wringing wet with somebody's waste. He went to leap into the crowd.

Thankfully, Security grabbed him. He never would have made it. The barricades were a good ten feet away from the lip of the stage. Would've broken his neck.

I had to turn away from the stage.

Truth?

I couldn't stop laughing.

Don't ever let an up-and-coming band tell you how they felt bad for the act that goes on

before them and fails. There is no feeling bad about it! It's a secret triumph. A big smile on the inside while the competition eats it, teeing up your band for greatness.

If you squander that opportunity, then you never deserved it in the first place.

Just as Louder's set dissolved into what could only be described as a slow-burning wind

down, the sky opened.

The rain fell hard and fast, as if to say What the fuck did you expect?

The crowd was a living thing. It drew a deep, belabored breath. It shifted and surged like a leviathan. Thousands of hands went up. Tongues wagged to catch the rain. Eye liner ran and suddenly the audience was rife with black-eyed, raccoon-looking maniacs scaling each other in some unhinged King of the Mountain. Heads disappeared. Surfaced a few yards away. I saw a three-some break out a couple feet from the barricades. No one stopped it. And there was no deference for the act itself. The people around the fucking trio crammed in around them. Bumped them. Grabbed at the male's hair. Tousled it. Yanked it. Spanked their asses.

All this under an ever-twisting shower curtain of torrential rain.

Baptizing the twisted masses in some secret, abominable rite.

"End-times," I said to myself.

"Huh?"

It was J.

I nodded to him. The winds cut through the shockingly warm rain and steered it into our

faces. We stepped back. I armed the wetness off my face. J yanked his t-shirt up to wipe his face dry.

"You believe all this?" I said.

J laughed. "I been backstage trying to patch things up between Davey and Gretch. The two

of them. An immoveable object and an opposing force. Just barely kept it all from going fucking boom!" Then he remembered the question he'd been asked and answered it in his signature J fashion. "Wait'll we take the stage. Everybody'll be fucking. Bunch of muddied monsters rolling around. Making Grifter babies!"

I shuddered.

"Nine months from now, huh?"

I nodded, stiffly.

He clapped a hand on my shoulder, his long sinewy fingers strong and spider-like from the

way he worked them into impossible chords Hendrix would've admired.

"So, is it safe to head back to the room?" I asked. "Gotta do my warmup."

J shook his head. I wasn't expecting it.

Or this:

"We're on next," he said. "Clean-up crew for Louder. They sent me to fetch you."

"You serious?"

"Yeah, man."

I blinked at him. My hands felt like two lumps of granite. Until I ran my scales on the bass, they would go on feeling like that. I usually spent a half-hour alone, running up and down the fretboard until my fingers reached full flexibility and my nerves settled.

"J, c'mon. I thought we had another hour."

"Don't look at me, Stevie. This is all Davey."

I surveyed the masses. A naked woman took a nose-dive off the sound tower. A beauty, caked in mud from head to toe. I thought of what it would look like if the sea of hands below parted. How would that be? Why did my mind go to that? Right to that? It's my nerves. Gotta get backstage and get on my bass.

"It's either this or Davey was going to split in that ridiculous RV of his."

"This doesn't make any sense. The guy made a big fucking thing about not headlining and now he's pulled a complete one-eighty and wants to just-I dunno-get this over with?"

"He came right out and told the promoter-you saw the size of that fucker! -he said this ought

to throw a monkey-wrench in the rest of the festival. Said we're gonna put on the kind of show no one's gonna want to follow us. Said it's gonna be one for the ages. Said the guy may as well call it a day when we're done. I'm *telling you, Stevie, we could not shut him up. I've seen him riled up. But this? This was different."*

I slapped a wet itch on the back of my neck. My hand came away with the crumpled thread-like body of a mosquito in my upturned palm.

"Christ," I sighed and flung it down in disgust.

The sky was a purple blood blister stretched wide when we took the stage.

The crowd had transformed into a sea of white, blinkless eyes and dilated pupils. The mud caked to their bodies erased the rest of them away. Cavernous mouths shouting for blood. Aware of Davey's penchant for holding up Grifter shows for the most ridiculous, and often undisclosed reasons. I think they were counting on Davey fucking up, just so they'd have an excuse to tear it all up.

Fights broke out or carried on in an endless array of pockets.

More people were fucking, their coupling more aggressive and animal-like than before.

Naked mud people propped up on shoulders stretched all the way back into the great oblivion beyond.

They kissed their middle-fingers, arced them outward for us to see.

I think if we had gathered Davey up and tossed him out into the crowd, they would have torn him to pieces.

I had the great pleasure of starting off "Knives for the People". I rolled out the riff without even having to look at my fingers. All muscle memory.

I caught sight of a lanky, bare-chested guy just barely escaping a nearby mosh pit.

Crimson glinted in the center of his face. He leered at me with a mouth full of—

Is that blood?

I shut my eyes, tilted my chin upward. Tried to disappear into the groove.

Chris and J's dueling guitars piled onto my riff in a madness of delay and wah-pedal. Their noise was a life-preserver for me. It lifted me up and out of my body.

The high of the live performance.

Davey swayed in my periphery, letting loose with his signature "horse-riding/whipping"

dance. Someone flung a handful of mud at him. It struck him in the chest.

I expected him to stop dead, to call it quits. He'd done it before, and for far less.

I held my breath.

Let it out.

He laughed.

Davey worked his hands in the mud, smearing it into a strange-looking symbol on his abdomen that looked half-Celtic/half-Greek lettering in origin.

Never missed a beat.

Kept on with that over-sexualized dance of his.

He turned to me.

We locked eyes.

He mouthed the words, "Watch this."

And I know what I saw.

I have since tried to convince the other guys in the band he did, in fact, say this right before all hell broke loose.

I know they believe me. But when there's a lot of money to be had, a lot of riches at stake,

the truth has a way of taking a backseat. Or barely making it into the car at all.

Davey started to sing:

> *I got a best friend who don't know how to live*
> *She's got a daddy who showed her how to die*
> *Never have I ever felt as disconnected*
> *As Penny when she says she don't know how to cry*
> *Her eyes got nothing but*
> *Knives for the people*
> *Knives for the people*
> *No room for tears*
> *She got the metal in her sights*
> *Sharper and sharper-*

A spray of bright red arced into the air above the crowd.

To my left.

A quick spurt. If I blinked, I would've missed it.

My stomach flipped over before I even knew what I'd seen.

I don't know what made me look for him, but I searched the crowd for that bloody mouthed

Ichabod Crane character from moments ago.

My fingers kept fretting.

My pick kept plucking the bass strings.

The act had turned into some kind of out-of-body experience.

And "Knives" kept on while I searched the sea of faces for that one fucking guy.

When the first body rose up, borne by bodiless hands and passed around, I found Bloody Mouth. He had been watching me the whole time. As he raised his hand in a horrid blur of motion and I saw the glint of the switchblade steel, my mind failed to translate what I saw. Then, another geyser of blood burst from the slashed carotid artery in the floating girl's throat. Her head lolled backward. Her mud-caked arms hung limp. Legs jerked about as the bodiless hands of the audience kept her afloat above their heads.

She was dying as they put her up to crowd-surf.

Then, a deafening chorus of shrieks and screams rippled across the sea of people.

They hadn't known.

Then they did.

My hands froze.

I surged to the front of the stage, waving my hands towards Bloody Mouth and the grisly

scene unfolding around him. The crowd who one minute had been buoying the dying girl one minute parted and her body disappeared into the crevice they created. Fans shrieked and shook, mopping the dead girl's blood off their faces and arms and throats and backs.

"Get em'-get em'-get em'!" I screamed, my cries deadened by the song that marched on.

A yellow-shirted, burly Security guard somehow heard me.

Then, an army of Yellow Shirts hopped the barricades and surged into the crowd.

Fans crowded up against the steel barriers, unseating them.

The mad scramble to some kind of safety had begun.

Another limp body rose up above the crowd. Maybe fifty or so yards west of the first one.

That's when I nearly lost my fucking lunch. And the bottle of Knob Creek whiskey I'd

poured over top of it all.

Bloody Mouth was too far away from the second body to have slit their throat too.

Had I really seen him at all?

"There's more than one of them!" I screamed.

The crowd had already devoured the Security detail. They had turned to flashes of yellow and glimpses of sweaty, bloodied brows, and matted crew cuts. Flying fists.

Chris and J came up behind me. I didn't even notice the music had stopped. Even Davey had

stopped singing. He stood there by the drum riser, gripping the microphone with white-knuckled fists, swaying from side to side like an idiot savant.

Big green eyes watching without seeing a damned thing.

Fissures in the crowd of seventy-five thousand widened into yawning maws of emptiness.

The Mud People grabbed for their friends, slung arms around their boyfriend or girlfriend or husband or wife or hook-up's neck. Yanked them in any direction other than the places where two dead bodies, one male and one female, had bled out to their favorite band. The sinking ground and the driving rain offered the fleeing fans no traction. The storm worked against them. Discouraged escape. But us human beings?

We want to live so bad.

Until the next hardship.

I unslung my bass.

Chris grabbed my arm.

J my shoulder.

J: "No way, man! No way!"

"I gotta fucking help them!" I remember screaming.

The east sound tower buckled.

I watched it shudder as wind and rain whipped at it. Swirling it.

Overwhelming it?

Chris: "-security's got it! We gotta get outta here, Stevie!"

I turned to Chris. I didn't recognize him.

I only heard the screams.

I knew people were dying.

People were trampling one another.

And I had lost sight of him. I had lost track of the source of all this fucking chaos.

A thick cluster of fans split apart, confirming my dread.

The subtle shapes of people pressed down into the soft ground shocked my eyes.

Facedown.

Still.

The further the opening in the crowd expanded, the higher the body count of the trampled

rose in wretched numbers.

I didn't even know I'd said anything. Later, J would tell me what I said. Right before Chris

Desmond and J physically carried me off the stage against my will.

I was raving, by all accounts.

"Bloody Mouth," I'd said. "Bloody Mouth did this. H-he was on The Mountain with us! I

fucking remember him now!"

Davey was the first one to leave the stage, his spell cast and the damage done.

What we discovered backstage?

Gretch unconscious on the ground and Davey standing by with the young girl, Allure, folded into his embrace.

I'm going to try and lay it out as best I understand it, even if I can no longer really trust my own memory.

The shadows are closing in.

They're black walls.

Forcing me. I don't want to say goodnight-not ready to go to sleep yet-Mom five more minutes

FORTY-TWO

Gretch takes the next exit to decompress at the nearest motel. She anticipated the long, solitary car ride north, which according to the maps spread across her passenger seat would take six hours, that her mind would wander. That certain memories lying dormant for the better part of a month could stir for no other reason than that she had nothing but time to think. She had brought along a duffel full of CD's and burned through five of them (one a double album) when even the music became an irritant.

When a light mist spits at her windows, she is relieved to have a reason to turn on the wipers. The *whoosh* of their blades breaks the silence. She finds a rhythm in their mechanical motion and taps the steering wheel. Hammers out a simple, lighthearted beat.

And this motion lulls her into a feeling, although fleeting, of optimism.

Everything is going to be alright.

Let go and let GOD.

But an anxious mind cannot abide hope for long.

The dread seeps back in, subtle and sinister.

The fear of the other shoe dropping.

The future fear that robs the anxious of present joy.

The unwanted memories, once deadened but activated now, ooze into the front of her mind. Her heartbeat accelerates, drawing further attention to the panic mounting in her tightening chest.

"Alright, you fuckers," she tells them. "Come on out. Let's see it. All of it. Don't hold back. Let's do this … once and for all—"

The Beast of Memory breaks the surface of the black pool that stretches endlessly onward for want of a horizon. Its visages shudder and shift and bulge as the faces of her nightmares, real and those imagined, fill the black void. Stevie's face is wet as he peers out at her with the pitiful expression of the aggressor playing at being the victim. His face is a mask of crimson, made wet by the tears that smear along his sunken cheekbones. This is not the handsome, chivalrous bass player who'd pursued her and rocked her world in bed. No, this is the dying Stevie with the lone tuft of gray hair that flutters atop his head like some threadbare feather. *Turn around and come back home. Rescue me. Gretch, I'm not the monster. The other guys … they swept me up in their bullshit. I tried to swim away, but their current was too fucking strong. The pull of celebrity. I'm. A. Victim. See me. Really see me for what I am. Gretch—*

Her palms slip and slide along the steering wheel, greased with sweat. She can't breathe.

Gretch scans the side of the road for the next green sign predicting a motel and rest stop within the next two miles.

Two miles? Two miles—

You really think you-Gretchen Solomon-a stupid Mick with generalized anxiety, a fucked memory, and a family history of depression is going to square up against … a fucking Old God? Older than civilization? Predating recorded time? The Beast of Memory is pale, cheeks sunken, and eyes grey as icebergs. Black, inscrutable irises that search her soul and seize on her weakness. Prod and poke at it. Stimulate it. Vex it. Her tormentor. And Burnside smiles his shark-toothed grin. Each sharpened into triangles with lethal edges. Gretch knows this is new and its inaccurate. It doesn't matter. His presence is enough to drive up her heart rate and drag her back to that warehouse where he'd done things to her so wretched her mind pity's her enough to block most of it out altogether. *You are NOT a worthy adversary, honey! Stay the fuck home.*

Hold your husband's hand while he slips away. That's your duty as a wife. This is a Man's game. Of course, you never did get it. You were never meant to be a part of the Man's game. Everyone up and down the Strip? They laughed at you behind your back. They all called you a fucking slit behind closed doors! Playing at managing a band? You should have bent over and served your real purpose —

Gretch screams from the soles of her feet. It holds for what seems like an eternity, emptying her lungs and leaving her lightheaded.

And doesn't it feel so *fucking* good!

Drives the Beast of Memory back down below the black waterline.

Gretch cuts the nose of her Land Rover across two lanes and just barely catches the off-ramp that will dump her out right beside the parking lot of a Hampton Inn.

Laughing like a loon now, Gretchen Solomon pulls into a parking space close to the hotel entrance. She rests her forehead against the steering wheel.

Gretch realizes she has been repeating the same string of words repeatedly.

"You're all fucked when we meet again."

Over and over.

No doubt in her mind.

SHE WASTES no time before sinking into a hot bath. Sluicing the body temperature water through her fingers and dunking her head under feels like a second birth. The bathroom is surprisingly expansive, much to her delight. She could have opted to stay at a lesser motel, but Gretch suspects she would have had to hunt for one. She needed to get off the road before she caused a pileup or ran the Rover into a ditch.

She was careful not to pop a sedative until after the bath. For good measure, she happily doubled her dose of Ativan, dry swallowing them while standing in a white terry cloth bathrobe she'd found hanging inside the bathroom on the door. It brushes against her bare flesh with all the tenderness of a lover's fingertips.

Gretch decides there is nothing left to do but sleep.

It is 1 p.m. She knows she will greatly benefit from a good five to six hours of shut-eye before hitting the highway again.

Slipping between the sheets and quilt, Gretch winds herself up in the bedding until her arms and legs are bound and immoveable.

She doesn't dream.

A side effect of the sedative. Dark, depthless slumber.

No mind-movies, as the psychiatrist from the hospital had put it.

It feels like she only just shut her eyes when she hears someone hammering at her door.

Her skull still stuffed full of cotton from the deep sleep she'd been ripped away from, Gretch is sluggish at first. Then, she remembers that element of danger that has entered her life of late and rebounds by setting her bare feet on the scratchy rug as lightly as she can.

She sidles up alongside the door to her room. She addresses the other side of the door.

At the same time, Gretch regrets she didn't think to bring her brother's snub nose revolver in with her.

"Who is it?"

No answer.

She drops her eyes to the narrow opening between the door and the floor.

The center is darkened. Someone is standing there. Silent and still

Whoever it is clears their throat. A decidedly male register if she had to guess.

Then, her darkened doorstep brightens as the visitor walks off.

Could be a trick.

The door handle feels colder, more slippery, than it was when she'd first come in. She cranks it down, opens the door a crack and peers out into the hall.

Listens.

For breathing.

The slightest hiss of respiration.

Down the hall, drunken female laughter sounds, followed by the clinking of ice cubes flung into a tumbler glass.

And the sign of life a mere three doors down is enough to bolster her enough to open the rest of the way.

Coast is clear.

Turning to go back into her room, her bare foot knocks into something on the floor.

A Maxell VHS tape.

Gretch snatches it up, sneaks a final glance up and down the hall.

She slips the tape out of its cardboard sleeve.

A piece of masking tape is stuck to the center of the cartridge.

The words *TIME SENSITIVE* written on it in black marker. A hasty, hurried scrawl.

THE ROOM IS EQUIPPED with a VCR that rolls out on a shelf under the television.

Once she feeds the tape into the machine and it leaves her grasp, Gretch feels like she needs to give them a good, hard scrubbing. Like she was just holding a lump of dung.

Gretch switches on the television. The screen sparks then shivers with the snow that begins every VHS movie she's ever watched. This gives way to a black screen.

She kneels before the television.

There is no picture for some time.

It's faint at first. But Gretch is soon certain she can hear someone moaning. Gasping.

And she suddenly wants to eject the tape at once.

To smash it. Before a picture fills the screen to match the sounds of agony.

Too late.

She gasps, hand flying to her mouth to stifle a cry.

The picture is grainy, the V-hold guttering like a candle in a draughty hallway. Off-center, nearly hugging the left side of the screen, the half-moon of Harrison's Hart face shudders violently like he's trapped in the Arctic. The other half is claimed by the shadows thrown by a low, barely-there light. He is panting, his lips bleeding and split. His eyes are roving. Wild. When they land on the camera's view itself, they settle and ooze into something of an odd comfort. Like the lens pushed up against him is a newfound friend or savior, even.

A horrid, gleaming gash runs through his left eyebrow. The beginnings of a black eye have settled into the puffy flesh around his eye. Flashes of purple and royal blue. The eye is lidded, not yet sealed.

It feels like Gretch is in the room with him. She even reaches for the screen like she means to tend to his many wounds. Kneeling beside him. She winces as Harrison shifts around and the dim light plays about the contours of his cheeks. Highlighting various bruises and contusions.

She wonders how it is he's still alive.

Gretch lays her hands on the glass.

Harrison Hart laughs weakly. Desperately. And she is briefly fooled into believing somehow, he sees her hand, feels her there.

"Hey … Red …" His voice is ragged. He pauses. She can see his throat working, swallowing something. *Oh, dear God, please don't let it be blood.* "I don't have a lot of time to deliver this message. Just bear with me … if you don't mind. There's no Q and A at the end so … really try to understand."

You put him in this bad spot.

Another life ruined. You. Are. Toxic.

She pulls her hand away, wanting to see his face while he speaks.

I never got over this man. I have been a fool.

"Burnside's here with me," he says. "Mm … we are on The Mountain. Inside the rehab." He stalls, licks at the deep red groove carved into his upper lip. He winces. "There's nothing here. And … Burnside has been—how would you put it—he's been taking his frustration out on—"

Something quick and black enters the frame as quickly as it leaves it. Harrison's head jerks violently to the left of the screen. A new wound is opened along his right eyebrow. Blood gleams within the dark shorthairs. He gasps. Pants. Cannot draw a productive breath. And once he does, he uses this new and sacred oxygen to laugh his signature impossible smartass laugh as he hangs his head low. "Guess I forgot myself there for a minute," he whispers.

Harrison lifts his chin, glares at the camera.

"Yeah, so there's nothing here but the wind rushing in and out of the many, many broken windows. A draught that whistles. Place is fucking creepy as hell. But there's no magic here. I don't sense anything. No … Muse. I'm sorry to report Stevie's been out of his mind for longer than I think any of us really knew. All the way back to when they were recording *Knives*. I know. Sounds impossible. But I don't want you to waste your trip. And I don't want you to try anything heroic." A pause. He shuts his eyes, opens them big and wide. "I've been told what's gonna happen to me. That's been made plain."

All Gretch wanted to hear is that Burnside has agreed to release him if he records this video clip on his behalf. Says the things he's required to say to earn his freedom. That he will walk away from this.

She can't focus. Black spots dance before her vision.

"I want you to know … I have no regrets for getting involved in all this," Harrison continues. "I also don't want to lie to you, because I don't think I'm ever going to see you again. I dunno. I wouldn't want the last things I say to you to be a crock of shit. So, here's the truth, no matter how shitty. I'm supposed to tell you *do not come*. If you're on your way here, turn back around. Go home. Burnside wanted me to tell you so. And I don't disagree. There's nothing for you here. Honestly, Red, just hang back and tend to Stevie. And-and *try* to take comfort in knowing that if he was delusional about The Mountain and The Muse, it would follow that his memory is all the way fucked and he never hurt anyone, let alone took a life. I think you should try to view this as a good thing. It absolves him.

"Davey's here. It's true. He and Burnside, let's just say they see eye-to-eye about a great many things. It's almost like they're hardwired into each other's minds. The way twins sometimes are. They've made it known they will kill you if you show your face here.

"They're going to *clean house* very soon. Davey says he will have no problem tossing you onto the pile of bodies if need be. They wanted me to make that clear to you. There's an endgame in place for Davey's wives. And … Christ, one of them looks like-*she can't be more than seventeen* at best—"

Harrison flinches, looks up to the right corner of the screen at someone off-camera. "Alright—*fuck!*

He gathers himself.

"Red, *don't come*. They say you'll only make new tracks where they've covered all the rest. And it won't go well for you." Pause. "I don't want to die without telling you the most important part of this fucking *hostage tape*."

Gretch feels the hot sting of tears. The pressure in her temples as they build behind her eyes. The cutting realization that she cannot stop them, at least not when it comes to what they've already done to him on the videotape.

She speaks through gritted teeth, "Leave him alone, you pathetic fucks."

"You should know I'm past you, Red. Over you."

"What?" Gretch feels the lump of confused emotions form at the base of her throat. She suddenly can't swallow. Her thoughts are thrown into chaos.

Why would he look to hurt me? Why NOW?

"—have been for a long time. I don't know if our spending that short time together these last couple of weeks meant any more than my trying to get you into bed one last time. That's all it was. So, I don't regret the time we spent, but it would have been nice to have you once more. I'm over it. There's nothing there now. So ... now you really *have* zero reason to come. Why look to save a piece of shit womanizer like me. A tiger does not change his stripe, Red. Never."

Her hands ball into fists. Drawing herself up into a standing position, Gretch watches the screen as if from a great distance. Across a great divide. Harrison Hart's words, scathing and shocking, gut her. Even as she stands there, hollowed out, Gretch can't shake the gnawing feeling in her gut that there is something else going on here.

He's lying. Isn't he?

They are his last words, a complete and total separation. A messy break, but one that feels like it will hold.

Because whether this is a ruse or not and she is missing a subtext to it, Gretchen can't deny how his words have harmed and traumatized her.

The screen goes dark.

Then static.

Gretch stands there, marooned between action and inaction. She takes these few seconds to steady herself. She shuts her eyes and focuses solely on slowing her heartbeat. Deep breaths. Opening and closing of her hands. Digging her nails into the taut, webbed flesh of her palms. It awakens a drive and a hunger within that her prehistoric ancestors would have channeled to hunt or to go to war with a competing hungry mouth.

This won't keep me away.

Wild horses … the Rolling Stones had the right idea.

"I could turn around," she says. "Head home."

The VHS tape finishes rewinding. Tiny wheels within the console squeak like robotic mice. They lift the tape up and push it out an inch, awaiting its return to its sleeve.

"Home to what? Exactly?"

It happens in slow motion. An out-of-body moment where she watches herself first lay two fingers on the top of the television. Then three fingers. Four.

Then the push, quick and assertive.

The television tips backward, off its stand.

Crashes to the floor, a high enough fall that shatters the back of it. The rear shell falls away, spilling glass tubing, cathode rays, and wire guts out the sides. The screen flashes white. Smoke billows from the set.

In a fog, Gretch eyes the tv power cord plugged into the wall.

Better get that out of there. Could catch fire.

Instead, Gretch turns and switches off the bedside lamp.

Climbs into bed and sleeps in fits and starts. The face that swims up out of the depths of her unconscious is not Harrison Hart. Not Stevie Darius. Not Burnside.

It's Allure, the girl she failed years ago to save from Davey and his grooming.

And its Allure, of all people, who pushes Gretch on with a renewed purpose.

A new but nevertheless urgent mission.

INTERLUDE (VII)

(From the Memoirs of Stevie Darius)

1990

Listen to me.

I saw Gretch on the ground backstage at The Mud Festival. Lying on her side. Bleeding from a wound hidden under her red hair.

And I had no idea who she was.

For almost a minute.

Staring. Slack-jawed.

As it would later be described to me by an extremely spooked John Germanian, I just stood over her with this blank expression on my face. He was pretty much describing the exact moment I believe this fucking illness of mine, the forgetful man's disease, first announced itself in my brain. J. says it was like "watching the lights go out in my eyes".

On-stage minutes before, I was all there. J and Chris had to literally pick me up and carry me offstage. Otherwise, I would have hung back, trying to wave Security towards where I was dead certain I'd seen the Bloody Mouth kid, that sick fuck who kicked off the chaos and the bloodletting out in the audience like an earthbound demon.

355

Prompted by whatever symbol Davey had written in mud across his bare abdomen.

It had cast some kind of fucking spell.

Kids slitting other kids' throats.

Jesus Christ, the memory of it! If only the dementia would wipe that shit away. No, it only seems to attack the cherished memories, like my wedding day or the first time I met Gretch. The day my mother bought me a second-hand bass from a pawn shop down the street for my tenth birthday. All the good days of my life. Shot full of holes now. I can't remember the specifics. The feeling in those moments. They are beyond my grasp. My understanding.

One of these days I'm just going to …

No.

"What the fuck happened here?" I shouted. "How'd a fan get back here?"

Yes, I thought she was a Grifters die-hard who'd somehow breached Security while they scrambled around to quell the crowd.

The woman on the ground was still a stranger to me: "We're gonna get sued!"

I thought she was a groupie or part of our entourage: "Somebody help me with her!"

J had already taken a knee beside her. He was exploring her scalp, searching for a hidden wound or an egg. Anything.

He brought his hand away. It was gloved in wet red.

"Oh shit! Shit-shit-shit!" He wiped the blood on his leather pants and stood like a shot. He wheeled on Davey. "What the fuck happened, man? Did you see anything? Who did this to Gretchen—"

Then I knew who she was. I needed J say her name and it was like the tape in my brain that had stopped recording switched back on. My girl, my world was hurt. She'd either slipped and fallen, an unlikely scenario given she lay clear of any stairs or a pole she could have run headlong into. For all intents and purposes, she was clear of anything to strike her head on so hard it would have knocked her out.

"Where the hell are Chris and Bobby?" I erupted.

Behind me, Bobby's low and monotone voice, answered. "Here. Jesus, we're so fucked! They can't stop it. Security's powerless!"

Somehow, I'd been so hyper-focused on Gretchen and her injury I'd managed to unconsciously tune out the deafening and terrifying sounds of thousands of concertgoers tearing at each other and breaking for the exits and trampling one another. The screams. The curses. The bedlam. People were dying. They'd been whipped into a frenzy. And my brain was so fucked and fried, I'd forgotten all about that freak sonofabitch.

Bloody Mouth.

I just couldn't hold onto more than one train of thought. The other threads that did not directly involve my girl just slipped out of reach.

I saw Chris post up right next to Davey and the jailbait, Allure. It couldn't have been more symbolic of how the chips always seemed to fall lately when it came to band business and voting for or against certain points of order. They'd both stood in perfect opposition against the rest of us when we'd ultimately voted to stop hunting. And just like then, Chris looked like someone who suffered from a learned helplessness at the hands of his master, Davey-fucking-Grifter. Dracula and fucking Renfield, no shit! With Glory and this Allure chick their Brides of the Vampire bit parts.

The whole situation had never felt more-well-unholy? There is just no other way to describe how alliances seemed to fall in line without any previous planning or consideration.

J, Bobby, myself, and Gretch against —

Chris. Davey.

The band was split. I knew there would be no coming back from this.

I suppose that's why I did not hold back. I hated Davey for a long time. It all just bubbled up.

I put that fucker on full blast.

It felt like levitation the way I crossed the divide between Davey and myself right then. I pounced.

Allure let out this gasp that only egged me on and infuriated me even more.

Chris put out his arm to hold me back. I took him by the wrist. Turned it aside and twisted him right the fuck out of my face and out of my way. If J hadn't lodged himself between us, we would have beat each other bloody. Maybe unconscious. Chris used to be my brother and there was a time I would have gone to the wall for him. He was the new guy for a while there, having replaced Johnny K who quit right before rehab and mere months before we signed with Atlas Records and everything went bonkers.

Backstage, I could have killed Chris.

I looked at Davey.

It was like I was seeing him, really seeing the bastard, for the first time.

"You did this, Dave! I can see it in your eyes! Motherfucker!"

Allure let out this chirp like a scared little bird. Davey shuffled her behind him like I posed some kind of threat to her. Honestly, the girl could not have been more irrelevant in that moment.

I only had eyes for her man.

I felt all the heat in my body gather in my head.

My cheeks stung with rage.

Davey spread his arms wide, taunting even as he gave me good reason to take him by the throat. "Asshole! She came at me like she was gonna claw my fucking eyes out! What the fuck was I supposed to do? Chick was ranting and raving about how I kidnapped Allure and I'm grooming her against her will!"

My hands closed into fists, but I held back. Still don't know how. "Christ, Dave! You're a textbook groomer! How old's this one? Where'd you find her? Do her parents even know where she is? We're all sick and tired of pretending our singer isn't a fucking ghoul! You are seriously screwed in the head, man! And now-now you put your fucking hands on our manager?"

"There's no we, Stevie!" Chris blurted behind me. J was restraining him. "You don't speak for me, jerkoff! You got no right!"

"Shut! Up!" J exploded. He flung Chris aside like a ragdoll and put himself between Davey and I. "Stop this shit! We gotta get Gretch to a hospital and clear out before the mob comes for us!"

Davey scoffed. "Why don't we leave her to Stevie! He's the one sticking it in—"

I hit him with a sloppy right cross. My knuckles crunched against his jaw and a lightning bolt of exquisite pain shot up my forearm. I didn't pull the punch. Davey's head jerked violently to the side at such a severe angle I thought I'd snapped his neck. His hand flew to his jaw and his eyes shut for a split second before fluttering open again and landing on me. There was fire in them. Murder. And I wondered in that split second if Calliope hadn't taken hold of him as it had so many times before right before a hunt.

Would he try to kill me?

Would he have a choice?

The hackles on the back of my neck stood up.

I was someone else's prey for the first time ever.

Then we were locked into a chaotic cloud of arms and swinging fists and gnashing teeth and inventions in profanity the likes of which would have made fucking George Carlin blush.

We were falling. Together.

I craned my neck around, put my mouth to his ear. "What did you draw on yourself out there? What does it mean? What did you say to me, you fucking maniac?"

My arms were wound around him. I felt his back muscles stiffen. "Don't know what the fuck you're talking about! You're fucking dead!"

Before I knew what I was doing, I sank my teeth into ear cartilage and bit down. Blood flooded my mouth, a handful of dirty pennies on my tongue.

Davey let out a high-pitched scream.

Hands found my waist, encircled, and dragged me off our singer. I watched in displaced fascination as a couple of the guys from Louder pulled Davey away from me. They hauled him off with Allure in tow, a little girl shuffling behind the entourage and sneaking a lone glance back at me. I swore I saw a certain satisfaction glimmering in her saucer-sized blue eyes. All around me, raised voices spun out and around, creating a din of panic and chastising bursts of anger and a couple of spare female shrieks thrown in for good measure.

I thought I'd somehow been transported to the seventh circle of Hell where torment lives.

But Hell had broken out in the crowd of mud caked, sweaty masses who'd come to check out their favorite band. None of us would come to know until much later that eight concertgoers, one of them a ten-year-old boy, had lost their lives in the fray. Not to mention, the innocent victims who'd gotten their throats slit, all of this goaded on by this Bloody Mouth character no one else had seen but me. To this day, I wonder if I hallucinated him. Another early symptom of what would come to be this fucking evil dementia wiping away my memories by slow, excruciating degrees.

Was he on The Mountain with us?

Gretch was airlifted to the hospital and died once on the way. She suffered a cerebral hemorrhage and lost the ability to speak for several days. Doctors feared the portion of her brain that dictates speech had been damaged beyond repair, until she managed to speak her first word to me one rainy evening.

That word: "Done."

I knew what she meant. It was a resignation, and it had been decided upon during her time away, buried deep inside her own subconscious. There could be no changing her mind, and I wouldn't have tried. I was done with Grifters Anonymous also.

Not because I was following her lead.

I didn't trust my own impulse control any longer when it came to Davey.

I had no interest in suing him.

No, I wanted to kill him.

Ultimately, the band breaking up shortly after the tragedy at Mud Festival and the attack on Gretch created a perfect storm of disintegration for the lead singer who I decided I'd never really known at all.

Grifters Anonymous, the great rock and roll machine that fed on innocent lives and spit out the bones of genius riffs and lyrical anarchy, was dead.

From there, the dementia has been making its advance.

I am convinced it is punishment.

I had angered Calliope.

That's why things went so wrong so quickly for the band.

Calliope was stripping us of all blessings. Not a mere stripping of our fame and success. We're still considered living legends. Instead, Calliope stripped us of our health and ultimately of our humanity. Our sanity. And nearly robbed me of the only woman I ever loved, for nothing more than to prove a point. That Calliope was and would always reign supreme over us mere mortals. That we could never best her or pull a fast one. We were weak and vulnerable for all time.

Still, I have no regrets for putting an end to the killing. None. And Gretch still has no idea the man I used to be. Any of the men she managed used to be.

We sang a song titled "Knives for the People" and still, no one put it together.

The title was and has always been a confession in plain sight.

No one got it. That's why these memoirs are so necessary.

No more guessing. No more gray area.

Calliope, I speak directly to you now.

The spell is broken.

I've made my penance in these pages.

What more do you want from me?

What does my freedom cost?

I will pay it, but I will not kill for you. Any longer. No. Anything else.

If you must continue to punch holes in my brain and wipe out great segments from my life's memories, then do your worst. If that's what will make us square, take it all. If I have to give my own life for stopping the sacrifices, then consider me the final one thrown into the fire. Be satisfied.

Be satisfied

Be satisfied.

Please

FORTY-THREE

Gretchen Solomon's headlights sweep across the chained, wrought-iron entrance gate just shy of midnight. It stands at the end of a long and winding dirt path that is bordered on both sides by dense forestry. Even with the oaks picked clean by the cold fingers of winter, they still form a cluster that forms a wall of woods.

It's Gretch's understanding that the rehab was fully functional as recently as six years ago. Yet there is no serviceable road of any kind that would have taken any visitor straight to the buildings parking lot, let alone its front entryway.

She is not ready to kill the engine or douse the headlights. The last roadside light she saw was a mile back. Once Gretch kills the Land Rover, she knows she will barely be able to see her hand in front of her face. Even the incline just beyond the gate, glowing with a layering of smooth, bone-white snow, fails to catch and reflect the moonlight.

Remaining in the driver's seat, her gloved hands gripping the steering wheel with a desperate ferocity, she shuts her eyes. To dig deep for the mental resolve that will move her to shut the vehicle off, shrug her pack over her shoulders (ever so gently so as not to jostle the locked magazine containing four blocks of C4), and cross beyond the gate to make fresh tracks in the snowy hill.

It begins as pins and needles up her arms.

Down her legs.

Then it builds into a centrifugal pull on her bones, her joints, her flesh. From this vantage, she can't set eyes on the rehab, but Gretch is certain that it is drawing her closer like a great magnet of doom. No doubt standing atop the rise like some darkened monolith, pulling at her every muscle and sinew and ligament and bone.

She braces herself, hands clutching the steering wheel.

She slows her breaths and pictures a babbling brook. A crystalline sky, unbroken by clouds.

It centers her.

The *pull* is gone, leaving an ache in Gretch's frame and a feeling of euphoria like she's just come out of a coma or exercised vigorously and well beyond her limits.

"Go," she tells herself. "Go now. While it's still *your* choice to *make*."

She cranks open the door, steps out, and circles around to the back seat. She climbs inside and scoots across until she is on the other side. She reaches around, cranks the passenger seat in front of her forward enough to provide the legroom she needs to change out her Doc Marten's for a pair of heavy, fur-lined snow boots. Gretch wraps herself in a black, billowing ski jacket. She screws a maroon beanie onto her head. With stiff little fingers, Gretch works her hair into a long-braided plait that hangs down her back.

She shuts and locks the Land Rover. She gingerly shoulders her weighted backpack on and turns towards the locked gate just as a fierce gust of wind smacks her backhanded across the face. The snub-nose revolver she tucks into the back of her black jeans. The kiss of oiled, jagged steel rakes the small of her back. She hikes her panties up to deflect or at least to soften the friction there.

Something white flashes in her right periphery, scuttering between the tree line and the weakened, leaning gate that she will come to discover spans the entire border of the forest running east and west respectively.

The white spark assumes the shape of a long white veil caught by the wind and carried off.

She swears it has left an imprint in the air as it disappears into the freezing ether.

Cold fingers touch the buttons of her spine.

It is not the gun.

She shivers violently.

And there's nothing to compare this feeling to, as she has never seen a ghost before.

Gretch thinks this must be what it feels like for anyone privy to such a rare sighting.

Is The Mountain haunted?

Before terror can sink its claws in, Gretch stuffs the thought down deep.

Gretch approaches the gate. One of the iron slats has been hammered to the side, creating a breach that could accommodate a waifish, female frame. It would make sense, as Davey and his Sister Wives have needed to come and go from The Mountain to gather provisions, barter with the locals, and to filch from their homes and businesses in the dead of night as they saw fit. Glory told her Davey had even begun to turn out some of the younger, prettier Wives for the sake of exchanging sexual favors for gasoline to power the fleet of generators he'd imported to the abandoned rehab. Glory also mentioned a ski mobile the women would use to come and go, but damned if Gretch could see any aperture wide enough to accommodate them. There must be another opening in the gate further down the border.

Of course, the question of whether he'd pressed Glory herself into this type of sexual exchange was never asked.

No need.

The hunted look in the young woman's eyes said it all.

JanSport backpack slung over her shoulders, a high-powered flashlight rustling up against the various food and toiletry provisions she'd packed from home, Gretch wonders why she would have packed for an extended stay when, in fact, to become stranded on The Mountain or taken prisoner there rivaled her worst nightmares.

Squeezing through the opening in the gate with relative ease, Gretch pitches her weight forward and climbs the snowy rise. Her calves shriek in protest. It is a sweet pain. The activity floods her with endorphins. She is so intent on cresting the top of the rise her eyes nearly gloss over the separate footprints in the snow, a mere three or four feet away from her own. Tracking up the hill.

She moves sideways, centering her mass to keep from falling.

Carefully lowers herself down to have a look at the other tracks.

Two separate sets of boot prints cut into the snow.

They run side-by-side. Four across.

There is nothing she can do about it if they are waiting for her at the top. Inside the rehab.

Gretch realizes how badly she needs to crest the hill. To fix her gaze on the rehab huddled before the giant landmass like a sleeping cub before a dozing grizzly.

Until then, she cannot bring herself to believe entirely that there is a Mountain *or* a Muse.

FORTY-FOUR

First impression?

The Mountain does not look like any natural formation she has ever seen.

Not to her tired eyes, obstructed even more by the skirling snowflakes flying at her face.

It most resembles some prehistoric sperm whale washed up and left to die. It is a bruised, eggplant color, mottled with white slashes of snow caught in its craggy surface. There is a sheen to the mountainside that further enhances its resemblance to that of a beached gargantuan sea creature lying on its side.

She feels like she has crept up on something she was never meant to see.

Like her mother riding her father when she slips into their room after a nightmare.

Like the time she was driving down the Pacific Coast highway in a mad rush to make a meeting with the brass at Grifter's record label, and there had been an accident just cleared off the road. Bodies sheeted and assembled all in a row along the breakdown lane. A corner of one of the sheets lifted when a passing tanker truck thrust a gust of wind at it. And Gretch had seen the body underneath. The shattered skull and brain peeking out like an Easter egg skeined with blood.

Like …

Like …

She is instantly sickened at the sight of it.

The sight of the rehab building shines a light on the blind spot the ECT treatment had formed in the cortex of her brain. Gretch swears she can feel the blood as it once more rushes to refresh a dead memory. A fleet of them.

The harsh winter winds slash and whip at her, jostling her ever so lightly. It is pushing back on her. Discouraging her. A pathetic fallacy? Maybe.

It is convincing enough.

"I could leave," she says.

If Allure is still alive?

Harrison?

Glory, for Chrissakes?

"There is so much that can go … so wrong."

She could well be entering the lion's den without a whip nor a chair.

The explosives could have deteriorated. Prove impotent in a life-or-death moment.

"All the more reason to turn back," she tells herself, hearing her own voice more inside her head than outside as the winds swallows every word whole. "Go home. Deal with Stevie. *You.* No one else."

Go home. Turn him in. Or kill him.

But be done with all of this.

You're not a hero.

What Gretch does not realize right away is her boots have already started walking her again.

They've made the decision without her. An unconscious one, but one she decides to submit to.

After all, some Higher Power has already meted out a proper punishment on Stevie Darius, as well as his cohorts.

She'll leave it.

For now.

FORTY-FIVE

The rehab and rest is a festering wound with gangrene threaded through its once fine sandstone structure. Gretch can barely imagine the exterior of the structure having ever looked healthy in its bones or the stone base having ever shined a healthy earthy brown. God would one day have no choice but to amputate this structure from the body of the earth, even though the stories and myths that swirl around it offer dreadful proof its evil and illness having already spread.

It's clear The Mountain is what has infected the edifice with its rotting disease.

Closing the distance now, it becomes clear to Gretch that the four-story structure does not merely stand in the immediate foreground of the Mountain.

The building runs into the base of the Mountain. She wonders if the cold and the disorientation of the moment have compromised her senses. There is no conceivable reason why any architect would embrace such an uncanny design. Gretch had simply assumed these natural structures were not hollow but rather solid conglomerations of shale and other various stone formations compressed through time by the shifting of the earth's plates.

The fact that the rehab runs directly into the mountainside allude to a hollow interior.

Four rows of ocular-shaped windows face out of the easternmost side of the building. They are surprisingly smaller in size than average.

They resemble the eyelets of a lace-up shoe.

What lies within? Not merely the rehab, which she fears will boasts its own horrors.

Inside The Mountain itself.

Precariously, Gretch approaches the massive double doors, each twelve-feet high, which comprise the entrance to the rehab building. The doors resemble a pair of makeshift flotation devices devised by the hands of a castaway. Thick tree limbs bundled together. Upon closer inspection, she can see they are far more solid in their structure than something Robinson Crusoe would have sailed away from a desert island upon. She lays her hands on their surface and recoils at the frostbite teeth that bite at the webbing of her palms. The massive doors face out from what looks like the southeasternmost corner of the building itself

The building does not extend back from the big, imposing doors as much as it *fans* outward.

Gretch wets her chapping lips, takes hold of the black, twisted iron rung fixed into the door. She grits her teeth, expecting the bulk to barely move in her hands. She plants her feet and pulls.

The door opens with unanticipated ease. Such a surprise that Gretch sits down hard in the snow and the door wheezes shut, but not before offering her a quick look inside.

"Fucking shit!" she shouts and finds her feet once more.

She seizes the door handle and yanks it back, annoyed by the fact the seat of her jeans is now soaked through.

Within.

The darkness yawns absolute within. It fills Gretch with such a total sense of despair she must draw an especially deep breath and brace herself against the threshold for a moment.

Then, she moves all the way inside, lets the doors wheeze shut.

Deep blue comes to lift the hard edges here and there out of the black. A reception area forms around her as if from nothing.

As if conjured.

It is her eyes adjusting. Pupils dilating.

Gretch carefully lowers her backpack down off her shoulders. Brings it around so she can gingerly rummage inside. Her fingers side-step the locked magazine housing the explosives. Eventually, she brings out a powerful, police-issue-type flashlight with the long, slim and black body.

She thumbs the switch to On. It cuts a sharp white swathe across the foyer. Beyond it to where a single step-down opens onto a wide and impressive veranda that would have invited so many to come and sit and warm themselves by a flickering fire if not for the vacuous nature of it now in the absence of people. And yet, from this vantage, it would appear everything has been kept as it was before its owners and staff fled the rehab and neglected to even bolt the entranceways in their hasty retreat.

Any notion of having stepped into an edifice free from a slow, encroaching ruin is stamped out by the quick, paralyzing assault of rot upon Gretch's nostrils.

She immediately claps her free hand over her nose, gagging.

"Oh God," she says, dropping her chin into the pocket of her throat as if this will stave off the rank odor of flyblown meat and runny shit.

Is it Davey?

What the hell happened to him?

The mighty have not merely fallen.

They've taken a one-way ticket to sociopathic.

But she's come this far. Gretch must bear witness to Davey's downfall, no matter its form.

Because if the bastard ever makes it off The Mountain, or attempts to revive his career, she will have all the motivation she needs not just to stop him but to assassinate his character once and for all.

So the sonofabitch won't even be able to snag a job at Taco Bell when I'm done with him!

She follows the flashlights cone of light. Steps down into what looks like the main hall of a ski lodge. Makes a flurry of sweeping arcs with her flashlight. Gretch passes by one of the four balustrades that support what is a vaulted ceiling of dizzying crossbeams hatched into something of a brilliant, entrancing pattern of alternating angles. The floor is hardwood and sturdy.

Gretch pauses and whips the light about once more. It splashes across a cluster of chairs stacked on top of one another along the easternmost wall. Just shy of the right stairwell. It would not have given her pause if the stacks of chairs did not rise to an impossible height, practically skimming the roofbeams four stories up.

How?

Why?

Something flaps its frantic wings high above.

A blur of black.

It ceases just as Gretch casts her beam up into the rafters.

Her thigh knocks into the side of something soft but immoveable. She aims the cone of light at the impediment. A three-seater leather sofa. Mocha upholstery with a thin layering of dust coating its surface. It is joined in a squared-off arrangement of a duplicate sofa, two wingbacks, and two loveseats that share the same chocolate upholstery and dusty second skin. An oriental rug ties it all together in the center.

Tiffany lamps arranged on four end tables mark the corners of the ensemble.

Everything in its place.

The absurdity of the expensive light fixtures and the Italian-leather-upholstered furniture disorients her.

Gretch starts to wonder if she is not actually there, but rather home in bed with a fever dream turning her mind sideways.

The risers of another stairwell to her left wink at her with their deep blue murk that has not yet been touched by the flashlight's beam. She hits it with a bit of light.

The left and right stairwells border a dormant walk-in fireplace.

"Oh *fuck!*"

A body lies facedown and splayed out before the hearth like some twisted variation of a bear skin rug.

"Fuck. Fuck."

What did he tell you? He said DO NOT COME! *And here you are—*

Slowly, Gretch approaches the body. The cone of light starts at their feet, clad in black chukka Doc Marten boots. The left foot lies at an odd angle, like someone tried to twist it off like a bottle cap from the mouth of a soda bottle. Black leather pants cover a pair of long, stilt-like legs. An army-green bomber jacket billows about their equally, long and lithe upper body.

The flashlight beam crawls up the back of the body, shifting as Gretch closes in.

Their right arm is tucked underneath as if in some last-minute, futile protective gesture. The left hand rests in a pool of blood that looks to have already begun to dry. It is not spreading.

The body has bled out. The heart is a busted pump.

The light beam illuminates the back of their head.

Wait-wait-wait-what the fuck is this?

The dyed white-blonde hair still holds its severe spiky style. No blood. No wound in the rear of the skull.

"Burnside," Gretch breathes, her mind drunk on a range of emotions.

She can't hold back the quick flash in her mind's eye of turning the body over.

Finding a face that looks like bloody sushi.

(*DO NOT COME!*)

Suddenly, Gretch Solomon is aware of eyes on her.

Her skin crawls. Blood runs cold beneath a sheathe of goosebumps that rise across her forearms.

Whose eyes?

Davey?

The Sister Wives?

Her mouth runs dry.

Harrison?

For all intents and purposes, the dead man on the floor with what appears to be massive head trauma, is responsible for upending her already messy life. It would suffice to move along from the body of Paddy Burnside.

Gretch needs proof of her tormentor's demise.

On stiffened legs, she hunkers down beside the body. Her pulse is a snare drum between her ears as she stiffly takes hold of the body's shoulders. Turns it over.

For a split second, she swears the dead man's arms shudder in her grasp.

A phantom sensation.

Paddy Burnside's face is peeled away from the bone. It hangs off the tip of his chin like bloody wax paper. The bone structure is ravaged. Chewed. Bitten. Torn away. Caved in. A black hole where the nose used to be. Both eyes plucked from their sockets.

And Gretch barely contains the scream that pushes out at the seam of her pursed lips

It is reduced to something like a chirp before she manages to suppress it entirely.

Someone answers with a whistled melody.

At first, Gretch turns her attention to the second-floor landing where the left and right stairwells converge. The whistling is continuous, as if powered by a pair of gargantuan lungs.

The tune is vaguely familiar. Its title stands on the tip of her tongue. One thing she is certain of is it's not of the Grifters catalog. *That would allude to it being Davey … hiding himself away. But fucking where?*

The melody breaks off abruptly.

Gretch stands and cocks her head in what she believes is the general direction of the disembodied sound.

Show yourself, you sonofabitch!

Her eyes rake the brick inlay that frames the walk-in fireplace. When she fixes her gaze on the interior of the hearth, the impossible ink black within tries to swallow her consciousness whole. She mentally pulls back, even takes an unconscious and precarious step back. Remembering the weight of something in her palsied right hand, Gretch raises the flashlight and aims it into the hearth. Vanquishing the black hole quality that so unsettled her. Entranced her for a moment.

There is an aperture in the back of the hearth.

A perfect break in the seam of soot-stained brickwork, revealing a passage beyond.

The whistled melody picks back up.

This time, Gretch Solomon shrieks.

She knows the song now.

Mother. Fucker.

Suspecting she will need shoes with better grip than what she has on, Gretch quickly swaps out her furry snow boots for the Doc Martens she brought along with her just in case.

She reaches for the revolver tucked into the back of her pants. Brings it around. Stacks the flashlight overtop of the snub nose and moves in the direction of the anonymous, taunting whistler.

Gretch surges into the hearth. She fits her fingertips into the seam of the aperture. Draws it wider apart until it will accommodate her. Slipping into the beyond of The Mountain, Gretch immediately notices the drastic change in temperature from mildly chilly to a burgeoning heat that intensifies with every forward movement.

It is bare earth just within the narrow opening. The terrain is worn smooth. Not a crag or imperfection or sinkhole in the compacted dirt.

Gretch enters the tunnel, casting a wide and mildly comforting cone of light out before her. Digging every nook and cranny out of the crude rock archway inches above her head. The rock is the color of loose stool. The smell of rot stalks her now. Fills her nostrils. Tickles her gag reflex.

The tunnel floor is a descending ramp.

Visions of hell, as she has come to understand and envision it in her lapsed-Catholic mind's eye, flash within her frontal lobe. Spooking her. The increasing temperature only adds to this preconceived notion of what Hell is and has always been.

And the fire somehow lapped at Stevie's bare feet. Seared the flesh red and pocked with white sores. From hundreds of miles away. Its reach is endless as it is terrible. A justice I never took seriously because I thought it was all in his mind.

None of this *was in his mind.*

The whistler urges her on like a pied piper.

She has no idea when she crosses into the belly of The Mountain. Somewhere she'd read that it only gets colder the deeper you plunge into the earth.

And yet, as Gretch rounds one of a seemingly endless number of twists and turns and slants in the pathway, she is sweating through her clothing. Her face is a mask of perspiration. Her red hair clings to her scalp. Her head aches.

The whistled melody does not soothe.

It commands.

But Gretch Solomon has something else in mind.

A fitting end.

FORTY-SIX

The sound of labored breathing as she negotiates the winding dirt path deeper into the belly of The Mountain. A hot breath fans her right ear and there is a rank odor of corpse-flower breath.

The whistling has turned to singing, a dirge that feels more like a siren song.

It's a deep cut track from Louder's first album. The song: "Better Not Tell". The delivery is pitch perfect.

The cone of her flashlight winks off and on again.

The gradient beneath the thick soles of her combat boots changes. Her ankle twists. If it wasn't for the hi-top leather support of her footwear, Gretch would have suffered a sprain or worse, a break. There are few worse scenarios she can imagine finding herself trapped in. She steadies herself, draws herself up as best she can.

Throws battery-powered light further down the path.

What the hell am I ... looking at?

Gretch stands on ground made uneven by a littering of what at first resembles colorful autumn leaves with flashes of white and grey and slashes of black here and there.

She hunkers down on her haunches to have a better look.

What she finds is something that makes no sense.

Until it does.

She casts the light to and fro along the cave floor.

Instinct holds her back from progressing any further.

Now that she can see what she will have to trample over and tread upon.

Half-realized paintings.

Sketches done in pencil.

Gretch sifts through the items nearest to her. She unearths papers and parchments and swatches of colored paper and used napkins and crumpled printer paper.

All of which bear everything from hastily scribbled lines of half-formed prose or stunted poetry to significantly longer blocks of writing. The mode of how the words are committed to the papers is varied as it is astounding in its implications.

Some are written in a calligraphic style, clearly the work of a quill.

Printed words in dot matrix style. Longhand is the most predominant form as Gretch digs through the discarded *false start* works of art littering the cavern floor.

A veritable trove of aborted attempts.

She stands, shines her light as far as it will project without obstruction.

It is a straight shot.

It is also a treasure trove chronicling the human creative impulse through time.

The first she's encountered since entering the cave.

The abandoned works of art cover the floor of the cavern for as far as the cone of light can reach.

This changes things.

Gretch lowers her pack onto the ground, unzips it, and begins to snatch up every spare, scrap item on the dirt floor before her. In mid-motion, Gretch freezes *and*—

The world turns to sudden, shocking white heat.

It erases everything.

The cave. Her overflowing backpack.

For an instant, Gretch knows what it is to lose her sense of hearing.

Then, she experiences the first few milli-seconds of her body exploding.

The rip and the tear and the bones splintering.

The big empty of the dead mind—

Stop! STOP! LEAVE IT!

PUT ALL OF IT BACK!

EVERYTHING LAST FUCKING THING—

Gretch snaps to. Her skull feels packed with cotton. Spring-loaded so tight a headache blooms right behind her forehead. For a moment, there is no line between what she just experienced in all its phantom, mesmerizing horror, and the reality she just returned to. The question of whether she did in fact explode the C4 blocks in her backpack lingers in the forefront of her concern.

It's only when Gretch recognizes the trusty, throbbing (if not sloppy) beating of her heart between her ears that she accepts she is still alive.

That she had just randomly hallucinated her own immolation.

That the cave has no intention of allowing for so much as a shred of parchment or broken piece of clay to depart without some form of inner war waging against the thief.

The cave did that to me?

Gretch understands the directive, no matter it seems to have come from an inanimate landmass. If she means to proceed any further, she should minimize the amount of damage she inflicts on the discarded art carpeting the ground before her. Carefully, she pulls her pack up her back and shrugs it higher up until it is grazing her neck.

The best she can do to oblige the will of the cave is to skirt as much of the discarded art as she can.

This will require hugging the wall of the cave as she progresses deeper inside.

This is no easy feat, as the craggy, unyielding rocks rake her jacket and shirt up and aside. It cuts and carves the soft flesh of her middle back. She struggles to hold the flashlight upright and aimed into the black before her. She imagines her back will look like she has been tortured, tied to the rack by some bad actor.

There will be scarring, even.

She leans forward as far as her center of gravity will allow for without tipping her headlong into the pile of broken canvases and papers and warped paper pads edged in the brown and yellow of age and decay.

Stooping slightly forward as she strains to traverse the darkness that surrounds her, Gretch's breath catches in her throat when she spots something sticking out of the discarded art works at her feet.

The heel of her shoe makes a sickening crunching sound as it tears and rends and crumples rare items with every footfall.

Dead dreams.

Centuries of failure.

Under foot.

It is a page of sheet music, the notes penciled in. It bears a title that has been scribbled out so fiercely it punched a hole in the top of the paper. The composer's name is partly obscured by another piece clinging to it like detritus on the forest floor. Gretch sees:

rshwin

A SHUDDER RATTLES her from tailbone to the nape of her neck.

"George … George *fucking* Gershwin?"

It's the first piece bearing a signature she has come across.

She contorts her body just enough to grab the discarded Gershwin page from the piling.

The awe borne of what she has found, a musical piece written by the genius behind *Rhapsody in Blue* and *Porgy and Bess* that will never see the light of day. And the implication in having founds such a relic here of all places? The famed jazzman? Under contract with the—

The what?

Calliope?

Jesus Christ!

Who else left something of themselves behind?

It suddenly clicks with her, the great ball bearing falling into place with an unnerving metallic sound. Gretch casts her gaze further down the cave path like she is surveying miles of deep blue sea and wondering what sunken galleons bearing gold in its broken wood bellies lie beneath the swells. *Sheet music to an aborted Hendrix song? Botched Dylan lyrics? A sketch or five or twenty-five, with Picasso scratched into the bottom right hand corner. The first few crumpled, handwritten pages of an Orson Welles script destined to remain buried and denied for all time?*

Not to mention the countless artists and creators and innovators of their craft whose work never surfaced at all. Never to be excavated and dragged into the light.

It is not even a question any longer.

In the presence of such relics, the power of the cave, The Mountain, rears massive and sheds its previous mythic description in favor of undeniable truth.

Tangible truth. In her hands. Under foot.

It takes a fair amount of time to traverse the remaining area of the cave bearing its lost, sacred items. She stumbles a few times, her boot nearly flattening a splintery piece of broken canvas with what looks to be a sad clown done in dreamy swabs of oil paint.

Once across, Gretch finds she needs to stop. To take a breath.

To steady her hands, cut up and coated in amber dust rubbed off the walls.

Surreal doesn't begin to describe any of this. I feel like I just woke up on Mars, for Chrissakes!

Another matter sits in the back seat of her mind where she had successfully stowed it away for a moment of clear thinking.

Am I really going to destroy these relics?

How the hell will I ever sleep soundly again, knowing I've done so?

Still, she cannot abandon her plan. Her purpose for being there.

To shut down the Mountain or at least disable it beyond immediate repair.

Then to somehow escape with her life.

The C4 charges.

She must prepare them now that she's crossed the divide formed by the works of art.

And if she successfully arms the C4 blocks with the detonator just like *The Anarchist Cookbook* instructs (she'd held onto her brother's books for a reason she only now understands), it set off a series of devastating blasts. In turn, the explosions will most likely trigger an avalanche. Cave-in.

The prospect of destroying every last remnant of it all, some perhaps formed by the hands of history's most noteworthy icons in numerous artistic disciplines.

It's all Gretch can do to keep from getting sick down the front of herself.

While she still has control of her nauseated stomach, Gretch buckles down, bites her bottom lip hard enough to draw a drop of blood, and settles down onto her haunches to lift out the magazine bearing the explosives, a block of putty, an assembly of wires kinky and colorful like they belong to a children's play set, and a detonator that Gretch still wonders who her brother tapped for such an illegal implement.

Drawing on her memory of the "cookbook's" instruction, she gets to work.

Gretch mops her brow more than once while she works. The temperature is climbing steadily. A rise just steady enough to be felt without shocking her system.

She is the frog in a pot of water slowly coming to a boil.

The bombs capped in putty. Charges set. The detonator has a safety-switch to keep it from closing the circuit before its time. She carefully stows it inside the inner pocket of her coat.

She has no idea she's been holding her breath for the last minute or so until spots dance before her eyes.

She blows out a great gust and doubles over.

The trap is set. Demolition arranged. And Gretch straightens with a renewed sense of resolve that fills her up enough to make an about face and turn the flashlight upon the remaining pathway.

The cone of light illuminates the man in animal pelts seconds before his hand comes up and falls.

There's not even time for Gretch to scream before the rock in his hand strikes her across the top of her skull.

Plunges her into a depthless darkness of the mind.

Nothing.

FORTY-SEVEN

"Wake up, Red."

Someone has taken to lightly slapping her cheek.

"C'mon. Open your eyes. I need to talk to you."

Something of small weight rests against her right shoulder blade. She can feel that she is sitting down, and as memory of her where and when bleeds back into her brain, Gretch realizes she is seated on the rough, uneven ground of a cave.

She opens her eyes.

A slash of pain rips through the center of her skull.

And Harrison Hart rests on his haunches before her, hands steepled across his bent knees.

The bruises.

The black eyes.

The bloody smears up and down his cheeks and the abrasions she'd seen on the VHS tape anonymously delivered to her hotel room.

Gone.

The revulsion Harrison's battered visage had filled her with hardens into something of shock.

Then comes a visceral hatred for him.

The only thing that mars his appearance in any way is the sheen of sweat coating his brow and his hair, now flattened to the contours of his skull.

The heat is in the room with them. *But where?*

Lies. You … how … why would you? —

A pinprick of light gutters in the middle of his dilated eyes. A lopsided grin pulls on the bottom half of his face. And even in the dim, Gretch can see the white that rings his left nostril. He's been into cocaine. Hopped up on *nose beers*, like they called it back on The Strip. Coke being the natural laxative it is, Gretch thinks it had been his stink all along that greeted her in the foyer of the rehab center and then led her deeper into the Mountain. *He shit himself!*

Harrison cocks his head to the right of her. Somehow, she had forgotten the small weight resting atop her shoulder blade.

"Fucking shame," he mutters. "Fucking *Davey.* Poor girl looks just like Stevie describes her in his memoir. Younger even."

Gretch cranes her neck to the right. She is startled by the top of a girl's bumpy, razor nicked skull. Resting on her shoulder.

"What?" Harrison says. "You don't recognize her?"

Now. I. Do.

Allure.

I couldn't save you.

I was so close to extracting you from him all those years ago. You were going to let me help you. To hide you. To out Davey for his predatory bullshit.

Then I woke up on the cement floor backstage at the Mud Festival.

So.

Close.

Suddenly, her muscles clench and adrenaline floods them. Fight or flight mode chooses its side and Gretch screams, a watery tear-logged sound, as she kicks out at Harrison. Scrapes open some new wounds along her legs as the small stones sticking out of the ground bite into her. She swings at him. He bends backward, thinking himself free of her reach. Until she tags his chin hard with a half-closed fist. And the screams become words, packed with rage and murderous intent the likes of which she has never experienced before. *"You fucking mother-fucker! All just one big mindfuck! You sick* fuck! *Murdering—"*

She's never witnessed nor been on the receiving end of Harrison

Hart's brute force until he seizes her by both wrists with all the agility of a martial artist. Before she can resist any further, he yanks her up the craggy cavern wall, stands her up, and spins her around so she must turn her face aside lest she tear the tender, thin flesh of her face on the sharp stones jutting from the wall.

He puts his weight into her. He drives his knee into the small of her back, pinning her.

Harrison Hart, panting like a mongrel now, runs her arms up the center of her back until they can no longer move without snapping like a pair of twigs in his grasp.

Gretch screams from the soles of her boots.

This round of shrieks travels and echoes and spelunks every crevice of the Mountain's interior, taking on a terrible life of its own.

Harrison spins her back around. Presses her downward to take her place once more beside the freshly dead corpse of Allure. Torches burn at eye level along the wall of the widened cavern, but their reach is surprisingly shallow and much of Gretch's surroundings remain hunker in shadow.

Is that ... a—

"I was worried you might do something like that," Harrison says, his eyes hooded. He reaches for his back pocket, and his hand comes back around holding a crumpled red and white bandanna. "Open."

She hocks a wad of phlegm across the white tip of Harrison's black Converse.

He is on her at once.

She is too late to clamp her teeth down. To purse her lips.

Harrison pins her arms back against the wall with his knees. He forces the bandanna past her lips and teeth. Crams it until it hits home and triggers her gag reflex.

Gretch smells the fumes and tastes the tang of the gasoline that saturates the rag.

Nononononono—

"I would hate to have to burn you up from the inside out, Red," Harrison says, and in a dark sleight of hand produces a Zippo. He brings the flame.

Gretch flinches, eyes wide and terrified.

Spit it out! Do it now!

Confused and vigilant at the same time, Gretch pushes her tongue forward, expelling the flammable bandanna into her lap. Her hands are not bound, but for some reason she had forgotten this detail. Otherwise, she would have ripped it out of her mouth with the quickness.

She can feel his eyes surveying her as she lunges forward, up onto her knees. She vomits the partially digested remains of coffee and a Nutrigrain bar into the dirt.

Spits.

And spits.

The gasoline has coated the lining of her mouth and top of her throat.

Harrison lowers himself down before her, lit Zippo guttering in his hands as he holds it a foot from her petrol-infested mouth and lips. He eyes the flame. Holds his eyes away from her. "Don't scream. Don't fight. And you just might make it out of here alive. I mean, c'mon, Red. You gotta know I always loved you. *That part* of my little VHS performance? That was the truth."

"There are people who know I'm here," Gretch sputters. "Exactly where I am. And they know to come looking for me if they don't hear from me at—" She fumbles a number out of her frazzled mind and snatches it up. "Twelve noon today. I've …" Gretch gags, the gas in her mouth dripping from her palette onto her tongue. She blinks tears out of her eyes. "I've … always been smarter than …"

More gagging. Bile burns its way up her throat. She can't speak.

"Listen," Harrison says, snapping the Zippo shut. "If I wanted you out of the way I wouldn't have given you a very clear, *very stern* warning to stay clear of here. I'm not looking to hurt you. Yeah, I had to do the thing with the gas rag. If it's any consolation, I made sure to use Super instead of the cheap Unleaded. Only the best for my Gretch. So … gather yourself. I'll wait. Understand there is no way you can get rid of every bit of gas in your mouth. That's what it'd take to be in the clear should I flick the Zippo. Jam it into your mouth.

"But you don't want to *hurt me*, Hart? Are you fucking so far gone that that makes any kind of sense?"

The Zippo comes up, the flame guttering once more. She can feel its bite on the ridge of her nose. She shrieks. Bumps her head hard against the rock wall behind her and stars break across her field of vision.

In the light of the artificial flame, Harrison's calm and expectant eyes burn bright.

"This goes away again when you answer my question."

Her breath short and staggered, Gretch's eyes light on his and flinch away. "You … shit! You haven't asked me any fucking questions!"

"Where the fuck is Davey Grifter, Red?"

Now, she feels the subtle heat of the Zippos flame on her upper lip. "How the hell would I know where that psycho is?"

"See, I'm asking because he was the one who brought you up here and arranged you next to Allure. He's the one gave you that nasty bump on your forehead. I want to know everything. What did you see? How did he look? Is he armed? And no, I wouldn't count a handful of stone as *armed*."

An image flashes across her brain pan like a warning shot across the bow of a ship. *A man decked in animal pelts. Buckled to his body. Lashed to his limbs. His head is dented. Like an oversized golf ball.*

Then the rock comes down—

Even with the flame so close to her lips, Gretch gathers some grit.

"Cut the shit, Harrison," she says, through a rictus grin. "You were working with Burnside all this time. No doubt in my mind you're both tied to that wicked fuck, Davey Grifter, too. What's the matter? Your dog off the leash? You'll have to be the one to put the stick between his teeth, asshole!"

Harrison grits his teeth. He snaps the Zippo closed. Then, he does something that does not put Gretch at ease. No, it is quite the reverse effect. She fears he might kill her with his bare hands.

The washed-up rock star laughs, a rich and boisterous noise from his gut.

He stands, lording his masculinity over her.

He starts to pace back and forth before her, all the while holding her within his periphery. Something about the raw intensity coursing through this unhinged version of Harrison Hart holds Gretch at bay without any need for restraints. This is not the same person who had sat across from her cross-legged in her home, helping her pore through the Grifter's vinyl catalog for any useable clues regarding Stevie's credibility.

This is a man who has a casual relationship with his own sanity. The Mountain has infected him with raw obsession. The promise of a comeback. A second chapter, this one far surpassing his time as the frontman for Louder.

"Oh, Red," he says, pacing as he flicks the Zippo lighter opened and shut. *Click-click-click-click.* "That mouth of yours. It may have helped to ink a shitload of improbable deals for Grifters in their heyday. Now? No place for it. I have no idea where Davey is. Turns out he's turned squirrely since I saw him last. He's kept himself hidden. And it makes sense. After all, he's responsible for … all … this. Let me show you. It's dark in here. Easy to miss."

Harrison walks to the opposite wall of the cavern. He lights the Zippo, lowers the flame until it illuminates the hidden horrors lining the wall. He walks, holding the light by his hip, and provides just enough illumination for Gretch to see.

To scream at the sight of them all.

To burst into tears.

"This isn't my doing," he says. "They were already dead when I got here."

FORTY-EIGHT

The women are arranged like fallen dominos all in a row, seated against the cavern wall with their head resting on the shoulder of the one next to them. So on and so on. Twenty of them. Maybe closer to twenty-five. Gretch couldn't possibly count them in this frame of mind. She wouldn't want to if she could. With the lowlight challenging her vision, Gretch thinks they range in ages from the late teens to mid-fifties. The upper echelon represented by one silver-haired woman, who Davey might have chosen because of the resemblance to his departed grandmother.

Everyone of their throats is slit from ear to ear.

All wear animal fur, secured to their dead bodies in much the same way as Davey's ensemble. They fit the women haphazardly. Little consideration is given to their modesty. Here and there, one of them sits naked on the stone floor with their legs spread. Bare breasts exposed. Blood, still tacky and brown, coats the front of them and has splashed down into their laps.

That's not the worst of it.

Not for the Sister Wives.

Gretch comes off the wall just enough to verify what her strained, tired eyes seem to show her.

Oh … God …

The women each hold a butcher knife in their hands, which rests primly across their dirty, naked knees.

And it becomes apparent, in all its ghoulishness, the women were not merely using their neighbor's shoulder for a pillow. No, they were offering their throat to the woman next to them.

To be cut open.

On and on. Down the line. The second in line did the first to maintain the fluidity of the ritual. Running clockwise and ending with poor, lost Allure.

Which begs the question Gretch quickly dismisses for fear of losing her nerve.

Why didn't Davey cut my throat before arranging me with the others?

Why was I spared?

She doesn't realize Harrison had stopped prattling on until his hands wrap around her throat and he drive her body up the unforgiving stone wall once more. Tearing the back of her shirt that saturates with blood from the fresh wounds opened by the craggy surface.

"Where'd you go, Red? Huh? You don't think I've got anything important to say to you?"

"Nah-ah—"

He shoves the heel of his palm up into her chin, almost clipping the edge of her tongue off.

"I'm acting a fool," he chortles. "A fool for love. It's not serving my purpose. I need your undivided attention. Time to turn you into a captive audience. I'd hoped not to but … you never *really* listened when I talked. You never took me as serious as you should have."

She doubles over. She can't breathe.

It does not compute right away. Until she vomits and her right rib cage flares with white-hot pain.

He hit me.

Harrison …

Punched me in the stomach.

Stooped over with the last of her sick rushing out of her, Gretch feels the pinch of a zip tie as Harrison, who has now become her captor, binds her hands behind her back.

"You done?" he says, craning to look her in the eye. "Good. Siddown and listen close." He clamps a hand on her right shoulder and presses her down into a sitting position. Only now, her hands are rendered useless.

Still struggling to draw a productive breath, shoulders heaving and torso clenching, Gretch can only hope her sick rinsed the rest of the gasoline out of her mouth. "I don't ... know ... I dunno anything—"

Harrison looms over her like a monolith. "You're made of some seriously strong Irish stock, you know that? You can take a punch? Not a tear. Not one. See, *I know* you *know* something about this place. Because I was right fucking there beside you during most of your research. You just never took any of *this* seriously. You doubted its existence, let alone it's power. And I can't say I blame you. Your husband's brain was already turning into Swiss cheese when he started writing the Nasty Bits. You chalked it up to that.

"I've read the missing pages from the memoir. I've got them. And they led me here. This perfect little enclave, formed miraculously by the shifting of tectonic plates just so. Perfect for a congregation of believers to gather and worship. Near Calliope Herself. Tell me that's not magical. You tell me that's coincidence. This is the Church, Red. This is the Church of Calliope. Just like the pages said. And there is a visible relic of The Muse somewhere in this immediate vicinity."

"Harrison—"

"Sssssssshh—Stevie stopped just short of *where it is. What it looks like?* I don't know if he's fucking with whoever eventually got their hands on his pages. I dunno. But he's got fucking right. No. *Right!*

"Husbands and wives like you and Stevie? I know your type. You don't hold back a damned thing from one another. You never go to bed angry. You make sure to compliment one another at least once a day. You love and respect each other. I think it's beautiful. The only reason all of it doesn't make me throw up myself is that I have no doubt he told you where the relic can be found. You thought of it as gibberish. Think back. Because it's fact.

"Drag your memory like your life depends on it," Harrison says. "Cuz' if you don't ... if you can't tell me ... I don't know what that'll make me do."

"I don't know anything about a-a relic I swear—"

He seizes the bottom of her face. Squeezes.

She can feel herself slipping into a blackout from the pain.

He slaps her hard across the face to rouse her.

"It'll come to you. I have faith. I do." Then it comes to him. She knows this because of the way Harrison stands, slaps a hand to his forehead, and does an about face. "Sonofabitch, you *wouldn't* know. Would you? You—fuck! —you went and had your memory wiped back at the nut house." He turns to face her again, his eyes flat and black. "You don't know shit. You're nothing to me."

"Why would you do this?" Gretch asks, body rigid and diction crisp and clear. "I can't believe you were taken in by Stevie's ... bull-shit. His *hallucinatory ramblings*."

"Oh, save it, Red. We are *way* past the verification stage. Your guy, Burnside? Turns out he is *very fucking excellent* at what he does. The poor bastard wouldn't have ever made it to the Strip with some of the shit he let me listen to of his. But he's like a dog with a bone when it came to his cases. Very much a *ducks in a row* kind of guy. He could've been the next fucking Columbo if he just let the music thing alone. It was never in the cards for him. But some people? They just gotta keep at it. Trying to ram that circle into the square hole.

"You know better than anyone word of mouth is God," he presses on, ignoring Gretch when she tries to get a word in. "It's everything. I want you to multiply that kind of power—that influence—by a fucking thousand when someone comes to you with definitive proof a place like *this* exists. After years of hearing whispers about what only ever came to be considered the stuff of myth! On par with Robert Johnson and The Devil at The Delta. Here comes Paddy Burnside to call at my home with his questions and his-his fucking quid-pro-quo and, with what would prove very quickly to be the most tiresome of all, hero worship of me. He was a starry-eyed fucker when I opened the door to him standing there in that rumpled suit of his. Before long, I turned the tables on him and the poor fuck was answering *my* questions and *only* mine.

"It's easy to alpha someone when they'd lap your balls for taking their demo tape. I accepted it from him, even though he came out with it faster than he should have. It reeked of desperation. This guy must have been at it for a long goddam time. Burnside ain't young. And he was trying to break into what is always gonna be a young one's game.

"I led him on. I blew enough smoke up his ass that by the end of it I could have rolled him up and smoked him!

"He was making the rounds, talking to all the other bands who were in some kind of contact with Grifters. Going all the way back to their salad days in that shitty apartment Bobby's rich daddy footed the bill for. You'd think by the time he darkened my doorstep, the stars in his eyes would have lost some of their brightness. Not with this dude. Paddy Burnside was there to ask me about my experiences with Grifters. Once I took his demo and popped it into my stereo ..." Harrison starts to pantomime this part of his story. "Started bobbing my head to his shitty guitar and vocals. Fragments of songs. So many stops and starts. Shitty finger work. Sloppy pitch. It was embarrassing. But he was beaming. He was busting. Because I made him believe I was so into what he was doing that I was going to help him.

'And not just *help him*," Harrison says, scratching at the underside of his stubbly jawline, eyes glinting with dark pride. "I told him I'd be very interested in writing some songs with him. Seeing how that goes. And maybe—you're gonna love this, Red—maybe we team up, and we recruit, er, Lindsay Turner from Windowpain and maybe-just *maybe*-we try to poach Tommy lee from Crue. Something about *Tommy wanting out* and word was going around.

"That's when I knew I owned the motherfucker. I mean, I never actually needed to hire him on as my PI. I did that out of the kindness of my heart. I even put him on a nice, generous retainer so the guy could—I dunno—buy a second suit and get the first one dry cleaned, for Chrissakes!

"You saw my leavings of Paddy Burnside up there, Red," Harrison says. "Does it look like that loser made good use of my money? He could've traded up for some decent threads with the kind of money I threw at him."

Gretch's eyes burn from the heat, an invisible entity hanging in the air. Her temper is flaring. Strobing. "How long ago was this?"

"Oh, I'd say right around the time the grunge died."

"Before we met up at Cantor's? Or after?" Gretch's mouth screws into a snarl of sorts.

"Hey, the guy came to me, alright? He fell into my lap like a perfect piece of ass. The more he prattled on about what he knew, and Stevie's papers, the more I realized I was going to do one of two things. I was either gonna hire him to investigate further the existence of The Muse and The Mountain, or I was gonna beat the cock out of him if he refused me. Luckily, he went along. Took my money. And got to work. Your little disagreement with him's got nothing to do with me—"

"You *fucker!* I *told* you what he did to me? H-He left me for dead. He nearly killed me! And you teamed up with that piece of shit!"

"You listen to me, you professional fucking victim!" Harrison says, launching himself at her and stopping just short of putting his hands on her. "You set yourself on the path to this very moment years ago when you decided to rep for Grifters instead of Louder. You weren't even open to making us a part of your roster. No, you wanted to focus all your goddam efforts on making those murdering creeps into legends. All the while, you knew our agent was a lightweight. We could have surpassed Grifters, and everyone would have been better off for it.

"Most of all, Gretch Solomon wouldn't be stuck in such a bad spot as this years later. You put yourself here, alright? You. Owe. Me!"

Gretch's stomach lurches. Her ass has gone to sleep. She wriggles about to wake it up.

The zip ties binding her wrists together snag on something. Absently, she yanks her hands aside to unhitch them from whatever has caught the ties.

She hears it.

She prays Harrison is wrapped up enough in his own thoughts that he *does not* hear it.

The sharp sound of plastic tearing.

Alright, so you found yourself a possible out.

Thank God for the craggy shale stone jutting out of the wall behind her, sharp and unforgiving as the inside of an Iron Maiden torture chamber.

Harrison does not appear to have heard the sound. He stalks to the far wall, roughly ten paces from where she sits, ever-so-subtly scraping her wrist ties along the jagged stone projection lined up just above the base of her spine.

Keep him talking.

Let him believe he's breaking you down.

Closer to what he's after.

Gretch says, "Did Burnside ever tell you what happened to Glory?"

He is lost in his own thoughts. Doesn't respond.

"Harrison!"

"Yeah, the … the fucking Child Bride. What!?"

He swivels his body back around to face her. He comes to stand in the center of the space. And a dark cloud seems to pass over his visage. His eyes seem to sink into their sockets, creating black rings around them. A lopsided grin slants his lips, granting him a surprisingly stupid expression.

"Did he? Tell you what he did with her?"

The dead body of Allure sitting within her left peripheral vision prompts her to press the issue. Yes, Glory Tizione had set all this madness in motion. Had she never shown up on Gretch's doorstep, listed her as sole emergency contact, it's possible Gretch would have been free to live out the rest of her days in blissful ignorance. Of the type of man she married. Of her own unknowing complicity in enabling five men in their murderous exploits undercover of night. She could have gone on to love Stevie, rather than to …

Well …

And yet, Gretch can't shake the concern for Glory's well-being.

Thieving druggie Glory!

You've always known she was the victim of Davey's charisma and his gaslighting and his manipulation.

If she can save Glory, the death of Allure at the hands of one of her own Sisters would not cut so deeply into Gretch's soul.

Of course, this requires proof of life.

She is almost afraid of Harrison's answer.

"The last I heard mention of her was from Burnside," she explains, her mouth a desert. "He said he kept trying to get rid of her. To get her out of his house. That she was leeching onto him."

"Sounds like *that* Glory. Go on."

"I'm asking … did he ever mention her to you?"

"Wha-whaddya mean? Why would he think to share that with me?"

"I would think he'd brag to you about fucking Davey Grifter's estranged wife. That she was obsessed with him. He worshipped you after all."

"I dunno. It's not like we ever got around to comparing notes or our body counts."

"You never saw him with her?"

"I think I'd remember that."

Gretch feels it in her bones. A tiredness. A weight. Signifying a loss. "… oh …" she mutters, barely managing to draw some renewed vigor from the loosening of the ties around her wrists. It won't be long.

She had said she was going to make her way back here …

Did she?

Gretch's back stiffens. Her arms are cramping up from the incessant scraping motion she has somehow managed to conceal from Harrison's notice. She tastes something like dirty pennies in her mouth. Filthy coin on her tongue. Stuck to her palette.

A bad feeling. It pushes any lingering hope aside.

She considers not saying anything, Then, Gretch realizes she's got nothing to lose and plenty to gain if luck breaks in her favor.

"One of the last things she said to me before she vanished from my home was how she was going to come back to The Mountain."

Harrison looks at her. Doesn't say anything.

"She left because Davey told her about his plans. For the Sisters. And she wanted to get back here before it was too late." Gretch pauses. "She was going to kill Davey before he could *work his last bit of evil* on them."

Harrison turns in place, waving his hands all about. "Does it look like she stopped him?"

Still …

"Unless … oh … *man* …" Harrison Hart fixes his gaze on the cave wall, along the ground. His eyes narrow.

"No … way …"

"What is it? *What?*"

He waves her back into silence. "Just hold on. Well-well-well. Shee-it!"

Harrison Hart crosses the cavern to the east wall. He takes a knee before what can only be one of the dead women positioned there, heads leaning on one another's shoulders in eternal sleep.

She watches him lean in, closer and closer, his head cocked in cold concentration.

When he reaches out to touch one of the bodies in the dimness, Gretch knows.

"Glory ..."

FORTY-NINE

After a moment that has nothing to do with reverence and everything to do with morbid fascination, Harrison Hart stands. He dusts his hands off on the seat of his pants, then claps them loudly together. They produce a shot like a starter pistol. "Glory," he says, planting his hands on his hips. He can't seem to take his eyes off the corpse of Gloria "Glory" Tizione.

Gretch is thankful for the dark of the cavern. It hides the body.

You failed all of them-you failed all these lost *girls—*

Gretch has heard of cave-ins triggered by a gunfire or a raised voice. Her stomach somersaults when Harrison starts in suddenly with shouting. Taunting.

"Davey!" he cries. "You *pussy*! Come on out! I promise I won't laugh at your … your new look. I hear animal pelts are the big new thing. You're just ahead of the curve, man! But this hiding? I used to envy you. I hated you and your thug-punk bandmates for stealing the crown. None of you wore it well."

He pauses, waiting for some sound hinting at Davey's stealth approach or at least his coordinates if he is hunkered down nearby. "You and I both know it's my turn now. Grifters Anonymous is going to keep selling fucking *Knives* for the next twenty-five years. It hasn't fallen off Billboard yet and you assholes broke up four fucking years ago!"

Pause. "I want the blessing. I want the same deal Calliope gave you. All of you. *I want it*. And thanks to Stevie, I know it will require laying my hands on the relic. In this fucking cavern!

"So, every minute you spend hiding," Harrison says, his voice tempestuous now, "I'm gonna desecrate a corpse. I'll make the rounds to all of them if I have to. And I'll make sure to sink to new lows when I get to your Glory. You may have mindfucked them into killing each other in some ritual sacrifice I don't quite understand. I mean, is this you offering twenty-one corpses to Calliope? You looking to re-up with Her?"

Harrison's breathing tears in and out of him.

"It's my turn! Davey! You fuck! Face me!"

Gretch can barely see through the tears in her eyes. It's all just too much. "Harrison, this is *not* you! Please, think about what you're proposing—"

"Shut up, Red! Either I leave this Mountain with a *blessing* or I'm gonna show you who I really am. Who I've always been while you were too busy wheeling and dealing for that band of sick fucks. Christ, had I known that's the kind of man you were into, I would have shown you the levels of my depravity back when we were still fucking."

"You're not being true," Gretch pleads, her blood running hot. "It's this place. The Mountain's working on you. Listen to yourself, Harrison! You won't recognize yourself if you just listen to the horrific things you're proposing—"

"Oh, honey, look at what I've done to you leading up to this point. All of it … hatched and planned out far away from this fucking place. *This. Is. Me*. Now SHUT UP!"

"I h-hope Davey *rips you to pieces!*"

Then there is only the sound of Gretch's sobbing as she scrapes the last half centimeter away from her wrist ties, eyes shut and bottom lip pulled defiantly up over her upper lip like a malcontented toddler.

Nothing.

Harrison nods, slowly and stiffly, casting his gaze to the ground. He hocks a thick wad of phlegm into the dirt. "Alright," he says. "Think I'll start with Glory."

He unzips his pants, works his hand inside the opening, and fishes out his limp dick.

The wrist tie has slackened enough Gretch recognizes it is about to break. She scrapes double-time now, desperate to stop what is about to happen to Glory's poor, defenseless corpse. She tries to stall him, pushing the button she knows will at least give him some quick pause. A stab out at his ego. "Burnside may have been a wanna-be but you're barely a footnote!"

Harrison wheels on her, wagging his cock at her and spraying piss in her direction. "Thirsty, Red?"

"It's all downhill for poor bastards like you. I can't think of anything more fucking pathetic than guys like you! The Strip reeks of desperation from all the assholes like you that time forgot!"

He chuckles drily.

Not the reaction she is after.

Performing a strange, giddy-up kind of swagger with his member out and the last of the urine dripping out of it, Harrison Hart moves his genitals nearer to Glory's lock-jawed mouth.

"Oh—shit—she's still warm! This is gonna feel better than I —"

A black shape appears, conjured as if from thin air. It trails what can only be compared to that of a cry of unhinged anguish in its wake.

The wrist-tie snaps apart.

Gretch gains her feet, ready to launch herself across the cavern at Harrison when the wailing Shape engulfs Harrison, shocked and paralyzed as a fish zapped by a jelly fish stinger. Her lungs seizing up, Gretch scrambles backward. Crowds herself up against the wall. She claps a hand over her mouth to stifle a scream as she watches the Shape appear to swallow the former lead singer of Louder whole.

FIFTY

The Shape is amorphous. Its movements as it wrestles and overwhelms Harrison Hart are human in their stilted motion. She cannot decide who she should fear more, this interloper or Harrison. Both pose their own brand of threat. Once The Shape finishes with Hart, who's to say if it will then turn its lethal attention to her.

Her backpack lies in a heap mere feet from where she'd come to. Gretch decides with the last bit of her shredded nerves that she will not lie down like a lamb. Not when she can arm herself and even her odds a little better.

Her lungs aching and mouth a desert, Gretch lunges for her JanSport.

The only sign of Harrison amidst the tangle of billowing black is a pale patch of flesh. That and the rapidly advancing puddle of blood advancing across the dirt floor.

The Shape wheels on her.

Or so it seems.

It's like I'm invisible. He's not looking at me.

A quick chill, cold fingertips, graze her cheekbones.

It is like the caress of a caring mother in the dark during a fever dream.

She slides her brother's snub nose out of her pack, relishing the way it seems to jump into her palm.

Gretch scans the adjacent wall for the source of the sudden burst of cool air across her face.

A seven-feet-tall aperture, a cleft, in the stone.

An opening.

A door?

That's where The Shape came from? There's nothing magical or supernatural about its sudden arrival.

Gretch aims down the small sight of the gun, pinning The Shape in her crosshairs as best she can considering its manic motion.

When Harrison's water-logged scream escapes the scuffle, Gretch knows a fear like nothing ever before. *"Gretch … run—"*

A dull thud ends Harrison Hart's pleading neat as you please.

Another thud.

A Casaba melon striking the ground after having plummeted twenty stories.

Sweat drips into her eyes. She arms it off, but it keeps coming, turning this nightmarish scenario into a blur of watercolor haze. Before she can prepare herself for it, her stomach clenches and vomit burns its way up her throat. It breaks the seal of her lips, doubling her over. It is all she can do not to drop the gun. She holds fast to it, somehow mindful to remove her trigger finger from inside the circular guard.

The struggle is over.

And The Shape crawls away, retracting its blackness to reveal the inert body of Harrison Hart on the cavern floor.

The Louder singer's face is ground beef and brain matter ground together. Housed within a half-shell skull like the singer's head is some strange delicacy hailing from a backward, nightmarish corner of the earth.

Gretch raises the weapon, placing The Shape into the crosshairs once more.

Two things happen at the same time.

A pale, gaunt face materializes amidst The Shapes' amorphous black.

And it speaks in a sharpened Eastern European accent:

"How did we get to here?"

The black hood of his long flowing garment slips to the back of his head. His head is shorn. Even in the spare light, Gretch can see the strange series of indentations that round the skull. She remembers she is holding a gun on him.

He does not raise his hands in surrender. Could it be he welcomes the bullet? The man's long, drawn jaw seems locked into that of an eternal frown. The mask of the sad clown when the laughter dies. His face is hairless, his eyebrows no exception. Sagging, tired eyes.

And his name, his appearance. It adds up.

"You're Stanislaw," Gretch says. "This was your clinic."

What he says next confuses Gretch to the point the gun wavers:

"I was the Wizard, and this was Oz. And I have since been relegated to the jester. The shine is off Emerald City. The green is gone. All gone to black ruin. And this Mountain?" He stands to full height. It seems to take a very long time and when it is evident the man is well over six and a half-foot tall, Gretch understands why. Monk-like, Karl Stanislaw in all his imposing stature, presents himself as a benign man. Of little to no consequence. A once grand sculpture hammered down into a flat mass of gray clay. "This room? This is where the lies were made. They spread across the world, from what I understand. Every creative of every discipline somehow learned of this place. This ... *miracle artist colony*.

"Never underestimate the sheer power of suggestion for the desperate, especially the blocked creative. To be blocked is to walk around with a fingernail shoved in your ear until you can find a way to pry it out again. Again, the suggestion brought them here. They've been coming for a little more than a century. You've seen their leavings, no doubt? In the caves? And they have kept coming.

"And every one of them? In the last four years? Not a one has made it off the Mountain alive.

"David saw to that. Your David."

"Whoa, he is most definitely not my *David*—"

"He sent out his army of young, brainwashed women to cut them down as soon as they'd appear.

"I have tried to explain to him. To convince him of the ruse. This long game begun by a traveling salesman whose name I—for the life of me—can't recall."

Without giving it any thought, Gretch lowers the gun as Karl Stanislaw turns away from her. He walks past the body of Harrison Hart, absently stepping in the pool of blood haloing the dead rock star's ruined skull and stamping his footprint into the dirt as he makes his way to one of the dead women lining the cavern walls. "But you? You held to your goodness. You tried to save them all."

It takes Gretch a moment to realize who he is addressing.

"My beautiful bride," he sobs, stooping to collect the body of the woman into his arms. "My beautiful child. I failed you. I. Failed. You."

Stanislaw shuffles his monolithic frame to the center of the cavern. He lowers himself back down. Lowers her legs just enough to free up a hand so he can spread his black robe wide. Then, he maneuvers her in such a way that he holds her upper body to his chest with her lower torso brought to rest on the soft folds of his garment.

It is a sculpture waiting to be realized, if ever there was one.

His young wife. He nearly killed Chris Desmond when he propositioned her.

His ... Jesus Christ! His Child Bride!

This is his fault. All of it. Because he continued it instead of dismantling it brick-by-brick.

In a tired, morose voice, Karl Stanislaw glares down at his dead wife and continues. "I won't open another Eye. Never again. Davey knows this. And he will kill me for it. I won't do it."

"Another Eye? What is that?"

"God's Eye. You might have heard it referred to as the Third Eye."

"Like ... what ... *chakras*?" Gretch's therapist had referred her to an article related to this topic. In the name of achieving some inner calm. "The eye that looks within. Turned inside out."

"No," he croaks. "No-no-*no*. Nothing so quaint. Benign. *No.*"

"Then I'm not following," Gretch says, her cheeks stinging with impatience. "Tell me how you fooled them all. So, I know exactly how to shut down fucking Wonderland once and for all!"

"In biological terms, God's Eye is a mere fingernails-length of gray matter nestled in the center of the brain. To look at it, you could not possibly imagine what power this sliver of oozing matter wields over men and women alike. Once The Eye is pried open? Once it is made to see? It becomes a conduit, eating suggestion and expelling genius.

"The Eye has been the tool of my trade and manipulation. For these poor, poor women. And for that bastard animal, David. All those years ago when he showed up on what *had been* my Mountain with his merry band of jerkoffs. And their walking, bottomless wallet. The mogul. Nolan-fucking-Royal."

Gretch slips into silence.

Stanislaw accepts this as a cue to elaborate.

FIFTY-ONE

The oversized man does not appear to fear the bullet or Gretch at all. He offers her barely a sideways glance before pacing. Rubbing at the back of his neck with a curious viciousness. Speaking in a tone of voice more at home in a church than a cave.

"It was not long after the rock band's time on The Mountain the clinic was swarming with inspectors, or so they'd claimed (I still doubt their credentials). Come to verify the clinic was operating within certain standards and protocols. Health inspectors, as well. They arrived in a fleet of black SUVs. A black ops feel. I expected the FBI on their heels, to satisfy the trifecta of intrusion.

"They scoured every nook of the clinic. Pored through every document they could get their hands on. Boxed and seized hundreds of sensitive files pertaining to various former clients and their treatment. Many of them high-profile. The health inspectors littered the kitchen with roaches *they* brought in themselves. They dirtied the surfaces of the cooking appliances, rubbing their spit and what have you into them. I know this because my employees watched them do this. They made no attempt to conceal these actions.

"After eight hours of humiliation and argument and the push-and-pull of my people with the so-called *inspectors*, they served me an extensive list of violations. They deemed the structure unsafe for business or habitation of any kind. Condemned the clinic. We would have to vacate the premises immediately. There was nowhere for any of us to go. Every employee, including myself … we lived here. On The Mountain. They marched us out into the snow. They afforded us no time to collect our things. They were firm and they were cold-blooded.

"An official document declaring the clinic condemned and scheduled for Demolition no later than thirty days from the notice, they chained the front and side doors. Before we could fully appeal, or plead for that matter, they left The Mountain in that same black brigade of unmarked SUVs. See, they had been there for eight hours, but somehow when they disappeared again it felt for all of us as if we'd all just experienced a collective nightmare.

"The hearth?" Gretch says. "What did they make of that?"

"What else would they have made of it? They saw a hearth and nothing more."

"Aah. Somehow, they missed the seam in the back wall where the bricks swing inward? You said they scoured this fucking place."

"Oh, they searched its interior. Felt along its brickwork. They never made discovery of any *seam*." Stanislaw raises a finger into the air like a lecturer about to put a fine point on his next sentence. "Once I realized their keen interest in the walls of the hearth and their extreme exasperation upon coming up short, I knew who'd sent them. They'd been deployed by one man in particular. For the sake of a very specific purpose. A certain aim. And I still wonder sometimes if they would not have condemned the clinic had they found what they were sent there to find."

"Nolan Royal," Gretch says, another tumbler falling into place. "And yet … still it stands. Rescued by a deviant with enough money to secure the deed. In retrospect, I would much rather have seen the clinic collapse like a paraffin house. I would dance on its ashes, knowing what I know now."

"I have tried to burn the clinic to the ground myself. Something about the climate. The elevation. It won't catch. I … I have tried.

"Your David—"

"Stop fucking calling him that or I'm gonna put one in your brain, you hear me?"

"Apologies," Stanislaw says, continues. "He caught me in the act of trying to set it alight. And I believe this is what sent him into a rage that has lasted for the better part of three years. It changed something in him. Something shifted. I'd created a new man, whose personality and impulses fell somewhere in between that of fascist and mystic. I'd convinced him I was *with* him. That I shared his distorted vision, his plans to reinvent the clinic. To align its purpose more fully with that of The Muse and The Mountain.

"Exile. That was my punishment. Banishment to the woods. And he thought I'd simply submit to this. Instead, I hid down here. Made a home of these dark corridors. And kept clear of him. I saw all. More than he could possibly fathom."

The mention of the missing party, the animal-skin clad apparition hidden within the cave presses an icicle against her beating heart. "Why would he hide now? If this all belongs to him?"

"Oh," Stanislaw says, "he's not hiding. He's waiting. Ever the showman. Waiting for the perfect entrance to present itself."

Gretch casts a panicked gaze all about the dim cavern. Her frustration mounts as she raises her weapon. Sights down while searching for something (anything) in the way of motion. A jerk. Twitch.

One of the dead women lining the cavern walls appears to raise and drop her sloped shoulders, heaving a small sigh. It chills her blood and Gretch stares at the corpse until it is clear the woman remains lifeless.

Trick of the mind.

Stanislaw continues:

"Davey mistook me for a kindred spirit when he arrived back on The Mountain, waving his deed in the air. I decided not to discourage this false belief, but to feed it. And when the time came for his overthrow and expulsion from The Mountain, he would never see it coming. It turns out, the bastard had it all perfectly planned out, from the time he got here until he wrested control from my grasp and forced me into a vulnerable position.

"When David first appeared, there were twelve males on staff here who also squatted here with the rest of us. Rockstar-Godhead insisted we plan a celebration. A feast, if you will. In honor of the *New Owner*. Himself. And the promising developments to come once he settled in. Now, mind you, there was something of *this* David in the younger version when he first came here with his band to get clean and—well—garner a new, wondrous inspiration, when all was said and done. There was a glimmer of the tyrant in his eyes. A certain way he set his jaw when things around him turned tense. But the man, with his shaved head and his gaunt face and burning green eyes, who made merry and *nursed* his bottle of seltzer water for hours? This was David fully transformed. The metamorphosis complete. Prometheus unbound.

"We threw this party with what little remaining beverages were stocked in the kitchen. It was all room temperature, as the electricity had been turned off. They packed it all on ice and in the snow. He sang songs for everyone. None of us wanted it. And he kept on long after one of us asked him to stop because they had a *splitting headache*. Davey slapped *her* (a woman, that's right) and sent her away sobbing. None of the men challenged him. You can't blame them.

"They were dying. They did not yet know it. All they knew at first was this sudden weakness in their muscles and limbs. Then a tremor in their extremities.

"One-by-one, all our men clutched their chests and fell over dead. Heart failure. They left behind spouses, four of them. A few were lucky enough to die in their wives' arms. I remember the screaming. The blur of women rushing to and fro, straining to attend to them after their hearts exploded. I ..."

Karl Stanislaw's mouth hangs open. His eyes are wet glass.

"Dear God ..." Gretch wishes her imagination were not so vivid. She might have been spared the mental reel playing back the mind movie produced by Stanislaw's descriptive power. The madness. "He poisoned them?"

"I still don't know how he managed to pollute *only* the men's beverages. It was some sleight of hand.

Just as sympathy takes hold of her, Gretch is instantly reminded of the *other* monster telling the story. Davey is not the only ghoul in the equation. Backstory does not absolve the big Eastern European of his part in all of this. His own sleight of hand. His reckless, ruinous ruse. Playing God through the manipulation of God's *Eye*. Crowning kings in their respective creative disciplines, while letting others waste away with false hope for greatness.

This confusion of sentiment won't allow for Gretch to shed a tear for Stanislaw, or for the men Davey poisoned.

"Once the women buried their dead (and we lived for weeks alongside the dead waiting for the ground to thaw), things moved very quickly. David worked his way into all the women's subconscious minds. The only evidence of this mental manipulation I ever witnessed were the times he openly whispered in their ears. Right in front of me. Words not fit for my ears. Only theirs. He saw no need to cast a spell with me. Again, he viewed me as his advocate.

"Because I didn't raise a protest. I didn't challenge him. That was not planned. It was … something about his arrival had—I dunno— locked me up. I felt neutered. Cucked. I acquiesced. Even when the women implored me to make a stand. And when I did not, it was not long before *they* acquiesced *to him*—"

A sudden pulse of impatience urges Gretch to raise her hand to stop him.

His words clip off.

"I want to know what *in the hell you* did to my husband. To Grifters? And, yes, to Davey! Because I have yet to hear you make *your* confession to *setting ALL OF THIS—YES, ALL OF IT*—in motion! I know whatever it was, you had your revenge for the way Chris disrespected your daughter-or your *wife*-or whatever the fuck she was or any of these women were."

"Let's not forget his reckless, dangerous behavior in tampering with the hearth. He had no idea what he was playing at. He needed to be shown."

"While I was never a big fan of Chris-fucking-Desmond, the life sentence you imposed on the five of them will *never* fit the infractions. Tell me what you did to them … *or I swear to God, I'll kill you!* It will be slow. And painful."

With his eyes downcast, greedily absorbing the death mask his young wife's face has become. Her head rests in his lap and he smooths her black hair back, clear of her forehead.

At first, she thinks he didn't hear her.

Just as Gretch is about to repeat the threat, Stanislaw says, "Don't you understand what this is, Mrs. Darius?"

"Damn you! Explain it to me!"

"The closest I'll ever get to someone who is clean of heart is here with you. Seated across from each other. In this bowel in the earth. Of course, this one in my arms maintained until her last breath she never murdered for David. Never had relations with him. Somehow—I have no idea how she managed it—my Yelena maintained her purity. Safeguarded her dignity. But she won't hear my penance. She cannot." Stanislaw raises his glacier-grey eyes and fixes Gretch with an imploring expression. "You are sitting for my confession. You've won this honor."

"An honor?" Gretch says, laughing darkly. "Fuck you. There's nothing *honorable* about a fucking snake oil salesman like you. I know many of these women were your wives before Davey whispered in their ears. They weren't married to the other men like you said. That would have leant the arrangement some small semblance of normalcy to this arrangement of yours. This cult you founded. But there is *nothing* normal about any of this fucking insanity! They were *kept* women. You and Davey are cut from the same depraved cloth. You're a predator who's been brought low."

"You have the upper hand," he utters, shutting his eyes. "Be gracious."

Gretch peels the hammer back.

"I'll be the last thing you see if you don't start talking."

"You still don't understand. I haven't made myself clear."

"Oh Christ, how *so*?"

"I don't fear death or your bullet," he says, plaintively. "I am counting on both once I've finished."

FIFTY-TWO

"I decided to explain to David what happened on The Mountain that night years ago. I knew I was taking a chance, but it needed to be done. I was his punisher that night. I punished him alongside his bandmates. And I didn't spare Nolan Royal, either. I spared none of them from a fate they would never fully be able to explain or make sense of. Something irreversible.

"With David, it became evident to me, the fool had no idea I was the one who'd *opened the Eye* inside of him. Blessed him. Cursed him. I held this information back from him. I acted as if I knew nothing of what he was talking about. Until it came time to trade in on these secrets in exchange for ..."

Stanislaw's voice trails off. He stiffens.

Gretch waves the snub nose at him. "Why are you stopping?"

"Y-you have to understand first," he stammers. "I stood no chance of freeing all of them. I had to make a choice and there was very little time. His Grand Sacrifice to Kalliope was already in its final planning stages. He still believed it would augment the creative blessings he had already been granted by The Muse of the Mountain. It would aid him in his musical comeback. The songs would come. And they would be brilliant like the ones before." He pauses, glances down at Yelena whose chin has taken on the texture of hardened clay. Rigor is setting into her body. "I bargained with Davey for mine and Yelena's safe passage from the rehab if I told him everything he wanted to know."

"Why only Yelena? She wasn't your only wife?"

Stanislaw gazed lovingly down at the body in his arms. "She loved me so well."

Gretch scoffs, repulsed. "And you actually took Davey Grifter- the deceitful sonofabitch-at his word?"

"All things considered, I was quite accommodating to Grifters Anonymous. I indulged Nolan Royal's damned incessant questioning as to what my net worth was. The greed in that old man! I hated him just as much as Chris Desmond. Still, I played the sympathetic, assertive director and clinician. I informed the rest of the staff I would be handling the Grifter's treatment personally.

"I wouldn't see anyone else subjected to the same abuse as my Yelena. But I had no intention of pursuing any sort of vengeance towards them. Not after Yelena. I still would have treated them. Housed them. Cured them. And they would have left with something of The Muse's blessing to help them as creatives. Had they not touched the hearth, I would have seen them off. Unscathed. Healed.

"The fire was not to be touched. That changed things dramatically. It burns at the only entrance to this cave. A natural barrier to its entry."

"Wait a minute," Gretch says, scratching her cheek. "I thought the rehab clinic was not only built *onto* the side of The Mountain. Doesn't it run right into the base of it as well?"

"The original owner of the building oversaw its construction and the drafting of its blueprints. It's my understanding he insisted on this arrangement. To enhance the illusion of the building and the Mountain and The Muse existing as one trinity. Much like the Father, Son, and Holy Ghost."

Gretch laughs, darkly. "Illusion. Now you use the word. Fucking damage done, cold bastard."

"Show me some grace, for the love of God—"

Gretch lunges at Stanislaw She does not stop until Stanislaw's hands are up, and the gun butte is cutting an imprint into his shorn, misshapen skull.

"Finish it!" she commands.

The words come fast and unbroken with barely a break in between them or a drawn breath:

"I saw the hearth was dark and something—it broke inside of me. My rage was something bone driven. I did not stop because I wanted to bypass any second thoughts. I wouldn't allow any introspection to cool my blood a second time. I made my preparations in a fog, working under the hypnosis of muscle memory. Then, I rushed into their rooms … one after another … the needle in their arm was what roused each of them. I might've made a decent physician the way I found the vein without a need to tie the limb off or for them to make a fist.

"They were in varying states of withdrawal. Coincidentally, Chris looked the worst for wear. Disabled by his own shakes and sweats. He was in the shit, more so than his *brothers*. I took the most pleasure in forcing him up and out of bed, almost as much as waking him with a hypodermic full of what I told them all was nothing more than Methadone. To treat their symptoms.

"I corralled them as best I could. They put up a small, trivial fight, but in the end, Nolan Royal —yes, I jabbed him as well and he did *not* question it, surprisingly—he led them into the main hall. The hallucinogen I'd pumped into their bloodstream—*woman, will you relax that damned gun before you split my skull with it*—it-it worked quick. By the time I commanded them to line up before me on their knees. Their minds were primed enough for what would follow. They were as submissive as a room full of beaten dogs.

"It was quite effortless. So much so I doubted its effects.

"I worked to restore the fire in the hearth. It was blazing, throwing off heat that seemed to have doubled in its intensity. I stood with my back to the blaze, a steady rivulet of sweat running down my back. Skating down my spine. It was glorious. The five of them. Lined up on their knees before me. Trapped in the throes of hallucination. The doorways to their unconscious gaping. They swayed, straining to remain upright. Their tongues lolled. Eyes bulged. Their long hair had already gone flat and fuzzy with perspiration as the hearth cooked them. By the time I began, the main hall must have hit one-hundred fifteen degrees. Hell on earth.

"I started with the young man with the poker-straight black hair and those—hmm—violet eyes. Like Liz Taylor. I clamped my hand down on the front of his head. And it took care of itself. He was chuffing like a dying horse. I thought he might stroke out. But when I drew my hand back, a great shudder passed through him and his eyes closed. I—"

"What do you mean *it took care of itself?*"

"Mm—?"

"What took care of itself?"

"Why … The Eye, of course."

"What about the—"

"It opened inside his mind. It's why he shut his eyes. There was no need to see through them. He wouldn't have been able to if the Third Eye was open."

"And … you just expect me to believe you? This is fucking horror show bullshit!"

"Then kindly blow my brains out and we can be done with this. Otherwise … I'll continue".

Sluggishly, Gretch relaxes her weapon, merely resting it against Stanislaw's head.

Stanislaw continues:

"I moved from one to the next. And the next. East to west. Pity none of them had any idea David, their fearless leader, was an epileptic. Prying open his pineal gland, The God Eye, left him sprawled across the floor. Flopping around like a fish with his tongue dangling out the side of his mouth. In any other scenario, I imagine his friends would have rushed to his aid. They did not even seem to notice when he fell into distress. He had no choice but to ride it out.

"I finished with Nolan Royal. I had never performed the Eye Opening ritual on anyone older than their mid-thirties. His advanced age put him at risk. Still, I knew I could not leave his mind unaltered, nor his memory of that night fully intact. No, I would have to fracture and complicate and skew his memory of their time on the Mountain as well. No witnesses.

"From what I have gathered from David, Old Man Royal has become something of a genius artist. I imagine before his Time on the Mountain, he could barely manage a stick figure.

"Their third eyes pinned wide open, I implanted suggestions and false memories of the most horrific and torturous and crippling I could possibly conjure. Imagine enduring an especially frightening night-mare, waking to the relief it was only a dream. Then, as you move through your day, that same nightmare plagues you with waking scenes and hallucinations of terror and torment. No escape. That was the curse. There are certain words, certain turns of phrase, when whis-pered in their ears that would shoot a pollutant through the very micro-center of the pineal gland itself. A Demon hormone, so to speak. It would not only pollute the section of brain, but it would also damage it well beyond repair. Allowing for higher-functioning capabil-ities. Paired with the very real, traumatizing visions run on a loop inside their minds. And no real way of shutting them off. Or sepa-rating out the false memory from the true ones.

"The equivalent of my reaching a hand into their brains, a hand that holds a pepper spray canister, and spraying their pineal gland, *their God Eye*, to permanent impairment.

"Know that I can sense your disbelief. This is the truth. And it is ugly."

Pause.

"This was the punishment I chose for them. They would all pay a price for the sins of the one. They are a band of brothers after all. Let them suffer the affliction. Perhaps next time they'd better police their own."

"These false memories," Gretch says, the start of a migraine pressing a steak knife into the front of her brain, "What did you show them?"

"Scenes of murder. The naked, primal act of taking a life. The cutting of wrists. Strangulation. Beatings. All of it happening at the ends of your band's hands. They were the killers in these false memories."

Now, Gretch takes hold of the gun with both hands and squares her stance like someone preparing to pull the trigger. She seizes her bottom lip with her teeth and chews it. Nearly draws blood. A low moan of anguish hums in her throat but does not make it up and out. It sounds even more terrible in its muted tone.

"You. Made them. You made them into *murderers*! My husband … Christ, *all of them*! They were only boys! You would have done them a kindness by killing them instead of sending them back out into the world as five time bombs!"

"Lower your voice, Gretchen," Stanislaw cautions. "Unless you're looking to bring millions of tons of shale down on our heads—"

"Say goodbye, you fucking *ghoul*—"

"You'd leave the story unfinished?"

"Fuck you!"

Gretch touches the trigger.

It has the effect as before.

Like she has yanked the pull start of a lawn mower, the eastern European spits words in rapid succession. They trip over one another like two left feet on a dance floor as Karl Stanislaw, who said he wanted the bullet to the brain, did his very best to stave off the end of all things.

"Manipulating the pineal gland has been my trade, my secret tool, for decades!" he rambles, his tongue catching between his teeth. "Never have I seen such a fallout as the one they experienced. The false memories would eventually fade with all the others. In weeks. And they were supposed to feel relief in turn. They came to their own conclusions about their time on the Mountain and what exactly happened here. I'm telling you, *they drew their own misguided conclusion that they had entered some Faustian bargain with a Muse of The Mountain! They* misconstrued their memories, and it became this arrangement whereby they are called to kill and give sacrifice to Kalliope in exchange for divine creative abilities. A life of rampant overnight success! A place in history!

"As I said before, darkness and light. Good and bad. Two sides of the same coin, Gretchen! And the only conclusion you, or I, or *anyone* with a critical mind could arrive at is your young men already bore a penchant for evil to begin with. I unknowingly woke it up in the lot of them. But the evil and the deadly impulses had to have been there all along. Otherwise, they would not have become what they turned into.

"There was never any *connection* between the lives they took and their level of success. They made that false connection, no doubt the result of minds long damaged by drugs and drink."

If Stanislaw were permitted to turn his head to look up at her, he would have found her glaring down at him with her once green eyes gone to black and darkness having crept over his visage.

Her jaw set. Teeth grinding.

"That lets you off the hook?" Gretch says.

"This is what happened—"

"No, you don't. You are *not* innocent."

"David has always been a dangerous individual. You've only ever seen the tip of that monster's iceberg. There is a bloated blackness hidden beneath the waves you would do well to run from if you've got any sense of self-preservation."

"I've got a bullet for him, too. Wouldn't want to leave him out. And this is a *long time coming*. We have our history. But you? Did you ever even make a goddam attempt to explain to Davey that everything you'd made him believe about The Mountain and—Jesus—the *Muse* was an elaborate con? Huh?"

Stanislaw tosses up his hands. "You don't think I did that very thing when it became clear I was losing my hold—my influence— over my own people? My *artists*? I told him everything, exactly as I've explained it to you. This and *more*. I rolled the curtain away entirely." He hesitates, making strange, strangling sounds in his throat. "It was *not* a con! I take great issue with the use of that word to dismiss—"

"Too bad. There's no other way to describe what you've been doing to innocent, desperate people."

"It was *never a con*—"

"Finish it!"

"It wasn't—"

A wave of red ire pulses behind her eyes and Gretch swats the end of the barrel across his skull, opening a thin crimson line. Stanislaw cries out. Blood drips down the side of his head, a scalp wound that will bleed almost as intensely as a carotid or a femoral artery.

"All of them?" he groans. "The men and the women came to me … came here … because they were blocked artists. All of them. This was once an artist colony, its very existence only as well-known as word-of-mouth would allow. Many of them were suicidal. They'd lost the ability to express themselves. The only outlet for their intense emotional buildup—closed to them. I'd studied with the masters. Tibetan monks. They schooled me in the practice of forcing open the Third Eye. I laid hands on them, but it did not work for any of them at first. I had not yet fully mastered it. I was unsure of myself still. They threatened to leave. Some even threatened to do me bodily harm, thinking me a charlatan. I had to give them good reason to stay. To just … to hold on. Give me time and I would help them.

"I gave them religion. I gave them hope.

"Of course, David did not take kindly to this revelation. It tipped him over into mania. He'd been teetering on the edge for a long time. I thought better of telling him what he could come to view as the worst of it. Then I decided it would be best to unburden my soul completely to him. To do this tearfully. With a palsy in my hands. Yes, I put all of this on. It was required … to convince him. I told him that the real price of manipulating the pineal gland, of prying open the Eye of God, was premature death. And that if a surgeon were to open him up, he would no doubt be riddled with tumors or a failing organ. Something that would kill him sooner than later."

The last time Gretch had seen John Germanian, in all his terrible, self-imposed deformity, she sensed the once legendary lead guitarist was not much longer for the world. She had even anticipated his request to smother him with a pillow or to hold her hands over his mouth and nose simultaneously, to put a period at the end of his wretched life sentence. The rest of the band were dead, all by their own hands.

When her mind turns to thoughts of J, the only other band member she adored beside her husband, a significant sense of emptiness suddenly forms in the pit of her stomach. Something akin to loss. And she is certain what this feeling signals:

He's dead.

Yes.

John Germanian is passed.

Nothing when she thinks of Stevie, in the brief interim of silence as she waits for Stanislaw to continue. *Stevie lives.*

In a beleaguered voice, Stanislaw says,

"When I told David everything I've just told you, I watched something shift in him. He had known something was physically wrong with him, but he'd chosen to bury his concern. Davey might have even come to consider himself invincible, beyond the reach of death. Then, my news drove it home. The aches. The pains. The headaches. Maybe the frequent shortness of breath. What have you. He knew then I was telling the truth. And he was, in fact, very sick. He was dying.

"It's no wonder, in hindsight, he exiled me from The Mountain. Cut me off from my people. Turned them against me. Polluted the very autonomy I had worked to create on The Mountain. He cast me as the villain in this story. The liar.

"My Yelena … she only pretended to believe him. I know this. She never turned on me. She snuck me food wherever she could. Drink. Sustenance. I would have died out there in the snow and the mud and the deep, dark woods if not for her." Stanislaw's chin drops down into his throat, and his watery eyes fall upon the face of his most-cherished bride. He smooths an index finger across her right cheek. The ghost of a smile touches his lips.

Every nerve ending in Gretch's body screams for her to pull the trigger. To offer him no quarter of any kind.

I'm not like them.

Not like him.

No.

So, she stands by, until he finds his place in the narrative for what will be the final time.

FIFTY-THREE

"He took all of them as wives," Karl Stanislaw says. "No ceremony. He simply claimed them as *his own* in what my Yelena describes as a series of awkward and ugly scenes. There is nothing binding between that bastard and one of the women. Not Yelena, although he no doubt feels differently.

"As hard as I pushed to convince David of my ruse, and the Muse was not real, he exerted even more pressure and influence over the lot of them in *proving* Kalliope's existence. He soon realized that his words would only hold them in sway for so long. That is the way of human beings. Eventually, they will come to demand physical proof. Their faith dries up, or it has been stretched well beyond its limits."

"Well, guess the life of a cult leader is not without its challenges," Gretch says, tongue firmly set in cheek.

"It's important you understand the clear distinction between what this Mountain was before David's arrival. Mine was an artist commune. His version was more akin to Jonestown."

"What proof could he possibly have shown to them that they'd accept?" Gretch says.

"It would be easier to show you. If you'll just relax your weapon."

"Now why would I do that?"

"I would need to cross the cavern. The wall ..." Stanislaw brandishes his hand in the direction of the south wall where the lifeless eyes of ten of the corpses stares at them like tipped human dominos. "The proof is there."

After some internal deliberation, Gretch Solomon lowers her weapon. Stanislaw gently moves Yelena's head and shoulders off his lap and rises to full height once more. He towers over her. Gretch feels her pulse quicken. It is like a building has just assembled himself and put her inside of its shadow. He does not move towards the wall right off, but stretches with a deep, guttural yawn like the action is painful to execute.

"David's first wife is the one called Glory, yes?" he asks. "When she fled the Mountain, she set off the series of events which eventually led to all the death you see in this cavern. If she were still alive, I'm sure she would have been praying for a quick end once she came to realize what she'd set in motion." Stanislaw crosses to the western wall. The dead, doll-like eyes, glowing white in the dim, seem to watch him.

To invite him to come closer so they can devour him.

From her vantage, Gretch sees him avert his eyes from the dead assembled before him.

There are a series of pops and clicks and it takes Gretch a moment to recognize them as the noises of the man's tired, worn joints as he stoops to observe something at his waist level.

"Glory left David, and he immediately pivoted, presenting a new, urgent dilemma to the Sister Wives that must be acted upon sooner than later. He convinced them all Glory had made a threat to him before leaving that she would be coming back with the authorities and they would not only evacuate all of them forcibly, but they'd also exploit the gifts of The Muse to such a crippling degree Kalliope would be reduced to nothing more than a giant husk inside The Mountain. It took a great deal of back and forth questioning and answering between David and the women. They did not immediately accept the premise. *How could any human being possibly kill a god? Not possible! We should stay and fight!*

"David entertained their questions until it was obvious he needed to reassert control over them all. There would be no *standing up to the authorities*. There was only surrender, but not before offering themselves up to The Muse to strengthen her in the face of what was an inevitable showdown between her good and *their* evil designs for her. Yelena was badly frightened—she did not want to die—I tried to convince her to remain with me in the forest—she insisted on returning to the rehab building—couldn't leave her *Sisters* behind to die—had to save whoever wished to be saved.

"I decided to make my stand. I kept this from her. I did not want her to worry. It was better for her to focus on her task at hand, instead of bearing the added burden of worrying about me and what could happen."

Stanislaw scrutinizes the stone wall with his head cocked to one side. Then he straightens, squares his legs. He fits his overlong fingers into a pair of grooves in the wall's surface, openings which would have escaped the notice of anyone.

His shoulders roll as he pries at the stone with his bare hands. The sudden ripe smell of blood wafts up Gretch's nose. He has cut his hands open on the craggy rock while struggling to wrest something from the cavern wall itself. Strangely, he makes no sound of pain or the slightest discomfort. His determination has crowded out all other senses. "It's … just here…"

"You were saying you made your stand," Gretch says, worried he might lose the train of thought. "How did all *this* happen then?"

"You know what happened, Gretchen. Is it so important to you that I admit to the failure?"

"It is. You're not the victim here. I don't want you to lose sight of that. Not for one minute."

Still preoccupied with the wall before him, his upper body now writhing like a serpent as he struggles against the obstruction.

"I did not pass them like a ship in the night, if that's what you're looking to hear."

"Hart and Burnside?"

"Is that their names?" Stanislaw says, letting out a quick grunt before Gretch hears what sounds like a dinosaur egg splitting open.

"Then, yes, they had already planted their flag in the grand hall. One of them had come armed to the teeth, no doubt expecting a lethal army of writers and painters to ambush them at some point. You know those damned *creative types*. So militant."

A terrible thought takes hold of Gretch. All this time, she'd sat idly by, weapon at rest, and for all she knew, Karl Stanislaw could have been opening a compartment in the stone and retrieving a weapon of his own. A cold, steely vision of the towering man wheeling around and sending a blade end over end across the cavern to wedge itself in her throat renders her breathless.

Worse than that, the oversized eastern European could turn and squeeze the trigger of a firearm in his palm that takes her in the forehead. What kind of shot is Stanislaw? Gretch does not want to find out.

There is also the fact that it would be suicide to fire any kind of weapon inside a cave. It could trigger a deadly cave-in.

Gretch stands and trains the gun on the back of Stanislaw's shorn, bumpy skull.

"Stop."

The big man either doesn't hear, or he's grown brazen in the last couple of minutes.

"I said *stop!*" Gretch cries. "Stop *moving!* Put your fucking hands up and turn around slowly."

Stanislaw bows his head, raising his hands partway in a display of confusion. "I-I don't understand. You wanted to see—"

"I changed my mind. I'm not interested in seeing anything you want to show to me! Hands up! All the way!"

"But___"

"*Now! Now! FUCKING NOW!*"

He plants his hands on his head, skirts to the side of where he'd been standing, and takes a knee without prompting.

It puts her off her game. These added steps of surrender.

He tips his upraised chin towards the cavern wall, says, "It is exposed. Have a look."

"You deaf? I said ...I ..."

She can't help it.

Gretch turns her eyes to the wall opposite the giant on his knees.

First impression: it looks like a massive elephant tusk embedded in the rock.

Then, at second glance, its sheer size hints at belonging to the long-extinct wooly mammoth.

It is like the rest of the world around her, shale and sand and death and sharp edges and the sudden first taste of claustrophobia falls away like a faulty set design come crashing down around her.

All but the white projection in the wall, which will not let her look away.

At least, that is how it feels.

Clouds eclipse one another as they cross her mind. They slow and deepen with every new drift until Gretch gives in to the pull upon her brain and body.

"What is it?" she asks, barely conscious she has even asked a question.

I have a strong notion of what it is.

And why I must lay hands on the thing that somehow burned my life.

"Careful." Stanislaw's caution does not register.

Gretch frees up her left hand, places it out before her. It leads her towards the bone-white gleam in the stone wall

In her periphery, the sound of stiff fabric snapping like laundered sheets whipping about on a clothesline.

All noise. All distraction.

Shut it out.

Shut it all *out and just—*

"Gretch … Gre-e-*e-e-e-e-etch* …"

Karl Stanislaw is at her elbow, a floating white head in the billowing black of his robe. He raises an arm. His talon-like hand emerges and the index points to the object of both their attentions. "None of them have ever asked me … or *David* … which part of the Muse's skeleton this bone belongs to. It is a fraction of a much larger bone. Maybe a thigh? Leg bone? An upper arm? But that's not the question I have been waiting for the lot of them to ask in all my time on the Mountain. Want to know what that is?"

"You're … you're telling me this—this is—"

"None of them have ever once asked if it is *real*."

"Is it?"

Stanislaw crosses into her field of vision. "May I?" he asks her. He doesn't wait for her blessing.

He moves touches the white projection with a fingertip.

The sudden urge to attack him and protect this (*whatever the fuck this is!*) shocks her in its intensity. Her lips part. She bares her teeth at him like some feral creature.

He scratches at the bone-white projection with a fingernail.

Stop him! Kill him! Now—

Two things happen at the same time.

Lightning speed.

He holds up his finger before her. The nail is packed with what looks like paint chips.

She brings the gun up. About to pin it to the side of his weird skull when Stanislaw sheds his ruse of acquiescence in favor of his hidden, hideous aggression.

He fans his other arm wide, connecting with her wrist as it comes up.

She cries out.

Her palm opens.

The gun drops.

Even with every muscle flooded with adrenaline and quivering with a collective urgency, Gretch Solomon's push back is broken at once.

Stanislaw arm-bars her across the throat and punches her in the stomach, doubling her over.

Hands in her hair, wrenching her head upward so violently something clicks loudly in the back of her neck.

Stanislaws bends at the hip with perfect ease, white circle of a face divebombing to mere inches from her wincing, upturned face.

In a sibilant, disarming voice, he says, "You would have made an obedient Sister Wife. You would have fit right in. *You* could have died beside these Sisters and your death would have meant something. Even you wanted it to be real. You disappoint me, bitch!"

Gretch tries to spit in his face.

Nothing.

Her mouth is a desert.

"Sometimes people want to believe *so badly*," Stanislaw says, *"they'll stretch that belief beyond all logic and reason.* You. Are. Weak. Not. Special."

A gunshot rings out.

Then, deep, bottomless black.

FIFTY-FOUR

and even before her eyes flutter all the way open, Gretch sees the white protrusion in the cave wall is vibrating like a tuning fork. Her head feels heavier than ever before. She cannot lift it off the hard ground. Not at first, anyhow. She does not exert any energy, and she does not press the flats of her palms into the dirt floor. And yet her upper body rises and she sits up. Gretch feels like a marionette. She waves one hand before her in search of a fishing line glinting in the gloom. Attached to her. Stitched in. For some much larger, profoundly imposing Other to animate her as they see fit. The cave is darker than before. But she is certain she is still in the same cavern where before she and —

who?

you know—

who?

-the-the-the-youknow-the—

No, why don't you tell me?

The ladle dips down into the memory well of her mind. When she tries to draw it out with the answer she seeks (that being his name) it is a word search that eludes her so completely she might as well have occupied herself with trying to hold onto a slippery eel. Even when she turns around, her head *listing to the left with its added weight, and Gretch finds the* he *in question lying in a heap of black cloak she still can't retrieve his name from the well.*

The ladle comes up dry as a bone.

The smell of cordite and dirty pennies and shit hang heavy in the air. It is so thick inside her nostrils Gretch is surprised she cannot see this conglomeration of stink given shape and form before her eyes. It is the stench of hospice care and used body bags and the unembalmed.

New death. Recent.

The cloak. He wore *one?*

You tell me.

I'm not talking.

Who fucking needs you then—

You do—

There's new death *under the cloak.*

Eyes listless and unable to fix upon anything in the dark, Gretch reaches for the wall nearest her. An especially sharp crag of rock carves a kiss into the flat of her palm. She doesn't feel it and slowly hauls herself up through of graceless motion. Tries to separate from the wall and a wooziness settles into her skull, stuffing it with tack filling.

If she means to move about the cavern, she will have to keep to the cavern wall. To inch her way along.

I feel drunk. Concussed.

And Gretch Solomon becomes aware of two things simultaneously.

A quick glance down the front of herself and she finds the hypodermic needle sticking out of her right outer thigh. How she'd come to miss it for as long as she'd been conscious (not very long at all) and its pinch as it waggles about. The needle submerged into the muscle halfway. Just shy of the bone. The Eye.

The Eye.

Go on—what about *The Eye*—

He … Christ, my eyes feel like they're going to pop out of their sockets. I can feel them bulging. They're growing. Swelling—

Can't tell you what will remedy that … but you'll get it—

Bastard!

There! Did you feel that!

Feel what, fucking sadist?

You blinked and the pain muted for a split second—

Would you just tell me—my eyes are-I'm gonna lose my eyes—

Blink ... longer ...

What does that even mean—

The pressure in her right eyeball becomes excruciating and her vision, already impaired to the point her vision has transformed into a letterbox-type square picture, shifts and shudders. Gretch can think of nothing to save the eye but to seal it off with its lid.

There ... the pain is gone.

I don't-I don't understand how I ... dear God ...

Yes, make no mistake. You are still seeing, even with your eyes closed. Why?

Gretch truly starts to panic. Her heartbeat gallops like a spooked horse. She can feel the blood coursing through her veins, the slight friction between the fluid as it rides the circuit of her circulatory system. A sucking, like thick and viscous fluid through a narrow straw.

Heart attack? Is this what it feels like to have one? A sudden sensitivity to your own blood-flow?

To admit she is now seeing *through God's Eye is quite possibly the most terrifying realization she has ever had to submit to. Words would have proven inadequate if she tried to describe the difference between eyesight and Eye Sight. A hallucinogenic?*

He *drugged* me?

Gretch stares down at what she perceives to be the hood of his—

Stanis-law!

It's him!

That's him!

She decides it's imperative she verify he is indeed dead. After what he'd done to her, any lingering sign of life would make him a threat and Gretch knows she'd have to put him down herself. For good.

Damon's gun?

Is it hiding from her or —

The cavern is plotting against me? Obstructing me from ...

What?

Stooping beside the prone lump of black cloth, Gretch reaches for the hood. She draws it back, tongue bitten between her teeth.

Sleep no more—

The head is horned and scorched an angry red the color of boiled lobster. Patches of pale skin gleam here and there around his (its) *skull. They look like skin grafts, barely covering a quarter of the monstrous visage and dented head. And if not for the cloak, there is little chance she would have identified him as Karl Stanislaw. The seemingly penitent Croat dead and stripped of Its earthbound disguise. Laid bare for what he had been all along.*

Not quite the Devil, *she suspects.* But one of his soldiers. Sent to sew doubt and confusion and stir the mud, shattering the reflection and sending ripples through it all. Then, departing.

What are you?

What the *fuck is* all of this?

Why *can't* I know?

Shifting her shivery, fuzzed God's Eye gaze to the left, Gretch can at least answer the question of where *he'd come from. Seemingly materialized from thin air in the cavern with her. That is not the case.*

Perhaps an aspect of deeper, more discerning vision and understanding is a blessing of God's Eye.

Whatever the reason, she never noticed the slightest fracture in the north cave wall. Towards the right-hand corner.

An enclave.

Ethereal light burns bright within the fracture, calling her closer.

Gretch obeys, scrambling along the wall, hand over hand.

Blind and not blind at the same time.

Greedily, she inserts her fingers into the aperture.

Pries at the slim opening.

The gap widens by painstakingly slow degrees to nearly a foot.

It is enough that Gretch can angle her head around the lip of this opening.

To peer inside.

Black as an abyss

It's not enough to satisfy her curiosity.

She backs her head out of the opening and tries prying it wider. After a series of stops and starts, Gretch pulls the door outward enough she thinks she can squeeze her whole body through. It eludes her understanding that Stanislaw could have emerged from this separate alcove, but that he'd managed to do it undetected and soundlessly.

This door cut into the wall feels as heavy cumbersome as the stone laid across the top of an old crypt. It hints at the eastern European having possessed a form of superhuman strength. It will only make her head hurt even more.

Scraping her way inside the adjacent alcove, a hot wind rushes towards her face the moment she enters. It takes her breath away and leaves her gasping.

Gretch remembers she has a lighter in her pants pocket, an implement she had bought on the road at a gas station, along with a now crumpled pack of Winston 100's. Eyes downcast and head hung low with guilt, she'd purchased the smokes and light, returning to a habit she'd kicked four years ago. Almost to the day.

She'd ended up tossing the pack, the disgust of her personal weakness too much to stomach.

Something made her keep the lighter.

Fishing it out of her jeans pocket, Gretch thumbs the little wheel, and a guttering little flame casts a meager circle around her.

A room?

There is a horizontal aperture cut through the stone wall. At eye-level. She steps up to it, must stoop to peer through it, and is not surprised to find it looks out onto the cavern of death.

The chamber of lies.

Then, she draws a conclusion she wishes she hadn't.

This is … what … a viewing room?

To view what? The poor rubes who have visited the cavern. To pray. To lay hands on the white protrusion in the far wall they've come to believe to be a fractional portion of the "Muse's" massive skeleton? Who would have hidden back here, gloating or laughing or perhaps checking to see whose faith might be breaking? Who hunkered down back here, listening to the pleas, the sacred and secret imploring of the faithful to this *false bas relief* relic in the cavern wall?

Which one of the sadists?

Davey? Stanislaw?

This little hidden viewing room could and probably does predate both men. Stanislaw says he is one in a long line of caretakers and overseers of this property. This land.

She knows she's not interested in any exhaustive history of this Hell on Earth structure. All that interests her is making her escape. Of exploding this Hell on Earth on her way out the door.

A question bubbles up from the depths of her consciousness.

How did Stanislaw come to die like he did?

Who is responsible?

And the question that sits heavy in the pit of her stomach: Where is Davey?

Before she can think twice, Gretch makes a mad dash for the narrow opening. Cutting bloody slashes into her shoulders, her sides, her back, she makes her return to the cavern of death.

Gretch hears the scraping sound, not unlike that made by the prying of the stone door open moments ago.

The grating noise, shale upon shale, confounds her at first.

Until she traces the source of the noise to its source.

An opening in the floor of the cavern.

The size and shape of a standard doorway made horizontal.

She scrambles towards it, kicking up clouds of silt in her wake. Only to discover someone is in the process of sealing it off.

FIFTY-FIVE

"Davey!" she screams, throwing herself upon the slab as it shifts into the cut out in the cavern floor. "DAVEY, YOU FUCKER! YOU THINK I'M GONNA LET YOU BURY ME ALIVE? YOU FUCK!"

The slab is not yet in place. A small opening, shrinking by the second, winks at her.

Taunts her, it would seem.

And Gretch wastes no time.

She sits on the lip of the opening. Slips both of her boot heels into the opening, plants both hands behind her for leverage, and kicks out at the stone slab. Employs her calf muscles to the point of instant cramping and sweet, swooning agony. She keeps on, legs quavering now.

And with the spare bit of wind left inside her, Gretch cries, "STANISLAW TOLD ME EVERYTHING! AND YOU'RE NOTHING BUT A USEFUL FUCKING IDIOT, DAVEY!"

A bullet whizzes past the right side of her face, a hornet with a rocket up its ass. Gretch retracts her feet from the opening, flattens herself onto her belly.

Rolls away.

One of the corpses lining the wall halts her. Just the touch, the give of whatever part of their rotting body she's come up against, sends a terrific *shiver up and down her arms. Lying on her side, she watches and listens as Davey unleashes a slurry of curses, most of them slurs for the female who'd met him on his own sacred ground and bested him.*

The rounds are flying around the cavern now as he sends them up through the opening.

Then, it is as if these metaphorical hornets have taken up residence in the back of her head where her skull meets spinal column. One itch in this area turns to all-out irritation like she's broken out in hives. Just as a person who has caught fire will try to outrun it somehow, Gretch finds her feet and runs around in ever-widening circles. All the while, slapping at the back of her neck. Then bringing her hand back around in the hopes of finding a crushed wasp flattened against her palm.

There is nothing there, no matter how many times she does this.

They are crawling, clambering overtop of one another just under the skin. Circling the knob of bone protruding from the back of her neck.

The incessant slapping turns her wrist temporarily limp and useless.

Still, she cannot stop.

A scream rips its way out of her, sounding like it left a jagged path of torn flesh in its wake.

Bullets are ricocheting all over the cavern.

One clips her ear. Blood flows at once. A fingernail's worth of cartilage sheared off.

A round nearly takes her in the inner thigh, dangerously close to her femoral artery.

The bees.

The hornets! Whatever the hell they are!

GETOUT-GETOUT-GETOUTOFMYBODY—

"Don't try to fight it, Solomon!"

Davey Grifter calls to her from down below. He's stopped firing.

She always believed her first words to Davey once she crossed paths with him again would be no words at all. A weighted silence as she empties her gun into his belly or gets her hands around his throat. The last thing she would have wanted in this moment is exactly what transpires:

"What's happening to me?"

Like laying yourself upon the mercy of the court as a guilty party.

Her legs are rubber bands, barely supporting her upper torso. She swears one of the hornets has somehow made its way into the back of her throat.

That its sting is next.

Stumbling about as she struggles to keep herself upright, Gretch gags and retches, trying to expel the little buzzing demon from the back of her mouth.

Gathering bits of Davey's shouting in between her dry-heaves, Gretch hears, "...you fight it ...get worse ...your gatekeepers *will turn their volume down soon ... the noise is too new ... gotta be patient ..."*

"You ... bastard! Whatever this ... is ... I don't want it!"

"Oh, I think you know exactly what this *is, Solomon!"*

Hyper-focused on the buzzing phantoms encased beneath the skin of her neck, she bites her tongue. Words are of no consequence now. Relief is king.

Davey dives into the silence. "Did you lay hands on Her?"

Her cheeks are burning. "Fuck off, Davey! There is no her! *Your oversized comrade told me everything so save it and tell me how to make this stop—"*

"'Whatever it is, I don't want it!' Fucking ingrate! You have no idea what you're talking about. And I have been listening to every flagrant, pain-inducing lie and deception and twisting of the facts Stanislaw passed along to you. I've been down here, the entire time fighting back the urge to enter the cavern unnoticed so I could shut that asshole up once and for all."

Tears flood her closed eyes. When she tries to open them, it is like she has been staring into the sun for an hour straight. The lids squeeze shut again, oozing the tears out from under their flaps. God's Eye does not like to compete with the human sense of traditional sight. That is made quite clear. Through a throat webbed in phlegm, Gretch says, "I-I think their volume is lowering. Can't be ... sure."

"Do you accept Kalliope's blessing? Do you enter the arrangement freely and willingly? I was never given a choice, so consider yourself lucky. None of us had a say."

"I don't—"

"I've got just the remedy for you in that case, Solomon."

"I—"

The cluster of frenzied hornets under the skin have softened enough Gretch can hear her inner voice when it issues its warning.

Tell him you accept. Make him believe it. It'll put him off his guard and it'll buy you time to maybe escape with your life.

"I accept the blessing," she says, a lump rising in her throat.

In that moment, all becomes still. The air thins. The world had been holding its breath and only now does it exhale. The decision, one she doesn't believe in and has used purely for a ruse, now feels like a die cast. Something is different inside of her. Not just the fact that the hornets have calmed.

It is a sense of loss. A death. A reaping of her very soul.

"Welcome to the fold," Davey says. "Now why don't you come down out of there so I can show you out. I want you off my Mountain."

The singer's words are a morning bell for Gretch Solomon, shaking her from her trance and clearing a good bit of the hallucinogenic cobwebs away from her vision and her mind.

Gretch laughs darkly. "I'll leave when I'm finished here."

Nothing

"Well, why don't you come down anyway," Davey says, sardonically. "We should really talk about that. Before things get any more out of hand."

Casting her gaze all about, her eyes glancing off the assembly of female corpses all in a row, she wishes he was standing there in front of him. Her hands itch to close around his windpipe. They open and close, hungrily.

An idea takes shape in her mind. She wonders at first if she has the stomach to see it through. It's not strong enough a scruple to dissuade her. This is do or die.

Gretch lowers herself down onto all fours. She sweeps the flats of her palms along the dirt floor. She skitters about, hands fanning around in search of something.

From below: "I really think you ought to come down."

"Yeah?"

"That's right."

The loose stone practically leaps into her hand. It is sizeable enough to give some heft to her palm. Solid. Dropped from the ceiling of the cavern, no doubt because of the gunfire from moments ago.

Alright. Here we go.

She crawls back to the lip of the rectangular opening in the floor where the slab has been slid three-quarters of the way across.

"Let me ask you a question," she says.

"Solomon, I—"

"No, humor me, Davey."

"What is it?"

Gretch begins hammering the stone in her hand against the wall to her immediate left. "Do you think your Muse will feel pain or she'll lash out—break free of the Mountain, even—if I were to hammer this exposed section of her skeleton with a stone?"

"That's ... not—"

"Does Kalliope—is it? —is she still capable of screaming in pain? What is pain to a god?"

The stone starts to crumble in her hands. Hoping Davey won't be able to figure out she is across the cavern from the exposed bone. *She is counting on sudden blind rage and the impulse to protect his god will override his sense of direction. She strikes the wall with the stone in such a way it glances off the shale, producing a spark. And another. Another—*

"What the fuck *do you think you're doing?" Davey erupts. "You* crazy *heretical twat?"*

"I think ... yeah ... I swear I can hear the old bitch really starting to squeal!"

"Stop—just—STOP—I'M COMING UP—BITCH—"

That's right, legend!

Come along!

The scrambling of feet as he scales the wall just beneath the opening in the ground. The only way he could possibly make such easy work of this would be if there are grooves cut into the stone he can use to climb with the tips of his bare feet. A vision of what the soles of his bare feet must look like flashes before her mind's eye. The rough, leathery bottoms layered in flaky, white calluses upon calluses. Fresh and aged cuts crisscrossing the bottoms of his feet, occasionally tearing open to color the entire sole crimson.

Then there is the question of the animal pelts he is wrapped in like some Mesozoic caveman breed.

Davey Grifter, whose prized pair of acid-washed black jeans are on display behind glass at the NYC Hard Rock Café. Whose tastes for the young and unguarded girl would have landed him in prison among rough company if he were anyone *else. Whose face graces nearly as many t-shirts as Led Zeppelin (talking the* whole *band), brings his head up just above the opening in the cavern floor. The same abnormally misshapen, shaved skull as Karl Stanislaw.*

Hinting at something else going on with both their brains.

Something she can't possibly wrap her mind around. A thin, gray mohawk, no longer than a half inch, runs from his hairline and down the back of his head.

They lock eyes in that moment of mutual realization.

Davey's emerald eyes, glinting and manic, widen.

Gretch smirks at him, the stone raised above her head.

And the two of them understand that this—*this full-circle moment—marks the true break-up of Grifter Anonymous.*

The band will die in this cavern. It doesn't matter that the other four members are dead.

And she swears he bows his head as she brings the stone down.

Like he knows he's had this coming for years.

FIFTY-SIX

here
  dig-helpmewiththis
  need every man
  mayjustbe- a leg with no body—
  shutupanddig

Snatches of statements.

Non-sequiturs buzzing above her.

Then it feels like she has just been freed from a molding that has held her in its paralyzing embrace.

No that's not right. This is what it feels like to be dug up after a premature burial.

Finally, her belly can expand. Lungs can fully inflate and deflate in meaningful, life-saving respiration. The non-sequiturs gather context and combine into frantic conversation. And while she cannot yet open her eyes (the shale dust has glued them shut in combination with her inadvertent tears), she can hear the men, maybe four or five of them, with their banter and it reminds her of someone she knows.

Knew.

Is he

Still dead

Was he ever?

Stanislaw and his eastern European accent, the vocal equivalent of an icepick stabbing at the air.

Arrhythmic.

Sharp-edged.

Frightening at once.

The distinct odor of sulfur hangs thick and heavy in the air. It packs itself up her nose. She gags. Tastes a mouthful of bile. Gretch manages to swallow it. It burns all the way down her throat like she's drunk a mouthful of one of those exotic flaming cocktails.

It's strange where the mind takes you in times like these. Paralysis. Frozen in place. Completely vulnerable.

Gretch worries that the smell in the air could be her own mess.

One of the eastern-European men lets loose a ragged, shredding cough. "Smell like all the shit of the world run through here, no?"

Dizziness takes hold of Gretch. Places her on an invisible carousel and a disembodied hand gives it a good, hard spin. She misses the quick, heated back and forth that takes place between the two Russians.

Then what feels like the start of a *release.*

I'm dying? Is this how it goes?

Are these Stanislaw's men? Relatives?

Who the fuck are they and why does it matter because they're saving my life, so—

(you sure about that?)

Even with her eyes sealed shut, she senses the change-over from dark to thin light as another jagged length of stone is lifted away from the mantel formation that has suspended it mere inches from her nose.

Something about the sudden freedom in having her face exposed prompts her to speak. Gretch doesn't know she's saying anything until her rescuers fall silent at once and there is only the sound of her weakened, gravelly voice spinning out above her head like her words are scribbling a messy, colorful yarn in the air. "Who're you with …

Stannis … laws dead … dunno if … Davey … he may've … dunnit … I—"

"Can you open eye, *Gretchen*?" one of them asks, his voice a deep baritone.

She opens her mouth. Its gummed up inside. Something like wet cement coats her inner cheeks and has settled into her gum pockets. She tries to say something and can only smack her lips together loudly. Then, Gretch tries again to answer. "I'm … afraid to …"

A lightness of being floods her limbs, crosses her chest and stomach.

They're digging me out. They are saving me.

(you sure?)

A flash of memory. Huddling on the dirt floor of the cavern while Davey fires round after round up through the opening leading to the lower cave maze.

Firing round-after-round—

A cave-in.

He triggered one. It caught me up.

Now, there is another exchange happening a short distance from her:

"—find all the bombs?"

"—they are contained—"

"—the detonator? —"

"—still searching—"

"When you free her, ask her about detonator? Where is *detonator*?"

Mr. Baritone, distinguishing himself as something of a representative for her, says, "And if she does not know?"

"Mm-hmm," the other seems to muse. "Nolan will need to be briefed. You will be the one. *Da?*"

A slurry of voices echoes through the passage from a seemingly far-removed space. Maybe they are all the way back at the entrance to the underground stone maze. Just outside the dormant hearth. The walls of the cave answer this hurried back and forth in a staccato Russian cadence by letting out a slow-building grumble that stretches for an alarmingly long time and swells into an all-encompassing growl of stone against stone.

The last of the weight piled on top of her is hauled away.

She is borne upwards by what feels like a hundred hands.

Mr. Baritone is in her ear: "You must. You must. Open your eyes!"

I can't explain. If the God Eye is open, I can't use my eyes. It will feel like a knife to the brain.

She grits her teeth.

Warily raises her eyelids.

An otherworldly greenish light hits her pupils in all its blinding harshness. A veritable 4th of July fireworks show explodes across her brain. And once she realizes what has sparked this frenzy of sensory overload, Gretch grabs and latches onto Mr. Baritone's right arm.

"Get that *fucking* light out of my eyes!" she screams.

"I turn away. I turn away, see? We go out now!"

Mr. Baritone is wearing one of those miner's helmets with a flashlight mounted to the top.

The garish light peels off her face and plays about the walls of the narrow passage like a restless spirit orb.

Muttering men behind her.

Beside her.

Leading.

It is an entourage.

The last thing she remembers was the sickening sound of the legendary singer's skull splitting open when she struck it with a weighty, jagged stone.

More loud back and forth Russian up ahead.

Closer now.

They are headed for the hearth.

The rehab.

FIFTY-SEVEN

Who are these men?

A militia?

Search and rescue?

Sent by who?

Instead, the question she asks surprises even her.

"Where's Davey Grifter?"

The muttering flanking her on all sides turns to a frenzy of loud, overlapping exchanges.

They know him.

Are they here for him?

One of the hands carrying her digs into her right calf muscle, then relents. She angles her eyes in the direction of this. Strains to see who it is.

Mr. Baritone.

He casts his gaze to the dark, narrow cave maze before him. Behind him, a man with a nasally, nagging quality to his voice rattles off a stuffy string of Russian words. Mr. Baritone sighs heavily, then tosses a measured response to this cohort over his shoulder.

Wait a minute!

Hold on—I could have sworn I just heard him say …

Can't be … Nolan Royal?

Adrenaline floods her arms and legs. Gretch's hands are suddenly climbing and clawing for purchase along the shoulder nearest her. Trying to pull herself into an upright position while being carried.

She puts the question to them repeatedly. She cannot stop.

"Did Nolan Royal send you?"

Mr. Baritone grunts. Nothing more.

"Is he … is he *here?*"

Gretch cranes her neck to seize upon the glowing rectangle of light at the end of the maze. It swells and broadens with Mr. Baritone's every forward step.

Mr. Baritone's small black eyes touch her before turning straight ahead again. Lips pursed. Face flushed.

"Karl?" Gretch puts to him. "Karl *Stanislaw?* Do you know him?"

Nothing.

The four men carrying her edge up to the yellow light of the rectangular opening and stall there.

A tendril of cold reaches through the opening to feel her face. To cup her chin. Smooth her cheeks.

She flails her right hand outward, palm open and outward to reach for the cold. To curl her fingers around it and pull herself through the rest of the way like a baby miraculously grabbing for their own umbilical cord.

Finally, the men cross through the dormant walk-in hearth. She can see them all better than in the dark passage.

All of them are powerfully built with shorn or buzzed heads. She experiences a flash of Stanislaw's skull, the oddly unsettling bumps and grooves encircling the oversized man's bald head. They wear the bulky, black loadouts of tactical gear. Her eyes pass indifferently from one to the next.

Are these her saviors? Her abductors?

The questions sizzle in her brain as she observes the mercenaries muttering into their wrists. Talking to who?

Where is Davey?

Stanislaw?

The bodies of the women?

The—

"-detonator is here!"

Her carriers stall again, stopping adjacent to the arrangement of leather sofas and dead Tiffany-lamps atop end tables.

A fair-skinned merc with six inches on Mr. Baritone and most of the other men surges across the dust-coated hardwood of the main hall. His shoulders run in a near-perfect straight line across, interrupted only by his neck. His face is red with frostbite. Blonde stubble stands at attention in a shoe-horn bald formation on his head. No eyebrows, or they are far too light for detection. Bright, gunship gray eyes.

He is carrying Gretch's black JanSport backpack.

Mr. Baritone nods, unimpressed.

His deep voice fractures slightly as he raises it to direct the other mercs.

"We clear out! Double-time! *Out!*"

He exchanges the slightest nod with the detonator-wielding merc, who then heads back where the rest of them have just come from.

He disappears into the gaping black mouth of the hearth.

Her voice weakened by her body, Gretch groans up at the mercs carrying her in a synchronized trot now. "Take out the girls' bodies first. They deserve … p-proper burials."

Mr. Baritone moves to the door of the rehab center, propped open to the snow-covered mountain plateau.

Gretch sees a helicopter outside, rotors whipping the air incessantly.

Four black SUVs.

A black Econoline van.

The air is thick with cold.

Gretch sucks greedily at it.

The change-over from dim to blindingly bright, sunlight reflecting off the snow and amplifying its white to a powerful shimmer, forces Gretch's eyes shut once more.

She wriggles her body, straining to be answered. Acknowledged:

"Where are you taking me?"

"Chopper," he says. "Take you up and out. Then hospital."

A figure standing just outside the opened sliding-door of the van comes into fuller focus.

They are canting to the left as they poke and prod at the snowy ground with a cane that propels them forward.

They regard her with something like curiosity.

"Wait … I … you—"

"Save your strength," the old mogul, Nolan Royal, advises her as Mr. Baritone moves past him towards the waiting helicopter. "We've got it from here."

A hand presses an air mask over her mouth. She tastes vanilla. And she is too weak in mind and body to hold her breath. She's got no idea what she is breathing in after all. It could be toxic.

Gretch's eyelids gain weight.

Flutter.

The last thing Gretch Solomon remembers is the sound of explosions like a fleet of 747's crashing into the mountainside.

FIFTY-EIGHT

In and out of consciousness.

The sky is a flat, pale eggshell surface.

Her eyes twitch. Open a slit.

Lying flat.

But moving.

Centrifugal motion tugs on her like eager, exploring hands.

There is a dull throb along her right rib cage that hints at several fractures. Her intestines are coiled tight as a snake. She is fragile and this is something she's never been comfortable submitting to.

They have fitted her snugly into a harness of some sort to stabilize her as she lies within the chopper's hold.

Sleep eludes her.

Or she is eluding sleep.

Gretch Solomon cannot leave it alone. Cannot flee The Mountain without some small semblance of closure. She knows she will soon have to learn how to live alone and that she is enough. It won't feel that way at first.

But if she can feast her eyes and look upon The Mountain that has been compromised, gravely she hopes, by the detonation of a series of

C4 explosives, then part of Gretch can start to heal. From there, more of the same.

I never got to trigger them.

Then what was that blast you heard before you passed out in Mr. Baritone's arms?

Plane crash?

No.

She opens her eyes. Cranes her neck in the direction of the mountainside and what is left of the rehab center.

"Oh … God!"

A man's pale face, one of her carriers, slides into view. "Keep your head still, Gretchen. We will still need to assess for any spinal or cranial injury."

Gretch has no idea she was trying to sit up. When she discovers a hand flailing around in the air to her left she does not put it together that it is her hand, brandishing in the direction of The Mountain.

"Do you see it?" she says, eyes wide and expectant.

None of the men answer her, which only succeeds in spiking the level of her terror.

The Mountain side no longer resembles the slick, gargantuan body of some great sperm whale washed ashore. Now, it looks like some gargantuan monstrosity of a cracked nutshell. A deep, if not terribly wide, fracture yawns in the stone. Hundreds of feet in height.

Within the massive aperture, a pale, sickly-looking something lingers. It looks like some prehistoric bone belonging to an impossibly gigantic skeleton. An enlarged stalactite? Discolored rock unseated by the explosion—

They wanted the detonator.

The men in black. They blew up The Mountain. The rehab.

This sets off a series of synaptic explosions across the inner circuitry of her brain as questions surface above a sea of black waves. *What of Burnside? Is he dead? Let me the see body! I must be sure! Davey? Should I have spared him? Tried to bring him out with me somehow? Am I evil now? I caved in his head—*

One of the men tugs on the straps that stabilize her body in its harness.

The chopper banks hard to the right.

Gretch is panting. "Do you—"

"Just relax," the same man (medic?) tells her as he clamps an oxygen mask over her mouth. "Breathe."

Gretch rolls her head back and forth along the cushion tucked under it. She tries to make a grab for the mask, but her hand falls away almost at once.

"Ma'am?" The medic draws her mask aside. "What is it?"

He leans in, straining to understand her above the *whup-whup-whup* of the whipping rotors.

"The Mountain ... blown open ... something inside ... tell me ... please ... is it moving?"

The medic raises his head, sets her with a sidelong glance like an impatient parent. Then, he casts his gaze out towards The Mountain. The horizon, now a burnished orange glow lining its apex like a layering of sticky sunlight.

"I ..." Clearly flustered, the medic shrugs his shoulders and grits his teeth. "I don't ..."

She's too weak to form the words, let alone push them out.

You don't what?

He glances down at her. Gretch Solomon will spend the rest of her days obsessing over what she sees in his eyes. She will sketch the medic's expression, the tightness of his lips and quick, twitchy widening of his green eyes. She will fill sketchbook after sketchbook with this moment in time and the man who holds the key to her understanding of the world and whether she suffers from some clinical delusion and paranoia. Does his expression confirm or deny her sanity? Gretch will even share her drawings with friends, acquaintances, and even her therapist. Casually putting the question to them and mindful to keep any trace of desperation out of her voice, even though she will indeed become desperate as the months go by.

"Is it belief in his eyes?" she asks anyone who will listen. "Fear? Impatience? Confusion? *What?*"

The expression evaporates. The medic raises his head, exchanges a knowing nod with a bearded team member who reaches out of her periphery.

The medic fits the mask over her mouth again. The oxygen tastes different. A dark chocolate aroma.

"Count down from ten for me?" He tells her.

You don't WHAT?

He wants her to *fucking* count down?

Was it Her? In the Mountain?

Is She real?

What did you see?

What did you

What

Wha …

FIFTY-NINE

"God*dammit!* I can't reach it! Help!"

Gretch can't reach the phone on the nightstand next to her hospital bed. The morphine drip put her down for four hours. Then, she had dreamt something that suddenly snatched sleep away from her like a blanket from a baby. And she knew there can be no further rest, no matter the condition of her body. While she can't remember what it was that had stirred her violently awake, Gretch has come to with a single, burning need to make a call.

A woman in a white lab coat appears at her bedside. Lays a hand on Gretch's arm. "It's going to be alright, Ms. Solomon. You're at Cedars-Sinai."

Ms. Lab Coat, whose nametag reads *Dr. Henrietta Dennison*, wheels the stand closer and turns the rotary phone to face the patient. Gretch tries to raise herself up into a sitting position. Her lower back protests, sending bolts of lightning up the bumps of her spinal column. Dr. Dennison loops an arm around her just beneath her pits and slowly hoists her up until she nods to signal she's good now.

"Here," Dr. Dennison says, lifting the whole phone up and setting it in Gretch's lap. "Better?"

Gretch stares blankly down at the phone.

"Would you like me to dial a number for you?" Dr. Dennison says.

"N-no. Just checking in at home."

"I'll be right outside," Dr. Dennison says, and exits soundlessly.

With an especially stiff index finger, Gretch dials.

The receiver feels like an icepick against her ear. Her heartbeat thrums thickly inside her head.

Eight rings.

The answering machine should have retrieved the call after the fifth ring.

There will be no hanging up. Not until she's waited through at least a hundred of these dreadful tones.

Gretch grasps the receiver with both hands.

Around the twenty-seventh ring, she is white knuckling it.

The thirty-fifth tone is neatly clipped off.

Shallow breaths on the other end.

They don't say anything.

"Hello?"

Nothing.

"Hello? Is this Pru? Hey, why didn't you answer the phone?"

After some time, the light and airy tone of that cornsilk-haired girl Gretch interviewed in her kitchen mere days ago answers her. "This is her."

"I want to talk to Stevie. Put him on. I don't care if he's sleeping. Wake him up. Now, you—"

"Oh, jeez, yeah, Mrs. Darius ... I don't know that's going to happen."

"You ... you don't ... *I said put my husband on the goddam phone now or so help me—*"

"Can't. It's not safe."

"What the *fuck* are you talking about? Who *are* you? Really?"

"I think you know exactly who I am, Gretchen. And who I was. *And* I think you were okay with that because you knew I'd do what you could never bring yourself to do. I'm here to tell you there's nothing more to worry about. It's over."

"Wait-wait-*wait!* What do you mean it's over? What are you saying?"

"I handled him," Pru Garland says. "Don't worry."

"What did you do?"

But you know. She's right. You always knew who she was. Yes, it's impossible. That she *would appear on your doorstep when she is supposed to be moldering away in some shallow grave along with all the others —*

"Prudence," Gretch says. "Lovebug."

"I had a round-trip bus ticket *back* to my hometown when they murdered me. Did you know that, Gretchen? I only said I was running away because I wanted them to like me. It was a lie. But that doesn't mean I should have died for it. Right? Cunt? You just had someone wipe it from your mind so you wouldn't suffer the guilt.

"You're ... dead ... how—"

"Because I *really* wanted to meet back up with you and your scumbag murdering hubby. So the planets aligned. Jesus H. Christ signed off on it. And here I am. Sitting outside your house in the driveway with your cordless phone and a tall glass of homemade lemonade. Watching the first columns of smoke rise off the roof. Oh—" The sound of Lovebug cupping the phone in her palm. "—oh, I just heard the first window blow out. It won't be long now."

You never could have. Never would have.

She's right.

"Prudence—"

"And Gretch ... I absolve you. Whether you deserve it or not."

The line goes dead.

There is a moment when everything stops. Then, her mind starts firing on all cylinders. Frantic, uncompromising motivation moves her to remove her IV. The pain is nothing. A bit of blood spurts out of her vein.

Then, the doctor is at her side, struggling to stabilize Gretch's arms while an RN chases the right with the IV needle.

Gretch's green eyes are wide and raving.

"I gotta get outta here-gotta get outta of here-while I still have a house to go back to!"

Black spots dance before her eyes. Her periphery narrows as her chest tightens.

"OhGod-ohGod-oh *—she really did it?*"

Exhausted beyond measure, the fight runs out of her. "Can't …
breathe …"

A prick in her hand as the RN finally puts the IV back in.

The doctor does not back away. She allows for the deeply troubled
ginger-haired woman to lean into her. "You've got to keep calm. Your
air will come back. You've got three broken ribs on your right side. A
concussion and multiple lacerations. Right now, I want you only to
focus on your air."

"I've …" Gretch pulls back, terror tugging at the corners of her eyes
and mouth. "I have to get home!"

Dr. Dennison stiffens. "I *do not* advise that. You were brought to us
on the brink of death, Ms. Solomon. Quite literally dropped off in front
of our ER by some rather callused individuals, I would say. Do you
remember what happened to you? Who did this?"

"N-nobody did this to me," Gretch says, a tremor running through
her voice. "Cave-in."

"A what? Did you say a *cave-in*?"

"Doesn't matter. I'm alive."

"For now," Doctor Dennison says. "I'm advising you to stay. That is
my medical opinion. You've got internal bleeding. Any number of
things could go wrong once you leave this hospital—"

"I'm still alive, Doctor. I'll sign whatever you need me to sign. That
I'm leaving against medical advisement. Would you please—just—
draw up whatever papers so I can be on my way?"

"Ms. Solomon, I—"

"Doctor, I just got off the phone with a woman who claims my
house is on fire. And she's the one who started it. With my incapacitated husband inside! So, I don't give a shit what kind of pain I'm
going to be in. Don't care if it costs me my life. I'm responsible. I have
to go!"

Doctor Dennison folds her arms, rubs at the bridge of her nose and
gives a stiff nod. The RN in the room, whose held her tongue during
the exchange out of respect for the chain of command, accepts the cue
from her superior. "I'll gather the forms." She turns to Gretchen, asks,
"Would you like me to call anyone for you?"

"No one," Gretch says, and her own words fill her with instant loneliness. "Call me a cab, please."

Jesus, if this is not full-circle, then I'll be fucked.

455

SIXTY

The driveway that once ran parallel with the front of Gretch Solomon's blue farmhouse now borders a smoking pile of rubble. The smell of burning rubber calls water into her eyes. Behind her, the cabbie struggles to pull a K-turn amidst the tangle of parked police cars and bustle of firefighters rushing to and fro in a perfect protocol of mechanical motion. Running a hose or wrapping one back up again.

She can't breathe. She stops halfway to the waiting cluster of police and plainclothes huddling with their coffees at the end of the drive. A pair of detectives clock her with expectant and hardened eyes.

Gretch doubles over, rushes to a stand of bushes to vomit.

The two detectives break from the crowd of milling police to *what—aid* her?

To hold her hair back?

You have no idea why the caretaker would have done this!

No. Idea.

Gretch arms her mouth on her sleeve and straightens. Turns around, the roof of her mouth still tingling with stomach acid.

The detectives' expressions are well-worn masks of practical concern. A young, dark-complexioned rookie with heavily pomaded hair. Paired with a more seasoned, grizzled veteran. They are a living stereotype of every cop drama ever produced for television. The rookie comes bearing not one but two uncapped cups of Circle-K black coffee. The veteran gives a stern shake of his head to the younger one.

The rookie reads his partner right.

He doesn't offer the second cup to Gretch and stands there holding both with a wry look on his face.

Gretch clasps her hands together like she is readying herself for a long address to a crowd of onlookers. "Did you … did you find him?"

"Mrs. Darius, I'm Detective Spiegel," the veteran says. "This is Detective Tranto. I—"

Detective Tranto cuts in. "Who are you looking for, ma'am?"

(*I handled him-don't worry*)

Detective Spiegel, through gritted discolored teeth, says, "You're looking for your husband?" He pauses, mentally referencing the name he had only just committed to his notepad. "Steven. Is that right?"

Eyes wide, Gretch nods.

"Right," Spiegel says. He casts a look out across the rubble, which extends all the way to the tree line in the absence of not only the main house but the separate wheelhouse as well. "You're certain he would have been home when the fire started?"

"He … he was bedridden. Final stages of dementia."

"I see," Spiegel says. He empties the rest of his coffee into the grass nearby, crumples the cup. Doesn't know what to do with it and ends up tapping it against his thigh. "Now, Mrs. Darius—"

"It's Solomon. I never took his name." She spews the words like venom. The vehemence surprises even her.

It's new, and it's appropriate.

"Your husband was incapacitated," the veteran reiterates, evidently crowding his younger partner out of the Q and A for an earlier spat the older man has not yet lost the sting of. "You were away, it's my under-standing."

"I was."

"You would have left him in the care of a professional during your absence? Live-in nurse? Relative? Who specifically?"

She feels the change-over in her mind and body as the long-buried actor inside comes surging to the surface to take the reins from then on out.

You can't say she came recommended by anyone, especially not Lori. They'll verify that. And you can't say she answered an ad. Same reason.

Think, Gretch—

"She was so young," Gretch sniffs, cupping her hand over her mouth. Her eyes water over. "I met her in a grocery check-out. There was a long line. We got to talking. She ... she noticed I-I was purchasing a hefty supply of adult diapers. Some bed sore ointment. She said she was a hospice nurse. In-between positions. Before we knew it, I'd scheduled an interview with her for the following afternoon. It was like kismet. You know what *kismet* is?"

Gruffly, Detective Spiegel answers in the affirmative. Pen and pad at the ready.

"She ..." Gretch extends her arm. One crooked index finger in the direction of the smoking pile. "... she would have been here. With ... *my* Stevie."

"And her credentials were in order?" Detective Tranto asks, exhorting himself.

"Of course. Of course."

Detective Spiegel pauses, continues. "Ms. Solomon, can you think of anyone who would have wanted to hurt you? Anyone you may have had an argument with or something more long-term. A grudge, maybe?"

Gretch opens her mouth, gut burning to tell the whole story.

Now is the time.

Last chance to atone.

The moment of truth whereby she will reveal to the detectives that she has been married to a serial killer and had only just discovered his secret. Or *rediscovered,* rather. They will no doubt see right through her explanation as to why she hadn't gone right to the police once she learned about her husband's double-life, and that does not concern her in the slightest. She simply does not believe she deserves to escape some sort of accountability. They may very well produce a pair of handcuffs just for her. She will put out her hands. Allow them to clamp them over her wrists. She will not resist, because this is justice in its most straightforward form. From there she will explain how the ghost of her husband's first victim showed up on her doorstep a few days before. That Gretch *had* known who the little waifish blonde was and what the future held for Stevie Darius in the hands of this spirit of reckoning and still she—

(*I absolve you, whether you deserve it or not*)

The words of Prudence "Lovebug" Haines before the phone connection went dead.

Her mind clears, a slow-turning fog of cognition that thins and then disappears. What is left is a strange sense of calm and resolve. Fear of the unknown and great, overwhelming trepidation for what picking up the pieces of her life will mean.

Then a surprising resignation takes hold of her. Shakes her psyche.

Fuck the house!

Fuck that life!

Fuck the lie!

Fuck the denial!

It could be the shock of the moment. The still-smoking tinder mere feet away of her once prized homestead.

The previous sense of profound loss is overshadowed by an even greater sense of relief.

Relief?

She did what I never could have. The house is collateral damage. I can rebuild. What I could not have done is to live with a murderer. To wipe his ass on command. Bathe his reptilian skin. He was turning into a snake before my very eyes. The balls of his feet burned as a prelude to the Hell he would soon call home. And I never could have brought myself to kill him myself. I never would have been able to turn him in to the authorities because all he would have had to do would be to weep. To grovel. To beg his Pretty Baby Ginger Girl to let him die at home. Not in a prison cell.

And Gretch would have hated herself for her weakness of emotion. Her acquiescing to a killer who deserved all the things he would ask her to protect him from.

She would have let him live.

No.

Justice is done. Messy, but oftentimes it shakes out that way in the end.

No need to awaken it when it has done its job.

"No," she says, meeting Spiegel's searching gaze. "No one." Then she adds, "And I can't believe it would have been the girl. The nurse."

She won't be in the rubble.

She's in the ether again.

The detective goes on to explain how they will have investigators pore over the remains and if there was foul play, it will be brought to light. Then, he tells her he will be back to talk with her further about this, as it is now deemed a crime. Something about an accelerant having been used.

As Gretch Solomon follows along behind the detectives, she casts her eyes out over the blackened bones of her home that are still standing. The ashes. The tendrils of smoke rising from the din, thin and frail. A light fixture winks at her, as does the crystal of the small chandelier that hung in the foyer. The glimpses of white and pale something or whatever, partially submerged in the charred pilings calls the horror of what lingered just inside the fractured Mountain back into her mind.

Alive. Dying. Or dead. Only three possibilities, but she prays the third is the most likely.

Bones in the ash. Like the impossibly long, lithe and starved limbs of an otherwise concealed old god who had burned Gretch's life, literally and figuratively.

Her mind tries to pinpoint where in the remains of the house Stevie would have been. Lashed to his bed? Tied to a kitchen chair? In the bathtub? Where? *Where?*

Oh where-oh where can my Stevie D be?

Don't lose it.

Look away.

Gretch does just that, averting her eyes the whole way, and only half-hearing the buzz of words and disjointed conversation all around her.

EPILOGUE

EXTRACT FROM *SPIN* MAGAZINE, Issue 726, 1995, pgs. 45-47:

THE DEATH OF ROCK SLEAZE AND DECADENT SPECTACLE: GRIFTERS ANONYMOUS' INEVITABLE FINAL CHAPTER
By Melissa Barry, staff contributor

ON THE MORNING of September 12th, 1994, paramedics responded to a call from the palatial estate of 1960's character actor, Vincent Santos, in Van Nuys: "unresponsive male in the guest house". Emergency personnel would find the body of Davey Grifter, singer for the multi-platinum selling, Grammy-award winning hard rock band Grifters Anonymous, hanged from an exposed beam in the cottage's modest attic area. The Los Angeles coroner would place time of death as somewhere within the last five days. The body of the late rocker had already started to mummify when found. Santos had been in Las Vegas on holiday during this time.

As with far too many suicides, this death of one of rock's most celebrated, enigmatic front men carries with it a series of unanswered questions. Sources have commented in much the same way, often using the same turn of phrase: "The guys in Grifters all lived like tomorrow it was all coming to an end." Many have made it plain, oddly enough, they have been living in quiet anticipation of the day all five members died.

That day is here.

This death signifies the final link in the chain of what has been a series of tragic ends for all five band members. While the suicide of Davey Grifter is considered by most to be the worst in terms of sheer shock value, this is only the case in that he was the most visible and recognizable of all the members during their heyday.

Davey was *not* the first suicide to rock Grifters, but it was the last.

Shall we travel further down the rabbit hole?

The body of Bobby Royal, drummer for the band, would be dragged from the River Thames two years ago. His would be the first of the deaths. He had tied a heavy cinder block to his right leg and drowned himself in full view of a badly shaken scattering of tourists. An American from Albany dived in and attempted to rescue the troubled musician. The Thames offers near-zero visibility. The brave tourist nearly drowned himself to rescue Bobby Royal. There was no suicide note. His father, billionaire mogul Nolan Royal, suspects a heroin relapse, claiming he'd funneled millions of dollars into various clinics to help his son. "The break-up of Grifters set him on the road to destruction," he claimed. "There was nothing to be done."

Six months later, to the day, Chris Desmond would be found impaled on a rebar stake at an abandoned construction site. According to authorities., he had been warned away from the site along with a group of homeless who would regularly gather to shoot up on the open second floor. One of the addicts who had been in attendance the evening of Chris Desmond's death confided in an LA detective he had witnessed Chris weeping as he stood on the edge. Then, he had put out his arms like a butterfly and taken the dive "free and willing", as the anonymous addict would claim.

Deeper we go. You coming?

Fast forward six more months. In what most friends and fans of Grifters Anonymous unanimously agree to be the most heartbreaking of these "intentional" deaths, John "J" Germanian suffered a very public fall from grace that kicked off onstage at the 32nd Grammy Awards ceremony. He was a presenter for Best Hard Rock Performance, alongside Cyndi Lauper. Heavily inebriated, the guitar god managed to sever all ties to the record industry with an expletive-laden rant aimed at everyone from the President of Atlas Records (Grifter's label) to the son of an executive at Columbia who had asked him for an autograph while he was out to dinner. From there, Germanian retreated into obscurity, his once handsome face and sculpted body now showing up bloated and slovenly in the handful of photos snapped of him on his property by paparazzi.

The next time the name John Germanian would show up in print would be in the report of a botched suicide attempt. The first in what would become a quartet of attempts and culminate in a final failure that resulted in severe disfigurement and a life led in quiet, humbled hiding until eventually he found his window to snuff it once and for all. Irresponsible comparisons have been drawn between John Germanian and the late, great Kurt Cobain's chosen mode of suicide. Both used a shotgun. There, the similarities end sharply and definitively. One was successful in their attempt. The other was not and lived for another year in what can only be considered a copy of a copy of an imitation of life. Murmurings among the rock press about Germanian having probably "copy-catted" Cobain's suicide are unfounded.

They've also managed to capture the rock community's imagination.

The death of Davey Grifter further spurred on what has become an intense speculation about the band and what fans, old and new, and rock journalists believe to be its "hidden history". It stands to reason that we human beings abhor a vacuum. We loathe the unanswered question. And the untimely deaths of all five band members of Grifters

Anonymous stands as one oversized, glaring question mark that has defied explanation until now.

If you're going deeper into the earth with me, hang a left up ahead …

RUMOR AND SPECULATION have long surrounded Grifters Anonymous. These unsubstantiated theories range from the benign ("all the Grifters take part in a ritualistic masturbation ceremony twenty-four hours before every show"; "the members take turns *taking one for the team* by screwing an ugly groupie every other show to keep the goodwill and good vibes flowing"; "Grifters is *secretly* a Christian rock band, with the Big Guy on their side") to darker conjectures that ("J Germanian was a Jimmy Page obsessive who traveled in the guitarists footsteps like some Catholics walk the path of Jesus' final steps, and this led him to The Crossroads where he struck a deal with The Devil himself like Page and Robert Johnson are rumored to have done"; "Nolan Royal used his money and a fleet of enforcers to get the band's songs put into heavy radio rotation in America and Britain"; "Davey's now infamous *Child Bride*, Glory Tizione, was a traveling Muse for the band and not of this world"). Most surprisingly, sources seemed more fervently certain of the latter explanations for the band's meteoric rise.

Stop here and turn back if you spook easily, Reader …

The most common fan theory, echoed by most members of the band' fan club, The Massengill Army (I'm not kidding!), is the members belonged to an underground religion, its tenets falling some-where between Satanism and The Illuminati. One anonymous source claims "People tended to turn up missing after they've been with the band on tour or-you know-just putting in their time with one of them. Here today. Gone tomorrow. It became an inside joke. And there was *always* an explanation. Nobody really gave a shit. We were all too enamored and honored to be making time with Grifters to worry about our own safety. Or if we'd disappear next." Our offices reached out to the Grifters Anonymous executor, Gretch Solomon, the band's manager, for a statement but could not obtain one. Upon making a similar effort to contact Nolan Royal, the mogul made it plain in no uncertain terms that this is "the stuff of myth" and "according to Bobby, people were constantly hopping on and off the Grifter's entourage. Going back to their lives. Doesn't mean there was any foul play afoot."

Royal also put a very fine point on the fact the Grifter's catalogue has been charting in the Top 10 on Billboard ever since Davey Grifter's sad end. "There are two things that sell records: an interesting mythos and an early death … or five of em'_„

II.

SHE MUST REDIAL four times before punching the correct series of numbers into her cordless phone. It's an international one requiring far too many digits for someone whose forehead is burning with rage and fingers are stiffened and clumsy. US exit code—+44 Scotland country code—0131—then XXX XXXX.

The old man does not answer his own phone. No surprise. He's got more money than he or half of the UK could spend in their lifetimes combined. On the world stage, the title of philanthropist has been bandied about to describe the old man. But she knows him well enough to have fully expected him to sprout horns before her very eyes when she laid eyes on him back on The Mountain. Standing just outside an idling black SUV. Surveying her as his mercs carried her past him to the waiting helicopter. Then, on to a series of hospital procedures and a fully funded month-long stay there as well to convalesce without the burden of paying a ridiculous bill.

Never one to talk down to a servant, Gretch breaks the rule before she knows she's done it.

"Put the old fuck on!"

The woman, who sounds not much younger than the mogul himself who is pushing eighty-one, lets out a squawk like a goose sent flying by the swift kick of a well-aimed boot. She is not accustomed to the language used, much less the complete and utter lack of deference aimed at her employer.

"Beggin' your pardon, young lady—"

"Just tell him it's Gretch Solomon," she says, fully aware of the weight her name will carry when the old man hears it. "Tell him I read the Spin article."

A sound like a turkey choking.

"Do as you're told, Millie," snapped Gretch.

"I—"

"Never mind the how. I've made it my business to know everything about everyone who's ever had *his name* in their mouth since your demented employer dragged me into court over Grifter royalties. Now, I want you to get him on the phone before I start the drip-drip-drip of intel surrounding his disgusting relationship with his late son to every paper from the *Times* to the fucking *Wall Street Journal.* Do you understand, Millie?"

"Yeh, hang-on-hang-on-*ang' on!*" Nolan Royal is on the phone. "You got her weepin', Gretchen! An auld lass, nonetheless!"

There is a smile in his voice. A laugh woven into his words.

"Davey's body? We both know where he *really* died!"

Nolan Royal goes silent. When he speaks again, any trace of the Glaswegian that had crept into his accent is vanquished. The power broker is on the line now.

"Oh, for fuck's sake, Red, I—"

"Don't *fucking* call me *Red!*"

"You know what I done so why call?" the mogul asks, the first, faint sound of a weakening vocal cord whistling through his words. "I'm dying, Gretch. You've got me on my death bed. I just—" A ragged cough rips its way out of his throat. It's the sound of a body making a sound that most cannot recover from. "You'll have to pardon me, Red. You'll let a dying ol' coot call you whatever he likes, eh? Red? See, you dragged me up and out of my bed because I couldn't have ya' harassing the help."

Gretch nearly asks him if his feet are burning. Almost.

"Nolan ... god-dammit. Tell me!"

"I-It's nothing to me, Red. I'd be happy to. Let me just ... send everyone out."

"You just said it was *nothing to you.* Why not come clean to everyone so they can watch you leave this world knowing full well where you're headed—"

He's not listening to her, his hand over the speaker end of the phone. Nolan Royal is trying to raise his voice above that of a complacent rasp and cannot achieve this. She can hear him, through the cracks in his fingers, as he tries to transmit the same old booming bark that closed million dollar deals and humbled even the most arrogant CEO.

He comes back on the line, voice splintered now:

"It's nothing to me—"

"You said that already. I get it. You'll never see the inside of a cell. So, fucking go ahead."

"You ever read my book, Red?"

"No, but don't take it personally. I never read Trump's *Art of the Deal* either. Billionaires creep me out."

"You know the title of it, though?"

Her mind has already conjured an image of the paperback, which featured the smug and gloating round face of Nolan Royal on its cover. He sits at the easternmost end of a park bench, and Big Ben looms in the background as if to qualify his location. The title shimmers in gold block lettering:

"*Guarantee Your Returns*. That right?"

"Good girl," Nolan says. "You might not have found yourself in such dire straits financially if you'd cracked open the book and taken a look."

"Oh, I'm just fine financially, you old fucker. And now that you're not much longer for this world, it's looking like the copyright squabble is going to go my way after all."

"Yeah … well … put a pin in that. My estate will be carrying on the good fight posthumously and all—"

Another unnerving cough, thick and liquid. He manages to clear his windpipe. "You know the title of my book, you know exactly why I did what I did."

"And what's that?"

"Oh, don't be daft. Doesn't suit you, Red. I … see … I *guaranteed my return*. I thought I'd accomplished that when I hauled the five of them, druggies all of them, into a rehab so they could clean themselves up and start writing something of value. I knew, even with this tin ear of mine, they never would have gotten to where they did and made me at least some of my investment back if they'd kept on the way they were. And The Big Russian … he came highly recommended in certain privileged, exclusive circles in the know. He was something of a miracle worker. Could unblock even the most stopped-up creative *and* dry them out at the same time. Had no idea how he did it. The *how* didn't matter to me. I might've asked some questions. We could've avoided the ugliness that followed."

"*Ugliness.* Christ. That's what you'd call it?"

"Yeah well …" The old man wheezes into the phone. Laughs weakly. The old man is somehow amused by the sounds of his lungs failing. Filling with blood. "Inside a month when we got back from The Mountain, things started to really happen. I'll admit … it frightened even me. The turn. It felt … it *felt* unholy. Like none of us deserved it, and still we were going to have it. I was very pleased with my investment in my son's band. You know, I'd only agreed to fund and manage them so I could keep tabs on my son. So he wouldn't snuff it. In the end …"

The old man's voice trails off, leaving a trill of wind in its wake.

I don't believe you, Nolan Royal.

You don't mourn your son.

It's a lie.

"You dropped them apparently. Once they started to make a name for themselves. That doesn't add up. Not to mention they made it a point of never—and I mean never—mentioning you were ever their manager. Was that your idea?"

"When I painted my first oil on canvas, you know I felt no pride? None. I was truly terrified. I knew what it was. And the pull was there. I was suddenly shackled to this new talent, an ability I never asked for. Never wanted. A curse. But Chrissy angered The Russian. Stanislaw took no prisoners when he … scrambled our brains. He lumped me in with the rest of em'. Cursed me. I never wanted to be an artist. I'm a businessman. I was chained to this gift, whether I liked it or not. It kept me up most nights. Ran my mind into overdrive. I couldn't think

straight. There were only the oils. The acrylics. The clay. The *fucking* …
the art."

When Nolan Royal pauses and a dark, gloating laugh fills Gretch's
ear, she knows what he's going to say next before he says it:

"But you know my pain, Gretchen, don't you?" He pauses for
effect, letting her sit with it. "Bet you were wondering just what in the
good fuck that buzzing in the back of your brain was? Probably started
up when you were in the cave. It was that cunt, Stanislaw. He got his
hands on your brain, just like with the rest of us. By the way, good luck
with your showing. The Vanti Gallery, Manhattan. Cheers, love. You
got the artist bug, too. Cheers I say—"

"Fuck off, Nolan," Gretch says, even as a small flame of pride in her
newfound talent gutters happily, its fruit looking upon her from all
four walls of her living room in uptown. "So, this was a revenge thing?
I always suspected rich pigs like you as being above something like
revenge."

A long pause stretches out between the two of them. It nearly
convinces Gretch she has lost connection with the mogul.

What he says next is an ice shard in her heart:

"Alright, love … here it is," he says, rasping now. "Let me lay it out
plain for ya'. You know I got endless resources to keep you tied up in
court over the damned copyrights until you're just about ready to join
me in the cemetery, eh? And I will exhaust your resources long before
then, so it's not a matter of *if* I'll get the rights but *when*. Now, I dunno
if Billboard is something you still bother to check. You're out of the
game now that you're in the New York art circle. But it's all gone
according to plan. I didn't get here by *hoping for the best*. No, I had to
arrange it so *all of it would break my way*. Call it a long game of chess.

"Davey may have died from a heart attack on The Mountain when the
cave came crashing down around him, Gretch," Nolan says. "But as far as
the fans and the brass at the record company, the public at large, will ever
know is the poor, deluded fuck hanged himself up in that guest house. It
was only a matter of preserving the body and moving it there. Staging the
suicide scene. My team's attention to detail is *legendary*, Red—"

"I said don't call me fucking *Red*—"

"I became very curious about what such a tragedy does for record sales when that Cobain bloke snuffed it. The surge in sales of their entire bloody catalog is the stuff of myth following his death. Ever since then, I've had that notion sitting in the back of my brain. Forming itself. Hatching. And it sprang from my skull fully-formed as a newborn baby born right on time. I knew I'd come to storm The Mountain with my team. We'd take possession of Davey by any means necessary. Imagine our relief when we came to discover the boy stiff as a board down in that cave when we arrived. My men thought they were going to have to kill him themselves. Although, you could have skipped cracking his head open like you did. It took a bloody team of reconstructive surgeons to put Humpty back together again and hide the injury."

A light, airy female voice sounds in the background just as Nolan pauses to take a breath.

Gretch's ears perk up.

Hackles that had slowly been rising on the back of her neck as the mogul outlined his exploits involving Davey's dead body stood on end now.

Straining to hear even as the old man cups the receiver in his palm again, Gretch catches snatches of a full sentence: "… didn't mean me … kept out … c'mon, Poppy—"

I know that voice.

Holy.

Shit—

"Nolan, you old fuck, who is *that*? Who are you talking to?" Gretch is screaming into the receiver now to be heard. "*Nolan! —*"

"Oi!" he squawks. "Bottom line is this! Billboard sales of *Knives for the People* have rocketed into the stratosphere. Within an hour of the breaking news about poor, suicidal Davey Grifter, they started pressing more vinyl than when the album first broke through. A 200% surge in sales, Red. And I won't see a dime of it in the end. That's gravy, my love—"

"Who the *fuck* is with you right now?"

"You know, I never thought I'd ever find love again. An old fool like me. I'm a selfish bastard and a terrible partner to boot. Still think

Bobby's mum died to get clear of me. Took me decades, quite literally, to realize I wanted someone to share my money, my life, and this fat Glaswegian cock with."

In the background: "Is that *Gretch*?"

Fuck!

Nolan Royal says, through a mouthful of blood and mucous, "We married five months ago. Before my diagnosis. Thought I'd have more time. But at least she'll have endless royalties from Grifters to spend in my name and, God-willing, my *memory*."

Gretch hears him hand off the phone: "Give a *hello*, love—"

The girl's voice is warm and gloating in Gretch's ear. "How've you been, Gretch? Well, I hope?"

"Prudence—"

"Call me *Lovebug*."

ACKNOWLEDGMENTS

Get those lighters up!

Thank you to my wife, Dana, for providing the tender-loving kick in the ass and still loving me when I happened to fall on black days. Thank you to my children, Ani and Isabella, for their ever-watchful gazes that have kept me keeping on. Enduring thanks to Lisa Vasquez, editor-in-chief for Memento Mori Ink and Mother of Monsters, for giving me my first break with *Broken Birds,* providing invaluable support and guidance, and for formatting *Knives for the People.* The interior shines because of Lisa and I thank her so much! As for the exterior artwork and book wrap, thank you to the brilliant Matt Seff Barnes for capturing in one startling image the down and dirty vibe of *Knives.* Cheers, Matt!

Big thanks to Isabella Perri, trusted beta-reader, for her invaluable insight into the novel, her spot-on suggestions, and keen eye for detail. A spectacular writer in her own right, keep an eye out for her. (Time to start that dark academia novel, ahem …)

I was eight years old when my friend's older brother introduced me to Twister Sister's *Stay Hungry* and Ratt's *Out of the Cellar.* Nine when I heard Motley Crue's masterpiece *Shout at the Devil* for the first time. I knew next to nothing about the band members other than they frightened me (in a good way). The Sunset Strip of the 80's (or any decade for that matter) meant less than nothing to me. I was twelve when I heard Guns N' Roses' mind-blowing *Appetite for Destruction,* forced to listen to it in secret through a pair of satellite dish headphones so Mom and Dad wouldn't hear the words to "It's So Easy" or "My Michelle". That album in particular opened my eyes to the musicians behind the songs. My fear of them transformed into an all-consuming desire to follow in their footsteps. It has been an even greater thrill to write about my childhood idols, now adulthood heroes.

Ah, The Sunset Strip.

The intimidating task of capturing the vibe, the seediness, and the decadence ingrained in the subculture of The Strip, a place I'd only glimpsed in video snippets and grainy photographs, nearly sank my efforts before I could begin. Then *Nothin' But A Good Time: The Uncensored Oral History of the 80's Rock Explosion* by Tom Beaujour and Richard Bienstock was published in the spring of 2022. I devoured the tome of a book. I scribbled meticulous notes along the way. Shit, I wish I'd been there. In the thick of it.

This novel would not live and breathe in terms of time and place if not for that book. While all characters and events presented in the novel are purely fictional and anything appearing otherwise is sheer coincidence, I also tossed *Walk This Way: The Autobiography of Aerosmith* by Stephen Davis, *Watch You Bleed: The Saga of Guns N' Roses* by Stephen Davis (also), and *The Dirt: Confessions of the World's Most Notorious Rock Band* (Motley Crue) by Neil Strauss, Tommy Lee, Nikki Sixx, Vince Neil, and Mick Mars, into a big ol' blender and the book you hold in your hands is the black, viscous fluid poured out after the puree.

Finally, thanks to you for shelling out your hard-earned dollar bucks to take a chance on me.

Alright … bring the lights up …

ABOUT THE AUTHOR

PETER MOLNAR is the author of three novels, including Broken Birds and the Splatterpunk-Nominated collection Rhapsody in Red: Two Novellas of The Damned, as well as numerous short stories, music, books, and video game reviews. He is a teacher and Creative Writing mentor in the secondary school system. He lives just outside Philadelphia with his wife and daughter.